"I hate you!"

"Why? Because you desire me?" Jeremy asked.

"I *don't* desire you!" Meredith lied desperately.

"The hell you don't." His words were low and thick. Not giving her a chance to protest, he ground his lips into hers. Against her will, her mouth opened, and their tongues clashed in a battle of pleasure.

She twisted beneath him, her fingernails digging into his shoulders. "Please, Jeremy, please."

"Tell me," he growled. "Say you want me."

"Yes," she gasped. "Yes, I want you. Oh, Jeremy, how I want you. Love me. Please."

Her words melted him. He could hold back no longer . . .

*Also by Lisa Gregory
from Jove*

BONDS OF LOVE
THE RAINBOW SEASON
ANALISE
CRYSTAL HEART

BITTERLEAF

LISA GREGORY

A JOVE BOOK

BITTERLEAF

A Jove Book/published by arrangement with
the author

PRINTING HISTORY
Jove edition / July 1983

ISBN: 0-515-06333-9

Jove books are published by Jove Publications, Inc.,
200 Madison Avenue, New York, N.Y. 10016. The words
"A JOVE BOOK" and the stylized "J" with sunburst are trademarks
belonging to Jove Publications, Inc.

PRINTED IN THE UNITED STATES OF AMERICA

BITTERLEAF

Chapter I

MEREDITH WHITNEY sighed and pulled out the straggling stitches she had just put in her usually meticulous needlework. Frowning over the sampler, she berated herself for having accompanied her stepfather to Charleston. The idea of a few days spent in town, with its fine houses and cobblestoned streets, its stores and their profusion of goods, had seemed rosy at the time. Why, she had even persuaded Daniel to take her to the theater. But now, after two days in the vapid company of her cousin Phoebe, Meredith regretted coming. Phoebe could do nothing but prattle of clothes, parties, and the young gentlemen who had come to call on her, and Meredith was unsure which she felt more, boredom or irritation.

Across the room from her, Phoebe Spencer, blithely unaware of the vexation she inspired in her cousin's bosom, patted her fashionably high, powdered coiffure and said, "However do you stand it out there on that deadly dull old plantation? I declare, I would melt in a day."

"It is rather warm in the summer," Meredith gravely agreed, "although the worst dangers are the swamp fevers."

"Oh!" Phoebe snapped open her ivory-handled fan and plied it gently. "Don't mention such things. Cousin Meredith, you know how sensitive I am."

"Sorry," the other woman replied dryly. "However, I believe it's worse to experience the fever than to hear about it."

Phoebe turned her large, rather protuberant blue eyes in the direction of the window, wondering how long she would have to put up with her dreary cousin. Of course, Mother always extended a standing invitation to the daughter of her dear dead sister Anne, even if it meant having to put up with the presence of Meredith's stepfather, Daniel Hurley. As Caroline Spencer was fond of saying, pressing her lips together in a thin, prim line, it was not her place to pass judgment on her late sister's marriage to that low, presumptuous Hurley. After all, Anne had done what she had to to preserve Meredith's heritage for her. Phoebe, however, found it difficult to envision any damp, moss-draped plantation being worth the humiliation of wedding a mannerless merchant like Daniel Hurley. And Meredith Whitney hardly seemed worth the sacrifice, either, although it was obvious that she needed her own land, for the gawky, plain girl would never marry.

Phoebe's gaze returned from the empty street outside to fasten on her cousin again. Meredith's plain blue silk dress did little for her. The boned bodice flattened her ample breasts, but the square neckline was not cut low enough to reveal the consequent upswell of her bosom, and the wide skirts held stiffly out to the sides by panniers merely made her tall, slender figure even more imposing. Her brown hair was pulled back unattractively into a tight coil atop her head. Unconsciously, Phoebe smoothed the fabric of her own sea-green sacque dress, form-fitting and fastened with cunning bows in the front and free-flowing down the back, preening at the thought of how well she looked compared to her wallflower cousin. "Tell me, Cousin, do you never powder your hair? Surely life in the country is not so behind the times as that?"

A telltale flush mounted in Meredith's cheeks, and she wished that her fair skin did not betray her emotions so readily. She hated to let a silly chit like Phoebe know that her words had stung. "No, indeed," Meredith replied, striving to keep her voice cool. "Many of the plantation women dress quite fashionably, in silks and laces and styles straight from the court, but I find the towering hairdos uncomfortable in the heat and damp."

She did not add that a wired, padded sweep of hair would add unwelcome inches to her already dominating height. As it was, she looked down at half the men in the county, and only her Whitney cousins topped her by more than an inch or two.

Phoebe smiled archly, a glint in her eye revealing to Meredith that she understood the unspoken reason behind Meredith's plain hairdo. Meredith glanced hurriedly back at her sewing, and almost cried aloud in dismay. She had dropped another stitch. Why did she let Phoebe provoke her so? Meredith was no longer the awkward, gawky girl she had once been, tumbling haphazardly into womanhood, all arms and legs, her stockings perpetually full of ladders and sagging at the ankles. At thirteen, she had towered over every child in the county, boy or girl, and seemed to run into chairs and tables wherever she turned, her long legs or arms perversely stretching out to bump into things that appeared to be safely out of the way. Shy and bookish, Meredith had slouched in a vain attempt to hide her height, and whenever company appeared, she fled for the safety of her room to avoid the pitying glances that would be directed at her mother, looks that plainly said, "Poor Anne Whitney, how did she manage to raise such a hulking lump of a daughter?" Since then, Meredith had lost much of the awkwardness and resolutely forced herself not to run from visitors. She had found her competence in other areas and took pride in the things she could do better than anyone else. She had straightened her shoulders and built a thick wall of aloofness to protect herself from the pity. But there were still times, as in the presence of dainty young girls like Phoebe, that she felt once again gauche, with more than the requisite number of elbows and knees.

Meredith concentrated on retrieving the stitches she had botched, successfully blotting out Phoebe's trilling voice until she recovered her normal calm. When she resumed listening to her cousin, Phoebe was blissfully enthralled in revealing her latest conquest. "Then Jasper said, 'I want three dances with you, Miss Spencer.' Of course, I put on an offended face and said, 'Do you want to ruin my reputation, Jasper Caldwell? What would people say if I danced more than twice with the same man?' Of course, I wouldn't have minded at all, because he's quite nice-looking, and one of the wealthiest men in Charleston, too. But it never does to let a gentleman know you're interested in him."

"Doesn't it?" Meredith inquired wryly. "It would seem rather difficult to reach a happy conclusion, then."

"Well, eventually you'd let him know!" Phoebe exclaimed. "But not right off. Once they think you're caught, they lose interest."

"Ah, so it's the joy of the conquest they seek."

"Well, yes, I guess you could say so. I declare, Meredith, don't you know anything? You're four years older than I am, and a person would think you had never flirted with a man."

"I know. I'm twenty-one and quite on the shelf. But then, I've never been very good at 'the hunt' myself. For enjoyment, I prefer to talk with Cousin Galen or play the harpsichord or read an enlightening book."

Phoebe wrinkled her short nose at such pursuits, but followed the one allusion that struck a chord in her. "You mean . . . Have you and your cousin . . . Do you have an agreement?"

"Really, Phoebe! Do you think of nothing else? Just because Cousin Galen and I enjoy each other's company and have the same interests in life, why must everyone persist in turning him into my suitor?"

"Isn't he?" Phoebe persevered, shrugging off the older girl's admonition. "Do you want to marry Galen Whitney?"

"I never thought about it," Meredith lied coolly. She had indeed thought about it more than once. She and Galen were well-suited in temperament, so alike in their tastes that theirs would be an entirely harmonious marriage. Galen respected her mind, her finer feelings, as none of the boorish young men in the county did. They had little on their brains besides drinking and gambling, or taking over their father's plantation and raising a family. Of course, Galen had never breathed words of love in her ear. He would do nothing so improper or forward. His first thought was always for her reputation. He would not tell her of his feelings until he asked for her hand. Meredith suspected that what held him back was the typically Whitney financial circumstances. Everyone whispered that Four Oaks was a step away from being gobbled up by the creditors. And Galen would not subject her to the humiliation of whispers that he had married her for her stepfather's prosperous plantation. Once Meredith had mentioned to him that since Bitterleaf had been her father's, even though Daniel Hurley had saved the plantation and her mother from ruin by buying and improving the land, she would always consider Bitterleaf to be Whitney land. However, Meredith would not go beyond that hint. She was content to continue as they were. Theirs was a quiet, contented sort of love, not the wild, tempestuous affair of poetry.

"Oh, please, Cousin Meredith, don't be so stuffy," Phoebe said, pouting. "How can you not have thought about it? The other night I heard Mama tell Papa it was as good as a settled thing. Everyone has known for years that you and Galen would marry. She said only marriage to someone as eminently respectable as Galen Whitney could wipe away the stain of the household you've been living in."

"What!" Meredith's head jerked up, red spots of anger staining her cheeks. "The Whitney name has never been sullied! Bitterleaf is as fine a house as any in Carolina, and no one would dare say otherwise!"

Phoebe swallowed, taken aback by the unexpected blaze in Meredith's eyes, which turned them from hazel to a penetrating green. Meredith's quiet demeanor had misled Phoebe into dismissing her as a mousy sort. "I didn't—that is—I mean, no one says anything about you. No one could think a Whitney did something wrong. It's Mr. Hurley and—"

"And who?" Meredith pressed, her head proudly high.

"You know. That woman. Mama says I mustn't ever say her name."

"Mrs. Chandler?" Meredith supplied coldly. "Mrs. Chandler is a friend of my stepfather's first wife. There is nothing odd or indelicate about his offering her the hospitality of his house when she fell on hard times. Nor is there anything wrong with being penurious. After all, Mama and I had patches on our dresses when Mr. Hurley came to buy Bitterleaf. If he had not fallen in love with Mama and married her, we would have had to leave Bitterleaf and would no doubt have been living on your mother's charity for the last eight years."

Phoebe raised one delicate eyebrow in amused disbelief. "Don't try to divert me, Cousin Meredith. You know very well what I'm talking about. People say that Mrs. Chandler is not a friend of your stepfather's first wife, but a penniless actress he found in Virginia. And they say that she's not living there on his charity, but is amply paid for what she does—and we can all guess what that is.''

Meredith opened her mouth to reply sharply, but stopped at the sound of footsteps on the marble floor of the hall. She recognized her stepfather's heavy tread, and she was not about to let him know the subject of their discussion—or he might treat Phoebe to a display of his swift temper. She clenched her teeth and assumed a pleasant expression.

"Meredith, my dear. Miss Phoebe." Daniel Hurley stepped fractionally into the room and acknowledged the girls' presence with the short nod he habitually used in place of a bow. He was of medium height and squarely built, his powerful chest and shoulders straining against the fine, brocaded waistcoat and jacket. In deference to his visit to the city, he had donned a powdered white queue wig, although at home he preferred to wear his natural hair. Beneath the wig, his eyes were dark and bright, alert to the tense atmosphere of the room, and his chin thrust forward pugnaciously, not because he sought to enter a conflict but simply because that had been his expression all his life. In earlier years the heavy, broad-boned face had held a certain rough attraction, but middle age had put its mark upon him, turning his cheeks fleshy and smudging brown shadows beneath his eyes. He was a prosperous plantation owner and his suit was of excellent material and fit, but Hurley did not look like a gentleman planter. He wore his clothes carelessly, and there was no refinement in his speech or walk or stance. He stood now with both hands on his hips, watching Meredith, ignoring the sweet smile Phoebe had pasted on her lips.

"Good afternoon, Father Hurley," Meredith replied politely while Phoebe giggled out a greeting.

"Pah!" The man's face twisted. "You make me sound like a papist priest."

"I'm sorry if it displeases you."

He snorted. "Don't put on airs with me, missy. I've never known you to be sorry a single time when you displeased me. Would you like to come with me to the Market? They're auctioning off a load of indentures this afternoon, and I thought I'd take a look-see."

"Why, yes, I would," Meredith replied, surprising even herself with her alacrity. Normally, she shunned slave auctions and the selling of servants' indentures, but right now she believed she would consent to go to hell itself in order to escape Phoebe's conversation.

"Come along, then. The Spencers' carriage is waiting for us outside."

Meredith quickly fetched her gloves and bonnet and rejoined her stepfather in the hall. Waving a cheery good-bye to Phoebe, she swept out of the house on Daniel's arm. Unconsciously, she heaved a sigh of relief as the black footman helped her into the carriage, and behind her, Hurley chuckled. "I thought you might appreciate a chance to get away."

"I do. I felt as if I were drowning in Phoebe's chatter. She can talk of nothing but tricks to catch a husband—as if a man so easily deluded would be worth having—and parties and scandal." She stopped uncertainly on her last word, remembering the scandal Phoebe had been rehashing.

Hurley caught her hesitation, and a faint smile touched his lips. "Was she blasting your ears about Mrs. Chandler?"

"Yes, but it was nothing, really. I assured her it was the veriest gossip."

He patted her hand affectionately. "You're a good daughter, Meredith. Mrs. Chandler and I appreciate your kindness."

Meredith bit her lip. It was all she could do to keep from snatching her hand away. What Phoebe had said was true, of course. The whole county—apparently the whole colony of South Carolina—knew of the liaison. It was wicked of Daniel to carry on with Lydia Chandler right there in her dead mother's house. And for him to thank her for trying to conceal the scandal added the finishing touch to the insult. It was not kindness nor regard for Daniel Hurley that made Meredith deny the affair. She had to fight to prevent the Whitney name and Bitterleaf from being dragged through the mud by the gossipmongers. But she could not expect her stepfather to understand her motives. He was fond of her in his rough way, and he presumed that she reciprocated the emotion, acting out of loyalty and love for him. The fact was that Meredith had resented him from the day he arrived at Bitterleaf and offered

to buy the plantation that had been in her late father's family
for almost seventy-five years.

Meredith lifted the corner of the carriage curtain and stared
out the window to avoid responding to Hurley's words. The
tall, thin houses of the Battery slipped by the carriage, deli-
cately tinted and adorned with grillwork, their high walls and
iron gates concealing neat little gardens where flowers grew
in profusion and fountains sparkled. The wooden shutters,
which could be closed against the lashings of wind and rain,
were now open wide to admit the fresh sea breezes, for even
though it was autumn, the air steamed. On the other side of
the cobblestoned street lay Charleston Bay, where the Ashley
and Cooper rivers flowed into the gray Atlantic Ocean. In the
distance on her right lay the docks where many masted wooden
sailing ships rested, the lifeblood of Charleston; they took the
raw riches of the fertile colony—rice and indigo—and brought
in return the finished goods and gold of England, providing
the commerce that made Charleston in 1761 one of the three
major ports of the American colonies and also one of its
largest cities.

The carriage rocked to a stop before the Market, the raised
platform where slaves were bought and sold. Beyond it,
Meredith could see the tall white spire of St. Philip's, pristinely aloof from the merchandising in flesh that lay before
her eyes.

Hurley climbed down from the vehicle, and Meredith watched
through the raised curtain. A crowd had gathered, mostly
men, although here and there one could spot a plumed or
flowered bonnet. The auction had begun. A man and woman
stood together on the platform, their hands clutched together
convulsively, their heads downcast, while the auctioneer rattled on about their merits as servants. Technically, Meredith
knew, the couple were not being sold as slaves. The shipping
company had given them passage to the colonies, and in
payment, the pair had signed an indenture promising to work
as servants in the new land for a period of years, usually
seven. The shipping company would then sell the indentures
to the highest bidders when the ship reached the colonial port.

However, no matter what their legal status, Meredith could
discover little difference between a slave auction and the

selling of indentures, except that these people's skins were white. They were placed on view before the crowd and bought like animals.

Meredith wished she had not come, despite Phoebe's chatter. The couple were sold, and a slight young man replaced them. He appeared too frail to be worth much, but he was purchased by Mr. Gladney, the silversmith, to be an apprentice. Meredith shifted in her seat. It was hot in the enclosed carriage. She opened the door, but even that did not lure the slight breeze into the boxy conveyance. Hurley glanced up. "Hot in there? Come out and stand. There's a pleasant enough breeze."

It was more ladylike to remain inside the carriage, but the sweat inched down Meredith's back, and she decided to do as her stepfather suggested. Standing beside Hurley, she was a good inch taller than he, and her high-brimmed straw bonnet made her even more towering. It was something Meredith had grown used to, just as she had become accustomed to the initial stare of a stranger or the discomfort of dancing with a man whose head stopped at her nose.

The boy was led off the platform, and a man strode across the stage to stop beside the auctioneer. He was taller than her cousin Galen, Meredith thought in surprise, and his shoulders were broad, his arms knotted with muscle. He wore no shirt, only ragged trousers, and Meredith could see the ribs that lay beneath his taut skin. He obviously had not had enough to eat during the passage over, and ordinarily Meredith's heart would have twisted with sympathy for the hungry man. But this one defied all pity. He walked cockily, his arms akimbo and he surveyed the crowd with an arrogant sneer. From his attitude, one would have thought him a well-dressed lord surveying the rabble, not a ragged, starved servant about to be sold.

"A fine-looking fellow," Hurley commented.

"Aye," a nearby man agreed, "but a mite too proud for me. That one's a troublemaker. He'll be off and running in a week."

"No, he wouldn't make a run-of-the-mill servant," Hurley replied noncommittally.

"Now here," the auctioneer began his spiel, "is a valuable worker. He has enough strength to put him in the fields. Look at those arms, that chest!" His fingers jabbed at the parts he extolled. "But that's not all. He can read, write, and do numbers. He's experienced with horses. Who'll start the bidding on such a fine specimen?"

"Ten pounds," a voice in the crowd offered.

The auctioneer grimaced. "Do you think to get him for free? He's worth at least forty pounds."

"Twelve." The bidding began in earnest, gradually creeping higher and higher. Throughout the bidding, the servant held his head high, his cold, arrogant face stamped with contempt. Meredith had to concede that he was as fine-looking as Hurley said. His hair might be clubbed clumsily at the nape of his neck, but the color was blazing gold. The lines of his face were clean and smooth, the cheekbones broad, the nose straight, and his blond-brown eyebrows curved above eyes of a piercing blue. A thick red-gold beard covered his jaw, the same color as the hair that matted his bare chest. But despite his handsomeness, he sent a chill through Meredith's stomach, and she agreed that the man was a troublemaker.

Hurley raised a finger, and Meredith whirled toward him in surprise. Before she could speak, her stepfather called, "I'd be willing to pay twenty-four pounds for the man, but first I want to hear him say something."

"Why? You think he's deaf and dumb?" the auctioneer blustered.

The man turned his bold blue gaze on Daniel Hurley, his mouth curling. "Is my speech so important?" he inquired coolly, his deep voice rolling out over the crowd, resonant and possessed of the purest of English accents. "Will it improve your profit any?"

Hurley met the cold eyes imperturbably. "Thank you. As I said, I'll offer twenty-four."

"Twenty-five pounds," said a man in the crowd.

The man on the block continued to look at Hurley as Daniel pushed the bidding higher, and the scornful gaze took in Meredith standing beside her stepfather. Slowly, casually, he inspected her, for all the world as if she were on the platform and he in the crowd, and Meredith flushed under the examination. A smile quirked the corners of his mouth, and he swung away to stare into the distance, above the heads of the crowd.

"Going once at thirty pounds," the auctioneer threatened. "Going twice."

Hurley lazily raised one finger, raising the price. "I have thirty-one pounds. Going once, going twice. Sold! To the gentleman in the blue coat and buff breeches."

"You're not serious!" Meredith gasped.

"Of course I am. Get into the carriage while I make arrangements to have our new servant brought to the Spencers' house." Hurley strode away.

Meredith glared impotently at his retreating back, then whirled around and climbed into the carriage, her skirts swaying. How could Daniel have been so foolish? She had thought her stepfather many things, but never lacking in wit. Couldn't he see that such a man would not stoop to hard labor? He'd escape into the swamp in a matter of days, and Hurley would lose his entire investment.

A few minutes later, Daniel entered the carriage, and it rolled away. Meredith folded her arms, her expression frosty. Daniel raised an eyebrow, and his lips twitched. "All right. What is it, lass? Your face would freeze a fire."

"What is it?" she repeated with heavy sarcasm. "That man, of course!"

"Jeremy Devlin?"

"Is that his name? So he's Irish as well. I might have known."

"As to that, I don't know. His name may be Irish, but he speaks like an Englishman."

"An English gentleman," Meredith corrected. "Don't you think there's something havey-cavey about an indentured servant who talks as if he were a lord?"

Hurley shrugged. "I see nothing wrong with it. Most likely he's an actor down on his luck, or a gentleman's servant who got thrown out on his ear. Maybe a tutor who got caught dallying with his charge's older sister."

"A tutor? With arms and shoulders like that? Huh!" Meredith's tone was scornful.

Hurley cast her a meaningful look. "Ah, so you noticed, did you?"

Meredith bit her lip and struggled not to blush. "How could I help it, when he had on no shirt?" she snapped.

"Well, you're right. Not many tutors have muscular arms. They're built along more willowy lines, like your cousin Galen. I've often thought he would make an admirable tutor."

"We are not discussing Galen Whitney. We're talking about the servant you bought. How could you?"

"Why, quite easily. That's why we came to Charleston, if you'll remember. I purchased three blacks yesterday, and I wanted an indentured servant, if there was a quality one available—"

"But why?" she asked, surprised. "You've never wanted an indentured servant before?"

Hurley smiled secretively. "Let's just say this Devlin fellow fits the requirements."

"He's a troublemaker, just as that man said."

"How do you know? You haven't even met him."

"It was obvious. He was arrogant, didn't show a sign of shame. Anyone else would, in his position."

"I don't want a weak man. Nor one whose spirit's been broken. When I got his indenture and arranged to pay the captain of the ship, I took a closer look at Devlin. His back was bruised and welted. Clearly, he's received a few blows aboard ship."

Meredith winced, but insisted stubbornly, "Which proves he's a troublemaker."

"No, it proves he doesn't buckle under easily. It doesn't mean he can't be handled by the right person."

"But to pay so much for such a risk—thirty-one pounds! I've never known an indentured servant to bring so much."

Hurley shrugged. "Other people saw his worth, too. Don't worry. We had a good crop this year. The captain was happy to take the money out in trade."

"Why do you need him? What can he do that isn't done by others?"

"He's a bright man. I might groom him to be overseer."

"You already have Caleb Jackson."

"Who does his best to cheat me at every turn. I'd prefer someone more reliable."

"But you can't just hand the overseer's job to an indentured servant!"

"I don't plan to start him in the position. Right now, he isn't well enough for field work. He needs a week or two of good food to fill out his frame. For the time being, I'll assign him to the stables.''

''But that's Sam's domain. He'll be offended if you put another man in there.''

''He'll do as I tell him and be quiet about it. Which is more than I can say for the members of my own family.''

Meredith pursed her lips and fell into a cold silence. After a moment, Daniel reached across to pat her clumsily on the knee. ''There, I didn't mean to hurt you. I like your spirit. I can count on you to stand up and tell me exactly what you think. It's the same quality I admire in Devlin. Come now, don't be angry. I took a chance on a servant. What does it matter? If you turn out to be right, I can afford the loss.''

She sighed, a faint smile touching her lips. ''That's true, of course. And I have no right to scold you on how you spend your money. It's simply that I took a dislike to Mr. Devlin.''

''Did you? It'll work out, I'm sure. Now, let's talk of something else. Why do you call me 'Father Hurley' in your cousin's house, as if I were someone you barely knew? I'd prefer you call me Daniel, as you do at home.''

''It seemed impolite. Aunt Caroline is so strict about propriety, you know.''

''Do I ever!'' He laughed shortly. ''She rang quite a peal over your mother's head ten years ago for marrying me. Said I wasn't Anne's class. 'Course she was right. Anne was always above my touch. But couldn't any man have loved her better or given her more. She was happy, wasn't she?''

''Yes, she was very happy,'' Meredith answered truthfully. Her mother had not seemed to see Daniel's coarseness or mind the lack of gentility and education that her first husband had possessed in such abundance. Even Meredith had softened to him, seeing the way he showered her mother with love and presents.

They pulled to a stop at the door of the Spencer house, and Daniel jumped down, then turned to help Meredith from the carriage. Her aunt's house was a soft pink color, decorated with stark white ironwork. Narrow and tall, it was set almost flush against its neighbor on one side and had a small bricked-in garden on the other. They climbed the front steps and entered the cool marble hall.

Aunt Caroline's modulated voice came to them from the drawing room. "Meredith, my love, how are you? I feel I've hardly seen you today."

Caroline Spencer raised her cheek for Meredith's dutiful peck. She was as small and perfectly formed as Meredith's mother had been, her slender hands graceful, her tiny waist still spannable by a man's hands. Few lines showed in her face under the fashionable makeup she wore, and the current style of powdering the hair hid any streaks of gray. She had not married a man who had wasted away his birthright as Benjamin Whitney had done, and her looks and personality remained untouched by the worries that had marked Anne. But neither did she possess her late sister's warmth and enjoyment of life.

"Phoebe positively monopolized your time this morning. I suppose you two were full of girlish things to confide."

Meredith could not imagine either having girlish confidences or exposing them to her flighty cousin if she did. But she did not say so, merely smiled at her aunt and murmured a noncommittal response. Aunt Caroline nodded briefly to Hurley and spoke his name, her typical greeting to the man Anne had married against her wishes. If it were not for the fact that she accompanied him, Meredith doubted that her aunt would have admitted Daniel to her house. Of course, then Daniel would have stayed at a public inn and doubtless been far happier.

"If you'll excuse me, I'll go to my room and tidy up. The Market was rather warm," Meredith said.

"Yes. I'm glad to see you wore your hat against the sun. When you were a child, you were quite careless. I remember how you threw me into absolute horrors, running out into the sun without a hat or long sleeves."

"I've become quite staid now, Auntie. I found I don't like to go about with freckles," Meredith responded. She bobbed her aunt a slight curtsy and left the room. Quickly she ran up the stairs, longing to unfasten her dress and lie down for a few minutes with a cool rag doused in lavender water on her forehead. It was the treatment her mother had given her whenever she came in with a pounding headache from too much sun or exercise, and she used it now to soothe the headaches that were more often brought about by people than by the sun.

Her maid, Betsy, appeared when Meredith tugged at the bell pull. "There, you look right peaked, Miss Merry. Have you had a bad day?"

"Not so bad. But sometimes my cousin wears on my nerves, and I had a slight disagreement with Mr. Hurley."

Betsy hid a smile as her fingers worked at the ties of her mistress's dress. It was not uncommon for Miss Merry to argue with the master. They both enjoyed it, and Betsy suspected that the argument was not what had given her the headache. More likely it was her silly cousin or the stuffy aunt. Betsy would be happy when they returned to Bitterleaf. When she finished unlacing the bodice, Meredith lay down and let Betsy gently massage her temples, then press a damp, sweet-smelling cloth across her forehead.

Betsy tiptoed softly out of the room, leaving Meredith alone with her thoughts. She wished fervently that Daniel had not purchased Jeremy Devlin. She had to admit to herself, even if not to Daniel, that she wasn't worried about his running away. It would serve Daniel right if he did, and she wouldn't be sorry. No, what bothered Meredith was having Devlin around all the time, knowing that this servant had boldly run his eyes over her and then dismissed her. He thought her beneath his notice, no doubt too tall and plain to bother with. How could she bear to face him when he had stood on the block, himself a piece of property being bid for, and contemptuously judged her and found her wanting!

Chapter II

JEREMY DEVLIN sat flat on the wooden deck of the ship and
leaned against the railing. The vessel plowed through the
thick gray-green water. A breeze caressed his face, and he
sucked in a grateful gulp of air. How could the colonials
stand to live in this hellish place? The air was so thick and
moist it was almost solid, and his lungs had had to labor to
breathe from the moment the ship landed in Charleston Bay.
And the heat! When he stood still, the sweat would pop out
on his forehead—and it was September, the truly hot months
past. He gazed across at the shore, where gnarled gray trees
clung to the banks, their roots writhing into the river like
great snakes. Gray strings of moss hung from their branches,
wafting in the breeze like tattered, dirty lace. He suppressed a
shiver. Even the landscape here was bizarre.

He had seen England, Ireland, and the Continent, but this
was a whole new world. Its strangeness shook his confidence,
a thing that had happened rarely in the past. A few months
ago, as Devlin sat in his favorite gambling den, his arm
looped casually around the shoulder of his latest mistress, he
would have laughed uproariously at the idea that he would
today be sitting on a boat on a river in the Carolinas, his
hands bound before him, three great, silent blacks crouched
not five feet away from him, possessions, like him, of the
man at the far end of the boat. His mind was still reeling from

the shock of it. He could not blame the old man, really; he
had become too much of a scandal to him. But he wondered
if his lordship would have paid the ruffians to knock Devlin
over the head and sell him to the ship's captain if he could
have envisioned what indentured servitude meant. Had he
known that his nephew, a man with Wrexham blood coursing
through his veins, no matter how illegitimately, would be put
up on an auction block and sold to the highest bidder? Devlin
closed his eyes at the memory of his shame, the final humiliation after weeks of starvation and beatings by the sailors that
his aristocratic attitude had brought upon him. When they
pushed him up the steps and onto the stage, shirtless and
dirty, exposed to the eyes of the eager crowd, he had wanted
to curl up into a ball, or to burrow into a hole and hide. But
his pride had held him erect, made him face them with head
high and mouth curling in contempt. They were peasants, he
told himself, not one his equal in bloodline, education, or
manners, and he had fixed his lordliest gaze upon them.

Remembering that time, he swung his gaze to the front of
the boat, where the girl sat idly toying with her closed
parasol. A green-and-gold-striped awning shaded her. Earlier,
before they rounded a curve in the river, she had opened the
parasol to block the rays that crept in from one side of the
awning. Her delicate skin must feel none of the sun that
blazed down upon his head until he thought his brains would
fry, Jeremy thought savagely. Just as her delicate derrière
must not suffer the rough planks of the deck. He smiled
involuntarily. As if delicate were a word that could ever be
applied to that one. He did not know her name, and in his
mind he called her "the Amazon." Truly, she could have
been a warrior queen. She was what Ferdy Worthing would
have termed a "fine, strapping wench." Ferdy always put
down his gold for the healthy, milkmaid sort at a brothel, a
girl who looked as if she might snap him in two. Not Jeremy
Devlin. No, he preferred a small woman, with dainty wrists
and a soft rounded form.

For a time on the auction block, the people in the crowd
had been a meaningless blur to Devlin. Then the man Hurley
had bellowed at him to speak, and Jeremy's eyes had locked
on him and the woman who stood beside him. Although he

had managed to retort, his whole being had been jolted by the realization that a woman witnessed his shame. He had stared at her, frozen with humiliation, until at last a saving anger burst in him. No woman of sensibility would come to gawk at humans for sale. She probably took a perverse, lascivious pleasure from watching half-naked men paraded and sold like cattle. He was surprised she hadn't asked to inspect the merchandise. The spurt of disgust had freed him, allowed him to turn his face from her. He had looked more closely at the crowd then, and found women scattered among the men. What a strange breed these colonials were. He'd lock up any woman of his before he'd let her view the sale of flesh.

The Amazon stood now and opened her parasol, then strolled over to the man who had purchased him. The man pointed to something on shore, and she laughed, revealing white, even teeth. Jeremy wondered how it would feel to have those teeth sink into the flesh of his shoulder, sharp with passion. The thought surprised him. Surely he had no desire for that giantess. Her head came clear to his chin, and she was plain and dull as ditchwater. Her dress was a lackluster brown, much the color of her hair, which she wore in a conservative knot on her neck, and her skin was colorless. Compared to the beauties he had known in London, powdered and rouged, blazing with jewels and satins, she was a country mouse. Moreover, she had seen him at his lowest point, stripped and treated like an animal. He despised her for witnessing his debasement and for the sick nature that made her enjoy watching it. How could he have any hunger for her?

And yet—perhaps he wanted to couple with her for that very reason. To have her beneath him, dominated, writhing, moaning, begging for the pleasure he could give her. Yes, to have the Amazon at his mercy would be suitable revenge. He swallowed, and his eyes sought her out again. What was she to the old man? Daughter? Wife? How would it feel to lie against a woman whose body was almost as long as his? It might be pleasant to rest upon a woman without having to support himself on his arms to avoid crushing her. He studied the girl, wondering how her body would look without the concealing dress. The stiff bodice flattened her breasts, but something told him they were full and ripe, and that the hips beneath the hoop were wide, the legs strong and slender. Simply thinking about it made the heat rise in his blood. It had been a long, empty time since those beauties in London.

It did not occur to Devlin to wonder if she would succumb to him. The upheaval in his life might have shaken him, but not to such an extent. He had always been attractive to women, able to smile and wheedle his way with them or take them as his right, whichever suited his purpose and mood. And once he'd taken them, they wanted him back again and again. It was something he'd inherited from his parents, he thought, for Jeremy Wrexham had had a surfeit of ladies until the day he died, and Bridget Devlin had never lacked for gentleman protectors. Once a friend had asked him his secret with women, and Devlin had said, grinning, "Simple: I treat the whores like ladies, and the ladies like whores."

The boat turned into an inlet, and both Hurley and the girl were gripped by excitement. They leaned over the starboard rail, gazing into the gloom of the lush undergrowth lining the banks. Jeremy looked in the same direction, but could see nothing. After a few minutes, a wharf came into view, with sheds for storing and a large wooden dock. Several small black children were on the dock, pointing and jumping. The ship pulled to the dock and was secured by two black men who waited there. They laid a plank from ship to dock, and the Amazon ran down it lithely, despite her encumbering hoop and skirts. Hurley followed her. The children clustered around him while he made a great show of searching his pockets and finally showered them with sweets. The children scrambled across the planks, picking up candies and stuffing them into their mouths, and Hurley and the woman stepped from the dock onto a beaten dirt path that curled into the undergrowth. A dark-haired man, casually dressed in shirt, breeches, boots, and a wide-brimmed straw hat, came down the path from the opposite direction and halted before the couple. He talked to Hurley for a moment, and Hurley gestured toward the boat. Jeremy noticed that the girl stood well back from the newcomer, almost behind Hurley. The man moved aside to let them pass, and the couple disappeared around a curve.

Two crew members strode back to where Jeremy sat. "All right. This is where you leave. Get up now."

Jeremy rose slowly, easing stiff joints. The three blacks stared at the crewmen with a blank lack of comprehension. One of the crewmen prodded at a black with a short club, and the other made rising motions with his hand. Finally the blacks rose. Jeremy quickly left the ship ahead of them. He'd never been around such as they before, and they made him uneasy. Better to stay far away from them.

The cluster of children had vanished. The man who had met Hurley on the path paced the dock, waiting impatiently for the new arrivals to leave the ship. He carried a long, coiled whip in one hand, which he tapped irritably against his boot. Jeremy straightened to full height and came to a stop before the man, staring at him squarely, his face carefully devoid of any sign of intimidation. The dark man glared, his eyes sudden pinpoints of hatred. The others padded onto the dock, their bare feet silent on the wood.

"I am Jackson," the dark man began. "I'm overseer here at Bitterleaf. That means I run things. You do as I say." He shook out the whip and snapped it across the dock with a loud crack. "Or else. Understand?" Jeremy waited silently, determined not to appear to give in to Jackson. He doubted whether the others had understood a word the overseer said, but clearly they understood the meaning of the whip. Jeremy did, too. The crew had used only their fists or clubs on him to crush his arrogance, but he had seen a disobedient sailor's back turned to pulp under the lash. Jackson gestured toward the path. "Walk that way. Go."

Again Jeremy took the lead, jumping lightly off the dock. He disliked obeying the overseer, but he wasn't about to group himself with the slaves. He trudged up the path, struggling to breathe in the thick air, his eyes on the lush vegetation around him.

Soon he could see the vegetation ending before him, and he glimpsed a green expanse of lawn. His footsteps quickened, and he emerged onto a wider walk paved with crushed seashells. Jeremy stopped abruptly, staring at the well-kept house and yard that interrupted the bizarre jungle landscape. For a moment he felt as if it could have been a dream, and he had awakened back at an English country home. He faced one side of a two-story, red-brick mansion trimmed in white. A cupola adorned the top of the house, and a fan-shaped, columned porch jutted out from the rear. He could glimpse the corner of the long porch, supported by tall, round, white columns, that ran across the front. Beyond the porch, on a wide green lawn, lay sheep, peacefully cropping the grass. At the end of the lawn curved a circular carriage drive, also paved in crushed shells, and from it a road stretched into the distance, shaded on both sides by massive oak trees hung with gray moss. A garden encompassed the side and back of the house, and though it was autumn, flowers bloomed in riotous pinks, reds, and purples.

Hurley stood on the small rear porch with two women, one the Amazon, the other a petite beauty several years older than she. Her red hair was piled charmingly on her head, and her face was dainty and dimpled, her smile bright. Now that was the sort he liked, Jeremy thought, his manhood swelling in his breeches. Soft, pliable, and sweet. She chattered vivaciously, her laughter tinkling out across the garden, and placed a small white hand on Hurley's arm. The gesture could have been that of a daughter, but Devlin glimpsed the warmth on her face, the curve of her mouth, and knew that she slept with Hurley. What a shame for her to be wasted in an old man's bed. The other woman must be his daughter, then, not his wife. But the redhead could not be her mother.

"Around behind the garden!" Jackson barked behind Jeremy, prodding him with the butt of his whip. Devlin tensed. Before his time on the ship, he would have whirled and taken the man down for the insult. But he had learned since then. Sucking in his breath, Jeremy suppressed his anger and started along the path that curved behind the garden to the outbuildings on the far side of the house. The tiny shells of the walkway bit into his bare feet, but he scarcely noticed as he breathed in the scent of the flowers on the other side of the hedge. Jackson gestured toward a side path leading to the outbuildings—the stables, storehouse, smithy, granary, cistern, and others Jeremy did not recognize.

When Hurley had purchased him, he had explained that Bitterleaf was a huge plantation worked entirely by black slaves, and that Jeremy would be the only indentured servant.

Jeremy could see by the number of outbuildings that the plantation was almost a town in itself.

"Jackson!" Hurley's voice called from the porch. "Leave Devlin here. The white. I want to speak to him."

Jeremy halted, turning. Jackson gave him a hard glare before he swung away, pushing the others before him to relieve his disappointment at having Devlin taken out of his grasp. Hurley left the women and walked toward him, stopping a few feet away to mop his red face. He motioned to Devlin. "Come here, boy. Let's sit in the garden."

Jeremy followed him, and Hurley sank onto a stone bench. Jeremy remained standing, his feet firmly planted apart, his bound hands clasped in front of him. He had also learned not to sit when others did. Like all his lessons, it had been hard won, and he had the bruises on his back to prove it. Hurley gazed up at him, shielding his eyes from the sun, and waved impatiently toward the other bench. "Sit. Sit. I don't want to crane my neck to see you."

He dropped onto the bench Hurley indicated and waited for him to speak, luxuriating in the color and scent of the garden. It was so long since he had been in the midst of beauty, and the flowers invaded his senses. Did they smell this sweet in England? Had he simply forgotten, or were the flowers here, like everything else, lusher, riper? He was jerked back from his thoughts by Hurley's voice. "I'm putting you in the stables, Devlin. I understand you do such work."

"I know horses."

"Sam is the head groom. You'll report to him, even though he's a slave. Do the blacks make you uneasy?" He chuckled. "Me, too, when I first came over. You'll get used to them, even find some of the women mighty pretty in their own way. But that's beside the point. What I wanted to talk to you about was running away." Jeremy did not betray his surprise by so much as a flicker of an eyelash, although his stomach quivered at the words.

"I know a man like you will be thinking of escape. You've

too much spirit to take to being a servant. When I first saw you, I liked the fact that you weren't cowed. A broken man won't do for me. But I'm asking you not to run. You won't be in the stables for long. Nor the fields, either. They kill a man, white quicker than black. No, I have things in mind for you far better than that.''

"What things?'' Jeremy asked, puzzled.

"No—can't tell you yet. I have to observe you for a while, see if you have the qualities I suspect you do. I know nothing about you, except that you sound like a gentleman, but you aren't, or you wouldn't be here.''

"No, I'm not a gentleman.'' Devlin's voice was tinged with bitterness.

"Well, it makes no difference to me. No gentleman myself. But I'm a good worker and crafty, and I know how to make money. I suspect you're the same kind. But I got to study you, see for myself.''

"So I'm to be a bug that you pin and watch wriggle?''

"Don't make the mistake of thinking I'm a crazy old man. I'm not. Nor am I soft. I could put you in the fields under Jackson and break you without a single regret. Don't forget that. But I want you to know there are possibilities ahead for you. It would be wiser not to try to run away. I imagine we'd catch you anyway. First few weeks here, a man has trouble breathing the air, let alone running.'' He stood. "I'll take you to the stables now.''

Jeremy followed him, wondering how Hurley knew his thoughts were already on escape. The old man was right. Everything was too strange now, too foreign. He had no idea where to go or how to leave. He wasn't physically up to it, unused as he was to this climate and weak from weeks on the ship. But give him a few weeks, and then he'd take his chances. No matter what Hurley said, he wasn't about to hang around here on the hope the old fool would offer him a better job than the stables. Any job in servitude was not for Jeremy Devlin.

Lydia Chandler fanned her face as she settled into the damask-covered mahogany chair. "My, my, it certainly is hot for September. Don't you think so, Meredith?''

"I suppose. I've lived here all my life, and I don't notice the heat as much as you do." Meredith paced the floor, unaccountably restless now that she was home.

"I envy you," Lydia replied with feeling. "Lord, but it's been ages since you left. You can't imagine how glad I am to see you. It gave me the chills, being out here all by myself with all the slaves—and Jackson, always giving me the eye."

"Did he bother you?" Meredith asked, surprised. "Tell Daniel, and he'll let Jackson go."

"No, no, he never says anything outright. Just little hints and glances, you know."

"No, I don't," Meredith retorted flatly. "I'm not the type who gets little hints and glances."

Spots of red stained Mrs. Chandler's cheeks. "If you think that I encourage him . . ."

"Don't take it that way," Meredith hastily assured her. "I wasn't implying you did anything wrong. I simply meant men aren't interested enough in me to hint or glance." Meredith smiled. She would hate to hurt the other woman's feelings, even though her morals were hardly what Meredith would wish for herself. When Lydia had arrived on her stepfather's arm after a business trip to Virginia, Meredith had been consumed with rage. How dare he bring his fancy woman into her mother's house and live with her openly, exposing not only himself but Meredith as well to all kinds of scandal! She was quite determined to despise Lydia. But though she deplored their liaison and resented the insult to her mother, Meredith found it difficult to dislike Lydia. She was a warm, open person, blunt and often coarse, but humorous and down-to-earth as well. She was competent and helped out whenever it was needed, but never imposed herself or attempted to run the house. Meredith realized that a more scheming woman would have tried to entice Hurley into marriage and persuade him to cut Meredith out of his will.

Gradually, Lydia had become more and more a friend to her. She persuaded Meredith to straighten up and carry her height well instead of slouching in an attempt to be shorter. "Be proud of being tall. Mary Queen of Scots was six feet tall, and she was considered a great beauty in her day!" she pointed out to Meredith. Meredith had replied tartly that it was despite her height, not because of it, but she came to believe that Lydia was right. It was better to be proud and plain and towering than ashamed and plain and towering. Slouching only worsened her looks.

"Tell me about Charleston." Lydia leaned forward eagerly. Meredith knew Lydia would have loved to go, but of course could not, since they had stayed with Meredith's aunt.

"Well," Meredith began hesitantly. "You know I don't much care for calling on people, or fashion, or parties."

"Meredith!" The other woman's voice vibrated with disappointment. "Do you mean to tell me you didn't do anything?"

"I did go to the theater," Meredith admitted, and a corner of her mouth twitched.

"You wretch," Lydia exclaimed. "You're teasing me. Tell every detail."

Meredith described her trip to the city, including an excursion to the theater and a visit to the millinery shop, concluding, "And I bought something there that might interest you."

"A hat? Oh, let me see."

Meredith went into the wide entry hall and up the mahogany-railed staircase to her bedroom on the second floor, with Lydia right on her heels. Inside her room, Meredith pulled a hatbox from the luggage and extended it to Lydia. Lydia pried off the lid, her mouth forming an "O" of delight.

"Oh, Meredith, it's beautiful!" She reverently pulled out the straw hat inside. It was shallow-crowned, its wide brim dipping on both sides so that it resembled a coal scuttle upside down. The edge was trimmed in blue satin, as was the low crown, and a froth of lace spilled down the back. "Try it on and let me see."

"You try it on. It's yours, you know."

"Meredith!" Lydia gasped in surprise, throwing her arms around the taller girl. "You're a dear." Running to the mirror, she set the bonnet on her head. The front dipped low over her forehead, coyly shading her eyes and accenting their blue color. The back rose precariously, pushed up by Lydia's piled hair and by the tall inner crown, so that the hat tilted saucily. She turned this way and that, admiring it in the mirror. "It's absolutely beautiful." She smiled at her reflection, then pulled off the hat and held it out toward Meredith. "But you try it on, too."

"I got it for you," Meredith protested.

"Then put on *my* hat," Lydia said with heavy patience. "I want to see how it looks."

Meredith made a face. "I can tell you how it will look. I'll seem ten feet tall."

"Please? As a favor to me."

Reluctantly Meredith accepted the concoction from the older woman's hands. "You must have been lacking in amusement while I was gone." Going to the mirror, she placed the hat in the same position Lydia had, although the back did not rise as much above her sleek head. Even so, the saucy tilt greatly increased her height. Meredith grimaced at her reflection. "See? I'm a giant."

"But a very pretty one," Lydia pointed out. "You may look tall, but it does nice things for your face."

Meredith searched the mirror again. It was true that the satin ribbons around the edge softened the firm, clean lines of her face, and the pitch of the hat gave an almost coquettish brightness to her expression. A faint smile curved the straight, wide mouth, then Meredith firmly shook her head. "No. It is pretty, I'll admit. But frills and furbelows are not meant for great, towering women. They're lovely on you, but on me they look silly."

Lydia sighed. "Honestly, Meredith, you are the most exasperating girl. You've never left this backwater parish, yet you think you know more about style than I, who's lived in London. You could be a pretty woman as well as a sensible one. What does it matter if you're tall? You can't fade into the woodwork by making yourself as plain as possible. You should go for the opposite effect—bright colors, a pretty face and hair. Then everyone would notice you with envy."

"Even Opal Hamilton?" Meredith said, invoking the name of the second wife of Angus Hamilton, who was much younger than he. She was the reigning beauty of that part of the country, a dainty porcelain doll of a woman, with pale blond hair and limpid blue eyes.

Lydia grimaced. "Yes, especially that stuck-up little fancy piece. She trembles with dread if any woman threatens her position. That's why she's so sharp-tongued and eager to gossip. I knew an actress like her, the foremost player of a leading company in London. She was a real beauty, but she was so frightened that someone might look better that she turned into a vicious hag, concentrating all her efforts on destroying others. But don't try to lead me astray. We weren't talking about Opal Hamilton. We were discussing you, and how pretty you'd be in this hat and other clothes like it."

"I'd look as if I was at a fancy dress ball," Meredith replied firmly, taking off the hat and replacing it in the box. "Even if you're right, I couldn't possibly carry it off. Everyone knows I'm plain Meredith Whitney, who does her stepfather's accounts, runs a household, and has been on the shelf for years. I can't be a tall, dashing *femme fatale*."

"You forget that I'm here to help you." Lydia strove to look outraged.

"You can teach me, but you can't speak for me or dance for me, or make me anything but stiff in the company of men. I appreciate your efforts, but I've been this way for years, and I'm content with myself. Why pretend to be something I'm not? My cousin appreciates me as I am."

"Oh, him." Lydia dismissed Galen Whitney as unworthy of her consideration. "You might as well marry a stick. I've never heard Mr. Whitney turn a pretty compliment or make a witty remark or look as if he'd die to get you into his bed."

"Lydia!"

"Well, that's what courtship and marriage are all about. All Galen Whitney can do is spout poetry and drone on about dreadfully dull books and ideas. Believe me, that won't keep your bed warm at night. He'd bore you to tears."

Meredith assumed a frosty expression. "Cousin Galen and I have a spiritual attachment. Our minds are in tune."

"That's what I'm saying! He's cold and deadly dull, and if you think you'd be happy married to such a man, you're only fooling yourself. For all you struggle to appear cool and unemotional, I know there is fire and passion in you. I've seen it creep out when you're fighting with Daniel or tending a slave's wound.''

"The first instance is anger, and the second is compassion. I fail to see what either have to do with carnal lust, which is what you seem to be discussing.''

"Do you think your emotions are that separate, that you can have some and not others, that you can deeply feel pity or raging anger or loss at your mother's death—yes, Daniel has told me how you cried your heart out the night she died—''

"He shouldn't have mentioned that to anyone," Meredith muttered, tight-lipped. She hated to remember the night her mother breathed her last. Meredith had turned from Anne's bedside, stumbled into her stepfather's arms, and sobbed helplessly, clinging to Daniel as to a lifeline. It was the one close moment she had felt with the man she had always thought of as a stranger in her home. It was also a time of heartbreaking despair such as she hoped never to experience again.

"Why shouldn't he talk of it to me? Because you act as if you dislike Daniel? Or because it doesn't fit your picture of yourself as a cool, contained person? Well, you did cry, and you did hurt, however much you prefer to deny it. And I can't believe you'd truly be happy with Galen Whitney, who doesn't need to fake his lack of emotion. Don't you want to pour out your heart to a man, feel his arms tight around you, and know he wants you so badly it makes him shake as though he had a fever? Wouldn't you like a strong, handsome creature with eyes that blaze right through you—for instance, the man Daniel brought home today. What's his name?''

"Jeremy Devlin?" Meredith's voice cracked in amazement, and color flamed in her cheeks. "You can't be serious! He's an indentured servant. Daniel bought him on the block three days ago.''

"Such things don't matter here. Daniel arrived in the colonies with barely the shirt on his back, but today he's one of the most respected and wealthiest men in South Carolina. Being a servant doesn't make a man less fine or less handsome. Your cousin has superior bloodlines, but he doesn't have warm blood running in his veins, and that's what it takes to be a man.''

"I don't condemn a man for being poor or attempting to better his lot by coming to the colonies, even if it means buying his passage with his own servitude," Meredith stated haughtily. "But that man is . . . He's . . . well, he isn't proper or respectful or respectable. He's . . ." Her hauteur vanished as she fumbled for a word to describe the arrogant man who had stared at her with thinly veiled dislike throughout the trip up the Cooper River.

"Handsome?" Lydia supplied. "Tall and broad-shouldered! Or is it that he's proud? That he looks at you not like a servant does, but as a man would."

"I don't know what you mean."

"Perhaps not. Certainly, your cousin Galen wouldn't know how to look that way at a woman, and you'd discourage any other man less bold than the one in the garden."

"Lydia, you sound as if you liked Devlin, as if you thought he was attractive."

"Well, of course I do. Don't tell me you didn't notice."

Meredith shrugged. "He is a fine-looking man, if that's all you're interested in."

"I think it's something that should interest a girl your age."

"I am not a foolish, romantic maiden, continually searching for a handsome man to sweep me off my feet."

"At least you *try* very hard not to be." Lydia moved to the window. She didn't want to argue with Meredith, even though the girl was being stubbornly blind. Besides, she had found that no one could budge Meredith once her mind was set. It was better to let the subject drop.

The stables were clearly visible from Meredith's window, and Lydia found her gaze turning toward them instinctively. Meredith might admit no attraction to the new indentured servant, but a jolt had run through Lydia the instant she saw him. He had fastened brilliant blue eyes on her, and her skin had grown as warm as if he had touched her. As Lydia stood watching the barn, Sam walked out, Devlin following him. He strode across to a wagon and lifted a heavy sack from it onto his broad shoulders. His skin gleamed with sweat in the hot moist air, and his muscles knotted. Lydia swallowed against the sudden constriction in her throat. There was something about that man—an aura of danger and sensuality—that excited and frightened her at the same time. She knew with a dreadful certainty that with his arrival the lives of those at Bitterleaf would never by the same.

Chapter III

MEREDITH AWOKE much later the following morning than she was accustomed to. Blinking, she stared, startled by the sun streaming in the window and across the polished cypress wood floor. With a sigh, she stretched, pushed back the gauzy mosquito netting, and hopped out of the high bed. She padded across the floor in her thin lawn nightgown to the open window, which looked down on the backyard of the house. Just beyond the brilliance of the flower garden and the white breadth of the crushed-shell driveway, the land fell into tangled undergrowth as it stretched to the water, a tributary of the broad, lazy Cooper River. The inlet, much narrower than the Cooper, was sluggish and serpentine. The sun glittered off the water in bright sparkles.

She breathed in the heavy, moist air as if it were the life-stuff of gods and gazed fondly at the broad oak trees with their tangled ornaments of gray moss. How lovely it was to be home. There was no place like Bitterleaf. The rice and indigo fields lay to the right beyond the outbuildings, and Meredith turned to look in that direction. Her eyes fell on the stables below, where the new servant was carrying a shovel of muck out of the building to add to the heap outside. The sun played across his broad back and blazed upon the bright gold hair. He paused, resting on his shovel, and wiped the sweat from his forehead with the back of one arm. Hairs had come loose from the tightly knotted queue and straggled against his face, dark with sweat. Meredith's chest tightened, and she realized with a blush what a picture she would present if he happened to glance up at the house. She was leaning out of the window, clearly visible in her thin nightgown. She pulled back quickly, striking her head on the window frame so hard it brought tears to her eyes.

Gingerly rubbing her sore scalp, Meredith strode to the large wardrobe standing against the far wall. Her bedroom was a large, open room not cluttered by furniture. The great bed, so high off the ground that one had to climb into it via a small set of steps, dominated the room with its tall columns and heavy canopy, or tester. Heavy brocade bed curtains hung from the canopy, pulled back and tied in the still-warm weather. When the days of damp cold came in deep winter, the curtains would be drawn tight against the drafts that flowed in around the windows. Both the bed and the massive wardrobe were beautiful pieces of mahogany furniture imported from England, as was the highboy chest of drawers. Only the frame of the chamber pot, the comfortable Windsor chair, and the large trunk at the foot of the bed were made from native hickory wood.

Meredith opened the doors of the wardrobe and dug deep into the closet for a plain, much worn, and discolored Indian cotton dress. It was an ugly thing that had shrunk through many washings until it ended unattractively at her ankles. It was not the sort of dress she usually wore, but she saved it for days like this, when she expected to be involved in several dirty tasks. She knew that in the mere week she had been gone the housekeeping had probably deteriorated. Lydia was a pleasant woman, but weak about issuing commands and anxious not to assume authority that did not rightfully belong to her. The servants felt free to largely ignore her few suggestions, detecting her weakness and aware of her uncertain position in the household. Meredith suspected the place had not been dusted since she left. She would have to inspect the whole house carefully, including the kitchen and the springhouse, where fresh meat and milk were stored, to make certain that anything that had spoiled was thrown away. In addition, there were probably several slaves sick in their cabins, with no one to treat them while she was gone. She would have to tend them, and she had no desire to get blood and other, even less appetizing, aspects of sickness on a good dress.

She slipped on her chemise and only one petticoat, pulled on light stockings and heavy serviceable shoes with sturdy square heels and broad toes. There was a discreet tap on the door, and it opened an inch, then swung wide, and her maid Betsy marched in. "Oh, Miss Merry, I didn't know you were up and dressing. You should have called me." She bustled over to her mistress and snatched the worn dress from her hands. "You never mean you're wearing this old thing."

"I certainly do," Meredith declared defiantly. Betsy was only slightly less anxious than Lydia to put her mistress into beautiful clothes. "I have a great deal of work to do, and I'm not wearing something pretty."

Betsy opened her mouth and promptly closed it, deciding it would be less than tactful to point out that Meredith had almost nothing that was pretty. "Yes'm," she agreed resignedly and stretched on tiptoe to drop the garment over Meredith's head. The dress had faded to no describable color, a pale wash of some former pastel. Its bodice was too tight, so that her breasts strained against the material. Betsy shook her head in silent disapproval. Meredith said nothing, merely sat down at the vanity table so that Betsy could brush her long brown hair and tie it back in a somber knot at the nape of her neck.

"What time is it, Betsy?"

"Almost ten. Master'll be in from the fields soon." Like most planters, Hurley drank a tankard of homegrown corn beer after he rose, then rode around inspecting the fields, returning home in midmorning for a full breakfast. Usually by that time Meredith had also attended to many of her household chores. This morning, however, she would barely make it in time for breakfast.

She hurried downstairs, arriving in the dining room as her stepfather returned from the fields. There was a noisy flurry of activity outside, and a few moments later Daniel stomped into the house, calling for his valet to remove his riding boots. He entered the dining room and nodded briefly at Lydia and Meredith. He had not put on his wig that morning but had gone about the fields in his soft, at-home turban, as many planters did. The wig quickly became unbearable in the South Carolina damp and heat. He sat at the head of the table with Lydia on his left and Meredith on his right. Meredith, glancing across the table, noted that Lydia looked uncommonly pretty and flushed this morning. Apparently she had received a pleasant welcome from Hurley. As soon as the thought came into her mind, Meredith jumped mentally and blushed. How could she be thinking about such things? Even though it was common knowledge Daniel often shared Lydia's bed, it was most unladylike for Meredith to either acknowledge the fact or contemplate what transpired between them. She turned her attention to the narrow board table covered with snowy damask linen.

In her childhood, a large ornamental silver salt cellar had stood in the center of the table, but it had been sacrificed, as had most of their possessions, when they fell on hard times. After Anne married Daniel Hurley, she had imported new salt cellars, this time the more fashionable individual ones sitting on three spindly legs. A black servant passed around the board with pewter chargers filled with meat and dished out venison, pork, and pigeon onto their individual pewter trenchers, then set the serving dishes on the walnut sideboard. Beside each trencher stood a leather mug known as a jack. These were filled with beer brewed on the plantation. The meal was rounded out by fresh bread. The thick, almost unchewable crust had been sliced off and would appear at some other time as a gravy mixture with milk.

There was little conversation at their meals, since neither Hurley nor Meredith were talkers. Lydia had long since stopped trying to promote discussion. Breakfast was soon over, and they wiped their hands clean on the huge linen napkins. A servant again passed by with a "voider," a deep wicker basket into which he tossed the diners' napkins, trenchers, utensils, and any crumbs swept from the broad cloth.

After the meal, Meredith toured the house, carefully checking out the floors, straw mats, and furniture for signs of neglect in the housekeeping. She enjoyed her walk, for she deeply loved this house, just as she loved the land and the Whitney name. Hers was an old, fine family, and even though it had a sad tendency to squander its fortunes, there was no better bloodline in the whole colony. Bitterleaf House seemed to her to epitomize the Whitneys. It had been designed by her father shortly after her birth. It had taken ten years to build and was done largely by plantation labor. Even the bricks had been formed and kilned right here on Bitterleaf. Only the glass windowpanes had been shipped in from a German settlement in Pennsylvania. The wooden floors and walls were Carolina cypress, the gray tree whose roots thrust above the swamp water like gnarled and knotty limbs. The walls were paneled, and around the fireplace the paneling was elegantly finished. All the walls were painted a gray blue, although squares of paperhangings had been added to the entry hall last year at Lydia's request. She had assured them it was the highest fashion in London. So now above the chair rail cut across the middle of the wall there rose a tangle of flowers and birds in vibrant colors, with no pattern repeated. Even Meredith had to admit it was lovely.

Bitterleaf House was large. It contained drawing, sitting, and music rooms downstairs, as well as a spacious ballroom. Upstairs there were several bedrooms and a ladies' sitting room. The staircase rose in broad, shallow steps and turned at two landings. The banister was smooth, polished oak. The house was a jewel, grander and newer than Four Oaks or any other plantation in the vicinity. Her father had spent a large amount of money building it, as well as slaves' time, neglecting the fields for his masterpiece. The farm had suffered as a result, and the expenditure had contributed greatly to the mountain of debt with which her mother had had to cope after Benjamin Whitney's death. Anne had clung fiercely to the house, determined to save it and the farm as her daughter's heritage. Meredith knew she would have struggled equally hard, for if she ever had to leave her home, Meredith was sure her very soul would shrivel and die.

As Meredith headed toward the back of the house, she came upon the very man she was looking for—Paul, the black majordomo who was in charge of the household servants. His face was as dark and oiled as wood, never revealing a thought or emotion. He was calm, efficient, and obsequious in a way that somehow managed to remain lordly. Meredith had never liked the man as she did their cook, Dulcie, or her own maid.

He strolled toward her in silent, portly dignity and stopped to gravely execute a bow. "Miss Meredith. I hope you had a pleasant journey."

"Yes, I did," Meredith replied. "However, I am not so pleased with the way things have gone here."

He assumed a look of amazement. "Here, ma'am? Is something wrong?"

"Yes." Meredith kept her voice firm. She was not about to be fooled by his air of innocence. "The floors haven't been waxed, though I left strict instructions they should be. Also, the furniture has not been properly dusted, and the silverware on display in the dining room cabinet is tarnishing. It should be polished. And I think it's time to carry out the straw matting and clean it. Then bring down the rugs from the attic, clean them, and spread them on the floors—after the floors have been waxed, of course. I'll be the one to determine when they are waxed sufficiently."

"Yes, ma'am."

She continued with her list of complaints and tasks, ignoring the older man's faintly hurt look. She had known Paul since she was a child, and he had seemed a grand, imposing figure to her then. Sometimes it was difficult to remember that she was in charge, even though she now rose several inches above his head. When Meredith was through, Paul nodded, resigned, and glided away, no doubt to release his wrath on the hapless servants under his authority. Meredith continued along the back hall and out the side door. A covered sidewalk led to the kitchen, which was wisely detached so its heat would not affect the rest of the house. Under the iron rule of Dulcie, the cook, the kitchen sparkled. Dulcie tolerated no slovenliness around her. She was Paul's wife, and a more different person than her husband could not be found. Warm and friendly, she was the confidante of everyone in the household, black and white alike. When she heard Meredith's footsteps, Dulcie whirled and threw her arms wide. "Miss Merry! You been gone forever! I thought you were never coming back."

Meredith smiled and stepped into the woman's bear hug. "You know I'll always return to Bitterleaf unless I'm dead."

"I suspect you might do it even then," Dulcie remarked.

Meredith chuckled and stepped back to glance around the room. The brick walls were whitewashed and lined with shelves on which were stored foodstuffs and pots and pans of every size, shape, and description. A door led to the large pantry, where cornmeal, flour, sugar, and other bulky or valuable foods were kept. The door was always locked, and the key hung securely from Dulcie's belt. One wall was entirely taken up by the huge, deep fireplace and the bake oven beside it. The continual fire burned merrily, and a pot hung over it on a crane. The crane could be swung out to have pots placed on it without risking burns to the cook's hands. Trivets stood in the fireplace on legs of various heights. The empty trivets were lined up beyond the fire. The others, supporting pans, kettles, and a large teakettle, stood in the coals. The trivet legs served to keep the pots above the coals and ashes.

On the mantel were several hooks from which hung long-handled spoons and ladles, useful for stirring food cooking in pots over the fire. Also adorning the hickory mantel were a long-handled waffle iron and a wrought-iron toaster rack. A plain oak cabinet in one corner held stoneware jugs, a few glass bottles, and various serving dishes known as chargers. The kitchen had a bright homey atmosphere, and despite the constant warmth, Meredith always enjoyed being in it.

"Would you like some tea?" Dulcie asked. "I've got the kettle on."

"Yes, I think I would." Meredith sat at the rough wooden table, which had only benches for seats. The large black woman solemnly poured the steaming water into the pewter teapot and put it aside to steep while she set out the sugar pot, creamer, and a pan of golden bread.

"Spoon bread, Miss Merry. Fresh hot. I just pulled it off the fire." Unlike loaves, spoon bread was made from cornmeal, dumped in a big lump into a pan, covered, and placed among the hot coals. The resulting bread was sweet and good, crispy brown around the edges and slightly gooey on the inside. Meredith could not resist dishing out a piece onto the small pewter porringer Dulcie handed her and covering it with sweet honey.

"What's happened since I left?" Meredith asked, knowing

Dulcie was cognizant of everything happening on Bitterleaf—and in the whole parish as well.

Dulcie tilted her head to one side, considering. "Well, that Sarah had a baby, fine big boy like his daddy."

"Good! Has there been much sickness?"

Dulcie shrugged. "There's always sickness. A man can't work those fields in water up to his knees and not get sick. If a water snake don't get him, the swamp fever will, or—" Her face closed.

"Or what?"

Dulcie glanced at her blankly. "Nothing, ma'am."

"Or Jackson?" Meredith guessed. "Dulcie, you can tell me."

Dulcie shook her head. "It gets back to him." She glanced at the child in the corner, who was twirling a makeshift top, and the young girl standing beside the child, cleaning vegetables in a crude earthenware sink. Meredith followed her gaze.

"Jewel," Meredith addressed the girl, "find Betsy and tell her to bring my medicine bag. I'll go to the cabins soon to tend the sick." Dulcie followed her lead and shooed the toddler outside to play. "Now, what is all this?" Meredith asked when they were alone. "Do you believe Jackson can hurt you for talking to me? I am the mistress here, you know."

"Yes'm, but the master ain't likely to let Mr. Jackson go without some big reason, not 'less he can find somebody to take his place. And the overseer can get back at me without your knowing."

Meredith sighed. She knew the overseer wielded great power, largely unchecked, over the slaves. Although Meredith was sympathetic, she couldn't watch his every move, and, as Dulcie said, her stepfather was unlikely to dismiss the man on a slave's complaint. Daniel didn't trust Jackson any more than she did, but he hadn't found anyone else as competent who would do the work. "Well, nobody's here to report what you say now. So tell me what you're talking about."

"There's a big field hand, an African, been here not even half a year. He's wild. Mr. Jackson thinks he'd run away, so he's always been in chains. His name's Neb, but he calls himself some funny African name. His back's a mess of scars on account of Mr. Jackson, he lashed him so many times. Neb got the swamp fever, but that overseer made him work anyway—he hates the man—til Neb got so sick, he couldn't crawl out the door." Dulcie shrugged her shoulders. "That's what Pearl tells me, anyway."

"Pearl? Who's that?"

"A field hand," Dulcie said dismissively. "She's no-account. She's big and strong, so Jackson sent her to live with Neb. He thinks they'll have good babies. Only Pearl's scared silly of the man 'cause he's crazy and wild. He's even crazier in his fever, thinks Pearl's somebody else and hits her. She comes up to the door near every evening and begs to bring him here for tending instead of staying at the field hands' quarters. But nobody here can say yes, so he stays down there."

"I see. Well, as soon as I finish with the cabins here, I'll go see him. But it sounds as though he can't be saved."

"Maybe not. But they think you do magic."

Meredith knew her only "magic" was the Peruvian bark she imported to the plantation at great cost and trouble. There were few doctors—or laypeople—who believed in it. It was considered a papist product and probably poisonous. Meredith had used it many times, knowing a London doctor had proved its efficacy more than a century before. She had no room for superstitious fear when there were lives at stake. She had managed to keep more than one slave from dying of the dreaded swamp fever by giving him the powdered bark.

Dulcie rose from her seat, commenting under her breath, "Maybe he'd be better off if you didn't save him."

Meredith considered her remark. Some of the wild ones never adjusted to the plantation. They ran off and were killed in the swamps or brought back to be punished. There was nowhere to go, and they were usually captured if they managed to escape the hazards of the swamp. Others pined away for their home and freedom. Sometimes she did feel they would be better off dead, but her instinctive belief in the sanctity of life would not allow her to step back from helping someone if she had the power.

When Betsy appeared moments later, toting the large leather bag of Meredith's medicines, Meredith rose, tied an old kerchief, or clout, on her head, and left the kitchen. She strode across the front lawn and down the driveway between the towering oaks, then turned and walked to the rough cabins housing the slaves who worked in and around the house. Two pregnant women tended the slave nursery under the shade of a spreading oak. They quickly gave her the children who were sick. One was a poor malformed infant for whom Meredith could do nothing but pray it would die easily and quickly. The other had cut his foot, and it had become infected. Meredith lanced the infection with a slender, sharp knife, then took out a pot of paste that she had made from moldy bread. Spreading the paste on the cut, she bandaged his foot.

In one of the cabins, she found a woman suffering from fever. It was not the deadly swamp fever, with its extreme chills and sweats, but a lesser fever known as "the burning ague," for which Meredith had no medicine. She instructed the women to bathe her with cool cloths. Her last patient was a young man with an aching jaw and burning fever. Gently prying open his mouth, Meredith inspected his teeth and concluded that one of them was the source of his illness. She gave him some whiskey to numb the pain and, when he was drunk, pulled out the offending tooth with a small pair of pliers.

Her chores at the cabins finished, she set off for the stables, where Sam came out to greet her, grinning broadly and bowing. "Miss Merry, Miss Merry, look at my leg!" He cut a caper for her, laughing.

Meredith smiled. Sam had been kicked by a mule a couple of months before, and Meredith had set his leg. The bone had knit properly, enabling him to walk without a limp, even dance, and he obviously gave her the credit for it. "It's not my art. It's your bones," she assured him. "Betsy and I need to ride to the field hands' quarters. Can you hitch up a cart?"

"Sure, Miss Merry, sure."

Betsy glanced at her mistress in surprise. "We're going to the field cabins?"

"Yes. There's a slave there who needs attention."

Betsy sucked in her breath. "That'd be Neb, ma'am. He's powerful mean. Maybe we ought to take somebody with us. I heard stories . . ."

"Nonsense," Meredith replied stoutly. If he really was as big as Dulcie said, no one would be able to restrain him except the indentured servant—and Meredith wasn't about to take him along. Devlin was as likely to turn on them as protect them. She glanced around casually, wondering where he was.

He did not appear as they stood waiting, and in a few minutes, Sam emerged from the stables leading an old horse harnessed to a small wooden cart. Betsy jumped into the back with the bag, and Meredith took her place on the seat, pulling on her gloves to handle the reins. She clicked to the old nag and they plodded off. It was some time before they reached the cabins of the field hands. Poorer, dirtier structures than the house servants' homes, they were set in the middle of the fields close to their work. The cart jounced along the narrow, rutted trail winding through the fields. On either side workers toiled in the flooded rice paddies, cutting the plants with scythes and loading the straw onto carts. When at last Meredith reached the cabins, a little girl with wide eyes directed them to the cabin where the notorious Neb lay. She backed off and refused to go inside with them. Meredith ducked to enter the one-room shack, which stank of sweat and sickness. A man was stretched out on the narrow cot. He was big-framed and tall, but his flesh had shriveled on his frame until the bones showed beneath the skin. He swiveled his massive head toward them and stared with huge black eyes, as blank and unreadable as deep pits. His face, shiny with sweat, was the color of ebony. Meredith noted a wide, flat nose, broad forehead, and square jaw. His nostrils flared when he saw them, and for one terrifying moment Meredith feared he would rise and charge them, but he did not. Instead he closed his eyes and rolled over so he did not face them. His back was bare, and Meredith winced at the sight of old scars crisscrossing the skin. She glanced at Betsy, drew a deep breath, and stepped around to the other side of the bed. Her maid gamely followed with the bag.

Betsy set down the leather bag, and the man studied her. Meredith pulled a gourd cup from her kit and sent Betsy to fill it with water. She laced her hands together to hide their trembling and exchanged stares with the black man until the girl returned. She mixed the dried powder of Peruvian bark with the water and approached Neb cautiously. She brought it to his lips as he watched warily, but he refused to open his mouth to drink. Sternly Meredith ordered him to drink, but it made no impression. Finally she drew back with a sigh. "You try it, Betsy."

"M-me?" Betsy's pretty dark eyes widened. "Oh, no, ma'am, I'm plumb scared."

"He hasn't hurt us yet. Maybe my color scares him. You try it."

Tentatively Betsy extended the cup. Neb's eyes fastened on her, a sudden warmth in their depths. He raised his head slightly and drank, one hand clamping around the girl's wrist to hold the cup steady. He made a face and mumbled something unintelligible, but continued to drink until the cup was empty. Betsy sprang back.

"Thank you, Betsy." Meredith smiled at her. "Now, can you wet a cloth and wipe his face and chest? It will help the fever."

"I guess so." Betsy appeared doubtful, but left the hut to dampen the cloth. When she returned, she carefully washed the broad, dark face, then moved lower to his heavy arms and wide chest. Neb watched her steadily and once uttered a statement in the same unknown tongue. Looking at the powerful chest and arms, Meredith was reminded of the indentured servant, despite this man's darkness. He was handsome in his own way, she thought, and as large and strong as Devlin. But more than that, a fierce confidence burned in his eyes, even though he lay at death's door. He possessed a natural arrogance, a barely leashed power that Meredith suspected could spill over into violence at any moment. That was like Devlin, too.

When Betsy had completed her ministrations, they left the hut, hurrying in relief to the waiting cart. "Whew!" Betsy exclaimed. "I like to have shook to death in there, he scared me so."

"He is strong, but he seemed to understand and appreciate what you did."

Betsy made a strange noise. "He liked it altogether too much, if you ask me. A sick man oughtn't to look at a person like that. He's scary."

"What do you mean?"

"I don't know," Betsy replied, confused, as she scrambled into the cart. Meredith took up the reins, and they started on their way. "Like he—like he had some right to me. Almost like my body wasn't my own. You know what I mean?"

Meredith swung around to stare at her. "Whatever are you talking about?"

Betsy flushed beneath her coffee-colored skin. "I'm not sure exactly, but he made my stomach squeeze up. I can't explain it, but it scared me. I felt like he wanted me, like he could make me his whenever the mood struck him."

Meredith swiveled back to face the track, blushing herself now. "Betsy, this is hardly the sort of thing to discuss."

"Yes, ma'am, I know. But it's how I felt. I ain't had but one man. I let him 'cause I wanted to see what all the fuss was about. It didn't seem much to me." Meredith's cheeks flamed, but she didn't silence her maid. "I never gave in to another man, and they daren't take me. They know I'd tell you, and you'd be on 'em like a hen on a bug. But this one, he looked as if he didn't care who I was or what I could have done to him or nothing. Like *he* was the master."

Involuntarily Meredith's mind flew again to Jeremy Devlin. He had looked that way—oh, not with any desire for her, far from it—but with an arrogance, a lordliness which announced that any woman could be his at the merest flick of his finger. As if he ruled. She shook the thought from her head. She and Betsy were both becoming fanciful. "Well, whatever you thought, it doesn't matter. He's a very sick man, and he'll likely die. He certainly won't be able to do anything to you."

Betsy sighed. "Yeah. But you know what? Even though it scared me, it was kinda nice."

Meredith rolled her eyes. "That's enough of such nonsense. When we return I'll send a couple of men to fetch him. We can look after him better in the main cabins. Unless you don't wish to accompany me. I can get another servant."

"Oh, no, ma'am, I'll do it," Betsy responded quickly. "After all, I faced him once. I can do it again."

When they reached the stables, Betsy jumped down from the cart, and Meredith followed more slowly. She handed the reins to Sam and turned to Betsy. "Go back to the house and lock up the medicine bag. I'm going to take a stroll along the river to cool off.''

"Yes'm." Betsy darted to the house, eager to regale the others with the tale of her dangerous visit. Meredith strolled across the yard and circular walkway to the rough wooden path leading to the wharf.

When she reached the dock, she sat down on the faded planks and removed her heavy shoes. Rolling off her stockings and pulling her skirts up around her knees, she dangled her feet in the cool water, luxuriating in the gentle lapping upon her aching flesh. She untied the cotton scarf and unpinned her hair, running her fingers through it and lifting the heavy mass to expose her damp neck to the slight breeze. Meredith dipped the clout in the water and bathed her face and neck, unfastening her dress down to the swell of her breasts. Goodness, but it was hot for September. She wondered when it would cool off. Once the autumn arrived, there would be many things to do—fall cleaning, picking bayberries, candle making, hog slaughtering. She rolled her head to ease her knotted neck muscles.

A sudden noise startled her, and she twisted her torso to see what it was. Hands suddenly appeared on the wharf planks a few feet from her, then a huge white body heaved out of the water. For a moment she stared open-mouthed in shock. Jeremy Devlin stood before her, gold hair dark from the water, the white-toothed grin plastered on his face, and not a stitch of clothing on his body!

Chapter IV

"Miss Mary," he said, parodying the affectionate name some of the servants called her. "Did you seek me out? Do you have need of me?" His words were irreproachably servile, but the mocking tone combined with his leer and utter nakedness lent a lewd meaning to his questions.

His words slapped her out of her trance. Meredith scrambled to her feet, blushing red as a poppy. She realized Devlin could see the blush spreading across her neck and chest. She clutched at the neck line of her dress, at the same time remembering how the dress had been hiked up to her knees, baring her lower legs and feet. Good heavens, what a humiliating situation! She blurted out the first biting thing she could think of. "My name is Miss Whitney to the likes of you."

"Oh," he replied gravely. "Now I've offended you. My sincerest apologies." He swept her a perfect, formal bow, rendered ridiculous by his nude state.

If possible, Meredith blushed even more deeply. What was she doing even speaking to him in this situation? The man had no clothes on! She whirled and darted off the dock. Dripping, Jeremy took two long strides across the dock and grabbed her shoes and stockings. "Miss Whitney!" he called after her, stretching her name mockingly. "You left your shoes and socks. Don't you want them?"

She broke into a complete run, and Jeremy chuckled. He

stretched out on the sunny wharf to dry, hands behind his head, and contemplated the blue sky. Gad, but the girl had looked enticing sitting there, her long legs and narrow feet exposed. Pretty legs. Too bad a plain girl wasn't allowed to show off her best feature. He'd enjoy having those long, muscled calves locked behind his back, pressing him into her. He groaned softly. It had been so long since he'd had a woman. That was doubtless why even such a gawky piece as the Whitney girl seemed desirable to him. But she had looked better than usual, even in that awful dress. The tight material had pressed against her bosom, forcing the breasts to swell upward, and the tops of the lush globes had been revealed by the unbuttoned neck. The nipples, hard and pointed, had thrust against the worn fabric. And her loose, flowing hair had been, not a mousy brown, but a rich chestnut, thick and tangled enough to beckon a man's hands. There was something to be said for her. It wouldn't be hard to bed her. No doubt she was a virgin and obviously skittish of a man, but he could break any mare and ride her. There could be pleasure in teaching a plain, dry stick like her to soften and flower. He'd be doing her future husband a favor.

Yes, first he would seduce the girl to salve his pride with the woman who had seen him degraded. Next he would take the other one, the dimpled, redheaded woman, simply for pleasure. And then he would run. He smiled, thinking of his freedom. No one could keep Jeremy Devlin penned like an animal. He sat up, rolling the sore muscles of his shoulders. Jesu, what a gruesome life. Yesterday Hurley had left him with Sam, the head groom—or whatever the position was named in this bizarre land. Sam was a middle-aged black man who had inspected Jeremy with disfavor and immediately set him to unloading sacks of feed from a wagon. He'd been given a most unappetizing supper of stew and coarse bread. Not even a bit of ale to wash it down. Later Sam showed him his narrow, dirty room above the stables. It contained a tiny chest of drawers—for what? he had no possessions—a stool, and a rickety bed that was nothing more than a rope laced between the sides of a bed frame and covered with leaves and straw, then topped with a rough sheet and blanket.

That morning he'd gnawed on some sort of domestic fowl for breakfast, so unevenly cooked it was black on one side and nearly raw on the other. He'd spent the morning raking out the muck in the stables. He'd heard the Amazon's clear voice, and Sam had trotted out to greet her, jealously guarding his right to fetch the mistress a cart. As if Jeremy wanted to cut him out of the job. What man would desire to appear before any woman as dirty and scraggly as he was, unshaven, unwashed, clad in nothing but torn, filthy breeches? Jeremy had lurked in the stables, peering through a knothole at her. Sam had called her Miss Mary. Such a calm, unassuming name for an Amazon. He had expected something more exotic. He had tried it on his tongue. "Mary." He wondered what would happen if he called her that. Would she turn Jackson on him? He was sure that son of a bitch would be quite happy to beat him senseless. Later Sam had given Jeremy a few minutes free. He'd lowered his pride enough to ask the man for a razor, a bit of soap, and a mirror. He almost ran to the river to shave off the scratchy beard. Then he had taken his courage in hand and jumped into the river to bathe. When he heard Meredith arrive, he had hauled himself over the side. Naked, he had the upper hand. Far better than appearing before her in the ragged breeches.

➤ Jeremy rose in one lithe movement and strode across the dock to the tree where his breeches hung drying. He had washed them in the river, but it had accomplished little. He pulled them on despite the dampness, grimacing at the discomfort and the unsightly stains. He could do nothing about those. At least the smell was gone. Jeremy ran his fingers through his wet hair, retrieved the precious soap, razor, and scrap of mirror and headed toward the stables. He stopped and returned to the dock, bending down to pick up her shoes and stockings.

Sam was tossing down hay to the horses when he entered, and with an inward groan, Jeremy joined him, carefully setting his booty in a corner. He wasn't used to this sort of physical labor. His robust physique was derived from sports and horse riding, not lifting forks. The skin on his palms was sore from gripping the unfamiliar tools. Before long he'd be as callused as a farmer. But that wasn't as bad as the sheer humiliation of it all.

He stopped in front of the last stall. A bay horse with a thin, elegant head stood far back in his stall, skin quivering and powerful muscles bunched. The ears went back and his teeth showed. "I've been wondering about this horse."

"That one?" Sam shook his head and laughed. "Leave him alone. He's a devil, that horse. A fancy stallion the master brought over from England, but can't nobody ride him. We'll have to use him for breeding is all."

"Beautiful piece of horseflesh," Jeremy commented once he finally managed to interpret what the other man had said. He found the black's thick accent difficult to follow.

Sam shrugged philosophically. "Sure, if he could be ridden."

"What's the matter with him?" Jeremy edged closer. "Was he broken badly? Did he savage a man?"

"No. Never broke that I can tell. He's just plain mean, like some people is mean."

"I've never met a horse I couldn't handle." The challenge danced before his eyes, beckoning. "I'm going to take him out and try him."

"Oh, no, you ain't," Sam declared firmly, grabbing Jeremy's arm with one hand.

Jeremy glanced at the hand and started to fling it off. He could easily overcome this man. But then there'd be hell to pay. Jackson would take his whip to him, and he'd have to pay for the disobedience with his flesh. His jaw knotted with anger. Damn! To think that he, Jeremy Devlin, must take orders from a slave—the shame twisted deeper in his vitals. Swallowing, he began again. "Why not? I promise I know what I'm doing. I'm an excellent rider."

"Master would have my neck if I let anything happen to his horse. You could get thrown off and tore up and get the horse tore up in the bargain. A horse and slave both? Uh-uh."

"I am not a slave."

"You is for seven years. And you'll do what I say!"

"Ask Mr. Hurley." So he was reduced to pleading, he thought. It tasted like gall. "Surely he can't want the horse to remain unexercised. If I could ride it, he'd welcome the opportunity."

After much shaking and scratching of his head, Sam agreed. "Tomorrow when he comes back from riding the fields, I'll ask him."

"Thank you."

Meredith ran all the way to the house, oblivious of the twigs and tiny stones that cut and bruised her tender feet. She galloped into the house and up the stairs as if the devil himself were after her, not stopping until she was safe in her room with the door closed. She sank into the lone chair, gasping for breath. Thank heavens she hadn't worn stays, or she would have fainted on the path. Slowly her breathing returned to normal and her nerves eased their frantic tempo. Meredith stared at her bloodied, dirty feet in dismay. How could she explain them to Betsy? The maid was sure to ask questions. She rose and dumped water from the pitcher into the washbasin, set the bowl on the floor, and sat down with her feet in it. She scrubbed them clean and eased her tender feet into new stockings. Then she lay down on her bed, arm across her eyes to cut out the light, and tried to sleep. Things would seem better when she awoke, she was sure.

But she could not sleep. She kept seeing Jeremy Devlin's naked, wet body standing before her. Their meeting had lasted little more than an instant, and at the time her mind had registered almost nothing. But it had retained the picture without knowing it, and now she remembered every detail, from the faint scar across one rib to the fine red-gold hair on his legs. It was the same color as his curling chest hairs, his beard, and that hair growing riotously around—no, she mustn't think about that. But how not to? She thought about his face instead, its clean lines revealed with the beard shaved. He was now even handsomer. His mouth was firm and full, sensuous, the teeth dazzling in their whiteness. How would his mouth feel?

Meredith jerked upright. Lord, what a thought! What was the matter with her that she was lying here thinking about being kissed by an indentured servant, she whose lips had never felt any man's, even Galen's? And why did she keep recalling the glistening broad shoulders, water streaming down from them, the arms bulging with muscles, the long, graceful thighs, the flat stomach, and—no, no. But she couldn't stop seeing it! Meredith clenched her hands. She had never seen a man naked before. It was curiosity, simple curiosity. So she might as well remember it, think about it, and then she could banish it from her mind. His manhood, thick and long, slightly swollen, springing from that bush of red-gold curls, as if it burst out of fire.

She pressed her lips together, trying to still the fluttering in her stomach. It was frightening, but strangely exciting. Perhaps that was what Betsy had been talking about earlier this afternoon. Oh, this wasn't helping at all! Meredith began to pace the room. Why couldn't she erase the vision of him from her mind? And why did she have the sneaking wish to view his back as well?

Daniel Hurley rode into the yard the next morning in his usual clumsy way and slid from his horse. God, the pain, he thought, but straightened, trying to turn his grimace to a smile as Sam approached to take his reins. Daniel had never been much of a horseman. He knew he was a comical sight to the native planters, some of whom seemed to have been born on a horse. Nowadays, he could barely sit on one for an hour without feeling as if he were being jarred to pieces. It didn't put him in the best of humors. Seeing his scowl, Sam quickly decided not to bother him with the white servant's request.

But Jeremy was watching as Sam turned silently away, and he hurried into the yard. "Mr. Hurley!"

"Yes?" Daniel turned, surprised.

"He's got a question," Sam explained disgustedly, pointing a thumb at Devlin. "He wants to ride Equilibrium."

"What!" The request was too astonishing to summon Daniel's ill humor. He stared blankly at Jeremy. "Are you serious?"

"If Equilibrium is the bay with the white blaze on his face, yes, it's true."

"You're mad. He's wild. Don't know why I bought him in the first place." He knew very well why he had ordered the horse from his factor in England. He had wanted to ride a beautiful thoroughbred to impress the aristocratic planters who looked down their noses at him. Then he'd gotten the damned animal and found that the most expert equestrian could not ride him, let alone Daniel Hurley.

"I'm sure I could do him," Jeremy pleaded, sternly repressing his pride. "Please. I'm an excellent rider. There's not a horse I can't ride."

Daniel snorted. "That's because you never tried Equilibrium."

"Then let me try him. If I fail, at least you'll get a laugh."

"It won't make me laugh much to see two valuable pieces of my property destroyed," Daniel retorted.

Jeremy flushed at the other's casual reference to him as a piece of property. "Neither of us will be destroyed. I promise you."

"Oh, all right, then," he snapped. "Take out the stallion and kill yourself. I don't care. But if you harm that horse, I'll take his price out of your back."

Hurley strode away, but stopped on the porch to watch. Was Devlin actually the horseman he claimed to be? An idea tickled at the back of his mind. Well, first he had to discover what Devlin could do. The back door opened and Meredith stepped out. "Daniel? What are you doing? Breakfast is ready."

"What? Oh, yes, be there in a moment. I want to watch this first."

"What?"

"Oh, that damn-fool Devlin is going to try to ride Equilibrium."

"Equilibrium!" Meredith gasped, one hand flying to her heart as if to still the sudden tumult there. "Oh, Daniel, you can't allow it. He'll kill himself."

Daniel shrugged. "He's determined. I want to see if he can do what he promises. He says he is able to ride anything." He shot a sideways glance at his stepdaughter, whose color was suddenly high in her cheeks. "Why don't you stay and watch?"

"Well, I'll certainly be needed when the horse throws him and pounds him into the ground."

"That's true." Hurley calmly fished out a pipe from his coat pocket, then a pouch and began to fill the bowl. Meredith shot him a simmering glance. How could he be so calm when a man was about to risk his neck foolishly, and he had the power to stop it?

Jeremy entered the stables eagerly. With a sour smile, Sam handed him a pair of worn jackboots, stiff riding boots wide enough in the leg to accommodate a man's foot, since they would not bend or give. Jeremy was sure the rough boots would gall his feet, but at the moment he didn't care. He might be shirtless and in ragged breeches, his footwear an old pair of ill-fitting jackboots, but the boots had spurs, and he was about to mount an excellent animal once again. He hadn't felt such excitement in years. Grabbing a bridle, Jeremy forced himself to calm down and sauntered into Equilibrium's stall.

The horse immediately skittered back, rolling his eyes, until he crashed into the rear of the stable. Jeremy talked softly to him, opening his hand to reveal a lump of sugar. He continued to speak in a low voice until the animal quieted. Although the horse eyed him suspiciously, Jeremy was able to slip the bridle over his head. Well, it was obvious he had been broken to the bridle at least. The saddle was more difficult. Equilibrium sidestepped pettishly, then came lunging back as though he wanted to grind Jeremy between his side and the stall. Jeremy dodged out of the way and approached again. It took several more minutes to saddle the stallion, but he was sure Equilibrium knew the saddle as well. He had been ridden, was trained. He was simply a difficult horse and used to having his way. Whatever doubts Jeremy might have had had vanished. He knew he could ride him.

Jeremy led Equilibrium into the stable yard, unaware of the couple observing intently from the back porch. "Got him saddled," Hurley declared, suddenly feeling as though he had backed Jeremy in a contest.

"Other people have saddled him," Meredith reminded him tartly. "They've even mounted. It's staying on that's the problem." She watched the lean, shirtless figure in heavy jackboots. One hand unconsciously curled into a tight fist of apprehension. She could envision Jeremy flying through the air, then the hooves of the horse raining down on him, hard and fast, until the white flesh was crimson with blood, the broad chest and proud head pounded to pulp. "Daniel, don't allow it. Please."

"I thought you wanted to get rid of the man," Hurley joked imperturbably.

"You know I don't wish to see a man killed!" she flashed back.

He smiled, watching Devlin ease one foot into the stirrup, all the while talking and stroking the horse's mane. The stallion's ears were laid back, but he was steady. Slowly the man mounted, his firm muscles lifting him inch by inch upward in the stirrup and over the horse's body, until finally he was in both stirrups and seated firmly on the horse's back. For a moment Equilibrium hesitated, as if surprised anyone had dared test him. Then he leaped forward in a headlong run. Devlin did not attempt to curb him but let the stallion run, concentrating on maintaining his seat. Equilibrium was, he agreed, a devil of a horse. He slid to a sudden halt halfway down the drive, nearly shooting his rider over his head. Devlin lost a stirrup, but regained it before the animal whirled and sped back full tilt to the stable yard. Equilibrium maintained this mad chase for several minutes before he began to buck.

Meredith's clenched hand flew to her mouth, and she chewed at her knuckles. Hurley spared her a speculative sidelong glance, then returned to the battle being waged in the yard. Devlin was a superb rider. He'd always heard the Irish gentry were. Could Devlin possibly be gentry? Where the devil else would he have learned to ride in such a manner? No actor or servant could afford fine horseflesh from childhood, and that's what it took, as well as skill, to ride the way Devlin did. He clung to the stallion like a limpet, outlasting every fishtail and jump and toss the animal tried. Finally the horse stopped, panting, his sides heaving, the muscles quivering beneath his skin. Then Devlin took control. He grasped the reins tightly, pulling up the stallion's head, and prodded him in the side. Equilibrium tossed his head once, but set off at a sedate trot.

Devlin put him through his paces, taking him from trot to post to full gallop, then back to walk, always in command. Meredith and her stepfather stared agape. "That man is a genius!'' Hurley exclaimed delightedly. ''By God, I've got a rider.'' He turned to Meredith, beaming. ''I have a rider!''

''A rider? What do you mean?'' Meredith was still stunned by the performance she had witnessed.

''For the race!'' he said impatiently. ''The fair race.''

''Oh.'' It was a race held annually at the time of the fair. It would take place this year late in November. Many gentlemen raced their horses, and everyone turned out to watch it and place bets. ''But surely only gentlemen can enter it. Not indentured servants.''

He grinned. ''We'll see.'' Faster than she could have believed possible, Daniel was off the porch and heading toward Jeremy Devlin, who swung down from the saddle, obviously weary but triumphant, unaware of Meredith's presence on the porch. He turned to speak to Daniel, and Meredith popped inside, afraid he would glance past Daniel and see her gawking at him. He must not think she had any interest in him—which, of course, she did not.

The rest of the day Meredith and Lydia heard about nothing but Daniel's new scheme. He would listen to no objections, and Meredith quickly gave up trying to convince him. If he wanted to make a fool of himself by trying to foist a servant off on the local planters, let him. She retired to her bedroom early, but it was a long time before she fell asleep. She kept remembering what she had witnessed that morning, the graceful melding of man and horse, the complete skill with which Jeremy Devlin had mastered the stallion. She wondered where he had learned the art, that combination of gentle, soothing calm and fierce control. What manner of man was he? He rode a horse like a gentleman, better than most, truth be known. He felt no embarrassment at a woman's catching him naked. He had been sold on an auction block. He spoke with the cultured accent of an aristocrat. He stared at her arrogantly, insolently, as if she were worthless. He'd teased her, laughed at her. He was a graceful, powerful animal. He was handsome. He despised her.

Turning on her side, Meredith burrowed her hot face into her pillow, willing her mind to leave Jeremy Devlin. But it would not, and it was the wee hours of the morning before she fell asleep.

She bitterly regretted her sleeplessness the next morning when she awoke. It was later than she usually rose, but still she felt drugged and sleepy. Why did she allow that Irish devil to dominate her thoughts? He certainly wasn't worth tossing and turning over. Meredith dressed hurriedly with the aid of her maid and walked downstairs. "Have you been tending the African?" she asked Betsy as she went.

"Yes, ma'am."

"How is he?"

"I think he's doing better," Betsy admitted in an amazed voice. "He still scares me, but he never does anything."

"Good. Tell me if he tries to harm you. Perhaps I should send a man with you."

"No. I think maybe he's better with only me. He knows he don't need to fear me, 'cause I'm so much smaller."

After breakfast Meredith settled down in the sitting room with Lydia, both occupying their hands with necessary mending of clothes. They chatted quietly, Meredith relating to Lydia the story of the sick, wild African and her visit to help him. Lydia shuddered. She hated slavery and could not become accustomed to the blacks. They frightened her, even as she pitied them. Meredith was used to it, had grown up with it, and had learned long ago not to think about the matter. It was a necessary evil to running the plantation. It was, thank God, Daniel's job to purchase them and turn them over to the overseer.

They had hardly begun sewing when there was an imperious knock at the front door. A moment later Paul came into the room to announce softly, "Mr. Galen Whitney, ma'am."

"Galen!" Meredith smiled and started up. "Oh, how nice."

"I showed him to the drawing room."

"Yes, thank you, Paul." The butler backed out, and Meredith turned to Lydia apologetically. "Lydia, if you'll excuse me."

"Of course." Lydia was aware that Galen would consider it highly improper to pay his call to Meredith in Lydia's presence. It hurt, but she was used to such slights. Besides, she disliked Galen Whitney and frankly preferred to avoid him. If only she could bring Meredith to realize he was not the man for her.

Meredith dropped the mending into her sewing basket and hurried from the room, not bothering to straighten her hair or dress. She walked into the formal drawing room, hands extended, a pleased smile curving her lips. "Cousin Galen."

A tall man stood gazing out the windows. He turned at her approach and returned her smile, although the movement of his mouth did not change his solemn brown eyes. His willowy frame was clad in dark breeches and a dark broadcloth coat and waistcoat. Galen preferred conservative clothes for the dust and wear of riding, which he had obviously been doing. Tall riding boots extended to his knees, and he held a slender crop in his hand. Galen's face was long and narrow, his eyes much the color of Meredith's. His lashes and brows were sandy, but one could not determine the color of his hair, for he wore a white bagwig. He moved forward and clasped Meredith's hand, bending over to place a light, dry kiss upon it as he sketched a bow. "Dear Cousin. I heard only yesterday that you had returned from Charleston. Of course I came posthaste to see you."

"I'm so glad." Meredith directed him to one of the stiff, velvet-upholstered chairs and sat herself down in another. "Tell me, how is Althea?" Althea was Galen's sister and Meredith's dearest friend since childhood. All her life Meredith had spent her social hours with her cousins. Although Galen was two years older than she and Althea three years younger, they had similar interests in music and reading that had set them apart from the children of most planters.

"Quite well, I think. She is sketching today. You must pay us a call soon, Cousin Meredith. Althea is anxious to see you."

"I wish she had come with you today."

Galen started to speak, glanced toward the hall, and stopped. When he began again, Meredith was sure his words were not what he had first intended to say. "I came to ask you to ride with me."

Meredith chuckled. "Why, certainly, if you can suffer the embarrassment of being seen with me on a horse. I have never been a very good horsewoman."

"You know I'm not one of the horsey set. I set greater store by those things which you do well."

"Thank you." She felt curiously deflated by his compliment. What were the things she did well? Reading? Running a household? Keeping Daniel's books? It seemed like nothing to set a man's heart beating faster. "Then, if you will excuse me, I must change into my riding habit."

Meredith left the room and darted upstairs, pulling the bell cord in her room to summon Betsy. She needed help to get into her riding habit. Betsy helped her out of the dress and hoops she wore. Meredith pulled on the riding skirt, which was of brown linen and cut very long on the left side in order to cover her legs when she was in the saddle. There was a loop on the hem that she could hold or put over her wrist to prevent the long train from dragging the ground as she walked. The top of the habit was, like most, cut along masculine lines. Meredith wore a white lawn shirt with a neckband to which a fall of lace was attached. Over that Betsy fastened a waistcoat of the same brown with gold designs embroidered on the front. It was sleeveless and cut as long as the jacket in front, but in the back was very plain and short-waisted. Betsy held out the jacket, which had turned-back loose cuffs and a long row of shiny buttons never meant to be used. Meredith slipped her arms into the sleeves, adjusted the sleeves and front of the coat, then sat down for Betsy to help her into her soft riding boots. The finishing touch was a tricorn hat, which she set on her head. Picking up her crop, she ran lightly down the stairs and into the drawing room.

Meredith secretly bemoaned the masculine cut of riding habits. She feared that with her tall frame and plain face she resembled a man too much already. However, in actuality the riding habit suited her well. The fall of lace beneath her chin softened her angular face, and the masculine cut of the jacket hung on her far better than on most women. The heavy combination of jacket, waistcoat, and shirt made shorter women appear positively rotund, whereas it merely emphasized Meredith's slimness. The mannish hat gave her a jaunty, almost playful look. But Meredith was unaware of the fact that she looked attractive, and so she felt no surprise when Galen Whitney did not compliment her.

Galen had sent a servant to order a horse saddled for Meredith and brought around to the front drive. Galen and

Meredith walked out the front door and down the steps. Their horses stood saddled and waiting for them. Jeremy Devlin held their reins. Meredith blushed when he turned his head and met her eyes. She couldn't see him without remembering the incident on the dock a couple of days ago. In her mind's eye he was naked again. Devlin grinned as if he realized exactly what she was thinking and was amused by it. Meredith circled around the horse's head to mount, Galen following to help her into the saddle. Meredith glanced away to avoid Jeremy's dancing blue eyes and stumbled slightly. Immediately Jeremy reached out to steady her with a hand on her arm.

He kept his hand there and unceremoniously shoved the reins of Galen's horse into Galen's hand. Stepping between the two, he effectively cut off Galen from his cousin. Galen gaped, his face flushing beet-red at the servant's insolence. Jeremy bent, cupping his hands. After a moment's hesitation, Meredith placed her left foot in his hands, and he lightly vaulted her into the saddle. Meredith settled into the sidesaddle and arranged her skirts, then took the reins from Jeremy's hands. Her riding gloves were thin, supple leather, and she could feel the electric touch of his fingers through the material. Unsettled, she touched the animal with her heel and cantered away, leaving Galen behind. Galen shot the servant a glance of pure dislike, mounted hurriedly, and trotted after Meredith.

Devlin watched them, smiling. He'd made an enemy of the pale, bony man, that was sure. He wondered what the man was to Meredith. Surely not her fiancé. Even the Amazon deserved better than that. She had been almost pretty today in her riding habit, cheeks flushed and eyes shining. But, Lord, she couldn't ride. His grin deepened to a chuckle as he watched the pair disappear down the driveway. Well, *there* was a matter he could do something about. Amazing how opportunities dropped into your hands if you waited. He strolled toward the stables, whistling.

Chapter V

"MEREDITH!" Galen called when he drew close enough to her to be heard. She glanced back and pulled to a stop, realizing with embarrassment how rudely she had set off without waiting for him.

"I'm sorry," she apologized.

"No need," he said. "I perfectly understand that you didn't wish to remain around that crude fellow. Who is he?"

"His name is Jeremy Devlin. He's an indentured servant Mr. Hurley acquired in Charleston."

"Well, he's a damned insolent scoundrel," Galen exclaimed heatedly. "Pardon my language, Cousin. I'm afraid I'm most offended by his rudeness. Did you see the way he practically shoved me aside and helped you to mount? Obviously it was *my* duty to assist you, not some ragtag boor with no manners."

Inexplicably Meredith was irritated by his tirade. What did it matter who helped her to mount? After all, Jeremy had been quite a bit better at it than Galen, tossing her not inconsiderable weight into the saddle as if she were light as a feather. Galen always heaved her up, which made her feel even more cloddish and grab desperately at the saddle to relieve him of her weight. "I don't know. I suspect his manners are excellent—or can be. He made me a perfect bow the other day." She forbore to add that the man had been nude at the time he did it.

"Well, I can't imagine why Mr. Hurley would bring such a type home. He is bound to offend a sensitive woman such as yourself. And running about half clothed! He's an obvious brute, too powerful by half to allow around ladies. If Hurley had to buy him, he should have placed him in the fields."

"I'm sure Mr. Hurley had his reasons," Meredith replied stiffly. What was wrong with her cousin today? She didn't like Daniel any better than Galen did, but it seemed in poor taste to criticize him in front of his stepdaughter.

"Come now, Cousin Meredith, I mean no disrespect to you. But when I think of the things you've had to endure from that man. The insults, the slights—and you a Whitney!"

"Because I am a Whitney does it make it worse if I'm insulted?" Meredith snapped. "Really, Galen, I haven't the slightest idea what you're talking about."

"It's hardly a fit subject to discuss with a lady." Galen's eyes flashed with indignation. "That's why I've never brought it up before. But you must realize what I'm saying."

"No, I don't."

"Meredith, you are an innocent, a perfect lady, but you have to be aware that Mrs. Chandler is—well, suspect."

Meredith's eyebrows drew together dangerously. "*What* do you mean?"

"I'm referring to Hurley's infamous liaison with that woman!" he hissed, lowering his voice as if someone might hear the awful words he uttered.

"Lydia Chandler is a . . . nice woman who has been very kind to me."

"Kind to you?" he repeated sarcastically. "You call it kind to damage your reputation and to subject you to things no lady should ever have to—"

"*Nothing* has been done in front of me which would offend me in any way," Meredith retorted heatedly. "You make it sound as if there were a wild bacchanalia taking place every night!"

"To even have such a woman in the same house with you is an insult! That's why I forbade Althea to visit you."

"You did what?"

"Surely you've noticed Althea and my mother no longer come to call."

"Now that you mention it, yes. I hadn't thought anything of it before."

"Father and I couldn't allow them to mix with Mrs. Chandler."

"You think it would taint them to breathe the same air she does?" Meredith was coldly furious now. There were times when her cousin's pride was all out of proportion to reality. The name Whitney and her good reputation were important to her, also. She had disliked Daniel Hurley's installing his mistress in the house. But the way Galen acted galled her. As if by her mere existence Lydia could somehow spoil a proper lady. "If that's the case, I no doubt ceased to be a lady in your eyes long ago."

Galen gaped, caught in the trap of her logic. "Now, Cousin Meredith," he began to splutter.

"No. I think we've both said enough. I'm going home now. I presume I'm still permitted to call on Althea, or would that damage her reputation also?"

"Of course I want you to visit us, Cousin. Please, let's not part this way."

"Whenever you choose to apologize, I'll be happy to receive you again." Meredith clumsily turned her horse and dug her heel into its side. The mare took off running, and Galen did not follow.

Tears burned in Meredith's eyes, whether from her spat with Galen or from the wind in her face, she wasn't sure. She galloped into the stable yard and pulled to a halt. Jeremy Devlin appeared in the stable doorway, a look of surprise on his face, and started forward to help her dismount. The last thing Meredith wanted was for him to help her down, so she jerked her foot from the stirrup and began to slide off. In her haste, her flowing habit became tangled around her legs, and she almost fell. Jeremy reached her in time, and his strong arms caught her. Inadvertently her hand touched his shoulder. His skin was warm and smooth beneath her fingers. She snatched her hand away.

"You look very pretty in your riding habit," he told her in a low voice.

Meredith flushed, sure he was making fun of her. "Set me down."

He complied, letting her slide easily to the ground. "However, you look something less than pretty on a horse."

"I beg your pardon."

"You're cow-handed, and your seat is atrocious."

"What! How dare you!"

He grinned. "I wasn't referring to your—uh, physical attributes, since I haven't seen the part in question. I was speaking of your riding seat. You sit a horse poorly."

"I'm sorry if I offend your sensibilities. Not all of us are either interested in or good at riding. I'll thank you to keep a civil tongue in your head."

Again he swept her a court bow, gracefully bending low. Meredith strode toward the house, back rigid.

"Oh, Miss Whitney!" he called after her in a loud voice. "Wouldn't you like your shoes and stockings? You left them with me the other day."

Meredith stopped in mid-stride, her cheeks flaming. He must have picked up the things she had forgotten on the dock in her haste to escape him. But he made it sound as if something had happened between them, as if she had been wantonly undressed with him! She whirled and shot him a venomous glance. He lounged against a hitching post, arms crossed negligently. "Have you no decency?" she hissed.

He seemed to consider the question, then answered, grinning, "Not that I've ever noticed."

Meredith was tempted to scream at him like a fishwife. He was outrageous. He didn't appear to have the least intention of acting as a servant should—or even as any human being should, for that matter. "You're vile," she spat, shoving back a stray bit of hair that clung annoyingly to her damp face. "Wicked."

"So I've been told." He was monumentally unconcerned. "Well? Shall I return your . . . uh, articles of clothing?"

Meredith fumed. She certainly didn't want her shoes and stockings in Devlin's possession. There was no telling what embarrassing thing he might do with them—show them to the other servants and tell them some story about how he had obtained them. He might even march into the house and hand them to her when guests were present! But much as she itched to have them safely back in her hands, she couldn't let him be seen giving her such intimate objects.

His mischievous grin broadened. He knew her dilemma and was obviously deriving a great deal of amusement from it. "Perhaps it's best I keep them. It wouldn't do to let other people see them. Of course, you can count on the discretion of a gentleman."

"What gentleman?" Meredith countered caustically, but much of the sting of her remark was blunted by the amused twinkle in his eyes. He had anticipated her remark, even enjoyed it. Meredith turned and stalked away. How she despised Devlin! He must have irritated Galen with his rudeness, or Galen would never have spoken so unkindly. Why had she defended Daniel's buying Devlin's indenture after she had strenuously objected to it herself? And why hadn't Devlin been issued any other attire? One of the maids could sew him linsey-woolsey breeches and shirt. There was no need for him to parade around in ragged breeches with his bare skin showing. It was positively indecent.

She swept into the dining room, where one of the maids was busy polishing silver. "Maisey, you're a fair hand with a needle, aren't you?"

"Oh, yes'm, I help Em with sewing sometimes."

"Good. It's come to my attention that Devlin has no proper clothing. See if you can find a pair of breeches and a shirt to fit him. If not, take his measurements and sew up something."

"Yes'm. Now, ma'am?"

"Now. Most definitely now."

The girl set down the silver cup and glided from the room. Meredith, suddenly weary, climbed the stairs to her room, pulling off her riding coat and hat as she went. She tugged at the bell rope to summon Betsy and began to unbutton the waistcoat. Betsy did not come, and Meredith shrugged out of the waistcoat, tossing it on the bed. Where was Betsy? It was next to impossible to pull off her boots without help. She opened the door just as Betsy pounded up the stairs. "There you are. Why didn't you—" She stopped in mid-sentence at the terrified look on Betsy's face.

"Oh, Miss Merry, you gotta come! He's up and raving," the girl panted, gasping for breath.

"What? Who? Neb?"

Betsy nodded. "Yes'm. All of a sudden, when I was dosing him, he rose up, yelling like a demon. He's in the worst fever I've seen. He shoved me aside and started tearing up the cabin. So I came to fetch you."

Meredith was already past the girl before she had finished speaking, dashing down the staircase and out the front door. As an afterthought, she called back, "Fetch Jeremy from the stables. Immediately!" She lifted her skirts and scampered down the drive toward the row of slave cabins. Behind her Betsy raced for the stables.

Meredith caught sight of the big black man ahead of her. He was charging past the cabins, headed for the driveway which emptied into the main road. Without stays, Meredith could run easily, even though it was not very ladylike to hitch up her skirts around her knees as she did. However, her only concern was Neb and the harm he might do himself and others in his fever. She raced along the driveway to intercept him. He was weak from fever and lurched and stumbled as he ran, falling down now and then.

"Neb! Wait! No!" she yelled as she drew close. He half-turned, staggering to a halt. Meredith slowed to a walk, gasping for air. "Neb, please, you're ill. You can't go anywhere. Come back to the cabin with me. Please? You'll feel better. You're too sick to be up and about."

The man watched her warily as she approached. Meredith extended her hands, speaking soothingly. He didn't know the language, but perhaps he would understand the tone. He, too, was tired and gasping, his eyes bright with fever, sweat pouring from him.

Meredith reached him, one hand going out to touch his arm. Suddenly, violently, Neb hurled her aside. She went tumbling to the ground, the wind knocked out of her. As she fell, she saw Jeremy Devlin pelting across the grass toward them, his face contorted with effort as he pushed for speed. He flung himself at the huge black, and they thudded to the ground. It was no contest, for Jeremy was as large as Neb and not weak with fever. Quickly Jeremy had the slave face down on the ground, both arms locked behind his back. He swung his head toward Meredith, tossing back the hair that had strayed from its queue during his mad dash.

"Are you all right?"

Meredith sat up slowly, one hand clamped to her side. "Yes, I think so." She drew a long, tremulous breath. "Except— except I'm out of breath."

"That was a damn-fool thing to do!" Devlin barked. "You might have killed yourself. This man could snap your neck like a chicken bone."

Meredith glared. She would have loved to retort as acrimoniously as he, but she couldn't waste the breath. Finally she gasped, "That's hardly the way for a servant to speak to me."

"I'll speak anyway I please! I practically had to break my neck to save you. Sweet Jesu, my feet are torn to ribbons from your abominable shell driveway."

"Don't worry, I'll doctor them," she retorted caustically, slowly rising to her feet. Devlin stood also, dragging Neb to his feet. "He's fainted," Meredith told Jeremy tartly. "Or you've killed him."

"I appreciate your thanks and gratitude. It positively overwhelms me. Come here. You're a good, strong wench. Help me hold him up."

Meredith's eyes widened at his casual description of her, but she hurried forward to support the sagging slave. Jeremy turned his back to the other man's chest, pulled Neb's arms around his neck, and, holding tightly to the black's arms, lifted him onto his broad back. "Lead me to his cabin," he grunted at Meredith.

She was startled by his action, but quickly led him across the smooth expanse of grass to the cabin Neb occupied. They found Betsy and the slave children there, gazing in wonder at the sight of the white giant carrying the black one on his back. Meredith shooed them out of the way and stepped into the cabin. It was a mess. Neb had even overturned the bed. Betsy and Meredith struggled to set the wooden bed upright again, and Jeremy slid Neb onto the mattress. He exhaled with relief and straightened carefully.

"I think I may have broken my spine," he grumbled.

Meredith shot him a withering glance. Betsy spoke up, "Miss Merry, he's waking up."

All three stared at the man on the bed. He was beginning to move his head, and his eyelids fluttered. Soon he was tossing and moaning and mumbling in his language. "Fetch my bag and some water, Betsy," Meredith told the girl. "Devlin, you stay here. I may need you again if he gets too wild."

When Betsy returned, she washed his face and chest with the cool water, which seemed to quiet him some, and Meredith mixed another dose of Peruvian bark. "I believe he's going through the crucial stage of the fever. If we can pull him through this, Betsy, he may live."

They studied him, Betsy chewing nervously at her lower lip. They continued to sponge him with cool spring water and tried to force some of it down his throat. Neb began to thrash wildly, and Jeremy sprang to hold him down. Neb was strong and insane in his fever. Meredith saw the muscles knot in Devlin's arms in his effort to keep the man in his bed. Finally Neb subsided. Then he began to tremble, until the tremors grew so great the whole bed shook with them. Jeremy glanced at Meredith, astonished.

"A chill," she explained tersely. "The swamp fever's like that. Fever and chills, fever and chills. The patient gets better for a while, as he's been doing, and then suddenly he's worse. It's a hard thing to fight."

"Yet you do."

Meredith shrugged. "What else can I do? Stand by and watch them die?"

"Some would."

Meredith began to pile blankets on the slave. Finally the tremors stopped, and he began to sweat again. They ripped away the covers. After another hour of raging fever, during which Jeremy again had to hold him down, Neb slipped into a deep sleep. Meredith touched the man's arm. His skin was cool and damp. She felt for the vein in the wrist, afraid he had died, but his heartbeat was there, faint but steady. She smiled tremulously. "I think we've made it."

"Oh, Miss Merry." Betsy hugged her enthusiastically. Meredith wondered if the savage had worked his way into

Betsy's heart as she tended him. Her sweet Betsy and that black beast? No, it was impossible, unthinkable.

Meredith straightened her aching back and motioned to Jeremy. "Come outside where it's light, and I'll work on your feet."

It was late afternoon, and the dying sun spilled onto the grass, turning it golden in patches. Meredith rolled her head tiredly as Jeremy set down the bucket of water and her medicine bag. She motioned for him to sit on the grass, and she knelt at his feet. Pulling up one foot onto her lap, she began to wash it with a cloth, dipping the rag into the bucket and washing again until his foot was clean. Jeremy watched her. Her hair had fallen loose from the knot and hung about her face in tangled curls. Now and then she brushed them back with an impatient hand. She was dressed in only her riding skirt and a thin lawn shirt, through which he could see her chemise. The sight of her lacy undergarment stirred him, but not so much as her posture before him and her gentle handling of his feet. His loins prickled and tightened. He knew that soon his manhood would strain embarrassingly against his breeches. He searched for something to think of beside the exquisite luxury of her firm, strong fingers holding his feet.

She had been kind to the slave in the cabin. It surprised him. Why did a woman who enjoyed watching human beings paraded on the auction block later tend a sick slave? Hers was not the careless charity of genteel ladies who rode in their magnificent carriages to the houses of the poor and sent their maids in with a basket of food for the wretches. No, this lady had hung over the bed and washed his face, mixed medicine and forced him to drink it, working until her back ached. And she had run after Neb like a madwoman, skirts hiked up to reveal the flash of long, agile legs. Neb could have killed her with one blow. Why did no one look out for her? No woman of his would be left to the mercy of slaves and stable hands. His woman. The heat in his blood increased. She *would* be his before too long. What he had witnessed this afternoon only made him desire her more.

Meredith, too, was aware of the sensuous implications of her washing his feet. She noticed that her hands lingered over the task. It was tiredness, she assured herself, merely tiredness. She would not willingly touch any part of this horrible man. Yet the scratch of his rough soles beneath her fingers sent a tingle up her arms and throughout her body. Firmly she pulled her hands away and brought out ointment to dab on the tiny cuts covering his soles.

"Miss Whitney," Jeremy began, his smile underlining the name she had proudly demanded he call her the other day on the wharf. "I am willing to correct your appalling skill, or rather lack of it, upon a horse."

"What are you talking about?"

"I'm an excellent rider. All my life, it's been my primary skill—my only one, my uncle told me. I am offering to impart some of my knowledge to you. I'll give you riding lessons."

"Why, how kind of you to offer," she replied with heavy sarcasm. "Since you are my indentured servant."

"Ah, but I am Mr. Hurley's servant. What claim does it give you? Your name is Whitney, so you aren't his daughter unless you're married—but no, it's *Miss* Whitney, isn't it?" His blue eyes sparkled with unspent mirth. She knew he enjoyed jabbing at her in retaliation for the arrogant way she'd taken him down for calling her Miss Merry. Grudgingly, she had to admire Devlin's nerve in speaking as he did to a woman who could have him broken under the lash if she so chose. Jeremy continued, "I thought you were either his daughter or his mistress." She gasped indignantly, and he chuckled. "Granted, you don't look the part, but who am I to judge another man's pleasures?"

"How dare you, you low, detestable—"

"Then I saw the other woman, and she is obviously sharing his bed."

Meredith blinked. "How could you possibly know that?"

"I saw it in her face. It's another area where I doubtless have more knowledge than you—unless, of course, 'the master' manages to keep two mistresses in the same household, both you and the pert redhead. Quite a feat, I should say, if he does."

Her hand lashed out to slap him, but Jeremy caught it easily and held her arm away. He considered forcing her back until she lay on the ground beneath him. How sweet it would be to sink into her firm body. But, no, he didn't want her to learn his touch in the midst of anger. She must melt willingly into his arms when the time came. So he simply gripped her wrist until her arm relaxed, then dropped it. Trembling with anger, Meredith turned away and yanked a long white bandage from her bag. Without a word, she lightly wrapped his feet.

"My offer still holds."

"After what you just said, how could you think I would come near you again, let alone take riding lessons from you?"

"Because you're proud," he answered. "Because you refuse to be intimidated by a mere servant. Because you enjoy doing things well and hate to turn down the opportunity to learn."

Everything he said was true, Meredith knew. And something in her urged her to accept his offer. But it was dangerous. Devlin was uncontrollable. He might use the lessons as an excuse to mount a horse, and once they were out of view of Bitterleaf, he could bash her on the head and escape. "I can't."

He shrugged. "Have it your way. By the way, you didn't tell me what your relationship is to the old man."

"He is my stepfather!" she snapped. "Not that it's any business of yours."

"I see. And who is the redhead?"

Of course, she thought. It's Lydia he's interested in. "Her name is Lydia Chandler. She is a friend of my stepfather."

He chuckled. "Yes, I know her kind of 'friend.' " She rose, towering over him, and he stretched out in the grass on his back. Meredith was certain she must have been mistaken, but for a moment something resembling compassion flickered in his sapphire eyes. "And does she make life miserable for you?"

"Why, no," she answered, startled he would think of it. "She is—quite kind to me."

"Unusual." He hesitated, then spoke in a voice so low she almost didn't catch his words. "Forgive me for what I said earlier. I was goading you."

"Why?"

"To watch you fire up, I suppose. I enjoy seeing your eyes flash. I like to bandy words with someone more intelligent than an ox, which is the mental level of most of my companions the past few weeks. But I knew you weren't Hurley's mistress."

"Your famous experience again?"

He smiled, a sudden, charming smile. It had the quality of a rainbow breaking across a gray sky. "Yes. You have the look of an untouched woman."

"I look like a spinster, you mean. Well, you're correct. I am. Good day, Devlin."

He flopped over onto his stomach and watched her walk away. She moved with none of a woman's delicacy. "My name is Jeremy," he shouted after her. Meredith hesitated but did not turn, then continued toward the house. Jeremy turned onto his back again, linking his arms beneath his head. The grass tickled his neck, and the air was tangy with its smell. He wondered if she would relent and come to him for lessons. It was a pleasant thought, a pleasant feeling, the first he'd had in a long time. He drifted off to sleep, his nostrils filled with the tart odor of green grass.

Meredith had no intention of going to the stables. She thought often of her lack of intention throughout the evening and the next morning.

As she dressed that morning, she asked Betsy about their patient. "How is Neb?"

Betsy's long brown face brightened, and she beamed at Meredith. "Oh, fine, ma'am. He passed his first really peaceful night last night."

Meredith stared at her. "You mean you stayed up with him all night?"

"I slept on a pallet on the floor, so I could hear him if he called. I been doing it ever since they brought him to the cabin."

"I didn't mean for you to nurse him round the clock! You'll wear yourself to a frazzle."

"I'm fine, really. He's so much better when I can bathe him in cool water ever so often."

"Betsy, do you have . . . some feeling for this man?"

The girl twisted the hairbrush she held in her hand and glanced away. "I respect him. He's strong—a fighter. I mean, not just his body, but his soul, too."

"He's just a field hand."

"That may be." Betsy's eyes flashed. "But he's got a lot more to him than most house slaves I know."

"He's a savage."

"He's wild," Betsy admitted. "But he's proud and brave. He's not tamed like the men around here. He's got *real* life in him."

Meredith shrugged. It wasn't her business if her maid chose to fall in love with Neb. She hoped the brute wouldn't abuse her.

Betsy saw the look in Meredith's eyes and said quietly, "Just 'cause he was free doesn't mean he's hurtful. He can be gentle as a child." The black eyes glowed, and Meredith wondered how far the relationship had gone. Surely they hadn't—No, he was much too ill.

Meredith stood up quickly, astounded to find herself speculating on Betsy's love life. "I hope you're right, Betsy. Now I must get a few chores done before breakfast."

Her work was dull. Meredith was surprised at her lack of appetite at breakfast. She felt strangely restless this morning. After the meal, she retired to the study, which was detached from the rest of the house, to work on the plantation books. Daniel was a money-maker, but he despised keeping records. Anne had performed the task for him and taught her daughter, so that after Anne's death, Meredith assumed the job. First she opened the record book containing the names and life events, such as births and deaths, of all the slaves. She added the names of the three blacks Daniel had purchased and on a separate page listed the white indentured servant. There had been very few others, as the almost blank page attested. All were gone now. When she was through with the book, she picked up the ledger to enter the prices Daniel had paid for them and the goods that had been taken in trade instead of money.

The ledgers contained the full history of the plantation. In them was listed every expenditure for either the farm or the

household, and every bit of revenue. Many of the transactions
were barter for goods and were duly noted. Meredith listed
the goods purchased for the house down to the last pin, as
well as the expenses for the farm. She also enumerated each
ounce of rice and indigo produced by the farm and its price.
Her records were so complete that she could tell at a glance
what slaves possessed what specialties, which were carpenters
or joiners or mere field hands, and recite exactly how many
pounds of pork (25,000) or bushels of grain (513) or gallons
of brandy (140) the plantation had consumed the year before.
She was exacting and meticulous, and she thoroughly enjoyed
the work.

She was happily engrossed in checking her figures for the
month of September when the door opened and the overseer
stepped inside. "Oh, Miss Meredith, I didn't realize it was
you. I thought your father was here." He smiled.

Meredith looked at him. She wasn't sure why, but for some
reason she doubted his words. Jackson made her skin crawl,
and she avoided him as much as possible. He was a sly, oily
man, and she distrusted him thoroughly. She replied crisply,
"As you can see, he is not. I suggest you look for him in the
house."

Jackson did not leave. Instead he sauntered over to the
desk, smiling. "That's all right. It happens I'd rather talk to
you."

"Indeed?" Meredith raised her eyebrows, endowing the
gesture with every bit of haughtiness she could muster. She
wanted to be rid of him quickly.

"Yes." He was oblivious to her manner. "I been thinking
about you for a long time. Thinking how when Hurley passes
on, you won't have nobody around to protect you and run the
farm."

"I am sure it will be some time before Mr. Hurley leaves this
world. And when he does, I can assure you I am quite
capable of both operating the plantation and taking care of
myself."

"Not like a man could, Miss Meredith. Woman needs a
man."

"This is hardly a fit subject for discussion, Mr. Jackson."

"Oh, I wouldn't want to offend you. No, ma'am. I'm not used to ladies and such."

"It's obvious."

"I'm a plain-speaking man. I tell you what I see, and that's that you're past twenty and still unmarried. Unlikely you'll marry any of the planters around here now, since you haven't already. Let's be honest. You aren't pretty and you're overly proud. It's a hard combination for some men to take." Meredith's eyes flashed. She was so angry she could not even speak. He went on, "But not me. I'm used to your ways. We could deal right well with each other. Fact is, I want to marry you."

"What!" Meredith jumped up, all thought of politeness swept away by her outrage. "You dare to suggest that *I* would marry *you!* Why, you wretched . . . beast! How could you imagine I would accept your offer? And phrased so prettily too! Good God, man, do you think I'm desperate?"

Jackson's bony face darkened, and his mouth formed a thin line. "You're no prize catch, you know!" he spat back. "There's not a man in the parish'd have you, even with all your land."

"I suggest you leave here immediately, or I'll tell Mr. Hurley of your 'proposal' and you'll be kicked off Bitterleaf before nightfall."

"I'd think he'd be glad to get you off his hands." Jackson turned and stalked from the room, leaving Meredith fuming behind him.

She whirled and plopped back down in her seat, then slapped the desk with both hands. How dare he! How dare he! As if she would let that crawly creature near her. She rose and paced the room. She should have called Devlin and told him to toss the man out of the room. Meredith smiled. That sight would have done much to soothe her ruffled feathers. She glanced at the ledger. She was useless for this work until she worked off her fury. Meredith closed the heavy book and wiped the quill pen clean. Then she left the study and went across the covered walkway into the house and upstairs to her room. Hardly thinking about what she was doing, she yanked her dress off over her head, unbuckled the belt of her hip-length "pocket" hoop, and tossed it onto the bed. She rang for Betsy to help her into her riding habit and boots.

Riding was precisely the thing to rid her of her ill humor, she thought. Anyone's company, even Devlin's, would seem pleasant after the snakish overseer. She rammed the tricorn on over her hair and sped down the stairs. Her face still set in its grim lines of anger, Meredith marched out to the stable yard. "Devlin!" she called, entering the stables, which smelled pungently of hay, leather, and horses. "Devlin! I've come to learn to ride."

Chapter VI

JEREMY STEPPED out of one of the stalls. Straw clung to his breeches and bare arms. "From the expression on your face, I thought you'd come to have me drawn and quartered."

"What? Oh. No, I was upset with someone else."

"I'd say that's putting it mildly. All right. Let me saddle your mare." He went into the tack room and emerged a moment later carrying bridle and saddle. With swift, sure movements, he fastened the equipment on the docile mare. Meredith watched, admiring despite herself the strong, agile movements of his fingers. He snapped a long leading rein onto the bridle and led the horse from her stall. In the yard, he cupped his hands and thrust Meredith up into the saddle, again making it appear effortless. He positioned her legs and feet, then handed her the reins, arranging her fingers around the leather straps. "No, not so tightly. You needn't keep a death grip on her. She's a steady horse with a nice, comfortable gait. Nothing to fear."

Meredith swallowed, disturbed by his hands touching such an intimate place as her legs, even through the cloth of the habit. However, he was obviously unmoved by the contact. His face and hands were purely businesslike as he frowningly inspected his work and minutely rearranged it. He was like an artist with a piece of sculpture. She might as well have been a piece of wood or clay as a woman. Meredith searched for something to say to dispel her own disquietude and seized on his remarks. "Mercy's a Narragansett pacer."

"Mercy?"

"Yes. Daniel purchased her from a Puritan. He named his horses after the virtues."

"Well, she's certainly merciful to you. Patience might be a more apt name, however. All right, now, tap her gently—*gently*—in the ribs. No need to go thundering off as you did yesterday." Meredith grimaced, but did as she was told. Jeremy stood at the end of the leading rein, stretching it taut, and Meredith circled him. He pivoted slowly, never taking his eyes from her. "Ease up on the reins. She needs little control. You don't have to fight a horse for mastery. Learn to *guide* her. Trust her, move with her. Now and then give her a little help by telling her where to go and how fast. Unclench your hands. You can't force a horse any more than you can a man."

"Indeed? I know some men whose wives lead them about by the nose."

"That's the important word—lead. You don't jerk and rowel and cut their mouths. Husbands or horses. You lead, you suggest, you guide. Haven't you learned that yet? I thought all women knew such basic wiles." He grinned at her, his tousled blond hair falling across his forehead.

"I'm not accustomed to using wiles," Meredith replied stiffly.

His grin broadened. "That's obvious."

"You're an impudent man."

"So I've been told."

"It is not an admirable quality in a servant."

"Ah, but then I am not an admirable servant, am I?"

"How can you speak in such a—a flip manner to me?" Meredith was amazed at his boldness. "It's not in the least appropriate."

"You mean I don't understand my position?" He relaxed the leading rein, and Meredith allowed the horse to stop as she stared at the man. He moved toward her. "I think I do. The sailors on the ship reminded me often enough that I was henceforth less than nothing. I'm no better than a slave, am I not? You may have me beaten for my insolence, or even put under the lash, which the estimable Jackson seems to have such a fondness for. Will you?'' He stopped at her side, his face upturned, the blue eyes piercing as though they would plumb the depths of her soul. ''Is it one of your pleasures to have a man beaten? Does the spurt of blood amuse you, as it entertained you to watch men sold? It fits ill with your careful nurturing of the slave yesterday. Which is you as you are? The woman who delights in the sufferings of captives or the one who tends a sick menial with unflagging gentleness?''

''I never—'' Meredith gasped, appalled at his words. ''How dare you say such things to me! Never in my life have I ordered a man beaten! I wouldn't dream of doing it. Nor am I amused by seeing men on the auction block.''

''No? Then why did you come the day I was sold?''

''To get away from my cousin,'' Meredith replied honestly.

''Your cousin? Not the skinny tutorish sort you rode with yesterday? Sam told me *he* was your cousin.''

''Heavens, no, not Galen! My cousin on my mother's side, Phoebe, who can prattle of nothing but beaux and dresses and parties until I am ready to scream. Even an hour in her company is enough to force me to do anything, even something I abhor, just to get away from her!''

Devlin thrust back his leonine head and roared with laughter. The sun glinted off his gold hair, and Meredith was reminded of some golden Greek god, Apollo or Mars, laughing and powerful. Belatedly she realized she had been conversing in a most inappropriate way with the indentured servant. She drew her face into prim lines. ''Not that it's any of your business. I came here for a riding lesson, not a discussion of my character. Who are you to judge me, anyway?''

''Quite right,'' he replied gravely, his eyes still twinkling. ''Your annoyance with Cousin Phoebe is quite above me. I am merely a humble servant, and I exist only to follow your command.''

''Meredith!'' A feminine voice floated across the yard, and Meredith twisted on her horse to gaze in the direction of the house.

''Here, Lydia!'' she called.

A moment later, Lydia Chandler rounded the corner of the house, a wide-brimmed straw hat protecting her head and face from the sun. She stopped when she saw Meredith. For a moment she started to return to the house, then walked toward them almost unwillingly. "I'm sorry. I didn't know you were busy," she apologized in her small, girlish voice as she drew nearer.

Devlin watched her approach, drinking in the woman's loveliness. She was older than Meredith by several years, older than himself as well, he guessed. But she retained a smooth complexion and endearingly girlish smile. China-blue eyes stared at him while trying to appear not to. Red curls bounced beneath the brim of the hat. Her figure tended to plumpness, but it had not yet exceeded the bounds of prettiness. She was dressed far more fashionably than the woman on the horse beside him, and she seemed a creature of the luxurious life that had been ripped from him so abruptly. There was nothing hard or challenging about her, only a dimpled gaiety and the promise of easy pleasure. A familiar heat began to surge in his veins.

Meredith watched Devlin's face as Lydia approached, and irritation rushed through her. Like all men, he was falling all over himself at the sight of a pretty face. "Quite all right, Lydia," she said tersely, drawing a startled look from Mrs. Chandler. "I was only taking a riding lesson."

It was apparent to Jeremy that Meredith had no intention of introducing him to Lydia. It would be "inappropriate," of course, to introduce a mere servant to a member of the household, he thought. So he swept the woman an elegant bow and boldly took the initiative. "Jeremy Devlin, ma'am, at your service."

Lydia giggled, her dimples flashing in her cheeks. "I'm Lydia Chandler."

A fetching piece, he thought, letting his eyes convey that thought. But obviously more lowly-born than Meredith. He wondered what she was doing in the house. This estate, while bizarre, was certainly as large or larger than most aristocratic holdings at home in England. Meredith's family must be one of the "nobility" of the raw land. So what was Hurley's mistress doing living as a member of the family? Surely the rules of nice society were not so loose even in the brash colonies. He wondered if Meredith was subjected to shame because of it.

Lydia, recalling her errand, tore her attention away from Jeremy and turned to Meredith. "I didn't realize you were busy, or I wouldn't have interrupted," she apologized. "But a boy brought a message for you from Mr. Whitney, and I thought you'd want to know. I presumed you were out in the garden or sitting in the arbor reading."

"It's perfectly all right," Meredith assured her. "I was finished with the lesson, anyway."

Devlin made no comment, merely grasped her waist with his sinewy fingers and lifted her from the mare's back to set her lightly on the ground. "Miss Whitney, may I expect you for another lesson tomorrow?" His voice and face were a model of servility, mockingly so.

"Yes." Meredith shot him a chilling glance and set off briskly for the house. Lydia trailed behind her, glancing back once at Jeremy, who thoughtfully watched their departure. Yes, Hurley's mistress was a tempting piece, and there had been a clear invitation in her round blue eyes, which he fully intended to accept. But instead of dwelling on her attributes, his mind skittered back to the stepdaughter. Meredith, Lydia had called her. So her name wasn't the plain "Mary" he had thought, but Meredith. It suited her. Dignified, almost regal, firm and strong. Unusual. He smiled. The slave must have been calling her "Miss Merry," not "Miss Mary." The nickname didn't suit her. She was not happy and laughing. Or at least she had not been so around him. He wondered if her personality was different around others or if it could change should her life assume a new course.

The note from Galen was, as Meredith had hoped, an apology.

Dearest Cousin,

I trust in your ever-generous Nature to forgive my hasty and ill-considered words of Yesterday. Of course, one with such a Nature as yours would see the Good in people, never the Evil. I applaud your Loyalty and Affection, and beg your forgiveness for my own appalling conduct. Please believe that only my Concern for you prompted me to speak when it would have been the better course not to.

Yours always,
Galen

The note was penned in Galen's spidery hand and signed with his usual flourish. Meredith read it once and smiled, then reread it again to fully absorb the style. What an exquisite little apology. She had been a fool to fall into the squabble with Galen yesterday. It had sprung from her irritation with Devlin, and she had unkindly taken it out on her cousin. He had been prompted solely by concern for her and her reputation. Anyone who loved her would despise the relationship her stepfather had forced upon her. Though she acquitted Daniel and Lydia of any malice, they had no understanding of the embarrassment it caused a person of her upbringing. She had been wrong to object to Galen's words, yet he was sweet enough to pen her an apology. How like him.

And how unlike the rude fellow in the stables. Her mind reverted to Jeremy Devlin. *He* insulted her casually, and though he was a servant in the house, he showed not the slightest regret for what he said. They might have been equals, or their roles reversed, the way he spoke to her. She ought to punish him for what he said. It was insolent and intolerable in an indentured servant. Yet if she reported him to Daniel, she feared he would impose strict punishment. Meredith could not bear to see a man lashed. And she could think of no lighter punishment she might impose herself. She considered transferring him from the stables to the fields or a more menial position. A demeaning position might reduce his swelled pride, but it seemed silly to take a man from the area for which his talents were most suited and place him where a man of lesser abilities, even a boy, would do as well. And the fields would harm him as much as the whip. Besides, Daniel had wished to put him in the stables, and she shouldn't remove him without speaking to her stepfather first. No, it was better to endure him until the lessons were over, then avoid Devlin. If his arrogance became too overweening, she would have him punished at that time.

Meredith shrugged. It was useless and ridiculous to allow a servant to occupy her mind so much. Instead, she decided to think about tomorrow. It was Sunday, and she would see Galen and Althea at church. It would be pleasant now that the quarrel between her and Galen was over.

The next morning Betsy helped Meredith into one of her nicest day dresses. She pulled on a chemise, petticoat, and stockings and buckled the short pocket hoop around her waist. It stuck out over her hips, flattening the silhouette of her skirt and holding it out wide to the sides. Over the hoop she placed the piece of clothing referred to as a petticoat. In reality it was an outer piece of clothing and in full public view. It was made of two layers of white muslin sewn together and puffed in a quilted effect. The skirt was dropped over the petticoat, draped back, and secured with bows so that the front of the ruffled petticoat was exposed. The dress was of chocolate-brown silk, the bodice parting to reveal a stomacher of brown silk embroidered with gold thread. The stiff, square-necked bodice was tight, as was the fashion, and pressed her breasts upward. Therefore a ''modesty piece'' of lace had been sewn across the neckline to conceal the tops of her breasts. On her head Meredith placed a frilled cap of the same brown silk. After slipping on brocade slippers of brown embroidered with gold, she was ready to leave for church. Picking up her prayer book, she ran lightly downstairs, where Betsy placed light clogs over her shoes. The clogs were nothing but wooden soles with a strap across the top, which protected the elegant slippers from the pervasive mud. She donned a light hood and cape over her head and body to protect her finery from dirt. The last item of clothing was long, soft leather gloves. When she was ready, Meredith left through the front door and entered the waiting carriage. Betsy took her place on the seat opposite Meredith. A few of the household slaves followed in a wagon.

In town, Meredith knew, all the slaves and servants attended church also, but on a large plantation it was an impossible logistical task. Bitterleaf had almost 150 slaves, as did several other large plantations, and the slaves of even one or two families would have overflowed the small church. Therefore, only the upper echelon of the house servants accompanied Meredith. Neither Daniel nor Lydia were church-goers. While the local Anglican priest was not the fire-and-brimstone Puritan of the Northern colonies, they did not wish to expose themselves to his contumely.

The ride to the church was bumpy, for the colonial roads were little more than rutted tracks. Usually the numerous waterways provided easier means of transportation. However, the church and a few plantations were reached more quickly on land. To visit these Meredith used the carriage instead of the family piroque, or large dugout. When they arrived at the small, pristinely white wooden church, the coachman jumped down from his high seat and helped Meredith to alight. She swept into the church, followed by her staff. The black servants sat on the rear benches with the other slaves, while Meredith proceeded to the Whitney pew, three rows from the front. Galen's family was already seated in the high-backed, enclosed pew.

The Whitney name was discreetly engraved on a small brass plate upon the door of the pew. Meredith opened the low door and stepped into the spacious pew, flattening her skirts to slide into place beside Althea. Their pew was cushioned in dark maroon velvet, and in the winter there were small metal containers filled with hot coals to warm the feet. The richly appointed church was a far cry from the simple, bare houses of worship in the New England colonies. South Carolina, like the other Southern colonies, was Anglican, following the church of their motherland. There were few planters in the area who did not attend the Anglican Church. The Hamiltons were the only dissenters of any importance in the area. They attended a small Presbyterian kirk, as befitting their Scotch-Irish heritage.

Althea smiled at her cousin. She was tall and slender, as were all the Whitneys, but in her face she resembled her mother, having pale blond hair and soft gray eyes. She was an attractive girl, shorter than Meredith, with a softer, more feminine look. However, there was a gravity in her demeanor that tended to mask her prettiness. Although Althea was not the wallflower Meredith had always been, her solemn manner, educated conversation, and the perennial Whitney lack of finances combined to make her a less than eligible mate. At eighteen, she was not yet quite on the shelf as Meredith was, but she appeared destined to become so.

"Meredith, how nice to see you." She smiled warmly and extended her hand to her friend and cousin.

"Althea. It's been ages since we've had a chance to talk."

"Yes, I hope you'll come calling soon."

"I will." Galen, sitting on the other side of his sister, turned toward Meredith, a question in his eyes. To answer him Meredith leaned across Althea, holding out her hand in greeting. He understood that all was well between them again and raised her hand to his lips, smiling as he did so. Galen's father, Francis, and mother, Veronica, also nodded and smiled warmly at Meredith. Francis had been Meredith's father's cousin, so their relationship was not extremely near in blood. But the Whitneys were not prone to large families, and their whole clan had dwindled to only these five people. Therefore, their relationship was close.

The priest emerged in his elegant robes and climbed the small winding staircase to his lectern mounted on a platform from which he could be seen by all the occupants of the high-backed pews. His message was mercifully brief, as his congregation liked, and the service was finished in little over an hour. Afterward, everyone lingered on the church steps to greet and gossip with people whom they hadn't seen since last Sunday. Because the plantations were large and spread apart, Sunday was often the only day of the week when anyone got a chance to talk to someone outside his or her family. Girls flirted with young men, fathers filled their pipes and swapped tales while they puffed away, mothers tsk-tsked over the escapades of the younger generation. Friends and relatives drew together, and the chatter rose, finally winding down as the parishioners slowly began to depart in carriages, wagons, and small open conveyances known as "chairs."

Meredith parted from the Whitneys as they pressed invitations on her to visit. She tried not to let it rankle that she would see them only if she visited Four Oaks, since they would not come to her house. She rode back to Bitterleaf in silence, disturbed by the sudden wave of loneliness that struck her. What would life be like if Galen never asked her to marry him? Daniel would die someday, and Lydia would leave. She would be left completely alone in the great house. Although she was a solitary person, capable of amusing herself, and with plenty of work to keep her busy, the idea of spending the rest of her life alone except for servants seemed bitterly unhappy. She needed companionship. She needed . . . love. Lydia was correct about one thing—Meredith was much more, emotional than she allowed herself to appear. Although Meredith doubted she possessed the passionate nature Lydia believed she did, she knew she was capable of deep emotions, of love and hate, sorrow and happiness. She wanted to laugh and smile, yes, even to frown and cry. Books and music would not be enough. She needed people. She wanted, Meredith admitted, a husband. When would Galen set aside his scruples and propose to her in spite of his financial condition?

"Miss Merry." Betsy broke into her thoughts as they neared Bitterleaf.

"Yes, Betsy?"

"Neb's been better the past couple of days. I thought you might want to stop and see him."

"It sounds like an excellent idea. Tell Joshua to stop the carriage by the cabins."

"Yes'm." Betsy leaned out of the window and called to the coachman above.

They turned right into the oak-lined drive leading to the house and stopped about halfway up it. Meredith climbed from the carriage, and Betsy scrambled after her. They walked across the springy grass to the cabin where Neb was housed. Meredith stooped to enter the cabin and was surprised to find Neb conscious. He stared suspiciously at Meredith, but his face softened when his gaze lighted on Betsy. Wherever she moved about the tiny room, his gaze followed her. Meredith checked his pulse. His heartbeat was no longer rapid, and his skin was cool to the touch. Although weak, he was improving. Meredith thought he would probably live, something she had not expected when she first saw him.

As she and Betsy returned to the carriage, Betsy began tentatively, "Miss Merry, he's not well enough to go back to the fields. Do you think when he's better you could find him a job around here? He could learn a trade. He's so big and strong I'm sure he'd make a good smith.''

"But we already have a smith.''

"Neb could be his apprentice. Learn from him, so when Martin is too old for such hard work, Neb could take over.''

Meredith hesitated. In the long run, would it really be doing Betsy a favor to keep him close? "Well, certainly until he's regained his strength, we'll find a less difficult occupation for him,'' Meredith replied carefully.

Shortly after breakfast on Monday, Meredith dressed in her riding habit and made her way to the stables. Jeremy Devlin was carrying in a load of hay as she approached. His tattered breeches were gone, and in their place he wore new breeches and a shirt Maisey had sewn him. Both shirt and breeches were made of rough linsey-woolsey, a combination of linen and wool material that was spun and woven on the plantation. It was the common attire of the servants. Neither breeches nor shirt fit him well. The shirt was too big and the breeches far too tight. These were even more embarrassing than his torn and ragged pair, for they clung to his buttocks and thighs in a most immodest way.

Devlin, of course, was as saucy as ever, no matter what his apparel. He bowed. "Madam, I understand I have you to thank for this elegant suit of clothes.'' He preened mockingly. "The material is a trifle rough, perhaps, but I'm sure it is the height of fashion for a slave, is it not? Just the thing for shoveling muck.''

"I'm sorry,'' Meredith retorted. "I thought you might appreciate having some clothes instead of running about next to naked as you have the past few days.''

He laughed, showing even, gleaming teeth. "There are times when nakedness can be quite appealing.''

"I'm here for my riding lesson. Shall we get on with it?'' Meredith reminded him sternly.

Jeremy inclined his head as though bowing before her wishes and strode back into the stable, returning moments later with Mercy. He repeated the procedure of the day before, lifting Meredith into the saddle, checking her seat and the position of her hands on the reins, then leading the easygoing horse around the yard, all the time correcting Meredith whenever she slipped from the proper position.

They continued in the same fashion the remainder of the week. Every day Meredith had a lesson that lasted approximately an hour. Devlin was insufferably insolent, but when he taught her, he was all business and even exhibited a patience that surprised Meredith. Once she rode well enough at a walk to suit him, he had her canter and trot, still circling the mare with the leading rein. "You're doing surprisingly well," he informed her. "You must have an aptitude. I take it no one bothered to teach you?"

"My father did," Meredith protested, but honesty forced her to add, "However, Daddy wasn't much of a horseman. I was so gawky I was ashamed to try to ride."

"Well, you know the rudiments. What you need now is constant practice. Go riding every day. I'll accompany you on Equilibrium."

"Accompany me!" Meredith exclaimed. "You most certainly will not."

He shrugged. "Suit yourself. I didn't think you were a quitter, though."

"I'm not quitting. I'll continue to ride, but I'll not spend the time with you."

"And who will watch your form? How often do I have to remind you to loosen up on the reins or straighten or relax your body? Without someone to correct your errors, you'll soon be riding the same old way. Since I have to exercise Equilibrium anyway, it seems the sensible thing to do. We'll go to a clearing where I can race my stallion. I must train Equilibrium for your father's race."

"Stepfather," Meredith corrected automatically. He cast her a curious glance, but made no comment. Finally she sighed. "All right. I'll be here Monday afternoon."

He helped her down, an amused twinkle in his eye. "Your sacrifice is most noble," he assured her blandly. She grimaced as she walked away. That man was really the most infuriating creature! How could she endure his company for over an hour every day?

Chapter VII

DANIEL SCRAPED up the last bit of gravy with a chunk of bread and popped it into his mouth. He sat back in his chair with a loud sigh. "Well, lass," he began heartily. "I hear you're learning to ride."

"Yes." Meredith finished her breakfast in a more dainty manner. It didn't surprise her that Daniel had learned about the lessons. There was almost nothing on Bitterleaf that he didn't know about. She wondered, her heart skipping a beat, if he was going to forbid her to take Devlin along. He might not want the servant gone so long each day, or he might fear Devlin would escape on Equilibrium. "We plan to begin riding farther afield this afternoon. I hope you have no objections. Devlin told me he needed to exercise Equilibrium, anyway."

Daniel smiled, a strangely merry, almost secretive smile. "Why, no, I have no objection. It sounds like a splendid idea. Equilibrium needs training if he's to win the race. I take it you like this Devlin fellow, to spend every afternoon with him?"

"Not at all," Meredith replied primly. The older man's expression annoyed her. However, the smile highlighted the dark circles beneath his eyes, and Meredith suddenly noticed how tired he looked. Now that she thought of it, he had seemed tired for several days. Her concern stifled the tart remark she had been about to toss back. "Daniel, are you all right?"

"Of course I am," he boomed. "Should I not be?"

"No, of course not. It's just—you've looked a trifle tired the past few days."

"Just the worries of the harvest." Lydia glanced up, a frown knitting her forehead, and for an instant she looked as if she would speak, but then pressed her lips firmly together and said nothing.

"Well, you ought to get more rest," Meredith admonished him. "You know, I could probably give you a medicine—"

"No!"

Meredith's eyes widened at his harsh tone. Why was Daniel so adamant, so anxious to dismiss the subject? His manner frightened her. "Whatever is the matter? If you're ill, you must go to bed, and I'll fetch something to help you. Now just tell me what pains you."

Her stepfather rose to his feet abruptly. "Enough of this nonsense. I tell you, I am *not* sick!" He frowned at Meredith and stamped out of the room.

"Well!" Meredith exclaimed, staring after him in amazement. She turned to Lydia. "Do you know what's wrong with him?"

"Don't you believe him?"

Meredith waved a contemptuous hand. "Of course not. Men hate to admit they're sick—or at least the ones I have acquaintance with do. But I'm sure he's not well. Even when we went to Charleston, he looked drawn and pale."

Tears sparkled in Lydia's eyes, and she lowered her head to hide them. "I don't know. Perhaps it's simply that he's getting older."

Meredith shook her head. "No. Lydia, what if it's something serious?" Her stomach twisted at the thought. Daniel ill? No, he couldn't be. The idea was absurd. He wasn't old yet.

"No, no," Lydia murmured reassuringly. "Surely he would tell us if it was serious."

"Yes, of course," Meredith agreed readily, eager to deny her ugly thoughts. "Certainly he would seek my help if it was bad. No doubt he has the flux or something equally embarrassing." She rose from the table in a rush of relief. "If you'll excuse me, I must see about one of the slaves who is sick."

Meredith went into the front hall, where Betsy waited patiently with her bag of medical supplies. They went out the front door and across the lawn to the small cabin where Em, the seamstress, lived. For several days now Em had complained of an ache in her stomach. At first Meredith had given her Jerusalem oak and honey for worms in the stomach. When it had proved to be of little help, Meredith had switched to snakeroot and wine. Neither had done any good.

However, this mroning Em seemed much improved and even smiled at Meredith when she entered the cabin. It just went to prove, Meredith thought wryly, that sometimes her patients improved *despite* her doctoring. Unfortunately, such was not the case with the other patient she saw that morning. Little Jim, so called to distinguish him from his uncle, Big Jim, was a teenager who was wasting away from consumption. She had given him turtle flesh, the common remedy, as well as asthmatic drops from the apothecary. But nothing helped, and he grew weaker daily. When Meredith came in the room, he brightened and began to talk eagerly about how much better he felt, but a wracking spasm of coughing cut off his cheerful words. Meredith agreed that he looked better, but the apparent improvement did not lift her spirits. She had seen the bright glow of health before in a consumptive's cheeks, and it usually signaled a decline in his condition.

It was a relief to escape the musty cabin and the false optimism of a dying boy. Meredith hurried across the lawn toward the kitchen, where the slave children were gathered. Organizing and sending out the children to pick bayberries would ease the heaviness in her chest.

Shortly after noon, Meredith presented herself at the stables. Jeremy pulled on stiff leather jackboots and saddled the horses, then helped Meredith into the saddle, a gesture she was becoming used to, though she could not be indifferent to it. He swung up onto the fierce stallion, and they set off down the drive. Meredith glanced at him from time to time as they rode, admiring the easy way he handled his horse. He made it look simple to control the spirited stallion.

"Where did you learn to ride?" she asked.

His head swiveled to her, astonishment stamped on his face. "What a civil thing to say!"

Meredith's mouth tightened. "I am capable of it, although I doubt you are."

He grinned. "If you can do it, I promise I can. Shall we call a truce? It's hard to ride together when you can speak nothing but cross words. It will be much more enjoyable if we pass the time pleasantly."

Meredith shrugged. "I never seek a quarrel."

His droll expression conveyed supreme doubt of her statement, but he did not say so. "To answer your question, I learned to ride from my father, who was one of the best horsemen in England."

"Really?"

"Yes. The Honorable Jeremy Wrexham, distinguished judge of horseflesh and women and far too fond of both. The only thing he liked better was brandy."

Meredith stared. "The Honorable . . . Your father was a member of the gentry?"

He grinned. "It's not polite to be so shocked by that revelation."

"But you—you're an indentured servant! Why would a gentleman . . ."

"Ah, there's the catch. As I assured your stepfather, I'm no gentleman. I am a bastard, madam, something which you no doubt realized already. However, I am legally a bastard as well as one in character."

"Oh." Meredith blushed to her hairline and turned her face away, striving for a cool unconcern.

"Tell me, is that worse than you imagined me to be or better?"

"I—I don't know. It doesn't explain why you're here. If your father cared enough to teach you to ride, surely he must have acknowledged you."

"He did. He loved my mother. If you'd seen her, you'd know why. She was a lovely, saucy, redheaded Irish flirt who could charm any man out of his money. Bridget Devlin. God rest her soul."

"She's dead?" Sympathy stirred in Meredith.

"Yes, she died, as do so many of the ladies who peddle their flesh—alone, graying, and past her prime, cursing the men who'd aged her, me among them, her only companion a bottle.''

"I—I'm sorry.''

He shook his head. "Nothing to be sorry about. It's the end of us all—the ones who live on the fringe of society, neither fish nor fowl. The finest blood in England runs through my veins, but I wouldn't be received in the best drawing rooms.''

"Didn't your father provide for you?''

"Oh, yes. I wore fine clothes and went to the best schools. I was the darling of his heart, as my mother had been. But he was married to a dry stick of a woman who bore him two sons, both as dull and dry a stick as she. They inherited the family name and received whatever money my father left. Whereas I—well, I speak like a nobleman; my manners, when I choose to use them, are impeccable; I can dance and court a lady to perfection. I am, in short, to all appearances a gentleman. I was educated enough to make a perfect secretary. Perhaps I could have made a match with the daughter of a merchant who wanted to add breeding to his wealth. I could have lived soberly and industriously on the allowance my uncle gave me. He's the head of the family, my uncle—Lord Wrexham. Instead, I chose to live as what I was not. I rode the best horses, kept the finest mistresses, gambled and lost, sometimes gambled and won, and dressed in the latest fashion. I frittered away my allowance the first few days each month and after that had to make shift as best I could. I became involved in some—ah, less than savory schemes. For a price, I guided wealthy buffoons through the treacherous shoals of polite society. I taught colonials to sound like Englishmen and helped Englishmen escape to the colonies. All in all, I became an embarrassment to my uncle, which was the one thing he could not bear. Finally I was found to have some connections with a notorious highwayman. It promised to brew up into a fine scandal. So milord had me knocked over the head, and when I awoke I was bound for the colonies as an indentured servant.''

Meredith stared. "Then you didn't—you aren't—"

"No, this is not the occupation of my choice. Much as I have enjoyed meeting you, madam, I find cleaning out the stables not entirely to my liking. And my clothes lack a certain savoir faire, don't you think?"

She didn't know what to say. It was amazing, unthinkable that one such as he should be laboring in the stables. Well-educated, the illegitimate son of a noble family, in all things prepared for the life of a gentleman—and now reduced to the life of a near-slave. It seemed manifestly unfair. He had not voluntarily committed himself to the indenture, nor had he committed a crime and been shipped over as punishment. He had been forced. He should not be here. Yet he *was* an indentured servant, and Daniel had paid good money for his indenture. Whatever misfortune had happened to the man, it had not been Daniel who committed the wrong. He could not be expected to pay for it, to release Devlin from his contract because Devlin's own uncle had thrown him to the wolves.

Meredith stole a glance at him. She wondered if she ought to tell her stepfather the story. Perhaps he would want to free Devlin. She also wondered if the tale he had just spun was the truth. For all she knew, he might be a tremendous liar who hoped to gain her sympathy. Jeremy caught her glance and grinned. "Can't decide whether to believe me? Wise girl. Actually, this time I am telling the truth."

"You sound as if it were a departure from the norm."

He shrugged. "I have never been a model for youth." Once again the winning smile flashed across his face. "Except, of course, as an example of what *not* to do."

The son had inherited a great deal of his mother's charm, Meredith decided. The crooked grin and the dancing eyes that invited one to share in his vast amusement were captivating. He belonged in the drawing room, not the stable. How could a man reared as he was bear the life he now led? Meredith tried to imagine how she would react if she was torn from her life, thrown onto a ship, and carried across the ocean to serve seven years of drudgery. Then she knew what he had in mind.

"You're planning to escape, aren't you?"

His eyes narrowed. "What makes you say that?"

"It's obvious. You couldn't live long as a servant."

"This fabric does scratch my skin," he admitted. "If I were to spend seven years in it, my noble flesh would be rubbed raw. Perhaps I should consider your suggestion."

"It wasn't a suggestion."

"Your father asked me to remain awhile. He has 'great plans' for me."

"What plans?" Meredith demanded disbelievingly.

"How should I know? They are Mr. Hurley's plans, not mine. However, as he pointed out, not being familiar with the country, I would probably be caught. I don't fancy having my back laid open by your charming overseer."

Meredith said nothing. He might wait for a while until he became more accustomed to the place and people, but Jeremy would run eventually. The most logical thing to do would be to flee on Equilibrium one afternoon when they were out for a ride. She wondered if he would simply race away from her, leaving her to go back and sound the alarm. Or would he knock her over the head or tie her to a tree to prevent her doing that? She decided it might be very unhealthy to ride out with Devlin. But surely it was safe for the time being. At least for a while, she could be with him without risking harm. She chose not to explore the reason she wanted to continue the rides.

They went out after that almost every day, and Meredith returned from the expeditions flushed with health and laughing. Daniel, seeing her, smiled to himself. Meredith and Jeremy talked almost continually on their rides. He corrected her mistakes in horsemanship and regaled her with stories of his former life in London, telling the latest gossip about the beauties of society and revealing the secret vices of great noblemen. In turn Meredith expounded on the colony in which she now lived, explaining how rice and indigo were grown and processed. He nodded sagely, sometimes asking questions and other times letting her talk uninterruptedly.

"Are you listening to me?" she asked suspiciously during one of his long, quiet intervals.

He smiled. "Of course. You were saying that indigo leaves must be picked carefully to avoid rubbing off the purple dye.

They are boiled in great vats, the leaves removed, and the liquid burned down to powder. Voilà—blue dye."

"Sometimes your eyes look so distant, I think you must not be listening."

"Just thinking about you."

"About me?" She stared at him.

"Yes. Is that so unusual?"

"But why?"

"Are you in love with your cousin? The servants' gossip is that you'll marry him."

"That's none of your busines," she replied haughtily.

"Oh, excuse me, are we the grand lady of the manor again?"

She glared at him. "I am not. You misinterpret whatever I say. But whom I love is *no* one's business but my own."

"And perhaps the man's."

Meredith didn't deign to answer. They stopped in a long meadow, and Jeremy jumped from his horse to help Meredith down. They had stopped here on their first ride, and Jeremy had ridden the great bay stallion across the meadow at various speeds to test both the ground and the horse. Since then, they had visited it on each ride. Meredith would dismount to sit on a large tree trunk that had toppled over and watch Jeremy race the stallion. Every time he put the stallion through his paces, the horse and man became faster and more attuned. Meredith suspected Jeremy would be able to win the race—provided he was permitted to enter it, of course.

Today, after Jeremy set her on the ground, his hands fell from her waist, but he did not move. She cocked her head up at him inquisitively. The look she saw in his eyes nearly took her breath away. She didn't know exactly what it meant, but it scorched her with its heat. She glanced away quickly. He reached out and took her hand. "I hope you aren't in love with your cousin." His voice was low and husky, and its timbre sparked little shivers along her spine. Meredith knew she ought to jerk her hand away from his—after all, no matter how noble his father, he was still her servant, and it didn't do to hold hands with a stableboy. However, her fingers defied her brain's message and remained, trembling, in his great hand. Gradually, meticulously, Jeremy removed her riding glove until her hand was bare against his. His skin was hot and calloused. Meredith wondered if those aristocratic hands had ever before held reins without gloves or wielded a shovel. No doubt they had once been perfectly smooth. He lifted her hand to his mouth and laid his lips against it, as if in greeting. But his mouth was as warm as his skin, soft and promising. The contrast between his rough flesh beneath her palm and his velvety lips above sent a longer, deeper tremor through her.

"Jeremy, what are you doing? Stop this at once."

He chuckled. "Your voice lacks conviction."

"You startled me, that's all."

An eyebrow quirked in disbelief. He dropped her glove on the ground and placed his hands on either side of her face, imprisoning her head and forcing her to look at him. For a long moment, he stared into her green-brown eyes, and then his face lowered. Meredith closed her eyes and sought to pull away, but his grip held her firm. Jeremy's lips took hers gently, moving upon them in exploration as if he had all the time in the world before him. Meredith tried to remain stiff, but could not. Instead she found herself thinking that at last she had experienced a kiss. It wasn't bad. Not bad at all. It was strange to be so close to a man, to feel the heat radiating from his skin, to mold her lips to fit his. Then the kiss changed, but that wasn't bad either, she thought. His mouth pressed against her in demand, and her lips parted, although she wasn't sure why. His tongue crept into her mouth, surprising Meredith, and she stiffened. It was strange, frightening, and yet—exciting, too. How hot his mouth was, moist and claiming. His hands slid down her shoulders and his arms encircled her, pulling her into her hard body. His hold flattened her breasts against his chest. She was glad for the cover of the habit's heavy waistcoat and jacket, or he would have been bound to feel the peculiar hardening of her nipples. His roaming tongue was beginning to shoot hot sparks throughout her body. Her loins melted like wax. She sagged in his arms, her fingers gripping the front of his shirt to help her stay upright.

When he finally released her, Meredith opened her eyes, now shining. Her lips were moist, barely parted. Her heart was drumming in her chest, blood racing along her veins. She didn't know what to do or say. Jeremy stepped back without a word, his face slightly flushed. His hands knotted into balls. "Damn." His voice was uneven. "I promised myself only one kiss. You make it difficult."

He whirled and leaped onto Equilibrium, who danced nervously at his sudden, impatient move. Horse and rider sprang forward, racing across the meadow. Meredith sank down onto the tree trunk, grateful for its presence because she was sure her legs would no longer hold her. She had never been kissed before, not even by Galen. She had had no idea that was how it would feel, that her body would throb and her lips ache for another kiss. Her fingers went to her mouth, as though his touch had made it different. Why had he done it? Had he actually wanted to kiss her, enjoyed it? But why? She was a gawky, awkward female. He must have known beautiful women in London, the best of courtesans and ladies both. Yet he had kissed her and claimed that her kiss had made him want another. Could it be true?

She sat bemused while he worked the horse, and by the time Jeremy trotted back to her, both horse and man sweating, she had regained some surface calm. She retrieved her glove from where it lay on the grass and slipped it onto her hand. Jeremy did not speak of the kiss, and neither did she. He dismounted and helped her up, then mounted again, and they rode back to the house. They began to talk as usual, Jeremy asking how the rice was milled and Meredith, grateful for a safe topic, explaining the process to him at length. When they reached the stables, he courteously helped her down. "Tomorrow?" he asked, and though the words were ordinary, there was a wealth of promise in his eyes.

"Yes." She ducked her head and hurried to the house. On the porch, she paused to look back. Jeremy was walking away from her into the stables, leading both horses. It was late afternoon, and the low sun caught his blond hair, turning it pale, almost white. The rough, ill-fitting clothes looked incongruous on him—as did the heavy jackboots. Such a rider as he was should wear better boots, ones that clung smoothly to the leg and allowed him to feel the horse and stirrup.

Suddenly it occurred to Meredith that there were great

stacks of clothes in the attic. Her mother had packed away all of Meredith's father's clothes when he died. Though they were several years out of date, at least they were of softer materials and cut to fit a man's figure. Her father had not been as big as Jeremy, but he was tall, and breeches had been worn a little looser then. She glanced at the clock in the hall. It was only five o'clock. Plenty of time before supper, which was always served at nine. She lifted her skirts and climbed the stairs, passing Lydia on the way. She smiled brightly at the woman.

"I was looking for you," Lydia began.

"Oh, nothing immediate, I hope. I was going to the attic to look through some clothes."

It seemed a strange occupation to Lydia, but she didn't comment. "No. I was merely lonely and thought we'd have a little chat. Some other time will do as well."

"Are you sure?"

"Of course."

Lydia continued down the stairs, while Meredith hurried to the steep, narrow stairs leading to the attic. Lydia had, in truth, not been so much lonely as tempted. She had been lounging in the upstairs sitting room, idle and bored, staring out the window, when Meredith and Jeremy clattered into the yard. He was laughing at a quip of Meredith's, and his lips were parted to reveal white, even teeth, his golden hair wind-whipped and sparkling in the sun. A pang of pure desire darted through Lydia's abdomen. She was more than fond of Daniel and had been faithful since they met, but this intensely masculine man disturbed and haunted her. She dreamed of him at night, and awakened empty and longing for his arms about her. She was ridden with guilt over her desires, both because of her loyalty to Daniel and because she hoped Meredith might become attracted to Jeremy. She would be betraying both her loved ones if she indulged her wanton yearnings.

She was grateful to Daniel for rescuing her from that failing troupe of actors and installing her in a comfortable home with beautiful clothes and a healthy allowance. She was grateful to Meredith for accepting her instead of turning a cold shoulder as many so-called ladies would have. She sincerely hoped Meredith would find happiness and suspected that this indentured servant might be the man who could give it to her. But despite Lydia's determination not to hurt Daniel and Meredith, as soon as she had seen Jeremy this afternoon, she was unable to quell the rush of desire. She had started downstairs to talk with Meredith, hoping it would allow her time to stifle her feelings, but Meredith was obviously busy.

Lydia strolled along the wide hallway to the back door and stepped onto the porch. The weather had cooled somewhat the past week, although her English blood could not get used to the unseasonably warm winters in Carolina. She gazed toward the stables. Perhaps if she strolled over just to talk, there would be nothing wrong. After all, Jeremy was a fellow Englishman, and she was hungry for conversation with one from her homeland. He could fill her starving ears with the doings of London, the fashions, the latest plays. She blithely ignored the fact that an indentured servant was unlikely to know anything about such things. Lydia scampered across the yard, her hoops bouncing around her in an ungainly way.

It was dim inside the stables, and for a moment she could see little more than shadows. As her eyes adjusted, she spotted Jeremy seated on a box, tugging off his jackboots. He glanced up and rose in surprise. "Miss Chandler?" His voice was as refined and modulated as those she remembered from England, the sound of fellow actors and gentlemen admirers who rushed backstage to offer her their attentions. A wave of homesickness swept her.

"Hello. I—I hope you will excuse my barging in here this way," she began.

"Your presence needs no excuse. It's too pleasant."

She smiled. "Thank you. I came to ask you . . . about London. I would so love to hear about it."

She came a few steps closer, her skirts held up to avoid the straw and dirt. He hurried to stop her. "Here, you mustn't walk on this floor; it's far too dirty for your skirts. Let's go somewhere else." He cast a quick glance around to make sure Sam was not watching, then took Lydia's hand and led her up the small wooden stairs to his room in the loft.

It was a bare, spartan bedroom, furnished with only a wooden bed covered by a patchwork quilt, a stool, and a small chest. There was no place for Lydia to sit comfortably, so they both remained standing awkwardly. She walked to the tiny, open window and gazed out across the fields. She swiveled to face him, her face an open appeal. His eyes widened, the breath catching in his throat. She wanted him to make love to her. Jeremy clenched his hands behind him, for once uncertain what to do.

This afternoon when he had kissed Meredith, his blood had unexpectedly boiled with desire. One mere kiss had set him off, creating a furor in his loins that even the furious workout on Equilibrium had not fully dissipated. He would never have dreamed that the tall, rangy woman could arouse him so. He, who had experienced the skill of the finest whores of London, had trembled with lust at the untutored kiss of an awkward country girl.

However, he had known better than to rush Meredith. He wanted her willingly in his bed. Only her complete surrender would satisfy the need to prove himself a man and make up for the degradation that had been heaped upon him. So he had moved away, biding his time, letting Meredith think about the kiss and remember it so that when he kissed her again, she would be eager for it. But his retreat had left him aching with unspent passion. Here was a woman asking to relieve the churning desire—yet he felt curiously reluctant.

Lydia swayed closer to him, still not speaking, her eyes fastened on his. Jeremy stood rooted to the spot, trembling with tension. He shouldn't take her. He must not ruin his chances with Meredith. The incident could easily get back to her. Then Meredith would refuse any advances. Lydia reached out, her fingertips grazing his shoulders, and a shudder racked his frame. God, it had been so long since he'd had a woman, and his loins were already writhing from this afternoon. She was lovely, desirable, her lips soft, parted, leaning toward him.

He bent and seized her, his mouth grinding into hers. Lydia moaned softly and moved against him, exciting him even more. He sank onto his narrow bed, pulling her down with him. Shoving down the neck of her dress, he cupped his hand around her breast and kissed her deeply. Neither of them thought of the open door behind them.

Meredith left the house, proudly carrying a stack of her father's shirts and breeches. She entered the stable quietly. She hoped she could manage to speak to Jeremy without disturbing Sam. When she could not find him in the stalls, she looked at the stairs leading to the loft. Jeremy had said he slept above the stables. Could he be in his room? She climbed the narrow stairs and tiptoed across the rough planks. It would be horrible if anyone heard her and came to investigate and found her in a servant's room! She reached his door and peered inside. The blood drained from her face, and she was barely able to suppress a gasp. She bit her lower lip until she tasted blood to keep from crying out. Jeremy and Lydia lay on his bed, kissing deeply, one of his hands surrounding Lydia's exposed breast.

Meredith turned away, sick and angry. He was making love to Lydia after having kissed her this afternoon. Oh, what a fool she'd been! He had been teasing her, playing with her. Of course the one he really wanted was Lydia. She had been aware of his interest in the other woman the day he met Lydia. And Lydia—Lydia, whom she and Daniel trusted!—was cuckolding Daniel, panting for her servant lover. It made Meredith ill to think she had been exactly like Lydia, swooning in the embrace of a stableboy, a bastard. She had trembled with hunger and wished he would continue to kiss her. She had even looked forward to tomorrow, hoping the same thing would occur again. How fatuous and naive she was to think he wanted her in return. Clearly his kiss had been purely pretense. He was amusing himself at her expense or hoped to use her in some way, probably to aid his escape. And she had blindly, foolishly believed the promise of his lips, simply because she wanted to. That was the worst of it, the fact that she had been so swayed by her own animal hunger she had not realized the obvious logic of the situation. She had been low, crude, as hot and yearning as any slut.

Meredith stumbled blindly back to the house and up to her room. It was several minutes before she had calmed down enough to speak. Finally she rang for a servant. When a young girl appeared, Meredith handed her the clothes she had carried to the barn. "Here, in about an hour or so, carry these out to Devlin in the stables."

"Yes'm."

The scrape of Meredith's heel on the stairs pierced Jeremy's haze of lust. He remembered that his door stood wide open and that anyone might come up the stairs and see them. The thought lessened his passion. He thought of Meredith and their kiss earlier that afternoon and realized that she had spurred his desire far more than Lydia's expert kisses did. That idea withered his lust even more quickly. Jeremy pulled away.

"The door," he explained and went to close it, glancing out first to make sure no one stood listening on the stairs. He turned back to look at Lydia. Her hair was tousled, her face flushed with passion, her breasts naked above the neckline of her dress. It should have been an alluring sight, he knew, but he remained curiously unstimulated. The truth was that instead of heightening his sexual excitement, the past few minutes of love play had lowered it.

Lydia sat up, tugging at her dress to cover her bosom. She, too, seemed adversely affected by their kisses. "Oh, God, what am I doing? This is insane! We could have been seen!"

"Yes," he replied noncommittally.

"Daniel wouldn't mind." Jeremy privately doubted that, but refrained from telling her so. "But I couldn't bear to cause him embarrassment, to have all the servants laughing at him behind his back." She sat still for a moment, staring blankly at the wall. Finally she went on in a low voice, "This is wrong. Daniel has been very good to me. I must go."

Jeremy said nothing. He knew if he reached out and took her into his arms again, she would melt once more. He could kiss and caress away her doubts and guilt. But he did not. All his desire had slowly drained away. When he made no move toward her, Lydia rose, saying a low, tear-choked good-bye. She fled the room and scurried down the steps. Jeremy flopped back onto his hard bed, one arm flung across his eyes. He couldn't believe he had passed up a chance to bed Lydia. Why? Because he wanted a girl whose conversation and wit he was coming to enjoy, but whose face and body should have left him stone-cold. He chuckled humorlessly. What in the hell was the matter with him?

Chapter VIII

MEREDITH DID NOT visit the stables for several days. Jeremy, expecting her the following afternoon, waited in vain. He worried that something had happened, then fumed because she had not sent him word she wasn't coming. By the time three days had passed, he was furious at her absence, desperate with worry, and almost sick with the longing that had built up inside him. He slipped away and roamed the garden and yard around the house, hoping for a glimpse of her, but he went unrewarded. He asked questions of the other servants as subtly as he could, but learned nothing except that all was normal at the big house. What was the matter with Meredith? Why didn't she come? Had her nerve failed her? Had deliberation made her regret that one impulsive kiss? Perhaps she liked to tease a man under her power, give him a taste of her mouth, then stay away and let him hunger for more. That would fit with watching men on the auction block. She might have lied about going to his auction only because her cousin drove her insane with her chatter. She could have been lying with her kiss that day. When his thoughts turned in that direction, Jeremy hated her. But, even so, he knew he still had to have her.

Finally, one day as he unobtrusively watched the house, he saw Daniel step out on the back porch with Meredith. Quickly he tossed aside the rake he had been pretending to use on the stable yard and strode to the porch. "Good day, Mr. Hurley." He bowed slightly as befitted a servant, revealing none of his anger.

"Why, Jeremy. How is my horse doing?"

There was only one horse as far as Daniel Hurley was concerned. "Equilibrium's fine, sir. He's the fastest horse I've ever ridden."

Meredith turned pale, then flushed when she saw Jeremy and would have turned to scuttle back into the house had her stepfather not blocked her way. She couldn't leave without shoving Daniel aside, which he would consider most peculiar. He must not get any inkling of what she had witnessed. When Jeremy bowed to Meredith, she forced a cool nod in response. But he was not about to let her off with that. "It's been some days since our last lesson, Miss Meredith. Have you been ill?"

"No."

Daniel turned to her. "Have you given up riding? Wouldn't blame you myself. I always thought it was damned difficult."

Meredith compressed her lips. Let Daniel believe what he chose, although it galled her to be thought a coward or incapable of learning. However, Jeremy would not let it rest. "Oh, no, sir, she's quite good. I've been pleased with her progress." He turned back to Meredith guilelessly, as if he didn't realize he was forcing her into a corner. "But you need to continue practicing, miss, or you'll lose it."

"Heavens, Meredith, why aren't you out riding, then?" Daniel asked.

"There's been so much to do. It's time to make the candles, since the children have picked all the bayberries. And there'll be the hog butchering and then the fall cleaning."

"You think they can't handle it without you? All you have to do is direct the workers, you know. You don't do the cleaning or candle making yourself, surely. Just give Dulcie and the others directions and take off a couple of hours. It'll do you good to get away."

"No, really, I don't think it's a good idea. I—It's not enjoyable for me."

"Nonsense. It isn't like you to give up."

"I'm not giving up!" Meredith retorted heatedly.

"Then why are you so reluctant? Don't you want to impress your next visitors?"

"My skill on horseback will not impress Cousin Galen."

He shrugged. "There are other chaps around. Very horsey, this parish—whole colony, in fact. I imagine you'd look damned fetching on horseback."

"Indeed she does, sir," Jeremy chimed in.

Meredith glared at him. She didn't believe his servile act one bit. Jeremy knew precisely what he was doing. He was aware she wished to avoid him, but he was forcing her into such a position that she had to ride. She couldn't explain to Daniel why she no longer chose to be in Jeremy's company. Stiffly Meredith said, "All right. I'll meet you in the stable yard tomorrow."

"Good!" Daniel boomed. "See that you do, girl. I'll be asking you about it at supper." He turned and reentered the house. Meredith whirled, right on his heels, and left without another glance at Jeremy. He strolled to the stables, a faint smile curving his lips. It had been enjoyable to get the better of her, but he still had no idea why she had developed a sudden aversion to riding. Well, tomorrow when they were alone, he'd discover the reason.

Meredith's stomach twisted with dread as she dressed in her riding habit. Betsy's constant chatter about Neb, whom Meredith had assigned to the garden while he recuperated, didn't relax her taut nerves any. At one point, Meredith almost screamed at her maid to be quiet, but she refrained. It wasn't Betsy's fault her nerves were frazzled. It was simply that she dreaded spending time alone with Jeremy. He sickened her. He was detestable. He was frightening.

She put on a bold front as she strode to the stables, determined not to let Jeremy see how he affected her. And no matter what, she wouldn't reveal her reason for stopping the lessons. She couldn't bear to talk about it, hated to even think of it, something she found herself doing all too often. When she recalled his large brown hand on Lydia's breast, kneading and stroking, his mouth locked to hers, Meredith felt physically ill. It was repugnant, disgusting—animal lust, with none of the finer feelings she cherished.

Jeremy sauntered out to meet her, the familiar crooked grin spreading across his face. His smile was devastating, and Meredith was sure he was fully aware of it. It was a game to him. Women were toys, playthings. He cared nothing for honor or trust or loyalty. Daniel had been kind to him, and he repaid him villainously. Meredith stared back at Jeremy without a hint of a smile. He frowned and snapped, "I'll saddle the horses."

When he returned, he helped her into the saddle without comment, his face as grave as hers. They cantered out of the yard to the driveway and were soon stretching out their horses at a run. Meredith was astonished at how wonderful it was to ride away her emotions. Anger and frustration flowed away as she bent over the mare's neck and urged her on. She had a sudden, heady realization that she was much improved as a rider, just as Jeremy had told Daniel. A few weeks ago she would have clung desperately to her horse's neck if Mercy had taken off at a run like this. Now she understood how to move with the horse and retain control through the reins.

They drew in at the clearing and allowed the horses to walk aimlessly for a few minutes to calm down. Jeremy dismounted and came to her side. Meredith barely gave him a glance. "I have no desire to dismount. Please finish your practice as quickly as possible, and let's go."

He tilted his head back. "What in the hell is the matter with you? Get down off that horse."

"Absolutely not!"

His anxiety, irritation, and frustrated lust of the past few days exploded. Jeremy dug his fingers into her waist and dragged her off her mount. He did not set her on the ground as he usually did, but pulled her close and let her slide to the ground, so that her body rubbed against his all the way down. When she reached the ground, Jeremy grasped her face between his hands and kissed her hard. His lips ground into hers, forcing her mouth to open and admit his tongue. Enraged, Meredith braced her hands against his chest and shoved as hard as she could. She caught him by surprise and he staggered back slightly, loosening his hold. Meredith struck his face as hard as she could, connecting with a solid thwack.

"How dare you, you—" she stammered, too angry to be lucid.

His nostrils flared, and bright pinpoints of anger sparkled in his pupils. "Bitch," he said almost dispassionately, his mouth curling into a sneer. She had tormented him for days, arousing him, then withholding herself. He had been gentle with her, slow and easy so as not to frighten her. He had even forgone the pleasures of the redhead's body. And she repaid him like this! "Teasing slut." He gripped her upper arms and jerked Meredith to him, his iron arms imprisoning her. Again Jeremy kissed her, forcing her to accept his mouth. At first his kiss was harsh and angry, more a demand than an expression of feeling, but at the touch of her soft lips it did not remain so for long. His lips gentled as he tasted the sweetness of her mouth. He worked at her with tongue and lips and teeth, exploring, hungry, until she responded with a whimper and her arms came up to curve around his neck. Her tongue met and matched his, easing tentatively into his mouth.

Jeremy shuddered, hurled violently into a realm beyond reason, aware of nothing but the supreme pleasure he held in his arms. He rained wild kisses across her face and neck, mouthing the soft flesh of her throat, nibbling her sensitive earlobes. Meredith moved in his arms, unable to absorb the multitude of delights he showered upon her. His hands came up, accidentally knocking off her hat, and dug into her hair. She could feel the pressure of his fingertips upon her scalp, the prickles of pain as the wooden hairpins popped from her hair. One hand moved downward, sliding along the smooth column of her neck, tugging away the fall of lace at her throat, and opening her shirt to his fingers. The stiff waistcoat impeded his progress. He fumbled at the buttons as he continued to assault her mouth and throat with scorching kisses. Meredith melted against the hard bar of his arm, head lolling back, exposing her throat to his mouth. She was almost swooning, hardly aware of where she was or what Jeremy was to her. She knew only that she ached for his touch in an inchoate, primitive way.

When Jeremy opened her waistcoat, his hand slipped inside the shirt's open neck, caressing the creamy tops of her breasts. He shoved down the sheltering chemise, popping the top buttons of her shirt. The ruffle of the chemise cupped her breasts, seemingly framing the rounded globes. The pink-brown nipples thrust out saucily, stiff and swollen from his arousal. Jeremy gazed at the naked flesh, savoring its beauty and promise, before he lowered his head and buried his mouth in her quivering breast. Meredith moaned and clutched his hair as his rough tongue encompassed the peak of her breast, stroking it until she thought she would burst. His mouth was sweet upon her skin, stray gold hairs tickling her blue-veined skin, his hot, panting breath setting her on fire.

Then a picture flashed through Meredith's mind, gone in an instant, but startling enough to jerk her from her daze. She recalled the scene she had witnessed the other day between Jeremy and Lydia as they lay sprawled upon his bed, her dress unfastened to the waist and his mouth feasting upon one breast as he did now with Meredith. The vision was as effective as a bucket of cold water dashed in her face. Jeremy was seducing her as he had Lydia, doing the same things to her in a no-doubt practiced way. First her stepfather's mistress, and now the mistress of the plantation. He was using her, demeaning her, and she had fallen in with his plan with a frightening alacrity. How could she have been so taken in by his lovemaking?

Meredith shoved against his shoulders as hard as she could, fury and shame sweeping through her and replacing passion, taking its intensity and violence. Her shove caught Jeremy off guard and sent him staggering. His heel came up against the large log on which Meredith usually sat, and he tumbled backward. He crashed to the ground, gaping at Meredith, bemused, his body throbbing with hunger and unable to adjust to the sudden switch in circumstances. "You pig!" she raged, incoherent with anger. He had humiliated her in a way that went far deeper than embarrassment, had made her own body a traitor, made her respond even though she did not wish to. "I hate you!" she spat. "I hate you!"

She dashed for her horse, tugging at her chemise and blouse to cover her exposed skin. Impelled by blind fury, Meredith managed to scramble onto the animal without help and dug in her heels hard. The mare jumped and took off at a dead run. Behind her, Jeremy stared blankly for a moment,

then charged to his horse and vaulted into the saddle. Had he
thought, Jeremy would not have followed on her heels but
given her time for her anger to dissipate, but he was pumped
full of desire and as wild and unthinking as she.

Equilibrium was by far the faster horse, and ordinarily
Jeremy could have caught her with ease. But Meredith had a
good head start on him, and in her elemental rage rode with a
natural grace and finesse, bending low over Mercy's neck,
almost one with the horse. The mare, quite frightened by the
woman on her back who was suddenly a stranger, raced with
all her might. Meredith thundered into the stable yard a length
ahead of Jeremy. She pulled Mercy to a sudden halt, sliding
from her back even as she stopped. Meredith stumbled and
fell to the ground, jarring her head and rekindling the tears
the wind had whipped into her eyes. As she struggled to rise,
Jeremy jumped off Equilibrium and yanked Meredith up
unceremoniously.

"What in the hell do you think you're doing?" he grated.
"Are you trying to kill yourself and your horse? Whatever
you want to do to yourself is fine with me, but why murder
the mare as well?"

"Let go of me! Why did you follow me? I wouldn't have
run if you hadn't chased me."

"Why did I follow you! God, woman, one minute you're
as hot for me as a dockside whore, the next you're screaming
imprecations and flying away like a madwoman."

"Oh!" Red washed across her vision at his description of
her desire. Not only had he humiliated her by proving her
weakness in desiring him when he felt nothing for her—for
how could he want a great hulking girl like herself?—but now
he was taunting her with her reaction! He would spread the
tale all over the servants' quarters. Soon everyone on the
plantation would know of her common, unbridled lust for a
stableboy, and then they would spread it through the parish.
She knew how gossip flew from slave quarters to slave
quarters and then to the main houses. Everyone would know,
and she would be unable to face anyone. She would be the
laughingstock of the parish: plain, gawky Meredith Whitney,
so wanton but unable to catch a man any other way, had
sought out an indentured servant. That was the only way she

could get into a man's breeches, they would laugh, by *owning* him.

Meredith jerked her arm from Jeremy's grasp and started across the yard, tears streaming down her red cheeks. Jeremy followed, grabbing her shoulders and whirling her around to face him. The overseer, unnoticed by either of them, was approaching the house, two slaves in his wake. He stopped and stared at the sight of the white servant who tended the horses actually laying his hands on the mistress of the plantation. Jackson's eyes narrowed, and a cruel smile touched his thin lips. Now Devlin had ruined himself. Jackson had disliked him at first sight and had regretted Hurley's taking him out of Jackson's hands. He would have enjoyed lowering that proud head a notch or two, but he had been unable to get his hands on him. However, Devlin, with his foolish lunge at Meredith—God knows, that gangly witch was enough to make any man fly into a paroxysm of rage—had gone too far. Hurley would approve of any punishment Jackson inflicted.

The overseer strode forward. "Miss Whitney, is this fellow bothering you? Do you want him punished?"

"Keep out of this," Jeremy snarled.

"Yes!" Meredith answered firmly, vainly trying to twist from Jeremy's grasp. "He's insulted me." At a motion from Jackson, the two slaves cautiously stepped behind Jeremy and grabbed his arms, hauling him back from Meredith. Meredith was positive his clutching fingers had planted bruises on her skin. She shook violently. "I want him punished for his insolence!"

Turning, she darted to the house, tears blinding her eyes and choking her throat. Oh, God, how awful, how awful! Behind her Jeremy shouted her name, but she ran on, bursting into the house and up the stairs. Devlin struggled to escape the two slaves, but both were strong field hands and retained their grip on him. For a moment the three men were locked in a silent struggle. Jackson shouted to another slave who had just emerged from the springhouse with a jug of milk in his hand. The black man stood rooted to the ground, staring at the scene, and Jackson barked at him again. This time he dropped the jug and rushed forward, not wanting any trouble with the overseer.

"Help them restrain that devil," Jackson told the slave. "Take him to the whipping post."

With the help of the third man, the slaves were able to overcome Jeremy and dragged him past the house toward the whipping post standing ominously among the small cabins. Jackson followed, a thin smile playing on his lips as he slid the coiled whip from his shoulder and fondled its smooth wood handle. He cracked the leather lash experimentally. He was going to enjoy this one, yes, even more than most. By the time he was through with Devlin, the man would be lucky to be alive. And Hurley wouldn't complain about losing an expensive servant when the fellow had threatened Meredith.

When Meredith reached the safety of her room, she slammed the door and threw herself across the clean white coverlet, careless of the damage her riding habit and boots could do to it. Tears welled under her eyelids and gushed out. Meredith clenched her fists and pressed them to her temples, willing the dreadful pounding of her head to stop and the fountain of tears to end. She could die from shame! No, that was the worst part. One never died from shame but was forced to live through it. And she would not be the only one shamed. Galen, too, would be ridiculed. Everyone knew the two of them were close. People often asked, as Phoebe had, when they would become engaged. Now everyone would laugh heartily at the idea that Galen's love had welcomed the embrace of a mannerless servant. Meredith squeezed her eyes shut. How could she have done it? She had acted like a slut, clinging to Jeremy and returning his kisses, delighting in the feel of his hand on her bare breast. Even though she was alone, Meredith blushed violently at the memory. She had permitted him to be intimate with her, to do things that no lady would permit a man to do until they were married. Worse than that, she had enjoyed it!

Her door burst open. Lydia stood there pale and agitated. "Meredith, please, you must come. Quickly. Jackson has taken Jeremy—"

Meredith tried to assume a cool air, wiping away the mute testimony of her tears. "I know. I ordered him to punish Devlin."

Lydia's eyes widened. "Meredith! But why? You can't mean it. Jackson's going to whip him!" Her voice rose hysterically.

Instinctively Meredith rose to her feet, her hand flying to her throat. "Whip him? But I—" She hardened her face. How dare Lydia champion her paramour's cause so openly! "It's no concern of mine. The man was insolent."

"Insolent!" Lydia gasped. "Good God, Meredith, you tend the smallest wound, you give the slave children treats, you stay up all night with a sick babe. You pour out your compassion on everyone within reach. And now you claim not to care if a man is about to be whipped?" Meredith remained stubbornly silent. Lydia stared at her aghast. Suddenly she set her mouth and grabbed Meredith's hand. "Come." She pulled her at a fast clip down the stairs and out the front door.

"Lydia," Meredith protested as she stumbled along in her wake. "Stop! What are you doing?"

Lydia did not stop, but plowed on, dragging Meredith with her along the drive. "If you want his back whipped so badly, then you'll watch it. If you delight so in spilling his blood, I'll make certain you're there to see it, every drop."

"What! No, Lydia, you've gone mad. I won't!" Meredith struggled against the other's grip. Being larger and more used to physical tasks, ordinarily Meredith would have overcome Lydia easily. However, this time the older woman had the intense strength of her emotions, and she was able to yank Meredith across the grass toward the cabins.

At one end of the cabins, just beyond the shade of the huge oaks, stood the fearsome whipping post. It was in reality two posts set side by side several feet apart. The wrists of the man to be punished were fastened with ropes to either pole. As they approached, Meredith could see Jeremy standing between the posts, arms spread wide and tied tightly. His head hung forward, and she could see nothing of his face but the bright fall of hair. He was shirtless, and across his back blossomed several red welts and one bleeding line where the lash had cut the skin. Meredith stopped dead, and Lydia released her hand, certain she had achieved her goal.

The two women stood to one side, unnoticed by the others.

Jeremy was in profile to them, as was Jackson several feet
behind him. Farther back several slaves had gathered, silent
and taut, eyes fixed on the white man between the posts.
Jackson gave the whip a little shake and raised his hand,
flipping the long lash back and then forward. It sang through
the air and popped against Devlin's back. The muscles in
Jeremy's arms and back knotted with the effort of remaining
silent, and his face contorted, lips drawing back from his
teeth in a grim imitation of a smile. His skin glistened with
perspiration, and the hair around his face and neck were damp
with it. As the whip dropped away, it left another bright red
stripe across his back.

"No!" Meredith screamed, horrified, and for the first time
Jackson and the others turned and saw her. "No! Stop this at
once." She hurried forward.

"Miss Whitney, I'm sure this is too troubling a sight for
your eyes," Jackson countered smoothly. "Perhaps you'd
better go back inside."

"No. I want you to cut him down."

Jackson's eyes glittered. "But you told me to punish him."

Meredith saw his hand go back and she realized that he
didn't intend to obey. He was too far gone in his blood lust.
As his hand arched up, she darted forward, flinging her body
between Jackson and his victim. Jackson had already started
the whip forward. With an oath he twisted his arm, and the
whip whistled harmlessly onto the grass beside her. Meredith
swallowed. For a moment she had thought the lash would
slice her, too. "Cut him down," she ordered, her voice
shaky.

"Miss Whitney, you're overwrought. You asked to have
him punished."

"Not like this. I didn't mean for you to whip him."

He smiled. "What other punishment would fit the crime of
laying hands on you? He deserves a good lashing. Your
stepfather would agree, I'm sure."

"My stepfather would agree with *me*. Now cut him down!"
The two stared at each other in silence, then Meredith looked
across at the slaves, her eyes lighting on one very recogniz-
able figure. "You, Neb. Cut him down, as I said."

The black face remained impassive, but he moved quickly

to the posts. His nimble fingers untied the knots, and Jeremy sagged. The big man held him up, and Meredith waved other slaves forward to help him. All were frightened of disobeying Jackson, but neither could they disobey the mistress. Two men helped Neb pick up Jeremy and carry him across the lawn to the stable yard. Meredith and Lydia followed, Meredith first sending a girl to fetch Betsy and her medicine bag.

The men laid Jeremy on his stomach on his bed, then scurried out. Neb remained, standing by the far wall, his hands linked together, silently watching. Meredith knelt at the head of his bed. She wasn't sure whether he was conscious. He must have passed out, she thought, for he said nothing. Tears streamed down Meredith's cheeks unheeded. Her hands twisted together in her lap. Gazing at his back laced with long red welts and the horrible bloody stripes, she was overwhelmed by guilt and remorse. Why had she ordered him punished? She should have known Jackson would jump at the opportunity to whip him. Indeed, Lydia had told her what Jackson was doing, and she had stubbornly refused to help Jeremy. Meredith covered her face with her hands. Dear God, what was the matter with her? She'd never had anyone whipped in her whole life. She hated the practice. Yet she'd condemned Jeremy to this punishment because of her wounded pride. Because she had kissed him like a wanton and was ashamed of it. It didn't matter what he'd done, that he had made love to Lydia and then tried to do the same to her, nor that he would spread her embarrassing tale all over the place. None of it was as cruel as what she had done in retaliation.

She stretched out a trembling hand and laid it lightly on the gleaming thatch of hair. Leaning close, she whispered, "I'm sorry. I'm so terribly sorry."

Chapter IX

BETSY ENTERED the room breathlessly, the heavy leather medicine bag in her hand. "Here, Miss Merry, What's wrong? What happened?"

Meredith looked up, wiping the tears from her cheeks with her hands. "Jeremy is hurt, through my fault."

Betsy handed her the bag and glanced wide-eyed at Jeremy's prone form. "It looks like he's been whipped."

"He has," Meredith replied shortly. She pulled out the jar of ointment that she made from moldy bread. "Get me a cloth and water." Betsy complied, and Meredith gently washed his back. Jeremy stiffened. Meredith knew her light touch was painful on the wounds. It was not as bad as she had first thought. There were only two strips where the flesh was actually cut and another three that were raised welts. She spread the ointment on the cuts to prevent infection, then dabbed a cooling lotion on the welts to take away their sting. With effort she turned to Lydia and for the first time spoke to her. Her voice was flat. "Lydia, are you staying to watch him?"

"Yes, if you want," Lydia replied, a little surprised. Normally it would have been Meredith who stayed if the patient's condition was serious or a slave girl if it was not bad. Why had Meredith asked her?

"Give him this for the pain." She extended a small vial

containing a sedative she had brewed from Jamestown weed. "Just a bit. It's potent. Put one drop in a glass of water and have him drink it. It will ease the ache." She replaced the other materials in her bag and rose.

Betsy picked up the bag to follow Meredith, and her eyes went fleetingly to Neb. A look passed between them, brief but clearly charged with emotion. Meredith, seeing the exchange, nearly sighed aloud. Betsy seemed to actually love the hulking brute whom she had tended. But how would it end for her? Meredith wanted to glance back at Jeremy, but refrained. She plodded down the stairs. She would not see Jeremy again, she was sure. She could not bear the shame of what she had done to him. He would hate her, as he had every right to. She thought of the gossip she had feared earlier. This was a worse, deeper shame. What she had ordered appalled her. Never in her life had she acted so impulsively and cruelly, condemning a man to whipping. She would have denied she was capable of it. Meredith wondered if she really knew herself at all.

After Meredith left, Lydia went to Jeremy's side and knelt to peer into his face. She brushed the hair from his forehead. His eyes opened, and he grinned crookedly. Tears sprang into Lydia's eyes. "Meredith left you something for the pain." She mixed the potion with shaking hands and helped him drink it. "She tended you."

"I know. I was awake."

"Why didn't you say anything?"

He shrugged, then grimaced at the pain it caused. "I saw no reason to."

"She was so sorry, Jeremy." Earnestly Lydia leaned closer, placing a hand on his bare arm. "Don't be angry with her, please. I've never seen her act that way. She's normally a very kind person, quite tenderhearted. I can't imagine why she let Jackson do it."

Jeremy studied her, his blue eyes unfathomable. "I guess I'm the first, then." He turned his head away. Moments later he slipped into a shallow sleep. Lydia sighed and sat down on the uncomfortable stool to wait.

*   *   *

"Where's Meredith?" Daniel Hurley glanced around the table, eyebrows raised in question.

"In her room," Lydia replied softly. She was tired from the long afternoon at Jeremy's bedside. He had awakened after several hours and taken another dose of medicine. Lydia had returned to the house and sent a servant out to sit with him, instructing the girl to notify her if Devlin needed the pain medicine.

"Is she sick?"

"Only at heart."

"What do you mean?"

Lydia explained the events of the afternoon, surprised at Daniel's chuckle upon hearing of Meredith's outburst of rage. "Daniel, what is the matter? Surely you can't be pleased with the way she acted."

He dismissed her objection with a wave of his hand. "Why not? It's one of the few signs of real emotion I've seen from Meredith."

"What do you mean? You and she lose your tempers with each other often."

"No, I mean real, ungovernable emotion, the kind that shows hate or love. Meredith's usually in full control. I'm glad to see she's not a plaster saint."

Lydia sighed. "Maybe so, but I had hopes that . . . No doubt you will think it foolish. But I had hoped Meredith and Jeremy might—well, that she might be attracted to him."

"If she weren't attracted to him, why would she get so angry?" Daniel answered obliquely.

Lydia stared. "Daniel, what are you saying? Would you condone—something between them?"

"Depends on what that something is. I've said too much already." He took a bite of goose and followed it with a hearty sip of beer. After a few more bites, he pushed away the pewter trencher, though it was still half full. "I'm not very hungry today. I think I'll go to the stables and check on Devlin's condition."

Lydia glanced at his dish, but said nothing. Daniel left the room, whistling tunelessly. He strode to the stables and climbed the narrow stairs to the loft. By the time he reached the top, he was panting shallowly. He stopped for a moment to regain his breath before he went into the room. Motioning for the girl watching Jeremy to leave, Daniel sat down gingerly on the creaky stool. Jeremy opened one piercing blue eye, then rolled to his side, more or less facing him. The old man had come to find out what he'd done to his stepdaughter, he was sure.

"I understand you got into a spot of trouble today," Daniel began. Jeremy only nodded. "What happened?"

"I was insolent," Jeremy sneered. "And for that I got the lash."

"Did Meredith order you whipped?" he asked.

"No. She told Jackson I should be punished."

"And should you have been?" Daniel sounded amused.

"Depends on your thinking."

"What did you do to make Meredith so angry?"

Jeremy stared at the man boldly. He knew Hurley would be furious if he learned Jeremy had kissed and caressed his stepdaughter. And the old man's punishment would make Meredith's pale in comparison. Yet he was too proud to lie. "Let Meredith tell you."

"Well, it would do me no good to ask Meredith. She never tells me a thing unless she wants to. And I don't think she will about this—she's locked herself in her room."

"Why?"

"Lydia says she's too ashamed to face anyone. Now, back to the matter at hand. What caused Meredith's anger?"

"I touched her hallowed skin," Jeremy tossed back sarcastically.

Daniel smiled a small, secretive grin. Jeremy gawked at him in amazement. Surely even a stepfather wouldn't be amused at a servant's treating a woman under his protection so lightly. If Meredith were his and any man made so bold with her, he'd have his head for it. "How do you feel about Meredith now?" Daniel asked, surprising Jeremy further.

A strange light sprang into Jeremy's eyes, but he didn't reply. He could hardly tell her stepfather it had made him want Meredith more than ever. Amazon, that was what he had called her at first. What a fitting name for her today when she had charged in between Jackson and himself, braving the whip to save him. He didn't understand why she had been so

enraged by his kisses, but there was no denying he caused
violent emotion in her. She had wanted him. He was certain
he wasn't wrong about that. But the desire had created conflict in her. Her infuriated order to punish him was an indication of the strength of her conflict and therefore the strength
of her desire for him.

Jeremy was determined that all her spirit and fire would be
his. But that was no answer for Hurley. Noncommittally, he
replied, "She also stopped the whipping and doctored my
wounds. I can't hate her for that, can I?" Again the light
flashed in his eyes, and Hurley had to bend to catch his
words. "No woman's had me in her power before."

Daniel tilted his head and studied the large man stretched
out before him. For an instant he wondered if he was doing
the right thing. God, he hoped he was not leading Meredith
astray. He wet his lips and said, "Devlin, once your back is
healed, you're to begin working in the house."

"What?" He had expected revenge. Instead he was being
elevated to a position in the house.

"You'll still ride Equilibrium in the race, so continue
training him, but except for that, your talents are wasted here.
You've book learning. I want you to take over the plantation
accounts. Can you do it?"

"I—I guess so," Jeremy stammered.

"Good. Then I'll expect you in my study when you're healed."
He stood up. "I'll send the girl back in. Good day."

"Good day." Jeremy watched him exit, still dazed by his
offer.

For the next few days, Meredith was subdued. She did not
venture near the stables, giving Betsy Jeremy's medicine and
instructing her to apply it daily to Jeremy's back until the cuts
were healed. Betsy stared in surprise, but did as Meredith bid
her. When she returned from Jeremy's room, Meredith questioned her in detail about his condition until Betsy wondered
even more why Meredith had not gone herself.

Though she questioned Betsy about Jeremy, Meredith did
not speak of him to Lydia. Once they had been friendly, but
now a restraint lay upon them. When they were together, the

silence was deafening. They broke it with only awkward, superficial phrases about the weather and housework.

Meredith was grateful that she had many chores to keep her busy. It was time for the annual candle making, which was done after the weather cooled enough so that the candles would not melt when they were put aside to set. The bayberries were boiled in large vats over fires outside, and the air was redolent with their sweet odor. Women skimmed off the tallow that formed on top of the water. The tallow was collected and allowed to congeal, then melted and refined over the fire again. When the process was finished, the resulting tallow was a transparent green. Bayberry candles were preferred to those made from the tallow of animals, for they burned more slowly and didn't melt in the summer heat, as well as adding a pleasant scent to the air. The kettles were then half filled with tallow and water and again boiled to a liquid consistency. Workers carried the kettles into a lean-to in the shade of the trees. There the tallow was poured into candle molds and left to harden.

A precious few wax candles were made from the wax of the plantation's beehives. Numerous candles were formed from animal tallow. They would be used in the kitchen and other places not frequented by the gentry. They were also used to make rush lights, strips of the outer bark of rushes dipped in animal tallow and allowed to harden, a cheap source of light for the slaves to use in their cabins.

When the candles had cooled, they were placed in compartmented candle boxes, covered, and stored in the deep, dark closet underneath the stairs, ready for use throughout the winter and next summer.

After the candles were made, there was barely a moment to draw breath before it was time to slaughter the hogs. This, too, was done when the weather grew cooler. Far behind the plantation house, so that the odor would not penetrate it, several men killed the hogs and dragged their carcasses to a large fire. Using a tackle hung on a tripod, the men tied the carcass to a rope that ran through the tackle and was hooked to a mule. When the mule moved, the carcass was pulled into the air and then lowered into a vast pot atop the fire, where it was scalded and scraped. Afterward the men gutted, beheaded, and halved the carcass and took it to the kitchen, where the meat would be cooked.

Every part of the hog was used. The fat was cut away and rendered into lard. The back meat was chopped and seasoned, stuffed into intestines, and placed in the smokehouse to slowly smoke. The ham, shoulders, and sides were soaked in large barrels of brine and later smoked. Even the livers were cooked and chopped fine to be mixed into a cornmeal mush known as scrapple.

Although Meredith did not participate in making the candles or preparing the meat for the winter, she was busy supervising the processes and tallying the total candles and meat for her records. Also, since the harvest was over and the rice was being slowly refined by hand, Meredith had to record the number of barrels of rice the plantation produced, how much was shipped by what captains and ships to Daniel's factor in London, and how much was sold directly to a merchant in Charleston. The same figures had to be kept for the indigo as well.

The work kept her mind off what had happened to Jeremy and helped her miss her daily rides less. However, one day as she sat in the study adding a column of figures, her sanctuary was invaded. There was a sharp rap at the door, and Jeremy Devlin stepped into the room. For a long moment she was too shocked to do anything but stare. Unconsciously her mind registered that he wore her father's breeches, stockings, and shoes. The breeches were a trifle too tight, but he looked more natural in them. Apparently the shirts and coats she had given him had been too tight for his wide chest, for he wore one of the rough linsey-woolsey shirts sewn for him earlier. Its sleeves were full and gathered at the wrists. The neck was cut deep, for it was made to be slipped on over the head, not having buttons. Therefore the shirt exposed a good portion of his chest. Meredith could clearly see his muscled skin and the fine, curling, red-gold hairs that adorned it. Her stomach quivered. She told herself it was the surprise of seeing him.

She didn't know what to say. She knew she should apologize, but she couldn't bring herself to speak so humbly to this man. The brief rapport they had established when they rode together was gone. Her pressing guilt froze her tongue and tightened her body, but her embarrassment kept her from admitting her guilty conscience. Jeremy appeared to have none of her qualms. He ambled into the room, his eyes roaming about, noting everything.

"A pleasant study," he commented, his hands clasped behind his back as he surveyed the bookshelves. "I had not figured Mr. Hurley for a bookish man."

"He is not. This was my father's study." Meredith eyed him warily. What was he doing here? He was not a house servant. But she hadn't the nerve to question him or try to put him in his place, not after the way she had punished his insolence. He walked without stiffness, substantiating Betsy's claim that he was healing very quickly. Had he come to tell her what he thought of her? Why was he not showing his resentment, the hatred he must feel for her?

"I see. And does the daughter take after the father?"

"Yes, I enjoy reading."

"I guessed you must. I wasn't one for books myself. I suppose I was always in too much mischief." He swiveled to look at her, his gaze sweeping over the navy-blue dress that did little for her skin or figure. "Why don't you wear brighter colors? And Molinist panniers instead of that pocket hoop? They're much better for tall women."

Meredith colored. "You shouldn't know about such things, much less discuss them with a lady."

"Beg pardon." His eyes danced in amusement, denying his words.

"What is the matter with you?" Meredith lashed out, her nerves stretched to their fullest, waiting for him to begin his verbal attack. "Why don't you go ahead and say it instead of keeping me in suspense like this?"

Jeremy lifted his eyebrows. "Say what?"

"Didn't you come here to take me to task?"

"No. Should I? Have you been naughty?"

"Stop treating me in that indulgent, superior way!" she snapped. "You couldn't be so calm inside. You must despise me for having Jackson punish you. Why don't you go ahead and display your rage?"

He bowed mockingly. "I am a mere servant, madam. How

could I dare upbraid you? I am entirely subject to your command."

"You seem to me more the type to seek revenge."

His grin was devilish. "Ah, but I will have my revenge in my own way, my own time." His eyes drifted over her body, giving a clearly sexual connotation to his words.

He meant to take his revenge out on her body! Was he planning to rape her? Or to demonstrate once more how quickly she succumbed to his advances? Fear, then anger, shot through her, followed closely by a heart-pounding excitement. Emotions swirled and boiled within her. She had no idea how to handle Jeremy. That required someone like Lydia, pretty and accomplished in the art of flirting. Meredith's hands gripped each other convulsively in her lap as she strove to mask her inner tumult, coolly asking, "Then what are you doing here?"

"Don't you know? Did Mr. Hurley not tell you? Your stepfather sent me. He wants me to take over the plantation accounts. You are to explain the system to me."

"What!" Meredith shot out of her chair. Daniel had given Devlin *her* books? "You're lying. That can't be true."

"Why should I make it up?"

Meredith tore out of the room and across the covered pathway to the main house. Lydia glanced up as she hurried into the sitting room, hoops swaying wildly in her haste. "Whatever is the matter, Meredith?" She rose, concerned.

"Where is Daniel?"

"I'm not sure. I think he's in his room, lying down."

Daniel? Taking a nap in midmorning? It sounded unlikely, but Meredith ran up the stairs to his room. Sure enough, at her strong rap, his voice called out for her to enter. She swung open the door and marched in. Ordinarily, since he was resting, she would have questioned the state of his health, but she was too angry and apprehensive to do so. All she could think of was Jeremy waiting below to steal her job.

"That Devlin man is downstairs in the study."

"He must be recovering quickly."

"That's not the point. He says you told him to do the plantation books."

"Yes. He's proficient with numbers and reading and writing.

Why waste an educated servant in the stables? Of course, every afternoon he'll continue training Equilibrium, but he can easily keep the books as well.''

"But that's my work!" Meredith protested. He couldn't take it away from her. He couldn't! Keeping the books was her most pleasant task. Supervising the servants and the household work could be a bore, but the accounts were interesting, different. They were important. It was part of her training to one day run the plantation herself. Hurt seared her. Daniel had taken from her what she enjoyed most and given it to a man she hated. She had wronged Jeremy, which made it even more difficult to have to sit by his side and explain her figures and the workings of the plantation. Did Daniel not know how much pain it would cause her? Or did he simply not care? And after she had taught Jeremy, he would know everything about what happened on her land, but she would know next to nothing. How could Daniel do this to her? Had he been pretending his affection for her all these years?

Coldly she inquired, "Are you displeased with my work?"

Seeing her aloof expression, he exclaimed, "No! Meredith, you mustn't think that. I want to relieve you of some of your burden. You've been a dear girl to help me, for you know I hate figures. But you shouldn't be stuck in a musty old office so much. You should be enjoying the things other young women do, dresses and parties and young men."

"Daniel, I don't care about those!" She went to him and earnestly clasped his hand. "Please, I'd rather continue to do the books."

He frowned. "Meredith, that's silly when we have a servant who would be perfectly good at it. I want him to get some experience in the financial end of the business."

"Why? What does it matter?"

"I told you that when I got him. I'm thinking of making the lad overseer. He'll understand his work better if he knows the dollar-and-cents value of it."

Meredith released his hand and stepped back. Daniel was set against her. "All right. Whatever you say. It is, after all, your plantation."

Daniel watched her leave, a worried frown creasing his face. He had stumblingly hurt her feelings, he could tell. He hadn't thought that that would be the result of his sending Jeremy to learn the accounts. He wished he could make her realize he hadn't intended it as an insult to her, but to do so he would have to reveal his plan. He wanted to put that off as long as possible. He sighed. Things got so complicated when he was dealing with Meredith.

Meredith returned to the study, firmly quelling her emotions. She must not let Devlin know how it upset her, for he would probably take great pleasure in that. She would be cool and calm, teach him the job as quickly as possible, and then get out of his sight. When she stepped into the office, she found Jeremy lounging gracefully in the blue wing chair. He rose politely, but without servility, his eyebrows raised in amused questioning. She shot him a glance that would have dampened any other man's pretensions. It had no effect on Devlin.

"If you will please come over to the desk," Meredith began formally, "we can begin our lessons."

He moved to stand beside her, far too near as far as Meredith was concerned. She sat down in her chair and opened the ledgers. "This is the tally of each day's finished product. Daniel brings me the figures each night. It's in terms of barrels. When we are through, I'll add the column to find the total production. There's a separate total for rice and indigo. This is the indigo sheet. When our rice is shipped to our factor in London, I place the amount shipped on this page. If Daniel sells some to a local merchant or ship's captain, I enter the figure here. When we're finished shipping, I total both figures. Obviously it should come out the same as the total of the finished product. If not, there's been a mistake or we've not sold enough or we raised too much."

"Sounds simple enough." He bent over the desk to gaze at the figures, so close Meredith had to lean away to avoid touching him. She could smell his scent, a mixture of horse and leather and the tangy smell of his skin. It reminded her of the day he had taken her in his arms and kissed her, and she writhed inside at the memory.

"Good, then we can move on," she declared tartly and turned the page. Jeremy leaned back reluctantly, although he remained far too near for Meredith to breathe normally. "This page is our receipts. Those in cash go in this column, those in merchandise go in these. Of course, the cash is totaled, as well as the more common merchandise received."

"Merchandise? Why do you accept that in place of cash?"

"Necessity. When we sell to ship's captains or local merchants, that's what we get. The goods sent to London are paid for in cash, but after the factor takes out the expense of all the merchandise he's shipped us from England, there's usually very little left. We are not wealthy people in the colonies in terms of coin. Our wealth is all in our land and possessions."

"I see."

Meredith guided him through the rest of the records, explaining the household accounts and the separate slave records. She hated being with him and she hoped they would finish as soon as possible, but perversely it irritated her that Jeremy caught on so quickly. She had to admit that had he not understood it, she would probably have been irritated by his stupidity as well. She knew she was so hurt and angry about losing the books to him there could be no pleasing her.

The following day Jeremy again reported to her in the study. His precise politeness to her was in itself a mockery. Since it was the end of October, Meredith decided to let him accompany her on the end-of-the-month inventory of the household goods. It was a dull, time-consuming job, but by doing it herself, she kept thoroughly knowledgeable about what went on in the kitchen and greatly discouraged thievery. Paper and quill in hand, Jeremy followed on her heels as she went first to the smokehouse. Obediently he counted the hams, bacons, sausages, and dried beef, noting the total on his ledger. The next stop was the springhouse, a small wooden structure built over a nearby stream. It was the coolest place on the plantation, and the things most likely to spoil were stored there: fresh beef, milk, the prettily molded butter. Here she recorded only the meat, for she kept no tally of the quickly changing milk products. In the root cellar, they counted barrels of onions, sweet potatoes, Irish potatoes, and other vegetables grown on the plantation. In the large pantry in the kitchen, they tallied sacks of flour, salt, sugar, tea, and cornmeal.

Jeremy worked quickly and efficiently. Meredith studied

him in surprise. "From what you told me I thought there wouldn't be a smidgen of industry in you."

"Why, what do you mean?" His eyebrows rose innocently.

"You said you never did anything gainful in England."

"I had no reason to there," he replied honestly. "Honest toil is not a quality admired by the aristocracy. A gentleman is raised to be idle and wealthy. Only the oldest sons, who will someday take over the land, receive any training in managing the estate. But someone like me, without land, name, or prospects, but also without training or incentive to work—what was I to do?"

"It sounds like excuse making to me."

He gazed at her for a moment, then smiled a sweet, crooked grin that Meredith was sure would stop any female heart. "Perhaps you're right. I was a rebellious, angry youth—and I wasted a great deal of time pitying myself." His look turned inward. "My experience on the ship coming over and here on this plantation has taught me to value things I once took for granted—freedom, health, kindness, control over my own destiny. Once I spent my time envying my legitimate half-brothers and my aristocratic companions because they had the things I could never have. Things that meant so much in London. Now, here, it doesn't seem so important. I'd give anything to be at home, comfortable, my own man again."

"And this time you'd appreciate it?" Meredith asked, patently disbelieving.

"You won't let a man rest, will you? I hope I would appreciate it. But your skepticism may be right. Within a few weeks, I'd probably be back to my old ways—envious, carousing, fighting. Anyway, it doesn't matter. I won't be there again, will I?" For the first time since she had met him, sadness crept into Jeremy's usually cocky voice. Sympathy washed over her, and without thinking she laid a hand on his arm. His huge hand covered hers, lightly stroking it with his fingertips. Her entire arm tingled from the contact, and she snatched her hand back.

"Must you misinterpret every gesture I make?" she snapped.

He sighed. "Damn, you're skittish. What makes you draw back from every touch? Why are men so abhorrent to you? It isn't lack of passion. I know. I kissed you. You wanted me quite badly.''

"Of all the conceit! I'll have you know it isn't men in the plural who are abhorrent to me, but *one man* in particular.''

"Why? Because I'm a servant? Because I'm a bastard?''

Meredith swallowed. She couldn't explain that she had caught him with Lydia, that she knew him for an inconstant lover, a man who added women to his collection as the Indians piled up scalps. The very words choked her. Her cheeks flushed with embarrassment. "I am not easy. I am not the sort of cheap tart you are no doubt used to. I value myself too much to fall into your arms and join your battalion of women.''

"Battalion? Good Lord, I haven't had a woman since I set sail from England. I've been so celibate I could qualify for sainthood—and you talk about being one of a huge number of women!''

He was a liar as well as a philanderer, Meredith thought, but she did not say so. She merely turned away to leave the large pantry where they stood. Jeremy caught her arm. "Or are you saving yourself for your precious Galen? Believe me, girl, it will be a waste. That dry stick will never give you a measure of the joy I can.''

"Do you think that's all there is to life? I have a purer feeling for Galen, as he does for me.''

"I have found that 'purity' is usually the lack of ability or the lack of opportunity.''

Her lips curled. "You couldn't begin to understand the kind of man Galen is.''

"No, I certainly can't. I'll never understand a man who's courted a woman as long as he's courted you and never kissed her. Don't bother to deny it. I can recognize a woman who's not tasted a man's lips before.''

Two red spots flamed on Meredith's cheekbones. "There's a great deal more to love than mere sex. You think that if a man and woman tumble in the hay together, they have done everything. Well, it isn't all. It isn't even the largest part of love. There's a meeting of the minds, a quiet companionship of spirit, a sharing of interests.''

"Maybe I don't know what love is. I doubt I've ever been

in that glorious state—if it exists. But I can tell you, there are things far grander between a man and his woman than the desiccated entertainments you propose." He placed his broad hand upon her stomach and let it drift over her abdomen. "Here is where it happens. The excitement, the glory, the shattering joy. Oh, yes, there are comforts that last longer and exist on a level far below the peak. They are such things as curling up beside a warm body all night long or seeing the light shine in your lover's eyes when she sees you or sharing laughter. Even arguing, when you know that all tension between you will be erased later in bed. A dog will do for quiet companionship of the spirit!"

The intimate touch of his hand and the low throb of his voice as it described his picture of marriage mesmerized Meredith. She drifted toward him, her chest aching in a way she had never experienced before. But her step forward broke the spell. She dropped her hands and almost hopped backward. "This is absurd. I refuse to stand about discussing 'love' with you." She whirled and started out the door.

"Have fun in your bed alone tonight," Jeremy taunted. "You can dream of all those delightful meetings of the mind you'll have one day with Galen while your heart turns to ice and your body withers."

Meredith almost ran from him. That evening at supper, she announced to Daniel, "Devlin is capable of doing the records alone now. I won't be teaching him anymore."

Chapter X

AFTER JEREMY took over the accounts, Meredith was left with far less to do. She wandered about the house almost like a ghost, wishing she could find more to occupy her than embroider pillowcases or mend rips and tears. Although she talked to Lydia some, the old companionship was gone. Meredith knew that no matter how funny or warm or kind Lydia was, Meredith could never forget the picture of her and Jeremy entwined on his low bed.

Once she stopped to ask herself why it bothered her that Lydia had slept—was probably still sleeping—with Jeremy. After all, she had always known Lydia's morals were not the highest. Why was it different that she knew Jeremy intimately? Meredith concluded that it was because Lydia had been unfaithful to Daniel. She did not expect Lydia to be a virtuous woman, but she had expected her to be loyal.

Some of her time was taken up treating the occasional sick person on the plantation. A couple of the blacks took sick from spoiled food. One day a boy cut his leg on a rake, and Meredith had to rush to him and apply green stickweed leaves to the cut to stop the bleeding. But the few illnesses and medical emergencies could not take up most of her days, and she often found herself idle.

One day she decided to visit her cousins. Taking the pirogue, she was poled down the river to Four Oaks, where the Whitneys lived. Since the main autumn tasks were over, Meredith had no qualms about taking up Althea's time. However, she had to admit it probably would make no difference if she had come earlier. Neither Althea nor her mother were the careful supervisors of household duties that Meredith was. In the same manner, Galen and his father were not good farmers or businessmen. They were a family who loved the graceful things of life and had little talent for or interest in the more mundane areas.

Galen and Althea were intelligent and even more well-read than Meredith, able to hold long, scholarly conversations and deep discussions about the beauty of poetry or the musical value of a piece of music. Meredith would never dream of discussing her accounts or problems with servants or the danger of insects to the crop with them. Meredith smiled indulgently as she stepped onto the wooden dock of Four Oaks and started up the path to the house. She had to traipse through weeds now and then, but what did it matter? The mind was most valued in this household.

"Meredith!" Althea's voice floated across the back garden, and Meredith looked up to see her cousin standing at a window. "Oh, I'm so happy. I'll be right down."

Meredith opened the back door and entered. She was one of the family here, not a visitor. The black maid desultorily sweeping the floor smiled a greeting at her. Althea swept down the staircase and hurried toward her friend and cousin, arms outstretched. "Meredith, it's been ages! I've been longing for a chat with you."

Smiling back, Meredith hugged her. "You look lovely today, Althea." It was true. Her cousin's eyes had a sparkle Meredith had not seen there before, and her skin positively glowed.

Althea blushed slightly. The color was becoming to her. "Thank you, Meredith. It is so kind of you to say so. Please, come into the sitting room. Mama is upstairs lying down. I'm afraid she has one of her migraines."

"I'm so sorry." She was quite familiar with her cousin Veronica's migraines, since the woman had them regularly. Meredith herself had always been unfailingly healthy. She had little idea what a splitting headache was like, although she was sure it must be dreadful. She quelled the traitorous thought that rose in her mind: was Veronica really that sick, or were her headaches convenient excuses to get out of doing something? They seemed to occur at the busiest seasons of the year.

Althea dismissed her mother's illness with a wave of her hand, an unusually lighthearted gesture for her. She pulled Meredith down on the sofa beside her and began to question her about her recent doings. Meredith could think of little to tell her cousin. Althea would no doubt find her dreadfully dull. She had been too unhappy lately to read. And she could hardly relate her misery at her exclusion from the accounts. For one thing, Althea would not understand why it would be anything but a relief. For another, all the Whitneys despised Daniel. She could not say anything against him around them, for she was too loyal to discuss Daniel with his enemies. And, of course, she could not possibly relate the things that had happened concerning Jeremy Devlin.

Before her visit, Meredith had wondered if gossip had spread to the other plantations. If Althea had heard anything, she would be too genteel to mention it, of course. But since she did not look at Meredith oddly or seem in any way different in her attitude toward her cousin, Meredith relaxed, sure she had heard nothing. Apparently the episode in the clearing with Jeremy had not yet spread beyond the plantation. Could it be—no, surely not—that Jeremy had, in fact, not revealed the way she had kissed him and molded her body to his, wantonly reveling in his caresses? Meredith shook the thought from her mind. She must not start ascribing a sense of honor to that scoundrel.

After their first excited rush of talk, they fell strangely silent. Meredith, realizing all the things she could not tell her cousin, felt a wave of self-pity. She was cut off from everyone these days—her cousins, Daniel, Lydia. And all of it was because of Jeremy Devlin. She had been fine until he arrived on the scene. It was as if he had brought an evil wind with him that swept away all her familiar supports. Her world was topsy-turvy. She wished, with an ache in her heart, that she could have it back again.

Galen came into the room a few moments later and greeted

his cousin with a pleased smile. "Meredith, I am so glad you came! I have a book you must read. I received it not a month ago from London. Remind me to get it before you leave."

They discussed a few local events. Finally Althea mentioned the upcoming horse race, which surprised Meredith. She had never known any of the Whitneys to be much interested in horses. She supposed Althea's comment was an indication of how sadly their conversation had dropped off. "I hear that Blaine Randall's Chimneysweep is the favored horse this year," Althea commented.

"Yes, so I understand."

"Has Mr. Hurley really entered Equilibrium?" Althea plunged on.

"Yes."

"But I thought no one could ride him!"

"That's not exactly true." Meredith had only the other night talked to her stepfather about the race. It was to be held during the fair, which was only a month away. She had asked Daniel how he could enter the horse when he had no rider. He had pointed out that Devlin would ride it. "But Daniel, he cannot. He's an indentured servant. They'll disqualify you. You'll embarrass yourself. You know they won't admit anyone but a gentleman to the race." Daniel had merely smiled mysteriously, and Meredith would have liked to shake him. Lately her pragmatic stepfather seemed to be turning into a lunatic.

"You mean Daniel will ride him!"

"No, of course not. He has a—rider, though."

"Really? Who? I'm sure Blaine—that is, Mr. Randall—will be anxious to hear about this."

"Must we discuss this idiotic race?" Galen cut in irritably. "Everywhere I go it is the only topic of conversation. I thought in my own house at least I would be spared it." He rose. "Excuse me, ladies. I will get that book for you, Cousin Meredith."

After he left, Althea leaned toward Meredith confidingly. "Forgive his ill temper. Lately Galen and Father have had such worries. They are afraid the factor in London cheats them dreadfully."

"They all do," Meredith replied cautiously. None of the Whitneys had ever mentioned finances before.

"Yes, but everyone seems to thrive except us. We are more and more in debt each day. Sometimes I think—I think we do not spend money wisely, or perhaps we aren't careful enough with what we grow." A frown creased her smooth brow. "You know, I am not the careful housekeeper that you are."

"A very merchantly sort of skill," Meredith said deprecatingly.

"No, sometimes I think it would be better if we were more practical. One cannot live on poetry and philosophy, you know, nor on the music of the harpsichord."

"Speaking of that, I should love to hear you play," Meredith said, changing the subject. It disturbed her to find changes or doubt in her dearest friend. "It's been so long since I've had the pleasure."

"Of course," Althea agreed with alacrity, rising to lead her to the music room. Meredith spent a pleasant half hour listening to the sweet, tinkling tunes of the delicate instrument. Galen joined them, and they sat wrapped up in the music, sharing their mutual delight. As she took her leave, Galen handed her the brown leather-bound book and urged her to visit them again. On the surface it seemed as it had always been. But there had been drastic differences, Meredith knew, both in herself and Althea. She was afraid her life would never be the same.

Daniel stepped into the study. Jeremy glanced up from the account books, and seeing who it was, rose politely. "Good. I hoped I'd find you here." Daniel advanced into the room. "How are you liking your new work?"

"It's quite tolerable," Jeremy admitted cautiously. In fact, he had found the accounts rather interesting, a far cry from anything he had done before. He could understand why Meredith enjoyed it. By looking at the accounts, he kept his finger on the pulse of the great farm. The business was beginning to intrigue him. However, Jeremy wasn't about to reveal that to Daniel. He didn't know what game the other man was playing, but as a general course he thought it wisest not to reveal too much of how he felt.

"Fine, fine," Daniel enthused. "I thought you might be interested in riding with me when I look over the fields."

Jeremy stared, but quickly recovered his composure. "Certainly."

"Good. Have Sam saddle me a horse. I'll meet you at the stables in twenty minutes."

When he left the room, Jeremy shook his head in bewilderment, but followed Daniel's instructions. Every time he saw the man, he did something stranger than before. Jeremy wondered where it was leading. Exactly twenty minutes later, Daniel arrived at the stables, where Jeremy waited with two saddled horses. Jeremy wore tan breeches and gentleman's riding boots, soft and fitted to his leg, with leather extensions on either side of the knees to protect them. Daniel ran an eye over his apparel.

"Where did the boots come from?" he asked.

"Miss Whitney was kind enough to give me a pair that belonged to her father. He was much my height, I believe. Fortunately, we had the same size foot, although the breeches and shirts are not as perfect a fit."

"Obviously," Daniel grunted and glanced again at the odd combination of elegant, outdated riding breeches that fit much too snugly, fine boots, and coarse, homespun shirt. "We'll have to get you garments that look a little more as if they were meant to be worn together."

Again Jeremy stared. "Thank you, sir." He struggled to keep the astonishment out of his voice.

"I'll have a girl take your measurements, and we'll order something from a tailor in Charleston." He clamped the reins in his meaty fist and strugggled into the saddle, with an assist from Sam. Jeremy swung into his saddle effortlessly, and they set out along the track leading to the fields. Daniel pointed to the now empty land as they rode along. "Rice fields. That's mostly what we grow, although we have indigo as well. I started the indigo not long ago. The government put a bounty of four pence a pound on it after 1748, to encourage growing it. Makes it worthwhile to cultivate it. Takes sandy soil. It couldn't be grown successfully in Carolina until a woman experimented with indigo seeds on her father's plantation and discovered what kind of soil it took. Eliza Lucas. I believe she married a Pinckney.''

Jeremy had grown used to the Carolinian way of inserting personal history about anyone they happened to discuss, as if the family he was from or the one he married into was of vast significance. However, Daniel's statement that it was a woman who discovered how to grow indigo startled him. The women of the colonies were very different from the women in England. It seemed as if every day he discovered how much they differed. "Unusual," he murmured.

"Yes, isn't it? Oh, there are some colonial wives who are just ornamental, but by and large they're hard workers. Real helpmates. 'Course, some men aren't strong enough for such a woman.''

Jeremy didn't know what to answer, so he said nothing. Daniel seemed to be hinting at something, but Jeremy wasn't sure what. The subject of strong women reminded him of Meredith, but Hurley wouldn't discuss his stepdaughter with a servant. A faint smile curved Jeremy's lips. He supposed Meredith could be quite a helpmate, if she chose to be. He imagined she would love as strongly as she hated. But he was beginning to wonder if he would ever feel the opposite coin of her emotions. He seemed to have lost his ability to win a woman's heart. Meredith's aloofness maddened him, making him do and say things that he knew would set her against him even more. Whenever Meredith turned her cold, imperious look on him or flashed her fiery temper, he retaliated in kind, too angry to cajole her. But when he responded sarcastically or insultingly, she disliked him all the more. Although he enjoyed pricking her emotions and making them flare to life, he usually ended up receiving an excess of them. It was difficult to make love to a woman when he was embroiled in a raging argument with her.

What did Meredith have against him? Until the day of the whipping, they had been developing a looser, friendlier relationship. She had relaxed and talked with him, even joked a little. He had discovered how wonderful it was to talk with a witty person again after months of deprivation. Then she had turned suddenly cold, as if a winter storm had swept over her personality. The change angered him, and he had kissed her, which led to the lashing. Jeremy had hated her in those moments when the whip bit into his back, but then she had rushed out like a virago, bravely positioning herself between his back and the whip. He'd seen the lash bite into the dust not inches from him, and he realized how close she had come to feeling its sting across her face and chest. His chest knotted whenever he thought about the danger she'd put herself in. Then she had bathed his wounds with gentle hands and applied the healing medicine, bending over him to whisper an apology. But after that she had cut herself off from him, no longer taking her riding lessons. It was obvious she had despised explaining the accounting to him. Why had she decided to hate him? And why was he so obsessed with her?

When he recalled all the beauties in London whom he could bed at the merest gesture, it seemed absurd that he should be panting after a tall, skinny, ill-tempered colonial spinster. Yet he was. He had even given up his plans of escape until after he had wooed and won her. Once he had told himself he wanted her so that she would help him escape, but he saw now that it was merely an excuse. It would be almost as easy to escape without her, and whatever help she could give him he could get as easily from Lydia, who had demonstrated that she was quite willing to crawl beneath his sheets. So why hold out for Meredith?

Daniel's words drew him back from his thoughts. "I have them plowed now, right after harvesting. Are you listening, boy?"

"Yes, sir."

"Good, 'cause I'm not talking just to hear my teeth rattle." He pulled his horse to a stop. Jeremy waited silently while Daniel gazed across an empty field, letting his mount's head wander to chomp at nearby weeds. "Some prefer spring plowing before they plant."

"When do you plant?" Jeremy inquired with polite interest, playing along with Daniel's game, whatever it might be.

"April, May, thereabouts. First you grow seedlings in beds, then transplant them to the paddies. When the plants are six inches high or so, you flood the paddies. You dam up a stream or divert the nearest river. These lowlands are easy to flood, which is why the country's perfect for growing rice."

Jeremy didn't doubt that. The land was so marshy he would have thought one wouldn't have to flood the fields to make them suitable.

Daniel rumbled on about the weeds, which were the worst enemies of the rice plants, and the blight. Jeremy listened, interested despite himself. Some of these things he had already heard from Meredith, but whereas Meredith had merely answered his questions, Daniel presented a complete lecture, covering every phase of the agriculture of rice. By the time he'd finished, Jeremy thought he must now know all there was to know about rice growing—but he was still in the dark as to why Daniel had told him.

He was even more mystified when Daniel continued his lecture the following day. They rode over every part of the large plantation, discussing rice, indigo, cleaning, milling, and polishing. At times Jeremy felt as though knowledge was being stuffed down his throat. Daniel took him along when he bargained with the ship's captain over selling him a cargo of rice. He had Jeremy read a letter from his agent in London and write Daniel's reply. Then, back at Bitterleaf, Daniel dug out all the letters he had received from the man over the past year and gave them to Jeremy to study, building a picture for him of his dealings with the factor.

Puzzled, Jeremy did as he was instructed. Daily he was drawn more and more into the workings of the plantation. He didn't understand why, and at times he resented it. It was far easier work than cleaning out the stables, granted, but he distrusted Daniel's secretiveness, and the whole thing seemed a terrible waste of time. Daniel's wanting him as a secretary made sense. He had an aristocratic hand, could read, and knew numbers. But why would a mere secretary have to be so knowledgeable about every aspect of Hurley's business? Why would one take a secretary on a tour of the fields and acquaint him with the work of the slaves and the number of workers the large plantation required? Why explain the methods by which a dishonest overseer could cheat his employer?

True to his word, Daniel had sent a woman to Jeremy's room to take his measurements. One day he took Jeremy with him to Charleston for a meeting with a merchant, and while there, they made a side trip to the tailor's to pick up the new clothes for Jeremy. Jeremy was thunderstruck at the quantity and quality of the clothes. Laid before him were numerous breeches, waistcoats, and jackets, clothes for all occasions and in every sort of material, from practical dark broadcloth to fine, colorful satins, brocades, and velvets. There were lawn shirts, linen shirts, neckbands, lace falls to be attached at the throat, and lace cuffs. There were several pairs of shoes with large, square buckles of gold or silver, as well as stockings, plain cocked hats, and two tricorn hats decorated with rich braid. Jeremy noticed that there were even several pins to attach the lace falls to the neckband, one of them decorated with a dark blue sapphire. He turned toward Hurley, almost too amazed to speak, his eyes blazing with questions. "You can't be serious."

Hurley laughed. "Of course I am. You think I had so many clothes made in this outlandish size for a joke? No one else could wear them."

That was true, of course. They were obviously made for him. He shot a suspicious glance at his companion. What was Hurley's aim? Could it be that he was the sort who preferred men to women? Jeremy had no false modesty; he knew he was a good-looking man. But he had thought that kind preferred beautiful striplings, not hard, muscular men in their thirties. Of course, in the colonies one's selection was necessarily limited. He gazed longingly at the profusion of luxurious clothes. He ached, actually physically ached, to feel the sensual rub of velvet against his skin, the feather-light weight of lawn, the smoothness of silk. It had been so long since he had worn anything decent. Sometimes it seemed as if the ill-fitting coarse, thrown-together clothes he wore were the emblem of his present degradation. It humiliated him for Meredith to see him dressed as he was, but he couldn't accept the clothes if what he suddenly feared was the price.

"Why?" he croaked out. "Why give all this to me? I'm nothing but a servant."

Hurley's brows drew together. "You're not going to turn all high-and-mighty on me, are you? Is your pride worth throwing these away?"

"Not everything can be bought. What do you want of me in return?" Jeremy eyed the older man warily.

Hurley passed a hand across his eyes, and it struck Jeremy that he looked exhausted. The circles beneath his eyes were dark, in complete contrast to the pallor of his skin. "Does it matter?"

"Of course it matters," Jeremy hissed fiercely, ignoring the amazed, avid stare of the waiting tailor. "I'm not an animal or a doll for you to amuse yourself with. I'm not a woman to be plied with presents and—"

Daniel burst out laughing, suddenly comprehending Jeremy's reluctance. "Good God, man, do you think I'm trying to lure you to my bed? That I am a pederast?"

"I don't know what to think," Jeremy retorted honestly. "I haven't the faintest clue what's going on."

"Haven't you? Well, it's no matter to be discussing here and now. Will it satisfy you if I promise not to force you to do what I ask? The choice will be yours."

"What choice?"

"You'll know in good time. I admit I'd like to sweeten the pot a little. Take the clothes. You can return them if you don't like my plan."

"You know that once I've worn them, they'll be much harder to refuse."

Hurley chuckled. "That's true. But, tell me, wouldn't you enjoy having everyone at Bitterleaf seeing you dressed like this? Think how amazed Meredith will be."

The last shrewd statement decided Jeremy. He could picture clearly how he would look in the new suits, how Meredith would stare. Some yearning for him would have to stir in her breast when he stood before her as proud and handsome as he had been in London. In these clothes he would feel almost himself again. With fingers that trembled, he reached out to pick up the garments.

Chapter XI

WHEN DANIEL and Jeremy returned from Charleston, Meredith and Lydia were sitting in the formal drawing room with Opal Hamilton. Opal was the young wife of Angus Hamilton, a dour Scotch-Irishman. He was middle-aged, with a lined, grim face and bristling eyebrows. After his first wife died upon presenting him with their eleventh child, he took for his bride a girl at the opposite pole from himself. Opal Hamilton was the undisputed beauty of the parish. At twenty-four and gratefully barren, she retained her youthful figure yet possessed a maturity that few of the other, younger belles could ever hope to possess. Her husband dressed her in the richest clothes and jewels, lavishing on her all the love and warmth his dry soul was capable of. Today she wore a dress of emerald-green satin, caught up with delicate silver pins over a frilled petticoat. Green-and-rose brocade slippers peeked out beneath her dress, accenting the green-and-rose pattern of her brocade stomacher. Her hair was high and stiffly wired and powdered in the latest fashion to reach the colonies. On top of the concoction was perched a ridiculous little hat, hardly larger than an iron and rather shaped like one, adorned with a clump of curling feathers. The green of her dress deepened the rather pale, grape-green color of her eyes. Her brows were plucked into a thin, arched line, and her cheeks and lips had been reddened.

Lydia and Meredith had giggled when they spied her emerging from her carriage in the driveway. To protect all her finery, she wore a huge pelisse that covered her from the neck down and made her resemble a great, shapeless lump. Over her high hairdo and hat she wore the expandable head covering known as a calash, so-named because it resembled the collapsible leather cover on the light, horse-drawn carriage known as a calash. It was a large, ribbed, dark satin cover that arched up and out over the whole hairdo, turning her head into a gigantic bowl with a face cut out in front. To protect her skin from the harsh rays of the sun, Opal wore a black satin mask and long black leather gloves. She moved stiffly in her abundance of clothes, looking like a creature from a nightmare.

However, coverings removed and seated daintily on one of the high-backed wing chairs, she was lovely indeed. She was also, in Meredith's opinion, vain, self-centered, shallow, spoiled, and had a good many other unpleasant qualities. Not content with being a beauty, she found it necessary to puncture everyone else's self-esteem. "How is dear Galen?" she asked Meredith slyly, preparing to describe his attentiveness to Opal at church, when the large bell outside sounded, announcing the docking of the master's boat.

"Daniel!" Lydia cried merrily, bobbing up and rushing to the window to look for him.

Meredith was relieved at the timely interruption, and she joined Lydia at the window. Normally both women would have gone to meet Daniel, at least stepping out onto the back porch, but they could not rudely rush from the room and leave their visitor by herself. So they waited for Daniel to come inside. Opal couldn't have cared less about Daniel's arrival. He had never shown the slightest interest in her, an unpardonable sin in Opal's eyes. Besides, he was old and unattractive, and Opal had enough of old, unattractive men in the person of her husband. She was interested only in young, virile men who could satisfy her voracious sexual appetite. In fact, that was the reason for her visit today. She had little liking for women, particularly pretty ones like Lydia who challenged her supremacy. Meredith was no competition, of course, but Opal disliked her quick wit and sharp tongue, of

which she was too often the victim. But she had heard gossip
about a handsome indentured servant at Bitterleaf, and she
had come to call in hopes of catching a glimpse of him. So
far, however, she had had no luck.

Daniel strode into the room a few minutes later, Jeremy
following on his heels. Lydia ran to greet Hurley, while
Meredith began, ''Daniel, it's good to—'' She broke off, her
reaction to Jeremy all he had hoped for. She stared at him,
stunned, and the silence in the room was deafening. Jeremy
was dressed as plainly as any planter returning from a trip,
but used as Meredith was to his manner of dress for the past
few weeks, the effect of the expensive, well-cut clothes was
dazzling. He wore a navy-blue broadcloth jacket edged with a
row of decorative pewter buttons. The coat was not designed
to fasten in front but hung open. Its wide, stiff skirts reached
the bottom of his hips, as did the more colorful, embroidered
waistcoat, revealed by the open coat. A white lawn shirt was
evident beneath the long vest, its lace cuffs emerging from
the wide, limp, turned-back cuffs of the jacket. There was a
fall of plain white linen at the throat, a pewter pin tacking it
in place. His breeches were also dark blue, so tightly fitted in
the new fashion that they had to be split at the knee and then
buttoned. Above his black leather shoes he wore white
stockings, their tops covered by the buttoned knee of the
breeches. Jeremy held a simple black tricorn hat in one hand,
and on his head was the soft, white wig known as the
Ramillies. It had a small puff on either side of the face and
was pulled back into a braided tail tied with a thin black
ribbon, unlike the bagwig favored by Galen, which had two
small rolls at each side and a bag enclosing the hair in back.

Meredith's chest contracted painfully. How tall Jeremy
was, how well-built. This must be the way he had looked in
London, elegant yet manly, unutterably virile in the fine
clothes. He was handsome—more than handsome. She could
not think of a word for it. Too big and strong for beauty. Too
well-formed and fine-featured for brutish strength. His lips
were firm, chiseled, his nose aristocratically straight. Sun had
turned the fair skin golden, and the darkened skin around his
blue eyes made them all the more striking. The suit was cut

exactly to his figure and emphasized the bulging muscles of his thighs, the width and depth of his shoulders and chest.

Meredith wondered how she could have been foolish enough to respond to his kiss—as if he could actually want her! No man who looked like that would ever have need of the plain Meredith Whitney. He could get any woman. Jeremy had been playing with her that day in the clearing, for his amusement or for some other devious reason. She had known it then and burned with shame at her reaction to him. But today, seeing him like this, the pain sliced through her freshly. She must have been mad. How humiliating—how he must have laughed at her breathless, naive passion!

"Miss Whitney." He bowed solemnly in his best drawing-room manner.

Meredith did not reply, merely raised her eyebrows frostily. Almost imperceptibly Jeremy's face stiffened, the faint smile disappearing. Daniel, uncomfortable around Opal, quickly made an excuse and departed, Jeremy following in his wake.

Opal turned to Meredith in amazement, eyes rounded and lips slightly parted. "Who was that?" she breathed.

Her fatuous expression irritated Meredith and she snapped, "Jeremy Devlin, merely an indentured servant."

So *that* was the man! Opal smiled. Rumor certainly hadn't lied. He was everything she had heard—and more. "An indentured servant. That must be amusing for you, Meredith."

Meredith narrowed her eyes suspiciously. "What do you mean?"

Opal tittered. "Why, surely even you must see the advantages of having one like that at your beck and call. Think how delightful it would be to give him orders, to . . . uh, reward and punish."

Meredith stared at Opal coldly. She had heard gossip of Mrs. Hamilton's infidelities. It was said Opal had sampled all the randy young bloods in the parish. Meredith had ignored the talk, but now she was certain rumor hadn't lied. The look on Opal's face was openly lascivious. It was obvious what she would require of a handsome male servant. The thought made Meredith shudder, but she reminded herself that Opal was the sort of owner who would have fit Jeremy's plans well. He had tried to gain control of Meredith by using his masculine appeal. With Opal, he would have met with more success.

"Tell me, Mrs. Hamilton, where did you get that dress? It's lovely," Lydia asked, breaking the awkward silence and diverting Opal's attention .

"Oh, thank you. I had it made in Charleston. Angus purchased a whole crateload of clothes! You can't imagine how that man spoils me."

"He must love you very much," Lydia remarked, patiently pursuing Opal's favorite topic: her fascinating self.

"Oh, yes. But sometimes he is so jealous, you just can't imagine."

Both Lydia and Meredith could very well imagine. Angus Hamilton was famous for his temper, and it appeared he might well have good cause to be jealous of his pretty young wife. However, they refrained from saying so. Opal lingered a few minutes longer, describing how the dress she had on had been copied from a "fashion baby," one of the little dolls dressed in a miniature of a London woman's dress. Such dolls were used by the colonial dressmakers to display London fashions. Since the transaction had been relatively typical and dull, Meredith quickly grew bored, Lydia only moments behind her. Fortunately Opal, having accomplished the purpose of her call, soon rose to take her leave, and they bid her good-bye with genuine smiles.

"Thank God!" Lydia exclaimed when she was gone, and Meredith chuckled.

"I always knew she was a vain bore, but until today I didn't know whether to believe what people said about her morals."

"Well, you can believe it. Did you see the way she acted when Jeremy walked in? I thought she was going to jump up and pursue him down the hall!" Lydia laughed.

"Yes. I'm afraid she must lead Mr. Hamilton a merry chase." For a moment their old camaraderie had returned in joking about Opal, but at the mention of Jeremy, the awkwardness of the past few weeks returned in full force. Lydia didn't have much room to talk where Jeremy was concerned, Meredith thought. She had betrayed Daniel quickly enough for him.

"I wonder what Jeremy is doing dressed so," Lydia mused, unaware that the stiffness in their relationship had reasserted itself.

"I can't imagine. But that's precisely what I'm going to find out—right now." Meredith marched out of the drawing room toward the detached study, her expression grim. She was pleased to find Daniel alone. Lately she had been almost afraid to enter the office for fear Jeremy would be there as well. Daniel looked up at her entrance and smiled. He appeared quite tired from his journey, but Meredith sternly quelled her uprush of sympathy. "What in the world is going on?" She confronted him, arms crossed across her chest, her back ramrod straight.

Daniel sighed. He had hoped Meredith had come in to chat as she had at times in the past. However, he could tell at a glance that she was there to fight instead. "What do you mean, Meredith?"

"I mean, why is Jeremy Devlin got up like a planter? How did he obtain those clothes?"

"I bought them for him."

"I guessed as much. What I want to know is why. He's a servant, for heaven's sake, not your son!"

"I'm quite aware of that. I'm also aware that it is my own business what I do with my money."

"But why? Why?"

"In case you hadn't noticed, his clothes were ill-assorted and ill-fitting. Why attack me? You gave him old clothes of your father's."

"Yes, but that's entirely different. They didn't cost money. They were just moldering away in the attic."

"Meredith, can't you be content with my answer? I bought the clothes because he looked bizarre in the others. Don't you find this an improvement?"

"Why should it matter what he looks like? I don't understand you. You drag him with you all over the plantation, take him to meet merchants and ship's captains, have him write your factor and keep the books. And now you purchase expensive clothes for him!"

"I have my reasons," Daniel said unyieldingly. "And in

due time, I will let you know them. But for now, suffice it to say that I chose to do it, so I did.''

Meredith pulled back at the rebuff. "Very well. It's obvious you have decided to cut me off from any knowledge of your business.''

"Meredith—" he began, realizing that he had hurt her, but she whirled and almost ran through the door to hide her welling tears. Daniel closed his eyes and rested his head on his crossed arms. He felt amazingly weak. He knew he would have to speed things up. There was no time for Nature to take her course. Slowly he heaved himself to his feet, knuckles flat against the oaken desk to support his weight. There was a deep, persistent pain in his belly. He tried to will it away, but it did no good. Sweat popped out on his brow, and he paled, but the pain gradually eased. He sank into the chair. It would have to wait until tomorrow. The trip had taken too much out of him.

Meredith stalked in high dudgeon to her room. As she opened her door, she spied Jeremy exiting from one of the guest bedrooms down the hall. Her eyes flashed. "What are you doing up here?" she demanded.

"Why, don't you know?" His blue eyes danced. "I thought you would go storming to your stepfather immediately.''

"What do you mean?"

"Well, surely he told you I was moving into one of the spare bedrooms.''

"What!"

As if to confirm his statement, a footman tramped up the stairs bearing a trunk and proceeded down the hall into the room Jeremy had just left. Jeremy watched her stunned face, his eyebrows arching and his smooth lips twitching into a grin. "I gather Mr. Hurley thought there would not be enough room for my new wardrobe in the room above the stables, not to mention the damage the dirt and heat would do.''

"Have you bewitched Daniel?" Meredith gasped. "Why is he doing all this?"

Jeremy shrugged. "I haven't the slightest idea. But I'm not about to question my good luck.''

Meredith whirled away and stumbled into her room, her

brain reeling from the shocks of the afternoon. Daniel must be going mad. Why was he suddenly lavishing gifts on a servant and offering him a bedroom with the family? Could he possibly hope the surrounding planters would believe Jeremy to be a gentleman visitor and so not protest his riding Daniel's horse in the race? Surely he must realize that word of what had happened here this afternoon would be all over the parish by tomorrow. Everyone would know Devlin was an indentured servant no matter what his appearance. The only other explanation Meredith could think of was that Daniel had taken a bizarre liking to Devlin and planned to adopt him. Some men were almost desperate for a son, and Jeremy had impressed him with his handling of the wild Equilibrium. But still . . . it was an absurd idea.

Meredith lay down on her bed and stared at the rough beam ceiling. She could think of no way to stop this madness. How had Devlin wormed his way into Daniel's confidence? He must be quite experienced at gulling credible people. He had already charmed Lydia into betraying her lover, and now he had convinced Daniel to make him almost a member of the family. He'd done his best to win her over, too. Meredith had to admit that if she hadn't caught him in bed with Lydia, she might have succumbed to his expert lovemaking that day in the clearing. It was only pure chance that she was not as infatuated with him as everyone else.

As suppertime drew near, Meredith realized that if Jeremy was sleeping in the main house, the odds were he would eat with them, too. She considered having supper brought to her on a tray, but Meredith didn't want to miss whatever went on at the dining table, so at nine she walked down the stairs and into the dining room. As she had guessed, Jeremy was there, dressed for dinner in a velvet coat the color of chocolate and black velvet breeches, fastened at the knee with bright golden buttons. The fall at his throat this time was lace and fastened with a pin as gold as the buttons.

Throughout supper, Meredith did her best to ignore him, all the time studying him covertly. He flirted lightly with her, spoke respectfully to Lydia but with the attitude of a stranger, and treated Daniel as older, but equal. Meredith could have screamed at his playacting. She would have liked to tell him she could see through his charade, that she knew he was as intimate with Lydia as Daniel was. But she couldn't embarrass Lydia or hurt her stepfather, so she kept her lips firmly sealed and ignored Jeremy's provocative, teasing statements and glances. She decided that the next evening she *would* have supper in her room, no matter what.

The next morning Jeremy sat in the study, his usually straight shoulders hunched over the account books, one finger running down the column of figures searching for the error he knew was there. Finally, with a triumphant smile, he found it: a transposed number. Carefully he drew a line through the incorrect number and wrote the right one above it. Now the column should add correctly. He began his addition again, but was interrupted by the door opening. Daniel Hurley stepped into the room, his face grave. Jeremy didn't know why, but suddenly his heart began to thump in his chest. The older man paused for a moment. Jeremy sprang up and offered him his chair.

"Thank you." Daniel sank into the chair with a sigh. "I need to talk to you, Devlin."

"Yes, sir?"

"I'm sure you remember I've told you I would reveal my plan to you. I wanted to delay it longer, but I see I must go ahead with it. I've given you these things, taught you what I have for a purpose." He paused, and Jeremy impatiently wished the man would get on with it. "Fact is, Devlin, I have a proposal for you. I hope the taste you've had of the quality of life here will help you decide."

"Decide what?"

"I want you to marry Meredith."

Jeremy's jaw dropped. Of all the things he had imagined Daniel might say, this was one he had not even considered. Marry Meredith! "What? Why? Excuse me, sir, but I can't understand why you'd desire your stepdaughter to marry a servant."

"I had hoped she would choose a good man who could take care of my land and herself as they should be taken care of, someone like Blaine Randall, say. But he's smitten with that Jezebel, Opal Hamilton, or at least he was. And Meredith is not—well, she wouldn't suit most men. Have you ever eaten a persimmon, boy?"

"What? No."

"Well, it's sweet inside, but the skin is so tart it puckers your mouth. That's the way my girl is. She's sweet inside, good and kind and full of love, but on the outside she's prickly, shy, and plain. She doesn't attract men. Hell, she towers over every man around except that limp-noodle cousin of hers. She's twenty-one. That's an old maid around here. She's not likely to marry anyone, but if she does, the odds are it'll be Galen Whitney. And I'm damned if I'll let him get his hands on my land. He'd ruin it just as his father has ruined Four Oaks, just as Meredith's father ruined Bitterleaf. The Whitneys are blessed with the good sense God gave a goat. Except for Meredith, of course. Thank heavens she inherited her mother's qualities. She loves to think she's like the Whitneys, but she's not dreamy enough. Too practical. Too full of fire. But she won't admit it. Always trying to cling to some crazy genteel ideal of hers. Lately I've realized I was going to have to force her to marry the right man."

"And I'm that man?" Jeremy raised one eyebrow skeptically.

"The minute I saw you, I knew you were. Handsome, distinguished. You speak good enough for Meredith and look good enough for any woman. Plus, you're half a head taller than she. Not many men can meet that qualification." A bark of laughter burst from Jeremy's lips. Daniel smiled. "And that's another thing. You have a sense of humor. A man needs one with Meredith. He has to be able to laugh and to make her laugh. I want her to enjoy her life, love it and live it to the fullest. With Galen, she'd dry up in a month. You can make her happy in bed and out. Give her children. Fight with her when she needs it, and pull her up short when she's too headstrong."

Jeremy was irritated at his words. "You talk as if Meredith were one of your horses, who had no say in whom she married. What makes you think she'll go along with it?"

"She will. Trust me."

"I'm not so sure," Jeremy replied with a twisting smile. "I think she despises me."

Daniel shrugged. "I doubt it. She's just fighting not to like you. Wouldn't fit her 'ideal.' She thinks she wants a goose like Galen Whitney. You'll just have to convince her it's really you she desires. Don't you think you can accomplish that?'' His voice taunted the younger man.

Jeremy scowled and walked to the window, his hands thrust into the pockets of his coat. "Damn it, I don't like dealing in flesh. I've never played the whore before."

Daniel groaned. "Not another idealist! Look, man, you're not peddling your flesh. You simply happen to be right for my daughter. You'll get your freedom and a huge chunk of land. You'll be wealthy."

"And that's not peddling flesh? What do you call it but selling myself?"

"It's an arrangement, like all the marriages of the aristocracy. You think they marry for love?"

"No." That was one fact Jeremy was very well aware of.

"Of course not. They marry to unite their properties or to put a name with a property or a name with a name. We're doing the same thing. You're the proper man to run Bitterleaf when I'm gone. You're strong, you're quick. I think you'll stick to it. You won't squander my land or fortune. And you'll give Meredith what she needs. It may surprise you, but you may discover that Meredith gives you what *you* need. She's deep, Devlin, pure gold. She doesn't have the looks her mother did, God rest her soul, but—"

"There's no problem with her looks!" Jeremy snapped. "I'm not holding back because I don't want Meredith in my bed. I simply don't know if I wish to be tied down so."

"Oh, I can understand your hesitation," Hurley put in sarcastically. "No doubt you find the life of an indentured servant far freer. You'd rather muck out the stables or work in the fields than own one of the greatest plantations in the colonies."

"I don't intend to remain an indentured servant long."

Daniel snorted. "Of course not. You'll run away—and then what'll you do? Not a penny in your pocket, only the clothes on your back. You'll get a job as a clerk with your book learning or physical labor with your broad back. You'll live on the edge of poverty the rest of your life."

"I'll get passage back to England. I had a good life there."

"Mm. So good you took on an indenture to get to the colonies."

"I was kidnapped." Jeremy stopped. What was the point in explaining the situation to Hurley? Even though he was mistaken about Jeremy's position in life, the true picture wasn't much less bleak. His uncle hated him, refused to send him any more allowance, and he had nothing except what his uncle gave him. Here he would own a huge plantation. He'd live the almost aristocratic life of a planter, managing his own land, overseeing his workers, dressing as he dressed now, and indulging in the other pursuits of the planters. From all he'd heard, they were a gambling, hard-drinking lot when they weren't working. He might find the life pleasant—if he could get used to the hellish climate, of course. And Meredith was part of the bargain, too. He'd wanted to get his hands on her since the day they'd poled up the river. It would be sweet indeed to be her husband, her lord and master. He could almost feel those long legs twining around his back, her fingers biting into his shoulders. He remembered the way her breast filled his hand, the hard thrust of her nipple against his callused thumb. Jeremy chewed at his lower lip, desire rising in his loins. He'd been strangely obsessed by the woman. There was no reason to feel this way about such a plain Jane, but there was no help for it. He had to have her.

"She won't agree," Jeremy pointed out. "This whole discussion is pointless."

"Leave that to me. Believe me, she'll agree. That's my condition for leaving her Bitterleaf in my will. She loves this place enough to marry you for it."

"Two people marrying for a piece of land," Jeremy remarked sarcastically. "What a delightful beginning for a marriage." Despite his caustic words, he was too familiar with the great marital alliances of the nobility for the concept to shock him. Peasants married for love. The higher classes married for advancement and kept women like his mother for love. That was his problem, of course: he'd seen the love in the eyes of his mother's "protectors." He'd wanted to feel the same emotion for his wife. The companions of his former life would laugh and call it the Irish in him. The red-haired peasantry from which Bridget Devlin came.

Weddings for material reasons were common, he told himself. They happened every day. His would be better than most in that he desired Meredith. Of course, it was likely that once he'd obtained her, her strange fascination would fade, and he'd be left with a woman he didn't want. But then Jeremy Devlin had never played the gentleman. If he wanted to leave, he would. Hell, he'd used women before. He could sell the plantation—as husband he would have full rights over it—and take off for England to live a life of ease. After all, he was a rogue, wasn't he? Always had been. He must look out for himself, for no one else would. Jeremy's face hardened as he remembered the haughty way Meredith had looked right through him yesterday. She knew he was a scoundrel. Contempt had been written all over her face. It wouldn't surprise her if he sold Bitterleaf and took off with the money. She'd expect it. He turned back to Hurley. "All right. I accept your 'proposal.' "

Daniel spoke to Meredith about the subject that afternoon. He was sure she would be the tougher nut to crack. But he also knew he held a trump card. He hoped he wouldn't have to play it. Meredith swept into the study at his summons, her manner deliberately cool. If Daniel wished to conceal things from her, then she would withhold herself from him. Daniel braced for the storm. "Meredith, I've come to a decision. I talked to Jeremy Devlin about it." He paused, but she obstinately refused to ask him a question. He continued, "I want you to marry him."

Meredith's eyes widened, and she gaped, rendered speechless by his words. "Have you lost your mind?" she managed, her voice cracking. "I wouldn't marry that rogue if he were the last man on earth!"

"What do you hold against the man? What's he done to incur your wrath? I never believed you to dislike a man because of his low birth or station in life."

"It's not his low station. Or low birth. If you must know, he probably has blood a lot bluer than mine in his veins."

"Then what's the problem?"

Meredith opened her mouth to say that Jeremy was a philanderer and she didn't want such a man for her husband.

However, she realized she could not express her opinion to Daniel without revealing Lydia's betrayal. That would hurt Daniel far too much. "I don't love him," she substituted lamely.

Daniel grimaced and waved away her objection. "No problem. It will come—a lot sooner than with that cold fish Galen Whitney." Meredith compressed her lips at his slighting reference to her cousin, but said nothing. "Look, Meredith." Daniel leaned forward earnestly, willing her to listen to him. "I'm interested in two things—the preservation of this farm and your happiness. Neither of those will come about if you marry Galen or if you marry no one. Those are the only options I see besides my plan. Am I wrong? Is there someone else who wants to marry you?"

"You know there is not." Meredith's cheeks burned. "Even with an extensive property, I'm not very marriageable."

"All right, then. Surely you see my proposal is the most reasonable alternative."

"That hardly follows," she snapped. "I am perfectly capable of running this plantation myself. I know and love Bitterleaf better than anyone else. I can handle it alone. And I'll be quite happy alone, too, thank you. I'll have my books and music and pleasant conversation with my cousins."

"Oh, fiddle-faddle," Daniel broke in irritably. "None of those things make up for a good man in your bed."

"Daniel, please, I am not a mare to be put in a paddock with a stud!"

"Don't you want children, Meredith? Can you imagine Devlin not giving them to you? Can you imagine their not being strong and healthy? Sweet Jesus, between the two of you, you'll raise a brood of giants!"

By now Meredith's face was crimson with embarrassment. "Daniel, this is absurd. I refuse to stand here and discuss my marital bed with you any longer."

"Oh, yes, you will, missy!" His face was as set as hers. "Because otherwise you're not getting Bitterleaf."

Meredith, who had begun to leave the room, halted and slowly pivoted to face him. "What?"

"I thought that'd take the wind out of your sails. This farm is mine to do with as I choose. I bought it from your mother.

She left you money, but I know it's this land you want. That's *my* decision. I can leave it to Devlin outright if I choose."

Meredith's face was stone. "Then why don't you?"

"Because you're my girl. I love you as a daughter, always have. Surely you know that."

"I thought so until today."

"I still do. You're too blind to see that what I'm asking is for your own good. Devlin is the man for you. Whitney won't give you children. You'll be lucky if you can drag him from his books and music long enough to get in your bed. Has he ever even so much as kissed you?"

"Galen's feelings for me are pure and respectful. He would never embarrass or compromise me in any way."

"Twaddle!" Daniel boomed rudely. "He's not interested in it. He'd rather talk about dead Greeks than kiss a woman. I'll bet Devlin's already tried to kiss you, despite the fact you could have him whipped for it." He shot her a sly glance. "Heh? Am I wrong?"

"I don't see that it recommends him as a husband." Meredith retreated to a haughty manner.

"Don't you? Which one do you think'll keep you warmer in bed at night?"

"There's more to marriage than—"

"It's the cornerstone of any marriage. What do you think I was able to give your mother? She was superior to me in every way—birth, breeding, intelligence, charm. But I pleased her in bed."

"Please!" Meredith gasped, shutting her mind to the mental picture of her mother in bed with him.

"Why? Do you think Anne was a saint? She was a woman, not a marble statue."

"I'd rather not discuss this . . . sordid subject any further."

"Meredith, listen to me." Daniel rose and grasped her by the shoulders. "I want the best for you. I want you to be happy. That requires a flesh-and-blood man. Not Galen Whitney. I know you. There are fires inside you that you won't admit. You're your mother's daughter. You can't be cold. You'll enjoy Devlin's lovemaking. It'll be your happiness, your reward, the source of your children. He's a strong man, capable of managing this farm and of managing you. There are few men who could claim that.''

''No man will manage me,'' Meredith retorted, her voice dangerously soft.

''Jeremy Devlin will.''

''Oh, no, he won't.'' She jerked out of his grasp and strode to the door, turning to toss back her parting shot. ''For I'll not marry him, not even for Bitterleaf.''

Chapter XII

MEREDITH CLOSED the study door and marched to the main house, her wrath boiling within her until she thought steam must surely rise from her very pores. How could Daniel propose such a thing! How could he so humiliate her! How could he suggest that Devlin's searing lips and hands could make up for the companionship and pure love Galen could offer her? She thought of lying in bed with Jeremy, of feeling his fingers all over her body, his melting kisses. She imagined the hot, pounding maleness of him covering her, his scent pervading her nostrils.

She stopped abruptly and clasped her hands against her flaming cheeks. How could she even contemplate such a thing? Sex would not make her happy, as Daniel thought. Besides, Daniel didn't know Jeremy. He didn't know that the woman Jeremy really wanted was Lydia. Why, if Jeremy married her, he'd have everything he wanted from the marriage. He certainly wouldn't bother to stay in her bed. No, he'd be sneaking into Lydia's bed, cuckolding the very man who had given him so much.

Sucking in a deep breath and releasing it in a long, tremulous sigh, Meredith forced herself to calm down. There was no need to storm around irrationally. She had told Hurley she wouldn't marry Jeremy, and that took care of the matter. Daniel would either give up the plan or do as he'd threatened and give Bitterleaf to someone else. Either way, she would be saved from the humiliation of a man's marrying her to win his freedom and gain a great plantation. She would be spared the pain of a philandering husband and the constant nuisance of Jeremy Devlin. That was gaining a great deal.

Meredith entered the side door and headed for the stairs. As she started up, she saw Jeremy lounging at the top, smiling as he talked with Lydia. A knife sliced into her heart. No doubt he was informing Lydia of his great good luck, describing the wealth he would one day have and share with her. Meredith stomped up the stairs toward them. Lydia, taking one look at her stormy face, wisely retreated to her room. Jeremy, however, stood his ground.

"I presume you've heard the news." His mobile mouth curved in amusement.

"You blackguard!" Meredith exclaimed. "You put this insane idea in Daniel's head, didn't you?"

"No! I was as surprised as you when he told me this morning."

"Ha! Well, I have another surprise for you, then: I'm not marrying you. You won't succeed with your scheme to get control of Bitterleaf."

"You mean you're willing to give up your beloved land rather than marry me?"

"I'd do anything rather than marry you," she spat back. "You're a vile, loathsome snake! How could you possibly think I'd fall for such a scheme? Are you so conceited, so swelled with self-love? Do you imagine you're irresistible to every female on earth? So desirable that I would offer everything I own just to marry you?"

"No, but, by God, with a sour tongue like yours, I can see why Hurley would have to pay a man to bed you!" he lashed back.

Meredith would have loved to slap him, but she had tried that before and she remembered how easily Jeremy had stopped her hand. It would only embarrass her to try. Pointedly she pressed her skirts to one side so as not to brush against him and swept past Jeremy to her bedroom, satisfying a tiny part of her rage by slamming the door shut behind her.

*   *   *

Meredith remained in her room the rest of the day and most of the next day as well. It went against her grain to hide like a sulking child, but she simply could not face the other three occupants of the house. Late the following afternoon, a knock sounded on her door, and Daniel stepped inside before she could inquire who it was. Meredith, who was seated in the Windsor chair staring down at the garden below, jumped up at his entrance.

"Daniel!" She crossed her arms, gripping them tightly. "What are you doing here? If you think I'll change my mind, don't bother."

He smiled faintly. "I'm well acquainted with your stubbornness, Meredith. You needn't warn me." He sighed. "I had hoped I wouldn't have to tell you this, but it's obvious you won't listen to me any other way. I have a . . . special reason for wanting you to marry soon. I would have liked for you and Devlin to fall in love naturally. I don't enjoy forcing the thing like this. But I have to see you married and settled quickly. I need to turn over the running of the plantation to you two soon. There's no room for the natural course of events any longer. Meredith . . . I'm dying."

Meredith was so shocked she almost giggled at the absurdity of it. Daniel dying? He was one of the healthiest men she knew, built like an ox. Her mother had gone quickly, burned up in a fever Meredith could find no medicine for. Meredith expected death to bring immediate devastation as it had in Anne. So she hadn't really noticed the gradual worsening in Daniel's appearance over the past few months. She saw it now. His cheeks sagged from loss of weight. His eyes were hollow, circled by dark. She remembered when she had noticed his tiredness and he had brusquely dismissed her comment. And the time she had found him taking a nap in his room at midmorning, so unlike the vigorous Daniel. Meredith glanced down at his hands. They shook slightly, knotted and veined and spotted with age. How had those hamlike hands turned so thin and frail without her noticing? A trembling began inside her and spread outward.

Meredith studied him with new eyes and saw a weakened, ill man. He spoke the truth. But she made one last, desperate denial. "No, you're wrong. It can't be true. What's the matter? I can physick you. I'm sure of it. You know my reputation."

His smile was a pale reminder of what it had once been. Meredith recalled his booming voice and hearty manner during their interview the day before. She realized what it must have cost him to act like his old self. One day had aged him terribly. "Oh, yes, I know that you are a healer surpassed by none. But no one can help a man whose belly's eaten up with fire."

"What do you mean?"

"I've had a growing pain in my gut for months now. Lydia knew—suspected, anyway. I haven't been a man for her in so long. . . .She never asked me, so I didn't tell her. She didn't really want to know for sure. My bowels are bleeding. My belly's swollen, though these stiff-skirted coats hide it. Everywhere else I've grown thinner. I'm bloated like a dead horse. Ah, Meredith, my girl, give up. Believe me. Even you can't change it, though if I know you, you'll drive me mad dosing me with potions."

Meredith pressed her lips together to stop their trembling. She was scared, so scared, just as she had been when her mother died. What was she to do? "A doctor," she suggested desperately. "I'll send for Dr. Drayton."

He snorted. "If you can't help me, what could a quack do? Drain the blood from my veins and feed me dried toads or some such rot? At least allow me to die in peace."

Meredith knew Daniel was right. A doctor wouldn't save her stepfather. He would let his blood, using a fleam so dirty and stained it turned one's stomach. Meredith would never believe, no matter what their learning, that medical men were correct in letting blood as a cure. How could it help to drain off one's lifeblood? As well say a fatal blow to the head would solve a headache. "I can at least relieve some of your pain."

"Can you?"

"Yes. Jamestown weed in small doses will do it."

"I'll tell you what will ease my pain: to know that you are married and settled before I die."

"Oh, Daniel, no." Her words were a low moan. She drew back, shaking her head slowly. "Don't ask it of me."

"I must. I have to be certain I've done everything I can to assure your happiness."

"Daniel, no. I promise you, Jeremy won't make me happy." How could she convince him? She couldn't reveal Jeremy's treachery in sleeping with Lydia.

"Please, Meredith. I ask it as my dying wish. Can you refuse a dying man?"

Meredith clenched her hands, tears boiling into her eyes and spilling over onto her cheeks. He was tearing her apart. She swallowed hard and spoke, her voice strangled by her tears. "All right, Daniel. I will marry him."

"Good girl." There was little of his former vivacity in his words. Meredith knew it was gone forever. But he smiled and hugged her. She clung to him like a child, pressing her face down into his shoulder. He smelled of tobacco and beer, as he always had. She remembered when she had cried on his shoulder before, and he had patted her back in sad comfort. Her mother had died then. Now it was Daniel. "You've made the right decision. I'm certain of it. A dying man doesn't have many chances. I know I chose correctly."

Meredith wanted to weep even harder at his delusion, but she swallowed her tears. Perhaps she would be able to make Daniel happy and yet not marry Jeremy. She could pretend she would marry—order gowns from Charleston, make wedding plans. It could take months, maybe a year. That was a respectable time for an engagement.

As if he had guessed her thoughts, Daniel pressed for a date. "I want the wedding soon. I'll see you married before I take to my deathbed. I aim to walk down the aisle with you."

"It will be unseemly to hurry so. People will think—"

"Damn what people think. I know you. If you don't marry before I die, you'll put it off for another year for the period of mourning. Absolutely not. Besides, I won't let you cheat me out of that walk down the aisle."

"Are you so anxious to give me away?" she asked, summoning up a tearful smile.

"Of course I am, you vixen," he teased, chucking her under the chin. "Now—how soon?"

"After the race sometime?" she suggested vaguely.

"Christmas! A perfect time for a wedding!" He thought

about it. "I can last that long. A little over six weeks. We'll set it the week before Christmas. How's that? And I want you to make plans for a party to announce your approaching nuptials."

"No! Oh, Daniel, please." Meredith groaned inwardly at the thought of her humiliation before the crowd of people. Daniel might as well announce publicly that he had to pay a man to marry his stepdaughter.

"I insist. I want everyone to know Jeremy will be my son-in-law. He's no longer an indentured servant, but their equal. After all, I have to make sure they'll let him ride in the fair race."

"But the race is three weeks away! I can't get a party together on such short notice. Everyone will have previous plans."

"Nonsense. Not come to the only dance we've given in years? Everyone will flock to it out of curiosity, if nothing else."

"Daniel, how can you care about a silly race?"

"Because"—he pointed a stern finger at her—"I intend to beat those high-flying bastards before I die. They've looked down their aristocratic noses at me from the day I married your mother. I couldn't ride like a gentleman, didn't know horseflesh. I was a merchant, a mannerless merchant. So I'm going to beat them—and with an indentured servant who has better manners than any of them'll ever achieve. Besides, I plan to tie you up tight, make you bound to marry Jeremy because you've told all your peers about it. Just in case I can't last the six weeks. I never take a chance." He lumbered to her door and left.

For a long time after he left, Meredith stared at the heavy door. Afterward she thought she surely must have memorized the grain of it. But her brain registered nothing. All she could think about was Daniel's dying. She was terrified. What a horrible mess her life was in. To please a dying man she had condemned herself to a marriage she was sure would be sheer hell. She stayed in her room throughout supper, too ill to eat, her thoughts bounding between the horror of marrying Devlin and the horror of Daniel's dying. She dreamed up potions to save Daniel and even told herself that he might be lying to force her to marry Devlin. Deep inside she believed in neither possibility, but she couldn't accept the idea that Daniel was dying.

It was easier to think of her impending marriage. Daniel no doubt believed he was assuring her of a husband to depend on after he died, but the truth was that she could take care of herself far better than Jeremy Devlin would. Why, the man hated her! He was bound to, because she had ordered him whipped. If he truly came from the background he had described to her, his humiliation would have been almost as great as the physical pain. He would exact a retribution for it when they were married. After their marriage he would have full rights over her and her property. She was familiar with the English canon of marital law: "Husband and wife are one, and the husband is the one." He could do what he wished with her and her plantation, short of murdering her, and there would be no retribution. What would he do? How would he exact his vengeance?

She wondered, too, what would be Lydia's reaction to the news. She had always been Meredith's friend, but she could not continue to be if Meredith married the man she loved. Did Lydia love him? Or was her relationship with Jeremy purely physical? That was one reason Meredith chose not to go down to supper. She didn't want to be there when Daniel announced her consent to Jeremy and Lydia. She didn't wish to see the look in Lydia's eyes—disappointment, hatred, jealousy, she wasn't sure what. But she didn't want to find out. Nor could Meredith face Jeremy and his gloating over his victory. Perhaps tomorrow she would be able to handle it better.

After a nearly sleepless night Meredith found she wasn't better equipped to handle anything. However, she couldn't stay in her room forever, so she dressed and glided softly downstairs, hoping to at least avoid everyone until breakfast. As luck would have it, however, she reached the bottom step just as Jeremy entered the back door, whistling cheerfully. When he caught sight of Meredith, he grinned impudently. "Ah, the glowing bride!" He crossed the hall, his hands reaching out and clasping her arms.

Meredith wriggled out of his grasp. "Let go of me."

"What?" One eyebrow sailed upward mockingly. "No kiss for the bridegroom?"

"No! Stop playing the fool. You must realize I have absolutely no wish to marry you. Who would want a husband who can be bought?"

The smile disappeared from his face. "It's a common enough practice. Money or land on one side, bloodline on the other."

"Daniel isn't interested in your bloodline."

"Mmm. He thinks I can 'handle' you." Again the cocky grin lit his face. "I warrant I can, at that. And speaking of being bought, you haven't much room to talk, my dear. You're selling your priceless maidenhead to inherit this plantation."

"I am not!" Meredith retorted heatedly. "I am doing it for Daniel."

"Such filial devotion." He pulled a solemn face.

"No doubt it's something you wouldn't understand! But he's taken care of me, been kind to me. I have a debt of loyalty to Daniel, and I couldn't refuse his dying wish."

"What?" He frowned. "What are you talking about? Dying wish?"

"Yes! He hasn't long to live. He begged me to agree, calling it his deathbed request. I was honor-bound to do as he asked. But I assure you that nothing less would have made me consent. I'd rather be fed to the wolves than marry you! Or perhaps it's one and the same." Meredith whirled and almost ran from him into the sitting room, shutting the door firmly behind her.

"Meredith! Wait, I had no idea . . ." Jeremy trailed off. She was already gone. He turned away thoughtfully. So . . . the old man was dying. That was the reason for his strange plan to marry Meredith to Jeremy. Daniel hadn't long to live and didn't have much choice. The only alternative was to let her cousin have her, and that was no alternative at all. Jeremy grimaced. He had learned about Galen Whitney from the gossip of the servants and from what Lydia had let slip at dinner. Cousin Galen, he decided, would spend his time on his poetry and music, letting the farm and Meredith go to hell. Meredith would be lucky if she maneuvered him into bed once a month. Jeremy was certain she'd receive no satisfaction from it.

Poor Meredith. What Jeremy had seen flash in her eyes was not loyalty to a stepfather but pure, unadulterated pain. She loved Daniel Hurley as a father, no matter how much she tried to pretend she did not. It gave Jeremy an insight into her personality. For some reason, Meredith refused to acknowledge her deep feelings. She felt love but denied it. She experienced passion but fought it. Somehow she had become convinced she should supress all vibrancy and emotion. He wondered what had happened to make her do it. Jeremy smiled, his eyes half closed in thought. He had no doubt he could change her reticence. He would bring forth every bit of lurking desire and raw emotion she had—and he would enjoy it all along the way.

While Jeremy remained behind her in the hall, thinking, Meredith leaned against the door of the sitting room, willing her breath to slow. She didn't notice Lydia seated on a straight-backed chair near the window, and she jumped when the other woman spoke. "Meredith! Oh, I'm so happy to see you. Come, sit here and let's talk."

"What? Oh, I'm sorry, Lydia, I didn't see you there."

Lydia beamed, and Meredith stared in amazement. This was hardly the jealous woman she had pictured. Lydia was smiling, almost laughing, her eyes alight with love and interest, one hand extended to Meredith. Meredith hesitated. Was she crazy, or was Lydia? She was about to marry Lydia's lover, and the woman showed not the slightest trace of resentment. She seemed, if anything, eager and happy. "Sit, and tell me all about your wedding plans. When's the date? Daniel was infuriating last night. He just said you and Jeremy were getting married, and didn't have a single delicious detail to offer."

"I—ah, that is, Daniel wanted to have it soon. Around Christmas, he said."

"Oh, how perfect! A winter wedding."

"We're having a party in two weeks to announce it. I don't know how I'll ever get prepared in time."

"Nonsense, I'll help you. I write a lovely hand, you know. My mother was a governess who eloped with an actor. We were penniless, but I had a lady's education. I'll help you address the invitations. We'll have it done in no time. The servants will be so excited, they'll clean everything until it shines without any urging. You and I can concentrate on your trousseau.''

''My trousseau!'' Meredith squeaked.

''Yes, of course. You'll need new dresses, at least one for the wedding and one for the party. You *should* have more new gowns, but I'm not sure we'll have the time.'' She frowned in thought. ''Some new nightclothes and pretty, frilly underthings.''

Meredith blushed. ''Lydia, really!''

Lydia laughed. ''This is no time for modesty, my dear. What woman wants a new husband to see her in drab, ordinary underclothes and nightgowns? Luckily you won't need all the new sheets, board cloths, napkins, and such that other brides do, since you'll be remaining here after the wedding.''

''Lydia, this won't be a normal marriage. I mean—there's no need for lace and frills. Jeremy won't—He's marrying me to get the plantation.''

''Oh, piddle. Does that mean you can't look enticing? Maybe it's why he's marrying you and maybe not, but if it is, you just have to turn his thoughts in a new direction.'' She smiled knowingly.

Meredith pressed her lips together. This conversation was incredible. Why was Lydia urging her to attract Jeremy? Surely she should be filled with bitter jealousy. She should want to hurt her rival, not help her. That was it! Obviously Lydia knew she had no reason to be jealous of her, Meredith realized. She was confident of her ability to keep Jeremy despite his marriage. Lydia could afford to be kind, knowing that any efforts Meredith made to entice Jeremy would only make her look ridiculous and awkward. She was no competition for Lydia, never would be, Meredith thought with a pang. She might be Jeremy's wife, but it would be in name only. He would lust after Lydia and save his sweet words and kisses for her. Meredith would be married and quickly forgotten.

Except for Jeremy's revenge. Meredith shuddered, remembering his reply when she asked why he hadn't taken her to task for punishing him. He had said he would take his revenge in his own time and manner, his accompanying leer making clear his sexual intent. Meredith wasn't sure exactly what he would do to her, but she was sure it would be painful and humiliating. And when he was finished avenging his shame, he would return to Lydia. No doubt Lydia would remain here as his mistress.

Tears of despair filled Meredith's eyes. How could she stand that! Not that she had any desire for Jeremy to grace her bed instead of Lydia's, Meredith quickly assured herself. Far from it—it would take an unwelcome burden from her. But all the servants would be aware of the arrangement, which meant that soon everyone in the area would know. Meredith couldn't bear the thought of living in that way, forced to endure her husband's infidelity under her own roof. For the thousandth time she wished Daniel had asked anything of her but what he had.

Summoning up the best smile she could, Meredith told Lydia, "Thank you for offering to help with the invitations. I'll draw up a list of guests immediately. But as for the dresses and—other things—we don't need them. I have plenty of things to wear."

"None suitable," Lydia replied firmly. "We are going to make you a dress for the announcement party, and I have exactly the material in mind—the beautiful pink velvet I purchased last year. It's gorgeous, but far too strong a color for me. It will suit you perfectly."

"But it's so bright!" Meredith protested.

"What's wrong with that?"

"I'll stick out. I'll be obvious."

"Well, of course you'll be obvious. You're supposed to be the center of attention. The party is to honor *you*."

"But I'll look laughable. I'm so huge, and in a flaming color I'll resemble a beacon."

"Nonsense. You're too sensitive about your height. I refuse to listen to another word against the pink velvet. Your coloring and height will make you able to carry it off. It would positively smother a little doll like Opal Hamilton, and it clashes with my hair."

"Lydia, please, no," Meredith almost moaned.

But Lydia was adamant, and for once she won out. Lydia

had felt guilty since the day she went to Jeremy's room. It was only sheer luck that had averted the disaster, or she would have destroyed her plans of getting Jeremy and Meredith together. If she and Jeremy had had an affair, eventually it would have gotten back to Meredith. Even though Lydia knew what would have passed between them would have had nothing to do with love, Meredith's jealousy would have ruined any chance for a marriage. But they had not gone through with it, and Jeremy and Meredith would marry. Perhaps the only reason for their marriage was the plantation, as Meredith claimed, but Lydia had witnessed the sparks between the two and was determined to do everything she could to foster their love. Her guilt spurred her even harder to help the match.

The next few days were occupied with making a guest list and carefully penning the invitations. Then Meredith and Lydia plunged into making the pink dress for the party. Lydia had a "fashion baby," which had arrived from London several months ago. The miniature representation of a lady wore the latest in fashionable evening gowns. Lydia took Meredith's measurements and laboriously traced a design on paper, using the measurements and the doll's dress as a guide. A slave girl cut the pattern from the cloth and did the rougher inner sewing. Meredith finished the more delicate stitchery around the cuffs, neck, and voluminous hem, while Lydia doggedly went on to redesign the style a little and cut a wedding gown out of ivory brocade.

Meredith protested at sewing up another new dress, but soon gave it up as hopeless. Lydia was not to be deflected from her aim. Actually, Meredith had nothing against new dresses, and she knew it was appropriate to have new ones for the occasion. But the bright pink of the lovely velvet made her uneasy. She was certain people would laugh and comment on "a stork trying to pass herself off as a peacock" or some such quip. But more than that, she hated to do anything to make the occasion special or like other weddings when it was purely a business arrangement on Jeremy's part and an obligation on hers. There was no love involved—in fact the opposite—and it seemed almost a sacrilege to pretend it was a joyous occasion.

However, since Lydia was unstoppable, Meredith grudgingly gave in to her plans. She even allowed Lydia to sew
several nightgowns of colorful silks, all shockingly revealing
and cut far too close to the figure. After all, Lydia might
make the nightclothes, but there was nothing to say Meredith
would have to wear them. She was sure Jeremy had no
interest in and would never see the delicate, lacy underthings
and gowns. It was an extravagant waste, but she would do it
to indulge Lydia. She supposed Lydia was attempting to salve
her guilty conscience, as if creating pretty clothes for her
would be an adequate exchange for having first claim on
Meredith's husband.

Meredith was constantly busy with either the sewing or the
numerous household tasks that had to be done to prepare the
house for a major party. Responses to her invitations streamed
in for days before the party, and she realized in dismay that
practically everyone in the parish planned to attend. Southern
colonials were notoriously fond of dancing and rarely missed an
opportunity to do it. Also, Daniel and Meredith had so sel-
dom given a party that everyone was curious to discover the
reason for their sudden departure from norm. Meredith had to
be sure the house was spotless and an enormous amount of
good food was prepared. The ballroom was opened up and
swept out, then the floors mopped and waxed thoroughly.
The long velvet curtains were taken down, beaten, aired, and
rehung. The furniture was dusted and the ornamental andirons
and fireplace tools were polished. The formal drawing room
and hallway were also cleaned, since the guests who were
resting or did not desire to dance might walk and converse in
the hall or sit in the drawing room. The staircase banister was
polished until it shone, and the upper sitting room also was
subjected to the cleaning, because it would be used by the
ladies to remove their outer apparel and retouch their hairdos
and dresses.

The pewter drinking cups were scoured with rushes, and the
elegant silver wine cups, tasters, tumblers, and mugs were
also polished and set on a large table in the hallway. The
silver beer bowl was set on one end of the table, and at the
other end they placed the rare porcelain punch bowl. There
would be imported burgundy and brandy for the men to drink,

as well as rum punch and homemade beer. There were also various fruity, homemade wines for the ladies.

An ox was butchered and hung in the springhouse until the day of the party. Hams were brought from the smokehouse and soaked for two days, then simmered all afternoon to make the tough meat tender. Slaves were sent out to snare game birds and catch fish. Several domestic geese and chickens fell beneath the hatchet. Meat pies were cooked in rectangular pans, either "trap" pies without upper crusts, or "coffin" pies, which had upper crusts. Stone jugs of sweet pickles and watermelon rinds were brought from the pantry, and potatoes, corn, and sweet potatoes from the root cellar. Dulcie and her helpers boiled and baked puddings and tarts and sweet candies. The day before the party, they lit a fire inside the bread oven beside the fireplace. When the oven was completely hot, they removed the coals and placed the pans and loaves of bread inside. Spoon bread was baked in covered pans placed among the coals of the fireplace.

For days the kitchen was fiery hot as the food was prepared for the feast. The house buzzed with activity. By the time it was sparkling clean and the food ready to be set on the long, damask-covered board, everyone, including Meredith, was exhausted.

Meredith had welcomed the work, though, because it gave her little time to think of Daniel's illness or the approaching marriage. Also, she was able to avoid Jeremy, declining all invitations to join him riding and after each meal scurrying off to work. She had to endure his presence only at mealtimes, where she carefully avoided speaking to him unless Jeremy spoke to her first. He noticed her efforts and acknowledged them with a wry, knowing smile. She might run, but they both knew eventually she would be his. He could afford to be patient.

When the day of the party arrived, late in the afternoon, Lydia dragged Meredith away from the kitchen and shoved her upstairs to clean and dress. Meredith went reluctantly. She dreaded the coming evening and the humiliation she would endure in front of her friends and family. What would Galen and Althea think of her! She couldn't bear to even imagine it. A cold knot grew in the pit of her stomach as

Betsy hauled up buckets of hot water and dumped them into a narrow, short half-tub. During her cramped bath in the small tub and while Betsy helped her into her undergarments and the new pink dress, the coldness spread to her hands and feet, until Meredith was icy all over.

Lydia insisted on arranging her hair personally. Although Meredith adamantly refused to allow her to pile it high atop her head, she did permit a softer style than usual. A long curl was draped over one shoulder from the low knot at the nape of her neck, and wispy curls framed her face. But Meredith refused makeup. Her face was deadly white, and any attempt at coloring would look absurd. She was sure that later there would be altogether too much color in her face. Hands trembling, she slid on lacy mitts, picked up her fan, and forced her feet to propel her down the stairs to face their arriving guests, feeling as if she was facing her doom.

Chapter XIII

JEREMY LOUNGED at the bottom of the staircase, talking to Daniel. He looked resplendent in dark blue satin breeches and coat. His blue brocade waistcoat was embroidered in gold, and the buckles on his shoes were gold. Although during the day he preferred to wear his hair unpowdered and tied in a simple queue, tonight he wore a formal white wig. A froth of lace at his throat and cuffs completed the picture of elegance. Meredith, seeing him from above, thought anew how heart-stoppingly handsome he was. Even if he weren't an inden-tured servant, she knew it would be obvious he was marrying her for her land. No man with his smoothly modeled face and excellent figure would marry a woman like her for love.

At the sound of her heels on the wooden steps, Jeremy and Daniel glanced up. Jeremy straightened unconsciously, a little stunned by the change in her appearance. She looked, well, almost pretty. No, not pretty. It was far too soft a word for her. She was striking, vivid—or at least she would be if her face were not the color of chalk. In the soft light of the wax candles, her hair was a deep, rich brown, and her eyes were large and dark. Although not entirely fashionable, her hair was arranged attractively around her face, softening her firm features. With her tall form and dark hair, she could carry off the brilliant pink color of her dress. The skirt was draped back to reveal a crisp petticoat ruffled in lace. Full sleeves fell from the shoulders, folding back to reveal cuffs of lace. The bodice parted over a stomacher of pale pink the color of the bows pinning back her skirt, which was embroidered in patterns of vivid pink birds. The square, low-cut neckline was edged with a single ruffle of lace. Since it was an evening dress, more bosom was allowed to show, and the tight bodice pushed up her creamy breasts so that they seemed about to overflow the dress.

Under Jeremy's regard, Meredith snapped open her fan nervously and closed it again, then grasped the banister tightly to walk down the rest of the way. Suddenly she felt extraordinarily clumsy. Jeremy watched her descent, and as she reached the last few steps, he extended his hand to help her down. "Your hands are like ice!" he exclaimed. It wasn't at all what he had meant to say, but he was startled by the cold touch of her skin. Meredith snatched away her hand, and Jeremy could have bitten his tongue for blurting out what he did. She must be dreadfully nervous to be that cold, and he had probably made it worse by seeming to criticize her.

"You're beautiful, Meredith," Daniel assured her, beaming with pride. "Lydia told me she was helping you dress. I can see her work."

Meredith's stomach turned colder, although a dull color began to mount in her cheeks. Jeremy knew Daniel's remark had been even more tactless than his. With all their good intentions, he thought wryly, they would soon have her in a state of nervous collapse. He again grasped her hand, clasping it too tightly for her to pull away. "You're beautiful tonight," he murmured. "A beautiful rose."

Meredith glanced away hastily, unable to meet the warm glow of his eyes. It was like staring at the sky on a too-bright day. She didn't know how to respond to either his gaze or his words. His voice didn't sound it, but surely he must be jesting with her. "A rather *large* rose, I should say," she reminded him tartly.

Jeremy's mouth tightened slightly. It was damned difficult to give the woman a compliment. She was determined to dislike him. He brought her hand to his lips, although she resisted, and brushed it in greeting.

How different it was when he kissed her hand from Galen's

polite, formal kiss. Jeremy made the ritual greeting intimate. His lips were warm and soft, and he pressed them against her hand a fraction longer and harder than was polite. Meredith prayed her fingers hadn't trembled so much he noticed.

He released her hand, and Meredith went to stand on the other side of Daniel, away from Jeremy. A few minutes later, just as the dock bell began to ring, announcing the arrival of the first guest, Lydia lightly ran down the stairs, out of breath, a vision of loveliness in pale blue satin, her red hair vibrantly unpowdered, but arranged in a fashionable high concoction studded with tiny blue bows. Meredith immediately felt like a huge, lumpy eyesore beside Lydia's pastel prettiness. "Oh, beg pardon," Lydia gasped, out of breath. "I'm afraid I'm late, as always. No one has arrived yet, have they?"

"No, my love," Daniel assured her with a smile and patted her arm. Meredith resisted the temptation to glance at Jeremy's face to witness his reaction to Lydia's beauty. She badly wanted to see it, but at the same time she couldn't bear to be certain.

Meredith placed Lydia between herself and her stepfather, judging it the safest place for her to be to escape any snubs. Normally Daniel would have stood beside the hostess, with their houseguest on his other side, but that would have made him introduce Lydia, and Meredith was sure he would do it far more clumsily than she. Besides, they would feel freer to ignore Daniel's introduction than a Whitney's.

There was the sound of women's laughter and the deeper rumble of male voices. Paul grandly flung open the door to the Craddock family. "Mr. Craddock," Meredith greeted him smoothly, extending her hand. "And Mrs. Craddock. How nice to see you. Do you know our guest, Mrs. Chandler? Lydia, Mr. and Mrs. Edward Craddock." Both man and wife were obliged to nod and shake Lydia's hand to avoid direct rudeness to everyone in the house, while Meredith went smoothly on to the Craddocks' teenage daughter and two sons. "Emily. Ned, Charles. How nice to see you." She passed them on to Lydia. Lydia, stiff and uncertain with the introductions, smiled mechanically and proffered her hand. Daniel pulled the guests away from her heartily, booming out

questions in his loud voice, then introduced the family to
Jeremy Devlin. Devlin was by far the smoothest in the receiving line. His bow was perfect and graceful, his clasping of the
ladies' hands somehow both respectful and intimate. He favored everyone with his charming smile.

The Craddocks were obviously taken aback by being introduced to an elegantly dressed, handsome man whom they
knew to be Daniel's indentured servant. Mingled with astonishment were a variety of other emotions, ranging from dismay to affronted pride to wary fascination. The women,
particularly, could not help but smile at him. They moved on,
the men handing their cloaks to a footman, the women going
upstairs to let the maids in the sitting room help them off with
pelisses or capes and hats. After the women returned and
joined the rest of their family at the refreshment table, the
next family, the Randalls, arrived. The father was dead, and
they were headed by their lively, active mother, Elizabeth.
Her husband had died while her sons were still too young to
run the plantation, so she had managed it herself, never
remarrying, until the oldest, Mark, was able to take over most
of the responsibility. Elizabeth was escorted in by Emory, the
second oldest, who was unmarried although in his mid-twenties.
He was a lawyer in the town of Greenoak nearby, and only he
did not live at home. Mark, the eldest, was there with his
very pregnant wife Felicity, followed by Blaine, Percy, and
Joseph. Elizabeth often said she had been blessed with five
sons, although Meredith privately suspected it had been a trial
rather than a blessing most of the time they were growing up.
Percy and Joseph were still in their teens, and Blaine was
twenty-two. He helped Mark run the huge plantation and was
one of the most avid horsemen in the countryside. His horse
Chimneysweep was the favored horse in the fair race this
year.

"Daniel," Blaine greeted the older man pleasantly, a winning smile curving his lips. "I understand you're entering that
wild stallion of yours this year."

"Why, yes, and here is the man who will ride him. Blaine,
meet Jeremy Devlin."

Randall stared at his rival, his face registering a shock that
was almost laughable. It boggled his mind that Daniel was

planning to put up an indentured servant in the race. For a
moment he struggled to think of an objection that would show
the preposterousness of the scheme without being outright
tactless. Blaine had always been a very polite young man,
Meredith remembered. Before he could get anything out,
however, Jeremy was smoothly bowing and saying, "It will
be a pleasure going up against you. I've heard Chimneysweep
is a magnificent piece of horseflesh."

Blaine goggled even more at Jeremy's cultured speech and
easy assumption of equality with him. "Yes—that is, thank
you. I think so. Though, of course, Equilibrium is a beauty."

"Oh, definitely." Jeremy smiled blandly.

Curiosity got the better of Blaine. "But he's unridable,
from all I've heard. Isn't he?"

Jeremy shrugged. "To most I'm sure he is. He and I seem
to have an affinity for each other, however."

Meredith thought it was an unusually modest statement for
Jeremy, but it struck Blaine as a cocky attitude for a mere
servant. He raised his eyebrows slightly and would have
looked down his aristocratic nose at Jeremy had Jeremy not
towered over him by several inches. He contented himself
with moving on to the table where he could sip burgundy and
become involved in a good male gossip about horses, women,
and the mystery of the indentured servant who stood in the
receiving line with the family.

After the Randalls, the guests began to arrive in great
numbers, one family following right on the heels of another:
the Waynes; the Littletons; the Campbells; the Hartwells; the
Thompsons, Ogilvies, and Kershaws, a clan of cousins so
intermingled everyone doubted that even they could figure out
all their relationships; the Jays; the Hindleys; the Phillipses . . .
The list went on and on. Meredith smiled until her cheeks
ached, mouthing friendly greetings to people she barely knew
and was certainly not friends with, exchanging compliments
and comments on the weather. There were so many so quickly
she barely had time to give a special greeting to the only
ones who meant something to her, her Whitney cousins.

When she spotted Veronica and Francis Whitney just inside
the door, followed by Galen and his sister, her first, unchar-
acteristically cynical thought was that apparently the Whitney

women were not tainted by Lydia's presence if everyone else for miles around was there also. Quelling the idea, she extended her hand warmly. Althea and Veronica leaned over in turn to place a cool kiss on her cheek. Meredith noticed that Althea's eyes sparkled with an excitement that she had never seen before. The girl glanced around as though searching for something or someone while trying to appear not to look. Meredith wondered what was happening to Althea. She *was* different, Meredith was sure of it. It wasn't her perception that had changed. While Galen bowed over Meredith's hand and murmured a low, personal greeting, her mind was so fixed on the change in his sister that Meredith hardly registered what he said, just smiled at him in the same fixed way she had used all evening. Galen moved on, acknowledging Lydia and Daniel with the briefest nods he could and still remain polite. But when he saw the insolent stable hand on the other side of Daniel, he stopped and stared as if he had been poleaxed.

"Mr. Whitney." Jeremy didn't betray any memory of their earlier meeting by so much as a flicker of an eyelash. Nor did he reveal his contempt for the other.

Galen shut his mouth, swallowed, and shot a horrified glance at Meredith. She regarded him almost as blankly as Jeremy, proudly refusing to indicate her true feelings in front of the others. Galen drew in a breath that pinched his nostrils and walked stiffly away. Fortunately there were other guests to be greeted, and Meredith didn't have the time to worry about Galen's thoughts or feelings. The monotonous flow of visitors continued for a time, then began to ebb. Meredith sagged gratefully as it became a trickle and at last stopped altogether. It seemed to be over. Of course the Hamiltons were not here, but she didn't expect them this early. They were always exceedingly late to any event. Meredith and Lydia privately agreed that the reason was Opal's desire to be the center of attention, which she could always achieve by arriving last.

Sure enough, almost half an hour after they broke up the receiving line and began to mingle with their guests, the Hamiltons were announced. Opal swept in, her spare, somber husband and three unattractive stepdaughters in her wake. She was dressed in a pearly iridescent satin, yards of material frothing around her slender frame. Her hair was high and powdered, held stiff by padding and wires. Rings sparkled on her hands, and a necklace of diamonds brought out the sheen of the dress. She unfastened her cloak and shoved back the calash on her head as she entered, so that everyone could see her magnificence. Meredith doubted that it was lost on a single person in the room, male or female.

"Oh, Meredith, I'm sorry to be so dreadfully late," Opal gushed, rushing forward with arms outstretched, the picture of delicate, feminine haste. Meredith supposed it must be an attractive picture, for all the men in the room beamed idiotically at her. All, that is, except Jeremy Devlin. In the corner of her vision as he greeted Opal, Meredith glimpsed Jeremy's amused face, sardonic eyes bright with mirth. At least he realized he was watching a performance, Meredith thought with some satisfaction. However, when Opal came to him in the quickly reformed receiving line, all drollery was erased from his expression. He gazed at Opal with warm, eloquent eyes, and Meredith's lips tightened in exasperation. Jeremy might be able to see through her, but it didn't stop him from snapping at her bait. Apparently Lydia wasn't enough. He wanted every pretty woman he met. A pain slashed through Meredith's heart. She would have to live with this the rest of her life, seeing his desire for other women, knowing he would satisfy it, that as a wife she would be betrayed over and over. What he did with other women didn't really matter to her, of course. She wasn't jealous. It was just that his infidelity would expose her to cruel gossip. Everyone would pity her, clack their teeth as they sorrowfully shook their heads and pointed out they had known it from the first—a man who married to get a plantation wasn't likely to be faithful. Poor Meredith.

Meredith chewed at her lower lip. She couldn't stand to be pitied. She wondered when Daniel would announce her shame to everyone. She hoped it would be late in the evening. She didn't want to have to face the sympathy, shock, and delighted, eager pity all evening. She moved to the refreshment table, where she sipped a glass of wine. Her throat and mouth were dry after all the greetings. Then Daniel led her out onto the floor, as was proper, to start the dancing. Other couples followed and formed sets for a fast country dance. Meredith always felt clumsy dancing, and Daniel was not a good partner. However, the fast movement of the dance covered a multitude of sins, and when it was through she thought with relief that she had escaped unscathed. She knew she would do little dancing the rest of the evening, not having been a sought-after partner even in her prime. Now she was considered quite on the shelf in a country where marriage at fourteen was not uncommon.

She quickly found out, however, that tonight was not to be an ordinary night, wherein she danced one or two sedate minuets with Galen and his father and spent the rest of the time talking to them. When she and Daniel had finished dancing, Jeremy appeared out of nowhere and clasped her hand, swinging her into line for the reel known as the "Sir Roger de Coverley." It was a favorite dance of the Southern colonists, especially the Virginians. A fast dance with a definite beat enhanced by clapping, it was easy enough to follow, and Meredith was able to stumble through it. She simply followed the strong pull of Jeremy's arm as they danced down the aisle between the other couples and watched the rest of the line of women out of the corner of her eye for cues to the few other movements. When it finally ended, she was breathless and flushed, feeling a strange mixture of excitement and embarrassment. She was afraid she had made a fool of herself with her clumsy dancing, but the swift, bouncing movement had been fun, too.

"There," Jeremy commented, taking her arm firmly by the elbow and steering her off the floor. "Now you look more like a happy hostess. In fact, in that dress and with some color in your cheeks, you're a handsome woman."

"Don't be silly," Meredith retorted, quelling the joy leaping in her at his compliment. He was teasing her or trying to flatter her, whichever fit in with his plan of the moment. "I looked like a dancing bear."

He made a snort of disgust. "You are the hardest damned woman to compliment. It's like taking a child's hatchet to chop down a tree. Hasn't anyone ever taught you that you don't *dispute* a compliment, you accept it prettily? You say, 'Oh, thank you, kind sir' and giggle or cast your eyes down in a maidenly way—not your style, I'll admit—or say 'Pray, don't flatter me.' Then I can protest how much I mean it and add to what I've already said in order to confirm it. What you *don't* do is squash a man flat.''

"I prefer the truth to vanity and flattery, thank you."

"Can't a compliment be the truth? You do look handsome tonight. I'm not saying you're a graceful dancer. Lord knows, *that* would be a lie. But your hair becomes you for once. The dress gives you color and style. And if you'll put yourself into my hands, I'll warrant I can even make a decent dancer out of you as well.''

"Thank you, I'm not interested. I generally prefer not to dance."

"What do you 'generally' do at a ball, then?"

"I sit and converse with—"

"Cousin Galen," he said, completing her sentence in a mocking, singsong manner. "Tell me, does Cousin Galen tell you how to dress and think and act? I wouldn't have taken you for a woman so easily dominated."

"He tells me nothing of the sort!" Meredith shot back furiously. "Galen is not domineering—" She paused, honesty forcing her to consider the fact that he had ordered his sister not to call at Meredith's house. "At least not with me," she finished lamely.

Jeremy guffawed. "Only because he doesn't have a ring on your finger, my dear. Whom does he domineer—that slim, reserved girl, his sister? What is her name?"

"Althea. Well, he has a brotherly tendency to guide her steps."

"And what makes you think he wouldn't feel a husbandly duty to 'guide' your steps?"

Her eyes flashed. "As we're not getting married, it doesn't make much difference, does it?"

"No. But since you seem to be languishing, forced to marry someone besides your precious Galen, I thought it would ease your loss to realize Galen might have been less than an ideal husband."

"Galen and I suited each other."

"Pardon me if I laugh. You forget—I've kissed you. I

know that pale, limp fish of a man could never keep you satisfied.''

Meredith gasped and whirled to face him, but his laughing, knowing eyes embarrassed her, and she turned away again. ''Your mind is in the gutter, just like Daniel's. No wonder he wants me to marry you. You're two of a kind.''

''He's provided for you as best he knows how.''

''I'm sure he feels he is doing the right thing. But the point is I don't need to be protected—except, perhaps, from the man whom he selected to be my protector!''

His hand, still lightly under her elbow, dug in. ''What does that mean?''

''It means I know you. There's no telling what you'll do to me and this plantation if we become in any way a burden to you. You're a selfish, self-seeking liar and cheat!''

His hand dropped away as if her arm were suddenly red-hot. His voice was light and sarcastic as he commented, ''Thank you for that marvelous endorsement of my character. Just the sort of loyalty a man desires in a wife.''

''What would you know about loyalty?'' Meredith asked bitterly and stalked away, joining a small cluster of guests, who were rather surprised to find the usually shy Meredith Whitney suddenly burst into their conversation and begin to talk animatedly. Jeremy eyed her balefully and retreated to the refreshment table.

The dancing continued until almost midnight, at which time the musicians at the violin and harpsichord stopped for the elegant repast laid on the board in the dining room. As people turned to stroll to the hallway, Daniel clapped his hands and roared for silence, jumping up onto the small raised platform where the musicians sat. ''Wait! Ladies and gentlemen, please! Before we adjourn to the other room, I have an announcement to make. I guess you've all been wondering what the occasion was that I decided to give a party. We have something special to celebrate tonight.'' He paused dramatically to let their curiosity build, then went on, ''My daughter Meredith has become engaged. Come here, Meredith.'' He extended his hand to her.

The whole audience swung in unison to look at her, mild interest on their faces. It was no surprise that she and Galen had agreed to marry, as it had long been rumored. Perhaps it was a trifle unusual that gossip hadn't informed them he had actually asked her at last, but that was all. Meredith flushed to her hairline, hating to be the cynosure of all eyes and dreading what was to come. On leaden feet, she stepped up onto the platform beside Daniel. He motioned in another direction, and everyone swiveled that way. Jeremy strolled through the crowd to the front and lightly jumped up to join them.

"You've all met Jeremy Devlin. No doubt you wondered why an indentured servant was receiving guests with us. Well, he's no longer an indentured servant." Meredith thought sardonically that Daniel was stretching the truth a bit so that no one would object to Jeremy's riding in the race. In fact, the wily Daniel wasn't about to release Jeremy's indenture until the knot was safely tied. "Ladies and gentlemen, this is my future son-in-law, the man who will have the honor and privilege of marrying Meredith. Jeremy Devlin!"

There was an audible gasp across the room as the entire assembly stared at them in blank astonishment. Daniel beamed. Jeremy bowed with a faintly mocking air and took Meredith's hand. Meredith stared down at the floor, her face fiery with shame. Jeremy squeezed her hand and hissed under his breath, "Look up, girl! Face it and be damned to them. You want that lot to realize they have the power to control you?"

Defiantly Meredith lifted her chin, more to spite Jeremy than to face anyone. Her eyes sparkled with tears, but stubbornly she held them back. She wouldn't make it obvious how miserable she was. Jeremy was right. No matter how awful she felt, it would be even worse if they knew she was miserable in her match. Her pride saw her through. She even managed a tremulous grin. The crowd finally broke from their stupor and began to hum like a swarm of bees as they gossiped among themselves. This was the most exciting, startling, unbelievable thing to happen here in years!

Gazing out over the crowd, Meredith caught sight of Galen's stunned, blank face and quickly glanced away. She should have told him about it before it was announced, but she had been too embarrassed. She couldn't face him, and like a coward had put it off and put it off until it was too late. She wouldn't blame him if he never spoke to her again. People broke from their groups to come and congratulate them, then hurried back to their clots of gossip. Then the crowd began to drift once more toward the doors into the hall. Meredith jerked her hand from Jeremy's grasp and jumped off the platform. She would have liked to melt inconspicuously into the crowd, but her dress and height made it impossible. All she could do was try to escape. She slipped along the wall toward the far doors that opened out onto the small side porch.

One hand on the knob, she turned to look back into the room. She was searching for Galen, but her eyes landed on Jeremy's looming form. He stood before Opal Hamilton, his head bent to catch her words. Petite and beautiful, Opal flirted up at him, plying her fan artistically, first snapping it open to cover her mouth, then closing it and softly rapping him on the knuckles for some ''naughty'' thing he had said. Meredith grimaced. Already he was chasing Opal, even though her husband was glowering jealously at them, and even though his engagement to Meredith had just been announced. Meredith could see her life with him was going to be one long, constant misery. Perhaps she would get lucky, she thought bitterly, and Angus Hamilton would kill him out of jealousy.

Meredith slid out the side door into the chill night air. She hurried down the steps and around the house. Obviously she couldn't stay outside, but neither could she face everyone at supper. Now that the congratulations were over and everyone had had a chance to digest the news, the dreadful questions would start. The women would giggle and ask about Jeremy in an arch way, all the time mentally laughing at her. Where could she hide from them? The study! She would be safe and alone there. She scurried across the walkway and into the study, chafing her bare arms to keep warm. Inside the study, she spent a considerable time starting a flame in the tinderbox in order to light the candles. She lit one candle in a bracket on the wall and another sitting on the desk, then sank into the wing chair, feeling quite at ease in the gloomy light.

It was some time later that Meredith heard the scrape of a heel outside and jumped to her feet. The door swung open to reveal Jeremy's large silhouette. He carried two plates of food. ''What the devil are you doing here? I've searched the whole house for you. Finally I saw the light here and decided it must be you. Here's your food." He set the plates on the desk and perched beside them, arms folded. "Well? What's your reason for hiding from a party in your honor?"

"It's not in my honor. It's to celebrate our engagement, which really has nothing to do with me at all."

"What drivel are you talking now? It has everything to do with you."

"No. It's Daniel's scheme—and yours. I never asked for it. I'm the one person who receives nothing from the arrangement."

"Why, thank you. It's nice to know I am nothing. Here all these years I thought I was more than that."

Tears suddenly burst from her eyes and poured down her cheeks. "Oh, God!" She raised a shaking hand to her face, vainly attempting to wipe away the tears. "I'm so ashamed!"

"Of crying?" he asked, amazed. "All the women I know are veritable watering pots."

"Well, I'm not!" she retorted fiercely. "But that's not what I meant! I'm ashamed because I'm marrying you!"

He was silent for a moment. "I see. Because I'm a bastard? Or an indentured servant?"

"No." She sniffed and began to search for her lacy handkerchief. "Oh, blast!"

"Here." Jeremy extended his linen handkerchief, embroidered with his initials.

Meredith reluctantly accepted it and wiped her face, then blew her nose. Oh, why was she always so inelegant, she wondered. She was sure Opal Hamilton would cry quite artfully without even reddening her eyes. Certainly Opal would never have to blow her nose. "I—it's not *you* I'm ashamed of. It's me. It's what everyone will think of me."

"And what will they think of you?" His forehead creased in puzzlement.

"Why, it's obvious! They'll say I'm so ugly and gawky no man would have me. Even my land wasn't enough inducement. Daniel had to buy, literally buy, a man to marry me." She began crying again and bent her head to hide her tears, pressing his crumpled handkerchief to her eyes.

"I see." He studied her for a moment, noting the long,

slender fingers clutching the white cloth of his handkerchief and the curve of her bent neck, accentuated by her softly knotted hair, giving her somehow a vulnerable look. He briefly pressed his lips together, then rose and went to her. Kneeling on one knee, he placed his hands on her hair, sliding them over the smooth mass and down to the nape of her neck. "Perhaps the spiteful will say something like that. Will anyone you care about be so cruel?"

"No, of course not. Althea will be pained because I've hurt Galen. She'll be embarrassed for me. But she wouldn't be cruel."

"Then if those you care for won't say it, why should it matter what the others think? It was fear of what others thought that kept you from riding, and I'll wager that's why you didn't learn to dance properly as well. I'm surprised you aren't a scurrying mouse of a woman."

"Me?" A giggle escaped her at the absurd thought. "A mouse?"

He chuckled, his hands stealing to her face to tilt it downward. Gently he kissed her. Unconsciously she grasped the lapels of his coat. Jeremy felt the timid movement, and his loins went hot and waxen. His kiss deepened. Meredith yielded to him, letting him tease her mouth open. His lips widened over hers, and his tongue glided across the sensitive roof of her mouth and along her tongue. Suddenly his lips dug into hers fiercely. He wrapped his arms around Meredith, pulling her down with him until they both knelt on the floor. Jeremy pressed her torso against his firm body, savoring the thrust of her breasts against his chest. "Meredith," he breathed. Holding her, he lay back on the floor, pulling her on top of him. It seemed to Meredith a surprisingly natural place to be.

With one hand he shoved down the bodice of her dress, and his mouth trailed down her neck and chest to explore her breasts. He made a soft, wordless noise as he took her nipple in his mouth and felt it harden at the touch. The sound stirred Meredith almost as much as his caressing tongue. She felt strangely weak and melting, itching, yearning. She pressed her legs together, and Jeremy laughed under his breath. "Here, my pet, this is what you ache for." He slipped a hand beneath her dress, sliding up her thighs and wedging his hand between them. Through the lace and silk of her underclothes his fingers pressed against her most secret, intimate place. Meredith relaxed her legs in surprise, then tightened them. He was right. Her flesh yearned for his touch. She moaned, part desire, part despair.

Jeremy drew back, panting. "God, you tempt me. But I won't take you like this, on the floor of the study. Not the first time. We shall be splendidly married and marvelously naked in our own bed. I wanted to give you a taste of what you're 'buying.' Perhaps there will be women who snicker, but you can bet there isn't one who wouldn't trade places with you, because you'll wake up smiling. They'll pretend to pity you, but in reality it's envy they'll feel, thinking about the nights you spend tumbling in my bed, well-serviced, while their own husbands are out wenching at the tavern or sporting with a slave girl or too tired or lazy or old to give their wives pleasure. They yearn, my love, they hunger for a young, healthy male like a mare in heat. Believe me, they'd grab at what you have. They'd pay any price to have the sleepy, well-loved look your face will wear. Maybe you bought me on the auction block, but I'll give you more than you could ever pay." Jeremy kissed her deeply while his thumb circled the nipple of one exposed breast until it swelled and hardened, thrusting out boldly to receive his touch. He threw one leg across her, securing her to him as his kiss lengthened. Meredith was lost in a swirling haze of sensations she had never known existed. He was hot, his breathing shallow and rapid. His heart thudded against her chest. She could feel something hard upon her thigh through the velvet skirt and petticoat. She knew with the inborn knowledge of the innocent that it was the essence of his maleness pressing her. Everything she felt or heard or breathed of him delighted her in its new raw maleness.

Tentatively Meredith slid her hands under his coat and across the thick brocade of his waistcoat to his back. Jeremy sucked in his breath sharply and groaned. "Ah, you witch, you torture me." Hastily she started to withdraw her hands, hurt and embarrassed. "No, don't stop. God, don't stop. I've been dreaming of this for weeks." Sensuously he rubbed his

pelvis against her, burying his lips into the delicate skin of
her lower neck. His movement and words, uttered in a shaken
voice, inflamed Meredith. She allowed her hands to drift over
his hard buttocks and muscular thighs. He rolled onto her
with his full length, his heavy body pressing her into the thick
rug. "Oh, Meredith, I want to feel you all over me. Nothing
lying between us." His eyes were glittering, midnight-blue in
their desire, as his mouth came down to claim hers, wide,
hot, moist, his tongue filling her with delight. Meredith ached
for him all over, the throbbing center of her yearning deep
within her loins. She realized, shocked, that she wanted more
than anything in the world to feel him inside her. Even the
thought embarrassed her, but still she longed for it.

"Jeremy," she sighed when his mouth released hers.

He nibbled at her earlobe, sending bright shivers all through
her. "Say it again."

"Jeremy?"

"Yes." His breath came hard, in short gasps, his skin as
burning and damp as that of a man in the throes of swamp
fever. "My name. You've never said it. Jeremy."

"Jeremy," she repeated in wonder that he should want her
to say his name.

"Oh, Meredith, Meredith." His mouth was running wild
over her neck and shoulders. Finally, with something like a
sob, he jerked away. "Sweet Mary, I want you." He rose
slowly to his feet, and fists clenched, stalked to the window.
He leaned his forehead against the cool panes of the glass,
speaking almost as much to himself as to her. "I don't want
to do it this way. I'm going to wait until our wedding night. I
swear it!"

Meredith sat up, her brain whirling from the land of insanity it had just visited. Horrified, she realized she had been
sprawled on the floor in wanton intimacy with Jeremy Devlin.
That man was a devil! How had he managed to persuade her,
to turn her into a—slut? She straightened her clothes, pulling
down her skirts and tugging up her bodice, and rose to her
feet. Jeremy turned and smiled wearily. His face appeared
lined and exhausted in the dim light. "Come here. I'll fix
your hair." Numbly she went to him, and almost impersonal-
ly—no, with the smiling indulgence given to a child—he

brushed back straying hairs with his hands, taking out a few hairpins and replacing them more firmly. "There, you look much the same—if no one notices the flush in your cheeks and the sparkle in your eyes. Think you're ready to brave the lions again?"

"Jeremy, what happened just now—"

He grinned and placed his palm over her mouth. "No need to talk about it. Just remember it, and know what you'll have while those sour old biddies lie in their empty, cold beds." He uncovered her mouth and playfully swatted her on the backside. "All right, get along now, or we'll start even more rumors."

Meredith's eyes widened at his effrontery. He treated her as if she were a tavern wench. She started to tell him exactly what she thought of his behavior, then closed her mouth. No, a little anger would help sustain her through the ordeal ahead. Squaring her shoulders and raising her chin, she swept forth to meet her guests.

Chapter XIV

JEREMY ESCORTED her to the side door, then circled to enter by the ballroom doors. Meredith knew it was the socially wise thing to do. People would gossip if they boldly entered the house together. However, in her present state she felt a stab of pain that he had wished not to be seen with her. She slipped in the side door and glided quietly down the hall. People were milling around in the main hall, eating and drinking as they conversed. The midnight supper was not yet over. Strange how little time had gone by. It had seemed like a lifetime. Beryl Wayne was flirting with Will Littleton. They nodded and smiled at her. Meredith was sure they wouldn't question where she had come from. It would never occur to anyone that Meredith Whitney had been engaged in a midnight tryst. In fact, she was sure no one had missed her.

Jeremy strolled from the ballroom into the hallway, cool and unconcerned. There wasn't a trace of what had happened on *his* face, Meredith noted bitterly. Opal Hamilton turned, saw him, and swayed coquettishly toward him. "Why, Mr. Devlin, there you are. I've been wondering what happened to you."

He smiled down at her, long masculine dimples appearing in his cheeks. It wasn't fair that any man could look so handsome, Meredith thought. And why was he encouraging Opal? Didn't he see Angus leaning against the wall, sternly frowning? Even as she watched, Angus shoved away from the wall and bore down purposefully upon the couple. Meredith moved quickly to intercept Angus as Jeremy replied to Opal, "Why, I was walking in the garden. I found it a trifle hot after the dancing."

"Alone?" Opal inquired archly.

"Of course, since you were not there," he told her gallantly. Meredith, overhearing the line, almost snorted. What drivel.

Mr. Hamilton, however, took the comment deadly seriously. He clamped down a hand on Opal's wrist, tearing her hand from Jeremy's sleeve. Jeremy stared at him, blue eyes suddenly blazing. "I beg your pardon," he began icily.

"You ought to! This is my wife you're flirting with."

"Now, Angus, we weren't flirting, just chatting." Opal pouted prettily.

"I saw what you were doing and heard it as well." He dismissed her and glared at Jeremy. "I'll thank you to keep away from my wife. No doubt you have the ideas and manners of a servant, but around Mrs. Hamilton I expect you to act like a gentleman."

Jeremy's jaw clenched, and Meredith knew he was about to make a hot retort. She managed to reach them in time, digging her fingers into the flesh of her fiancé's arm so hard that Jeremy jumped and swung to look at her. "Jeremy, dear, I hate to disturb your chat with the Hamiltons, but I must ask you a favor. Would you fetch me a glass of punch? I am dreadfully thirsty."

Of course he couldn't refuse such a request. Meredith knew from the twinkle in his eye that Jeremy understood what she was doing, even approved. He bowed graciously. "Of course, my love. Excuse me, Mrs. Hamilton. Mr. Hamilton. It's been so enjoyable talking to you."

Opal shot her a venomous look, and Meredith retreated, almost running into Althea, who was talking quietly to Blaine Randall. "Oh, excuse me."

"Meredith!" Althea exclaimed, smiling. Her friend looked unusually pretty tonight, Meredith thought. Althea positively glowed. "You sly, secretive thing. Why didn't you tell me?"

"What?"

"About your engagement, goose. You could have knocked

me over with a feather when Mr. Hurley announced it. I never suspected.''

"I—I'm sorry. It was—ah—a sort of spur of the moment thing.''

"Here you are, my love,'' Jeremy interrupted smoothly, coming up behind them to hand Meredith a glass of red punch.

"Oh! Thank you.'' She hadn't expected him to do as she asked, since it had been a ruse to extricate him from the situation with Hamilton. She stood awkwardly, unsure how to act with Jeremy in front of others.

Blaine Randall studied Jeremy. Now he understood why Daniel believed he could have the servant ride Equilibrium in the fair race. A fiancé of Meredith Whitney would have to be considered gentleman enough to ride in the race, no matter what his questionable past. Here was a real threat to Blaine's expected victory. No one knew how fast Equilibrium was because no one had ever seen the horse race, but it was whispered that he was exceedingly quick. If anyone could master the wild stallion, Jeremy Devlin could. He was a hard and powerful man, with a look of determination. But how the devil would a servant know how to ride respectably, let alone conquer Equilibrium? Perhaps it was one of Hurley's lower-class jokes. Blaine began to talk to Jeremy about the race, hoping to elicit some answers to his questions.

Since Blaine was taking care of the problem of conversing with Jeremy, Meredith was able to devote her full attention to Althea. Her friend didn't appear hurt by her betrothal, thank heavens. "I'm sorry I didn't tell you,'' Meredith began.

Althea chuckled. "I was teasing. It's all right. I could tell there was something different about you last time you called on us. I'm glad to find out it was pleasant.''

"No, you deserve an explanation. You must think I'm crazy.''

"Not at all.'' An almost mischievous smile flashed across her face. "Mr. Devlin is most handsome—and from his manner, my guess is he's more a gentleman than a servant.''

"Then you don't mind?'' Meredith stared.

"Of course not. Why should I? Whomever you choose is fine with me. I had hoped you and Galen would marry one day, but . . ." She shrugged fatalistically. "I told Galen he moved far too slowly and that if he wasn't careful, another man would snatch you from under his nose."

"Well, it wasn't exactly like that," Meredith murmured, glancing down at the floor. She was stunned by her friend's attitude. What a dear, kind girl Althea was! Believing Meredith to be following her heart, she was happy, instead of blaming her for not marrying Galen.

"Come, Meredith," Althea teased. "You and I are too much attuned. It's obvious to me you feel a great deal for Mr. Devlin."

Meredith refrained from telling Althea precisely what she felt for Mr. Devlin. *That* would really shock her. "Thank you, Althea. Your approval means a great deal to me."

"The dancing is beginning again." Jeremy turned from Blaine to the women. "Meredith, will you do me the honor? Now that everyone knows we're engaged, it won't raise eyebrows no matter how often we dance."

Meredith shot him what she hoped was a properly frosty glance. However, she submitted to his tucking her hand into the crook of his elbow and escorting her into the ballroom. They danced a slow minuet, their bodies almost brushing in the close, intricate steps of the formal dance. Jeremy guided her skillfully, almost forcing her to dance better than she normally did. When the dance was over, Jeremy did not lead her off the floor, and she looked at him inquiringly. He smiled, holding out his hands to begin the next dance. Meredith drew back hastily. "No, please. You can't mean to dance another one with me. I'm sure I stepped all over your feet."

"No. I can see, however, that I shall have to give you dancing lessons as well as riding lessons." He grinned. "We seem to be constantly teaching one another. Do you think you'll teach me to be a good husband?" He ran a caressing forefinger down her cheek, his smile turning devilish. "I'll wager I can teach you to be a good wife."

"There's more to being a good wife than skill in bed," Meredith snapped. Instantly she regretted her bold statement and turned her face away.

Jeremy laughed. "Ah, Meredith. If you have that one skill,

the others don't seem to matter so much.'' Despite her protests, he pulled her into a set forming for a country dance.

The dancing continued until the wee hours of the night, and Jeremy led Meredith onto the floor again and again. Meredith grew somewhat used to it and began to feel slightly less clumsy and self-conscious. There was the added advantage that as long as she remained on the dance floor, she could avoid the questions and sympathy of their guests. Slowly their guests departed, except for the two families who had to travel so far they were spending the night at Bitterleaf. Wearily Meredith turned from the door and dragged herself upstairs. She would have liked to shake Jeremy's company, but he escorted her to her door. There he left her after a kiss that shook her to the core. She stumbled into her room and hurriedly undressed, fingers shaking on the fastenings. Her heart was thunderous in her ears. She dropped her clothes on the floor and left them where they lay. Betsy would pick them up in the morning. She crawled into bed, certain she would be asleep as soon as her tired head touched the pillow. However, thoughts of Jeremy kept her awake, tossing and turning in bed until almost dawn.

Daniel considered the dance a great success. Even Meredith had to admit it had gone well. Now that it was past, however, she had more time to dread her wedding day. She concentrated on sewing her wedding dress and embroidering the sheets and pillowcases, trying very hard to ignore the seductive nightclothes that Lydia was spending her time on.

The fair was the week after the ball, culminating in the race the following Saturday. Jeremy took Meredith and Lydia to the fair on Friday, as Daniel did not feel well enough to accompany the ladies. Meredith normally visited the booths that sold various wares, ignoring the entertainments. This time, however, Jeremy insisted she see everything, dragging her from the booth where brass bowls were sold to watch the acrobats and jugglers. Meredith stared at the men balancing on each other's shoulders, then doing flips off them, both backward and forward. Unconsciously she clutched Jeremy's arm. He patted her hand soothingly. ''It's all right,'' he assured her. ''They're talented men, my pet.''

She grimaced at his endearment and, realizing how she was gripping his arm, dropped her hand and moved several inches away. He glanced at her with clear amusement, but Meredith raised her chin, refusing to let Jeremy embarrass or intimidate her. She was furious to note that her distance didn't bother him at all. He merely turned and talked to Lydia, who stood on his other side. Meredith fumed, her mind dancing with jealous images. She was surprised. Jeremy and Lydia hadn't contrived to "lose" her so they could spend the time alone. Meredith spent the rest of her visit to the fair in a disgruntled mood, made worse by the fact that Jeremy completely ignored it.

She was so irritated by Jeremy that she considered not attending the race the next day, but soon decided it would be an insult to Daniel if she did not. Besides, she had to admit she had a stirring of interest about the outcome. Although Meredith was not the sporting type, she wanted to see Equilibrium race after all the times she had watched him run across the meadow.

The race began early the following afternoon at Creighton Meadow, an almost perfectly flat piece of land on Carroll Wayne's plantation. Wayne used it to pasture his cattle, so the grass was cropped down. It was the best place to race for miles around. The spectators lined up in their carriages and open "chairs" on either side of the raceway. Daniel's coachman maneuvered their carriage into a prime spot at the end of the course, where they would be able to see the winner clearly.

Meredith, wrapping her full cloak around her against the cold, peered at the starting line at the far end, where several men walked about, leading their elegant horses by the reins. It didn't take her long to spot Jeremy among them. He was taller than the others and broader of chest. His hair, lacking powder, blazed a bright gold in the sun. He walked over the course, examining it, as did several other men, leading Equilibrium to keep him warm and relaxed. When Jeremy reached the end of the course, he turned in the direction of the carriage and made a slight bow to Meredith, a white smile flashing across his face.

Meredith colored, and was grateful for the way her broad-brimmed hat, shaped rather like a shallow bowl turned upside down, shaded her expression. She watched as Jeremy mounted Equilibrium, the muscles of his thighs knotting. He had discarded his jacket and waistcoat, wearing only a thin lawn shirt and breeches above his supple riding boots. Meredith could see the bunching of the muscles in his arms and chest as he grasped the reins, forcing the powerful horse to a slow walk. Equilibrium was sheer, raw power between his legs, and Jeremy ruled him with rock-hard thighs. Meredith smiled, something akin to pride warming her chest. For the first time, she had a small dart of satisfaction that hinted at the feeling Jeremy had described to her at the dance. Jeremy was her man, and it made her proud, even smug. Any woman seeing him mounted on Equilibrium would have to thrill to his essential maleness—and be envious because he would soon be *her* husband.

Meredith couldn't believe what she was thinking and tried to turn her attention away from Jeremy. She nodded at friends and acquaintances, listening to the good-natured betting and bantering going on around her, but not indulging in it herself. Daniel paced beside the carriage, nervously cracking his fingers. Lydia remained inside the carriage, protected from the chill winter breeze. Meredith supposed it would be more ladylike to seek its shelter, too, but she was amply warm in her cloak. She glanced around, reassuring herself that several other ladies waited beside their vehicles. She shaded her eyes, squinting down the long meadow to where the men and horses were now lining up. Equilibrium's coat glinted in the sun. Beside him sat Blaine Randall, his hair as black as his horse. Ned Craddock was on a gray that was smaller than the other two horses. He loved to ride, but he rarely won, not being the best of judges regarding horseflesh. Her eyes traveled along the line, noting the proud white stallion belonging to Kenneth Littleton and the chestnut gelding of Purdon Wayne. The white was the only horse that was a real threat to Blaine and Jeremy, but she was certain Kenneth Littleton lacked the skill to compete with Jeremy. She knew Blaine was a skillful rider, having seen him in past races. Though slimmer than Jeremy, he had delicate hands on the reins as well as remarkable firmness. His slight frame belied the steel in his arms and legs.

As she watched, she caught sight of Galen and Althea beside their father a few carriages from her. Galen turned and, seeing her, stiffly bowed. Meredith sighed. It was obvious her cousin was disappointed in her. However, Althea was not paying Meredith or anyone else the slightest attention. She had eyes only for the starting line, and her hands were clenched into tight fists at her side. Meredith recalled her friend's unusual interest in the race when Meredith had called on Althea a few weeks earlier. Other things Althea had said and done suddenly clicked into place in Meredith's mind, and she smiled. Why, she believed Althea had a romantic interest in Blaine Randall! She had been standing with him the other night at the ball, her face glowing. And they had danced together more than once. Meredith wondered if Randall reciprocated the feeling. He hardly seemed the type for the shy Althea, for he was not intellectual, his primary interests being the plantation and horses. He wasn't a carouser, though— thank heavens—the way his brother Percy appeared to be. But would he satisfy Althea? And would he appreciate her quiet charm in the midst of other, much more flagrant beauties? Meredith devoutly hoped Blaine would. If he was whom Althea desired, Meredith wanted her to have him.

A hush fell over the crowd, and Meredith shaded her eyes to watch the far end of the field. Her throat was dry, her stomach icy. She pulled out her handkerchief from the cuff of one sleeve and twisted it nervously between her hands. The riders were aligned, the horses held in check, and Emmet Littleton, who would start the race, raised his hands above his head, a square linen handkerchief in one hand. Swiftly his hands dropped, and the horses sprang forward.

Equilibrium was nervous, and it showed in his run. He jangled his head, wanting to take the bit and run. Both Chimneysweep and the white stallion were in front of him, and his competitive spirit balked at Jeremy's restrictive hand. Jeremy kept the stallion close to Chimneysweep, but did not try to pass him. The white outdistanced them all. But as they neared the finish line, Kenneth's horse was obviously tiring and began to fall back. It was then that Jeremy gave Equilibrium his head, and the bay hurtled forward. His nose reached Chimneysweep's saddle. Meredith crushed her handkerchief into a ball and grasped the decorative railing of the carriage to stand on a spoke of the wheel for a better vantage point. Her heart thudded as wildly as the horses' hooves.

Jeremy bent low over Equilibrium's stretching neck, his muscular body one with the horse. As she watched him, excitement rose in Meredith, and a peculiar warmth blossomed in her abdomen. She was taut, quivering, oblivious to everyone around her as she watched Jeremy urge his stallion forward until it was neck and neck with the dusky Chimneysweep. She did not witness Galen's stare of amazement when he glanced over and saw her perched precariously on the carriage wheel, her face glowing and her eyes fixed on the race.

Jeremy brought down his crop one time on Equilibrium's withers, and the stallion lunged forward. Suddenly he was head and shoulders in front of Chimneysweep. They thundered across the finish line, and Meredith flung up her hands with a shriek, tossing her much-abused handkerchief to the winds. She leaped to the ground as the riders hauled back on their reins, wrestling the charging horses to a halt, and hugged Daniel, who was grinning from ear to ear. Daniel swung her around. "Oh, Meredith, my girl, I did it! I knew that Irish devil could win!"

"Of course," Meredith quipped. "He and Equilibrium are soul mates."

Daniel roared with laughter and hugged her again. He released her to accept the congratulations of the people crowding around him. The riders trotted back toward the crowd, and several men and boys dashed out to greet them, chattering excitedly about the tremendous pace of the contest and its spectacular ending. Meredith, not thinking about what she was doing, darted onto the field with them, hurrying to Jeremy as quickly as her encumbering hoops and boned bodice would allow. He stood in his stirrups and gestured to her, his face flushed with victory. Ignoring the congratulations of others, he rode straight to Meredith. When he reached her, instead of dismounting he swooped down and with one arm caught her around the waist to lift her up. For a moment Meredith's feet dangled in space, and then Jeremy firmly plunked her down in the saddle in front of him. Equilibrium rolled his eyes at this strange new burden, but was too tired to protest.

"Oh, Jeremy, you won!" Meredith's eyes sparkled.

The hand that had lifted her up fastened behind her neck and turned her to him, his mouth sinking into the softness of hers. The warmth that had mushroomed in her belly now shot through her entire body. Meredith didn't give a thought to the other spectators. Instead, she wrapped an arm around Jeremy's neck and pressed her lips against his. He was hot, his shirt damp beneath her hands. Her nostrils were filled with the pungent odor of horse and sweat. Boldly, instinctively, her tongue flicked out to scoop up the tiny droplets beading his upper lip. Her movement interrupted their kiss, but Jeremy didn't seem to mind. He made a startled, almost animal growl deep in his throat. His free hand slipped beneath her voluminous cloak, straining her against his body, and he kissed her with even more passion, his tongue raking her mouth. Finally his mouth broke from hers. He whispered, "Witch! What are you trying to do to me?" His words were stern, but his mouth smiled and his eyes were blazing blue. "How can I dismount and face the crowd with the bulge you've put in my breeches?"

"Oh!" Meredith gasped and swallowed. Suddenly she realized how scandalously she had behaved in front of almost everyone she knew. Her face flamed to the roots of her hair. Jeremy chuckled, a warm, lascivious sound that made her stomach curl with yearning. "Oh, no," she groaned and buried her reddened face in Jeremy's chest. He discovered he liked the feel of her soft cheek and mouth and fluttering eyelashes upon his chest where his shirt gaped open.

He nuzzled her hair. "Don't worry. An engaged couple is forgiven anything."

"It's so embarrassing." Meredith's voice was muffled, and the movement of her lips on his skin as she spoke created a trembling along the arms holding both her and Equilibrium steady. Jeremy's skin was salty upon her tongue, and Meredith wanted insanely to run her tongue across his chest. It took all her self-control not to. What was the matter with her?

"You can hide your face all the rest of the day," he whispered huskily. "I don't mind. In fact, it's rather enjoyable."

"Oh, hush," she whispered tartly even though she felt the same stirrings within herself.

"You're not answerable to them." Beneath the protection of her cloak, he kneaded one breast, his calloused fingers seeking and finding the hard button of her nipple. "From now on, you answer only to me. Isn't that the ultimate propriety, to follow your husband's wishes? And I wish you to continue what you're doing."

"Jeremy," she murmured, dazed with pleasure by his probing. "Please, no. You mustn't."

"I don't think I can wait until our wedding night," he groaned against her ear. "I'll come to your bed tonight."

"No!" Meredith exclaimed in horror. "You mustn't."

"Who would know we preceded our wedding by a few days?"

"Betsy," she answered promptly. "By the sheets."

He understood her meaning. "Ah, yes, my dear, sweet virgin. Or should I say my dear, very dear, very astringent virgin?"

"Don't say either! Just put me down."

"All right," he sighed reluctantly and pulled to a halt. Kissing her once more, he set Meredith on the ground, his arm biting into her midriff like iron.

Meredith tilted her hat to hide her face and scurried through the throng of men and horses, ignoring the hoots and whistles exploding behind her as the men teased Jeremy about their kisses. Jeremy took it easily, too full of joy and victory to mind what they said. His desire for Meredith was a dull, sweet ache in his loins. He knew he would wait until their wedding night to protect her from the servants' gossip. But then . . . then. He swallowed hard and summoned a shaky smile.

Unlike Jeremy, Meredith could not face the knowing looks. Head down, she almost ran to her waiting carriage and climbed

inside. Lydia beamed at her, and she blushed again. Miserably she huddled in a corner of the carriage while Daniel
strolled around accepting congratulations and basked in the
glory of his horse and rider. Meredith berated herself for her
hasty actions and swore that she would never be able to face her
neighbors again.

Chapter XV

FORTUNATELY MEREDITH did not have to face her neighbors until her wedding, and on that day she was too nervous to care what anyone thought. She also did not have to face Jeremy much. He had taken on more and more of Daniel's responsibilities—meeting with captains and merchants to sell the last of the crops, riding the fields, supervising the overseer—as well as continuing to maintain the plantation records and meet with Daniel for long hours in the study to discuss his work. He was glad to be so busy that he hardly saw Meredith except at mealtimes. It grew harder and harder to keep his vow not to make love to her until the wedding night. Even after an exhausting day, he lay awake at night, thinking of Meredith in her bed just a few steps down the hall, and he wanted desperately to go to her.

Why did that woman fascinate him so? He groaned and buried his head in his pillow. He had had other, prettier women. He had known experienced whores who could turn a man into quivering jelly. Yet this tall, plain colonial lass fired his blood more than any of them. Perhaps it was because he had been so long without a woman. But why then had he not taken Lydia up on her offer? Or why not accept the advances of the very willing, beautiful Opal Hamilton? It couldn't be entirely deprivation. He wanted Meredith. He dreamed of the deliciously long legs and full breasts hidden beneath her dull dresses. He smiled at the idea of turning her tart asperity into soft, loving sweetness. Remembering her tentative, inexperienced touch the night of the party sent him into a dizzying swirl of longing. Was it her freshness, her power, the glimpses of an attractive woman beneath the shy rigidity? His desire to dominate an indomitable woman? Or was it because he simply enjoyed her company—her witty quips and unexpected, clear laughter, their spirited verbal sparring? He wasn't sure. All Jeremy knew was that he tossed and turned in his bed at night, torturing himself with images of a naked Meredith flushed and writhing beneath his hands.

It wouldn't last, Jeremy reminded himself. He had desired other women heatedly and been excited by the pursuit. But after he caught them, their beauty grew familiar and boring. Even the wiles of the best whores soon palled. Then he went on to greener pastures, just as he was sure he would this time. Once he had thoroughly satisfied himself on the statuesque body and taught her to please him, once she admitted she loved him, he would doubtless grow less and less attentive. He would begin to look around at other women.

The work would lose its appeal, too. At the moment, the colonial life did not seem dull. Running a farm was new, a challenge, just as Meredith was. It was a pleasure to be released from the grind of the stable work, but eventually it would start to bore him, just as the fillip of delight at suddenly becoming one of the landed gentry would fade. Everything in his life did sooner or later. Even cards or drinking or the most sophisticated woman. He knew his present attitude would not last, and he must prepare himself for that. What would happen when he looked around one day and noticed that Meredith was a great, unappealing wench or that the colonials were dead bores and farming sheer hard work and nothing more? What would he do then, tied as he was to the place? The land would be his to do with as he pleased, although left to Meredith. A husband had complete control over his wife's property. Jeremy knew he could sell the land, take the money, and sail to London. Return to his old haunts. Whenever he thought of doing that, he felt a bitter, inexplicable weariness. Was his life to be nothing but carousing and spending money? He recalled Meredith's tenderness as she had bathed and dressed his wounds. He didn't want to hurt her. If he made her love him, she would suffer when he left. What could she do if he sold Bitterleaf? With no property and no husband, she would be left to the charity of relatives. He knew how unkind that could be. Being married, she could not find a new husband, and a woman couldn't survive with dignity by herself. She could become a governess or take in sewing, but his heart ached at the thought. Or he could take her with him. But would that be any kinder? She would be a fish out of water in London, scorned by the sophisticates, miserably lonely for the people she knew and the farm she loved. For the first time, he thought of the consequences of his careless actions, the hurt he might inflict on someone else, and realized how loathsome he would be if he went through with it. Yet he knew himself to be a selfish, pleasure-loving creature. His uncle had told him so enough times. When he grew bored, Jeremy imagined, he would think only of himself.

Such uncharacteristic self-analysis brought Jeremy from his bed to go to the window. A peculiar bitterness pierced his vitals, and he wondered if he had it in him to behave better. For once, instead of accepting his whimsical, careless doings without a thought, he was filled with self-disgust. Meredith would be better off marrying her dull cousin. Denial surged within him. No! He would not allow her to be wasted on a milksop like that. Nor was he about to pass up his chance at freedom, wealth, and access to Meredith's bed. No, he'd learn to live with what he did. He had in the past. The past weeks of slavery had softened him, that was all.

Meredith, unaware of the desire boiling in Jeremy and the restraint he exercised in staying away from her, knew only that she rarely saw him. She sewed until her eyes burned and she thought her fingers would fall off. The hem of the wedding skirt was yards and yards around, and the stiff brocade was clumsy to work with. She also had to inspect the cleaning of the house and the preparations for the wedding feast, which was to be even greater than the party a few weeks before. Though her hands were busy, the work did not occupy her mind. It returned again and again to Jeremy. She was certain he was avoiding her. He must have decided that he had been overcome by temporary insanity the day of the

race. He had not entered her room that night as he had
threatened (though, she reminded herself primly, she had no
wish for him to.). He no longer teased or kissed her or even
shot her a speaking glance. If he had ever had desire for her,
it had obviously died.

Meredith looked at Lydia as she sewed and told herself she
was crazy to think Jeremy wanted her when he had such a
gorgeous woman as Lydia at his beck and call. Considering it
with the cool logic of hindsight, Meredith was certain Jeremy's
kisses after the race had been the product of the excitement of
winning. She, too, had been carried away by the glory of
victory. Imagine how much more so must have been the man
who had actually ridden the horse. When she had run to him
like a brazen hussy, Jeremy had seized the opportunity. Any
other woman would have done as well. He simply needed a
release for his exhilaration.

There was a good explanation for the other times he had
shown passion for her as well. Before their engagement he
had no doubt been trying to inveigle her into helping him
escape. Perhaps he had even had visions of a marriage such
as Daniel had suggested. The night of their engagement party,
he had been afraid she would back out of the engagement and
had made advances to her to persuade her not to. Jeremy
couldn't actually want her. The idea was ludicrous.

As the days passed, Meredith worked herself into a state of
fright. The idea of marriage and her wedding night scared her
simply because she had little knowledge of either. She hadn't
really considered that she might marry, except perhaps Galen,
a union that would have held nothing surprising or bizarre.
But Jeremy might do something awful once he had her under
his power. Or she might humiliate herself by succumbing to
his kisses as she had before. She worried about his continuing
the affair with Lydia, thus embarrassing her before the whole
parish. He might even take up with Opal Hamilton as well.
The way Opal pursued him, he would certainly have ample
opportunity.

By the time the wedding day dawned, Meredith was numb
with terror, moving like a zombie as she dressed for the noon
wedding. Betsy helped her into the hoops and a multitude of
petticoats. Everything Meredith wore was new, from her lace

and silk underthings to the ruffled petticoat and stiff brocade
dress. The brocade was ivory, as was the underlying petticoat,
which showed delicate lace ruffles. The stomacher was embroidered in gold, and ivory lace dripped from her cuffs and
lay in ruffles across the square neckline. Gold satin bows
caught back the skirt. Dainty brocade slippers peeped from
under her skirt. Lydia insisted on fixing Meredith's hair,
arranging it in a froth of curls intertwined with silk orange
blossoms.

"You're making me look like Ceres," Meredith protested.

"And what's wrong with looking like a goddess?" Lydia
countered.

"It doesn't suit me."

"Bosh. I'll decide that. You're lovely and very bridelike—if
only you'd pinch some color into those cheeks. You're pale as
a corpse." Suddenly her good humor faltered.

Meredith knew Lydia had thought of Daniel after she said
"corpse." A wave of sadness submerged even Meredith's
fear for a moment. Daniel was getting worse by the day,
growing thinner and more gaunt-cheeked until he hardly looked
like the same man. Both women knew he was clinging to life
just to see Meredith married. They feared that after the wedding he would decline even faster.

Daniel waited for Meredith at the top of the stairs. Although he was clearly thinner and his facial skin slack, there
was a glow of pride on his face that gave him a falsely
healthy appearance. He reached out to tuck Meredith's hand
under his arm and beamed at her. "You're lovely, my dear.
You, too, of course, Miss Whitney," he added to Althea,
who had followed Meredith from her room.

Althea was her maid of honor and wore a lovely pale green
velvet dress. Lydia had hesitated, awed as always by the girl's
reserve, but finally had screwed up the courage to ask if
Althea would like Lydia to arrange her hair also. To her
surprise and delight, Althea enthusiastically agreed. Lydia
had arranged Althea's pale, flaxen hair in an intricate series
of rolls with pale green ribbon winding through them. Although the effect was charming and fashionable, it suited
Althea's personality.

Now Lydia, flashing a smile at the other three gathered on

the landing, floated past them in a rustle of bright green satin. Out of politeness Meredith had invited Lydia to be one of her attendants, although she dreaded having Lydia's glowing beauty standing in mute comparison beside hers. Lydia had declined quickly. Her heart was warmed by Meredith's offer, but she was aware it would scandalize the neighborhood. She wanted Meredith's wedding to pass smoothly.

They descended the staircase, Althea in front, and entered the ballroom. It was the only place large enough to house their many guests. Althea flowed gracefully along the aisle to the front, where the Anglican priest awaited them. Meredith, knowing she couldn't hope for grace, strove to maintain a look of dignity. Daniel's pace was slow, and she knew it was taxing him to make the long walk. He leaned unobtrusively upon her arm. Meredith glanced at the front where Jeremy stood, resplendent in a rust-brown velvet coat with ivory breeches and a handsomely embroidered waistcoat. Lace spilled down the front of his shirt, secured by a single pearl pin. Meredith had given him the pin as a wedding present. He had given her a dainty silver ring so small it fit only her little finger. The ring was intricately carved, and in the center lay a deep blue sapphire. It was a beautiful ring, but Meredith knew the presents were formal and meaningless, especially since Daniel must have purchased the ring for Jeremy.

When they reached the priest, Daniel transferred her hand to Jeremy's arm. Jeremy's face was unusually serious, his eyes steady. He looked at Meredith, quickly taking in the slight tremor of her hands and the pallor of her face. The service began. It was overly long, and Meredith found herself clinging to Jeremy's arm for support. The priest spoke of the duties and responsibilities of marriage, the blessings of children, and comfort in one's old age. When the time came to repeat their vows, Jeremy answered firmly. Meredith barely stumbled through it, at one point completely forgetting what she was supposed to say. Her trembling increased, and Jeremy laid a warm, calm hand over hers. Strangely—since it was marriage to him she feared—the gesture provided some comfort.

Blaine Randall stood with them as Jeremy's best man. After he had lost the race to Jeremy, Blaine offered Jeremy his friendship. He was not a prejudiced or vengeful man.

Jeremy's riding skill was more than adequate to admit him to
Randall's circle of friends. Meredith glimpsed Blaine exchanging a glance with Althea that confirmed her earlier suspicions.
Clearly the other couple was imagining standing in their
places.

When the service ended, Jeremy strode down the aisle,
sweeping Meredith along with him. With Daniel and their
attendants they formed a receiving line for the guests as they
passed from the ballroom to the dining room, where the long
board was laden with food. Dulcie had outdone herself for
this feast. There were several meats, including ham, roast,
fish, goose, pheasant, and venison, as well as meat pies.
There were also sweet potatoes, white potatoes, and corn,
johnnycake, biscuits, and loaves of bread. To top it off there
were sugary candies and pies oozing with raspberries and
cherries, mincemeat pies, and sweet-potato pies, one of Dulcie's
specialties.

When they finished greeting their guests, Jeremy solici-
tously seated his new bride in a wing chair in the drawing
room and brought her a plate heaped high with food. Meredith regarded the plate with horror. She was sure she could
hardly swallow a mouthful, and the mountainous repast he
had provided made her ill. "I couldn't possibly eat this
much," she protested in a low voice.

He grinned. "Then don't. I'll finish it for you. I have a
prodigious appetite today." The twinkle in his eyes added a
double entendre to his seemingly innocuous statement. Meredith glanced away, wondering if he had meant it or if it was
only her wild imagination. Jeremy extended a glass to her.
"Here, have a sip of brandy first."

"Oh, no. I never drink brandy. It's too strong."

"It'll do you good. Keep you from fainting."

"I never faint!"

"Then today may be a first, because you're pale as death."

"Thank you very much."

He grimaced and waggled his hand. "Drink."

Meredith's lips thinned. If she continued to refuse, she
wouldn't put it past Jeremy to create a tremendous scene. She
took the glass and sipped primly. Warmth immediately flooded
her veins. She hadn't realized how cold she was. The plate of

food seemed less overwhelming now, and Meredith began to eat. Jeremy chatted casually, for all the world as if it were an ordinary day. She marveled at his coolness. They had committed their lives. Did it have any meaning for him?

She ate about half the food he had brought, and Jeremy polished off the rest. Grinning, he remarked, "I had too many butterflies in my stomach this morning to eat." He didn't add that his appetite had fallen off the past few weeks because of the desire that ravaged him.

"Indeed?" She was surprised. "I thought you were quite unconcerned."

"Only better at acting. You see, I had to survive in society." He stuck a last forkful of cherry pie in his mouth. "Delicious. This must be an invention of the colonies." Meredith watched him upturn a tankard of beer and swallow it in deep gulps. His Adam's apple bobbed. She had never noticed it before. But then, neither was she familiar with the line of his jaw and neck. The skin there was much softer than on his hands and face, more vulnerable. He was a huge man. And he was right: he was a man of great appetite. Meredith imagined the hand that held the tankard on her breast instead, the wide mouth drinking in her nipple. She shivered unconsciously. He was menacing, fierce, hungry. He lowered the mug and turned toward her. Their gazes met, and his eyes reflected her thoughts, a blue fire starting deep in them. Jeremy raised her hand to kiss the palm. His lips were searing, carrying a wealth of promises she sensed, but did not understand. Shakily she pulled away her hand. "It looks as if they are about to begin the dancing."

"Ah, then we must go." Jeremy arose readily and helped her from the chair. "We have to lead it off."

Meredith had not considered that. Her feet turned leaden at the idea. By custom the bride and groom danced the first dance alone, with everyone watching them. She would be the cynosure of all eyes. Everyone would see her dreadful clumsiness. They would remark how graceless and awkward she was. She wished there was some way she could get out of it, but it was expected. Jeremy's clutch was too strong for her to escape, and besides, she couldn't make an even bigger fool of herself by running away. Jeremy led her onto the floor as a minuet began. Expertly he guided her through the motions, whispering instructions for the particularly difficult movements. Meredith managed to get through it without disgracing herself and at the end flashed Jeremy a grateful smile. "Thank you."

"Don't mention it. I'm only sorry I haven't had the time to teach you as I promised."

Other couples joined them on the floor. Jeremy handed Meredith to her stepfather while he danced with Lydia. Meredith watched the handsome couple with a distinct pang of jealousy. They were much more suited to one another than she and Jeremy. Next Blaine claimed a dance as the best man, then Jeremy led her into the sprightly Sir Roger de Coverley. He urged her to dance again, but Meredith begged off, pleading shortness of breath. In truth, she only wanted to get away from the crush of the crowd and Jeremy's overwhelming presence.

Leaving the ballroom, Meredith wandered into the empty sitting room to stand staring out the window blindly. Moments later there was the sound of a step on the hard wood floor, and she whirled to see Galen standing in the doorway. "Galen!" She was pleased he had sought her out, but still uncomfortable in his presence. She hadn't spoken with him since the night of her marriage announcement.

"Cousin Meredith." He nodded gravely and advanced into the room. "I came to offer my congratulations . . ." He paused. "If that is truly what's in order."

"What do you mean?"

"Is this really what you want?"

"Yes, of course. Why else would I do it?"

"I don't know. Perhaps Hurley bullied you into it, though why he should wish you to wed a common servant is beyond me."

"Jeremy is not common," Meredith retorted instinctively. "He's far more well-born than either of us. His uncle is a peer of the realm."

Galen cocked one eyebrow sardonically. "Of course. It's a common practice among the nobility to be shipped to the colonies as indentured servants."

"It's true. You'd realize it if you talked to him. He was

obviously raised as a gentleman. His manners surpass anyone's here.''

"A clever rogue can ape his betters.''

"He is the illegitimate son of Jeremy Wrexham, who was brother to Lord Wrexham.''

"Meredith, please, you needn't try to excuse or justify him to me. I have no interest in his antecedents. He could be the Prince of Wales for all I care. What concerns me is your happiness. He's a vulgar, encroaching, crude—''

"Galen, he is my husband now,'' Meredith reminded him.

"Yes. I'm sorry. I understand you feel a certain duty to defend him—though you may rest assured he will never have the same sort of loyalty to you.''

Tears stung her eyes. Galen had hit much too close to the mark. "You don't understand.''

"No, I don't!'' he barked with more emotion than she had ever seen him display. "Why did you agree to marry him? I would have thought you, of all people, would be the last to be lured by a handsome face or manly physique. It's a low, gutter reaction typical of a female such as Opal Hamilton. There can be nothing in Devlin to please your mind or soothe your soul. Why marry him?''

Meredith felt an inexplicable pang at his reaction. He seemed more appalled at her social blunder than jealous of another man's taking her away. She reminded herself that the news had been a severe blow to Galen. They had grown up together, yet suddenly he found himself more or less cut out of her life. It had been taken as a matter of course that they would someday marry. Even though Galen had never spoken of an engagement, surely he had felt betrayed. She knew she would have if their situations had been reversed. Her face softened. "I am sorry, Cousin Galen. Truly I am. I should have told you before the party. It's something I—have to do.''

His eyes widened in shock. "You don't mean—''

"No!'' Meredith gasped. "How can you even think such a thing?''

"I don't know what to think!'' he shot back.

Meredith sighed. He wouldn't understand if she explained Daniel's request. He would hate Daniel for forcing her to

marry Jeremy. He couldn't conceive of her having enough
feeling for her stepfather to marry someone because he wished
it. She gnawed at her lip, frowning. "Galen, I can't explain."

His face was etched with disappointment. "I never dreamed
this would happen to us."

"Of course not. How could you?"

Galen sighed and turned away, walking out the door without a backward glance. Meredith sank into a chair. She felt as
though her heart was breaking. She was losing everything she
knew and held dear—Galen, Daniel, the plantation. What
was to become of her? Daniel believed his scheme would
ensure her protection. In truth, it put her at the mercy of a
man who probably hated her. She closed her eyes.

"Well! Have you run away from the party?" a voice
drawled sweetly. Meredith opened her eyes, embarrassed that
anyone had found her hiding. To make it worse, it was Opal
Hamilton who stood in the doorway, resplendent in a gold
velvet dress with matching golden butterflies in her padded,
powdered hair. Opal swayed into the room, and Meredith
wondered how she managed to swing her skirt so seductively
with every step. It must have required a lot of practice.

"I was a trifle tired, so I thought I'd rest from the dancing,"
Meredith replied, struggling to maintain a cool air.

"I'm sure it's wise to rest, considering the night before
you," Opal said with a smirk.

"What?" Meredith stared. Even Opal did not usually make
such blatant remarks.

"I mean, with a man like Jeremy, an . . . inexperienced"—
she chose the word so carefully Meredith was sure she had
some other, less complimentary word in mind—"girl like
yourself will have her hands full."

"Really, Opal, this is hardly a proper subject to talk about."

"Since you have no mother or other female relative to
advise you, I thought I should prepare you for the wedding
night." Opal lowered her eyes and raised her fan in a modest
gesture. "Of course, I am of an age with you, but having
been married four years, I think I'm qualified to give you this
little talk."

Oh, yes, Meredith thought savagely, I'm sure you're more
than qualified to speak of sex, not only with your husband but

with any other man who'd bed you as well. Meredith clenched her hands into tight balls, but managed to swallow the biting words that rose to her lips.

"Now, don't be shy," Opal teased. "Surely you have questions you'd like answered."

"No." Meredith's voice was strained. "I'm fine, Opal. There's no need for you to—"

"Tut, tut, think nothing of it!" Opal cut in. "After all, we're all sisters under the skin, aren't we? Women have to help each other through this ordeal, that's my opinion."

"Ordeal?" Meredith repeated, despite her resolution to cut off the conversation.

"Yes. What husbands require of us in the—ah—marital chambers. It's different, of course, if one is not *married* to a man. Then he's full of love and witty sayings, always trying to amuse and please you." She leaned back her head and stroked her bare white throat with long, bejeweled fingers, a sensual gesture that spoke of many such relationships with men. "But they require something altogether different in a wife. A mistress is cajoled, a wife is commanded. And therein lies the whole difference."

Meredith bit her lip. She would have liked to stop Opal, but she was caught in the web of Opal's words. She yearned to hear more about the subject she so dreaded and yet strangely longed for, too. What would Jeremy demand of her in bed? Would it be the heart-stopping pleasure he had given her before or something awful, painful, humiliating?

"A man enjoys his pleasures, especially one like Jeremy Devlin." Opal shot her a knowing look that pierced Meredith. She'd suspected he had slept with Opal, but had not wanted to face it. Jeremy wouldn't pass up such a willing bedmate as Opal Hamilton. "He's a man of voracious appetites. Such a huge, strong brute!" Opal's eyes glittered, and her pink tongue stole out to wet her lips. "May I speak frankly, Meredith? Remember I am talking to you in place of your mother. The pain tonight will be vast, for he will shatter your maidenhead. It's always so the first time, and with a man the size of Devlin! Well, I can't begin to tell you."

Opal was being spiteful, Meredith knew. No doubt she disliked the idea of her lover in another woman's bed. But there was truth, too, in Opal's warning. She remembered a young slave girl who had been raped by one of the field hands. The girl had been torn and bleeding, sobbing with pain. Meredith recalled Jeremy's muscled thighs controlling his horse, his iron arms lifting her into the saddle with ease. Opal was right. He was huge and strong. The chances were he would tear her unmercifully. God knows, he would have no consideration. She feared Jeremy would even take a savage delight in her anguish. Perhaps it would be his means of revenge.

"Men love a maiden for a wife. A mistress is for pleasure, but a wife is to do her duty, just that. Woe betide the wife who seeks her own pleasure in the marriage act. Do you understand my meaning?"

Meredith shook her head. "I don't think so."

"Men want virtue and innocence in a wife, not lust. They expect a woman to be a stick if they are married to her, because anything else means she has a licentious nature." Opal frowned, marring the perfection of her face. Meredith guessed she was speaking from personal experience, for she heard the ring of conviction in her voice. Apparently what she related was true for Angus. But then everyone knew he was a dour, righteous, strict Scottish Presbyterian. Would what was true for him be the same for other men, especially a laughing, passionate one such as Jeremy Devlin? Well, it didn't matter anyway. She wouldn't have to worry about appearing inexperienced and lacking in lust. It would be the truth. "So remember, my dear, if you feel desire for Devlin, you mustn't appear to. He wouldn't like it in a wife, I assure you."

"Opal, I appreciate your desire to help," Meredith began.

"Oh, it's nothing, I assure you. I would do the same for any motherless girl. Or woman, I should say in your case, for you are rather older than most brides, are you not?" Opal stood, her movement releasing a faint cloud of lavender scent. She smiled graciously, and Meredith managed a wavering smile in return. For a long time after Opal departed, Meredith sat thinking about her words. Each repetition increased her fears. In vain she assured herself that Jeremy wouldn't seek her bed, that he could not possibly desire her. But he had said he would seek revenge. She thought about the hurt and the unknown.

They would sleep together, Meredith knew. But what else was involved? Would Jeremy see her unclothed? Could she keep on her nightgown? Or would he strip her even of that? She trembled with embarrassment at the thought of a man viewing her naked body. It would be bad enough to be so exposed even if she were beautiful. But to have him look at the ridiculous length of her legs and torso, her whole lanky, clumsy body—it was almost too terrible to contemplate! She was sure Jeremy would laugh, first at her ugliness and then at her gaucheness in bed. She would do everything wrong, and he would laugh and poke fun. Doubtless he would humiliate her with the memory every chance he got. Meredith almost sobbed aloud. How could she bear it?

Finally Jeremy disturbed her reverie. "Ah. Here you are! Hiding? Come, you must dance with me. Everyone is wondering what's happened to the blushing bride." His eyes were glittering and his face was flushed. When Meredith went to his side, she could smell the brandy on his breath and see the dampness around his hairline and dotting his upper cheek. He looked wild, reckless and far too drunk for her ease of mind.

Placing her hand on his arm, she let him lead her into the ballroom for a country set. It was growing late in the afternoon, but the revelry was barely in full swing. The celebration would last far into the evening, even after the bridal couple had retired. The guests would drink and feast and dance, all the while making ribald jokes about what was transpiring in the bridal chambers upstairs. Meredith danced several more times with Jeremy and other men, but escaped at every chance to stand against the wall or stroll through the hall and other rooms. She nodded at several ladies and conversed with others, hardly aware of the pleasantries she uttered.

The banquet table was constantly replenished, and the guests returned to it again and again. The liquid refreshments also disappeared quickly and were as quickly replaced. Meredith noted with a jaundiced eye that Jeremy stopped by the refreshment table frequently. He was in tearing good spirits, laughing and joking with the other men, obviously turning their distrust and doubt into friendship. She was also very aware of the two dances he had with Opal Hamilton and the one with Lydia, as well as with every other woman in the room. It hardly seemed proper behavior for a bridegroom, but Meredith wouldn't give him the satisfaction of remonstrating with him. He would smirk and tell her she was jealous. Of course she wasn't. Nothing could be further from the truth. It was just embarrassing for him to seek the company of other women so assiduously, that was all.

The afternoon wore into evening, and Meredith grew more and more tired. She had to smile and look cheerful, even though she felt sick inside, a queasy stomach, which sapped her strength. Dancing and standing on her feet didn't help, and neither did her lack of sleep the night before. However, the physical discomfort was mild compared to her mental anguish. By the time dusk fell, and they had to light the wax candles in the tiered candelabra, Meredith was icy with dread. Another hour passed, with her growing colder and stiffer, before Lydia glided up and placed a confidential hand on her arm. "Come, Meredith, it's time for you to slip away, don't you think?"

"What?"

Lydia smiled. "It's late. Time to prepare for bed."

"Oh! Yes, I—I guess so."

"All right. Go on up. I'll tell Jeremy in about half an hour."

Lydia strolled away. Meredith dragged herself from the ballroom and up the stairs on wooden feet. It could no longer be postponed. The reckoning was upon her. Her heart hammered madly, and she thought she might freeze from her terror. The flight of stairs had never seemed so long before. Finally she reached her bedroom door. Inside she glanced around, her gaze drawn to the central, dominant feature: the huge, high four-poster. For the first time in her life she would share it with a man.

Chapter XVI

B<small>ETSY BOBBED</small> up excitedly from her stool. "Miss Meredith!"

Meredith turned and attempted a smile. "Hello, Betsy."

"It's the first time I've seen you, ma'am—since you got married, I mean. I'm so happy for you, Miss Merry."

"Why, thank you, Betsy."

Betsy grinned, white teeth flashing in her dark skin. "I'm sure you'll have a good life, with a fine-looking man like your husband."

"Looks aren't everything."

"No, but they help," Betsy added irrepressibly.

Meredith had to chuckle at her words. "I guess you're right, at that. I—I'll dress for bed now."

"Yes'm. I've laid out one of the gowns Mrs. Lydia made for you." Betsy moved behind her to unfasten the multitude of buttons. Meredith glanced at the bed, where Betsy had laid the nightgown. It was beautiful, and Lydia had made it especially for her wedding night. Betsy would think it odd if Meredith asked for an old, thick nightgown. After all, Betsy didn't realize that her wedding night was not to be like other wedding nights.

Betsy helped her out of the gown and hung it in the wardrobe while Meredith removed her petticoats and hoop. Betsy put away her things, all the while chattering about Jeremy and the splendid night ahead for Meredith. "Oh, Miss

Merry, you're a lucky woman. That one'll be good in bed. Big and strong, like my Neb. Very much a man."

Very much a man. Too much a man for me, Meredith thought wryly. But she said nothing, merely clenched her teeth and tried to shut out Betsy's words. When she was undressed, she bathed in the small slipper-shaped tub Betsy had hauled upstairs and filled with water. Betsy heated it by pouring in a kettleful of boiling water, and Meredith stepped in. She washed mechanically, musing on how ridiculous it was to prepare herself for a bridegroom who despised her. Betsy added a splash of perfume to the water, and even after Meredith stepped out and dried off, it clung hauntingly to her skin. Betsy dropped the thin nightgown over her head, then started to unpin her hair.

"No, I'll take it down," Meredith told her curtly, snatching out the blossoms Lydia had sprinkled in her pinned curls. "You go on to bed, Betsy."

Betsy grinned conspiratorially, surmising that Meredith was anxious for her to leave so Jeremy would come to her. In truth, Meredith could not stand her chatter any longer. When the maid was gone, Meredith timidly approached the mirror. She was appalled by the sensuality of her image. The gown was sheer white lawn, not quite transparent, but the closest thing to it. It revealed the lines of her body as if through a haze. The neckline was low-cut and exposed the tops of her breasts in all their fullness. Her dark nipples were obvious beneath the gauzy material. They tightened now in response to the chill air and her cold dread, and their rising was clearly visible.

Meredith wrapped a warm velvet dressing gown around her and slid her feet into fur-lined slippers, then sat in a chair to await her doom. It seemed as if hours passed, and still he did not come. Would he? She felt a fool to sit up waiting for him. Why should he come? That night in the study during the party had been mere playacting. He had wanted to sweeten her to the marriage. How well he had put on the hoarse voice and ragged breath, how convincing his low moan of desire. He had played her like a fish, reeling her in and letting her out. But now that they were married there was no longer any need to pretend. He didn't want to seek her bed. He would choose another room. Probably he already had and was fast asleep in bed. But no, she heard his quick laugh amid the revelry continuing downstairs.

Meredith clasped her hands together. She ought to go to bed and get some sleep. If she had dark circles under her eyes tomorrow, there would be lewd comments. But if Jeremy did happen to come, her being in bed would make her seem overeager, like a wanton tart. She chewed at her nervous lips, trying to still her leaping stomach, but she could not. Her hands grew icier by the moment, as her mind bounced insanely between fear that he would come and fear that he would not.

The door opened, cracking the stillness, and Meredith leaped to her feet as if she had been shot. Jeremy paused on the threshold, one hand upon the frame. Someone down the hall hurled a laughing comment to him, but he paid no attention. His gaze was fixed on Meredith, the heavy lids drooping to conceal the expression in his sapphire eyes. Meredith curled her fingers into a fist, steeling herself for whatever would come. Jeremy's coat was off and slung casually across one shoulder. His waistcoat was unbuttoned, and the fine lawn shirt hung outside his breeches. He swayed slightly. Meredith wondered how much he had drunk. Was he mean in his cups? Or would he sprawl heavily on the bed and pass out?

"Jeremy!" a man's voice hallooed from the stairs. "Shall I help you undress?"

Jeremy grinned. "You'll not get a sight of what's inside this room. My wife will valet me."

He moved inside and shut the door behind him. Meredith wet her lips, watching him like an animal in a trap. He tossed his coat over the back of a chair, then shrugged out of his waistcoat and dealt with it in the same fashion. His hands went next to his neckband and the attached fall of frothy lace, his eyes steadily upon her as he unfastened and discarded it. He said nothing, not trusting his voice to speak.

Finally, driven to desperation by his silence, Meredith burst out, "Jeremy, what do you intend? You can't seriously mean to sleep here."

He blinked. "Where would you like to sleep?"

"*I* will sleep here, of course. It is my room."

"Mine also now, unless for formalities' sake you wish me to have my own room. But I warn you, I'll not spend much time in it."

"Why not?"

"Why not? Meredith, don't be silly."

"You can't want to bed me," she said, pursuing the topic doggedly.

"Why can't I?" He grinned as he sat down and undid his shoes and stockings. "It's precisely what I want to do." His relentless fingers began to work on the buttons of his shirt.

"No!" Meredith almost shrieked. "Please, don't."

He frowned, then rose and came closer, one hand reaching out to tilt her face up to his. "You're actually scared, aren't you?" His voice softened. "Don't worry. I shall be very gentle when I introduce you to the pleasures of love."

"Love?" Meredith repeated sarcastically. "I'm not naive. We both know how little love has to do with *this* marriage. You married to gain your freedom and a great deal of wealth. I married to please a dying man. There's no point in continuing the farce in the bedroom. Let us have separate rooms and live our lives as civilly as we can."

His mouth quirked, his eyebrows lifting. "Living our lives 'civilly,' as you put it, is not my main goal."

"Jeremy, please, allow me a little dignity."

"Dignity won't keep you warm at night—or give you children. Don't you want children—heirs to Bitterleaf?"

The thought stopped her for a moment. She hadn't really thought of it. What would happen to her beloved plantation when she died if there were no children? She could leave it to Galen's or Althea's children, if either of them happened to marry and if they also happened to bear children. "The Whitneys run to small families," she murmured, following her line of thought.

"I can see why, the sort of pursuits they're interested in." Jeremy grinned. "I think I can promise you several strong sons to inherit your land. Between the two of us, we should produce giants, shouldn't we?"

Meredith dropped her eyes nervously at the intimate topic and backed away a little. "Jeremy, please, surely you can't really want to bed me!"

"Why not? I thought I made my feelings on that score rather clear." He stepped closer until he was mere inches from her, his strong masculinity looming above Meredith, overpowering her. She licked dry lips and looked everywhere but at him. Lightly, insinuatingly, Jeremy ran his fingers up her arms. His voice was low and husky, mesmerizing. "I intend to claim my full rights as a husband. Your land is not the only thing you have to offer."

His hands went to the sash of her dressing gown, untying the knot and letting the belt fall. Slowly, savoring the moment, he shoved back the heavy velvet robe, exposing her body clad only in the almost transparent nightgown. She heard him catch his breath and glanced up. His face was flushed, the eyelids heavy, shuttering the intense blue gaze. The dressing gown crumpled silently to the floor as he studied her. All mockery fled from his face as he looked at the swelling mounds of her breasts, nipples dark against the thin material. His eyes moved downward, taking in the smooth line of her stomach and its gentle flow into slim hips, the long shapely legs, hazily revealed beneath the cloth, all the more tantalizing for their faint concealment. Meredith watched him, braced for a jest or offensive remark, but none came. She sucked in her lower lip. Jeremy's eyes darkened to a deep midnight blue. "Meredith."

He pulled her against his lean, hard body, not pressing, but letting her rest against the warmth of his skin and the rocklike muscles beneath it. Meredith had never before been so intimidated by the size and strength of a man. Physically he was capable of doing whatever he wanted to her, and legally he had the right. In an agony of fear, anxiety, and trembling excitement, she waited. "Your hands are cold as ice," he murmured. "Like the evening of the party. Scared again? There's no public this time. Just me." He hypnotically massaged her palms. "I'll take good care of you, sweeting." His lips brushed her temple and forehead, light as moths' wings. "The first time is always scary. My knees knocked together like castanets."

An involuntary giggle escaped her lips at that unlikely picture. "You've never been scared a day in your life."

He laughed. "Tell that to the lightskirt who gave me my

manhood.'' He guided her to a seat on the bed and settled beside her. His hands went to the pins still holding her curls in place. "Do you mind if I take down your hair? Stiff like that, a man can't get his hands into it."

Meredith shook her head silently, unable to speak.

He continued in the same light, bantering tone as he slid the pins from her hair one by one and tossed them onto the table beside the bed. "I remember the tart took off her blouse as soon as we entered the room, and she had huge breasts. I'd never seen a pair like them. In fact, I'd never seen any bare. I stared and suddenly turned as shaky as a babe taking his first step. She must have wondered what had happened to the randy youth who'd agreed to her price so readily." His deft fingers in her hair stirred Meredith, and the ribald tale did strange things to her stomach. She knew she ought to be shocked at his telling her such a story. It should offend her maidenly ears, and a nice woman would order him to stop. But Meredith was curious to hear the outcome, and his humorous account relaxed her, made Jeremy seem less fearsome. "What happened?"

Jeremy chuckled. "I could hardly unbutton my shirt and breeches. I stammered and blushed. But she just laughed and said my size had fooled her. She hadn't realized I was only a green boy. Very kindly she helped me undress and led me to her bed." Jeremy finished with her pins, and Meredith's hair lay loosely tumbled across her shoulders. Jeremy paused to retrieve her silver-backed hairbrush from the dresser, then began to brush her hair in smooth, even strokes. His voice was rich with fond memory. "She taught me what I needed to know and more. I was young, had no control. In the course of her lesson, I must have peaked four times. But she didn't care, just kept stroking me, whispering in my ear, guiding my hand over her until I learned a woman's pleasure spots." Meredith closed her eyes, swallowing. Her husband was describing his experience with another woman. It should be distasteful to her, but the words, delivered in his low-timbred voice, merely made her feel warm and weak inside. Her tongue was too thick to speak, even if she could have thought of something to say. "Everyone should have an experienced teacher," he told her. "Someone to make it beautiful, not frightening." He smoothed her thick mane of hair and lifted it in his hands. She had turned slightly to aid his hair brushing, so he sat behind her on the bed. Now twisting the hank of hair around one hand and wrist, he raised it and bent to plant a soft kiss on the sensitive nape of her neck.

Meredith shivered in mingled delight and fear. She wished he would stop. She hated for him to see her naked, to view her absurdly long legs and sturdy torso. Perhaps if he only saw her clothed he would retain some delusion that she was fragile underneath. Jeremy nuzzled her neck, and she had a flashing picture of a stallion as he pursued a mare in heat, savagely gripping her by the neck with his teeth, subduing her. Meredith's hands twisted together in her lap.

"Relax, my love, relax," Jeremy whispered. "Trust me. I'll take good care of you."

"No, Jeremy, please." Her voice was desperate.

"Why are you terrified?" He sounded more puzzled than angered. "Am I such a monster?"

"No. Yes. I don't know. You told me you would exact your revenge for—for what I did to you."

He was stunned into silence for an instant. "You think I plan to hurt you in retaliation? You think I'm cruel enough to turn your first loving into a hell?"

"You—you laughed as if you meant you would punish me in bed."

"I did not say 'punish.' "

"You said you would take your revenge!" she insisted.

Jeremy sighed and pushed Meredith flat on the bed, staring down into her face. "So I will—but it doesn't necessarily mean punishment. My revenge could be pleasuring you so you regret your lashing."

"I already do!" she moaned wretchedly.

"Good. You should. Then perhaps my revenge simply will be for you to know me as your master and yearn for my touch. I'll break you to my gait so well you'll take no other."

"I would never be unfaithful to my husband!" Meredith protested sharply.

"I know you would not. And I'd kill anyone who dared touch you."

She was startled. There was no puffing, no bravado to what

he said, just a calm statement of fact. She didn't know how to respond to it, so she reverted to his earlier remark. "You'll *not* be my master."

He chuckled low in his throat, speaking to her in a voice as velvety as his lips upon her neck. "No? Already I know how to fire you up. Tonight I'll learn how to please you. What else will I need to know?"

"A thousand things you wouldn't be capable of." She was losing the thread of their conversation. Jeremy's hand lay flat across her stomach, its heat penetrating the flimsy cloth of her gown. His mouth nuzzled the side of her neck, his tongue circling erotically over her skin. Meredith felt fuzzy and confused. "Why do you bother? Why should you care to please me?"

"Because I enjoy it," he returned honestly. "Later I will teach you to give me pleasure. But for both of us to enjoy it, I must first teach you to *have* pleasure." His hand drifted up the plateau of her rib cage and hovered tantalizingly at the soft undercurve of one breast. His fingers crumpled the cloth, inching the neckline down until the pink circle of her nipple peeked above it, dark and engorged. He stopped the constant journey of his lips to gaze at the partially exposed orb. Meredith closed her eyes, embarrassed, yet prickling with heat. The heavy, avid look on his face as he studied her was more disquieting than her nakedness.

Jeremy sat up, his hands going to the straps of cloth across her shoulders and easing them down. Automatically she grabbed the neckline with both hands. He swallowed. "I want to look at you, Meredith. I won't hurt you. I just want to see you— all of you." His voice was hoarse, and a faint tremor hinted at more emotion than his words expressed.

"Please, no," she whispered, despising herself for pleading with this man. "I—I am not a possession to be studied."

"*Admired*. Perhaps you are not a possession, but you belong to me. You are my wife. And you saw me stripped before a crowd."

"Not completely naked."

"No, but robbed of every vestige of dignity. On public display. Truly a possession, as you just said."

"I am sorry. If there were any way I could take that shame

from you, I would." She opened great, tear-filled eyes. "But must you subject me to the same humiliation in order to ease your pain?"

"It's not the same." One callused hand stroked her stomach and legs persuasively. "I am the only one to see you here. There is nothing shameful when you do it freely. It is force that makes nakedness a humiliation."

"You are forcing me."

"I am asking. I am your husband. We are one now, remember?"

"Do you believe that?"

"That we are one body, one flesh?" He cocked his head to one side, considering. "Soon we will be joined. You'll feel the difference, the specialness of the union."

"Yet you have done the same thing thousands of times with other women."

"Never with my wife," he countered. "Meredith, how can I explain? There is a uniqueness, a specialness to each time. You'll see. And you'll learn, too, that there is no shame between lovers." He raised her hand to his lips and pressed a blazing kiss in the center of her palm. "I burn for you. Let me remove your gown."

"All right." Averting her eyes, Meredith rose and began to pull off her nightgown, but Jeremy stopped her and performed the task with his own hands. He eased the gown off her shoulders and down her torso, past her hips, then let it drop onto the ground. His mouth was parched as his gaze lingered over her body, taking in each detail: the pink-crested, heavy globes of her breasts, the slender waist and tight, spare buttocks, the long, well-shaped legs. Meredith found that if she closed her eyes and did not watch his face, it wasn't so bad. Then she couldn't witness his disappointment or amusement.

But Jeremy was not content with watching. Starting at her neck, he trailed his hands down her body, sliding over the thrusting breasts and soft belly to the joinder of her legs where the hair burst forth, thick and springy. Her cheeks flamed when he touched her there, and she emitted a startled gasp. Jeremy smiled at her innocence, both touched and excited. It would be damned hard to go slowly. His heart pounded at the sight of her ivory flesh, supple and slender, and her deliciously long legs tantalized him. Yet he knew he must take his time and open her up gently to pleasure. He must not give in to his pounding, mindless yearning.

Jeremy glanced away for a moment, focusing on the rest of the room, in order to ease the swelling bulge beneath his breeches. Meredith sensed something was different and couldn't resist opening her eyes. She saw his face turned away and realized with resigned horror that her body had disgusted him. As soon as he saw her naked, he had stopped the daring, sense-shattering things he had been doing earlier. Meredith reached for the gown to cover her rejected nudity. Jeremy turned back at her movement.

"Are you cold? I am sorry." There was nothing but concern in his voice as he pulled back the bedcovers. Before she could question or protest or slip into her clothes, he pulled the covers up over her. Tossing her discarded gown onto the Windsor chair, he began to undress. Meredith's eyes widened, and she averted her face. "It's only fair, don't you think," Jeremy remarked blithely, "that I should face you naked as well?"

"I'm not interested. I've seen you that way before."

He grinned. "So you have. But, as I recall, you didn't take much time to look." He divested himself of shirt and breeches and stood beside the bed, engaged in a clash of wills with his wife. Eventually Meredith's curiosity won out over her determination to appear unconcerned. She shifted her eyes to steal a peek. She saw the red-gold curls matting his chest, the scar she had noticed before slanting across his ribs, the flat stomach and heavy chest. The Carolina sun had baked his upper torso to a golden color, the tan ending abruptly at the waistband of his trousers. There was another difference: now, thrusting from the fiery ring of hair between his legs, was his distended manhood. It had looked only half that size the day she had caught him swimming. She stared openly, astonished into forgetting her vow. "What is it?" Jeremy asked quickly at her horrified expression.

"How can you be so—large? Before you did not seem—so—so—"

He realized what she was spluttering about and laughed aloud. "My dear, then I had seen only your bare legs. Now

I've explored your whole lovely body. That's desire, my pet."

She swallowed and unconsciously shrank back into her pillow. Her fear intensified. How could he keep from hurting her? She knew the essentials of lovemaking from the farm animals, and she was certain he would never, ever fit. She shook at the thought of him ripping away the tender membrane and forcing himself into her.

"Don't worry," he said, guessing her thoughts. "There won't be much pain. I'll be careful." He slid into bed beside her, one arm curling under her neck. She lay stiff as a board as he leaned over her. Meredith took in every detail of Jeremy's face: the blue eyes almost black in the dim light, the cheeks faintly shadowed by a day's growth of beard, the thin, straight nose, the golden skin. She could smell his scent, a tart combination of shaving soap, leather, and his skin. Tonight the odor of brandy blended subtly with the others. He loomed closer, his face huge in her vision, and she closed her eyes. Then his lips touched her mouth, pliable, almost tentative. He seemed to seek, to explore with infinite patience, his mouth gradually building her dormant fires. He moved his mouth on hers, pressing her lips apart, and his tongue began its dancing possession of her mouth. She could taste the residue of brandy on his tongue as his kiss assaulted her senses, spinning her into a wild vortex of pleasure. He seemed to kiss her forever, tasting and discovering her lips until her legs twitched restlessly and she arched up, searching. At last his mouth left hers to cover her cheeks and neck with faint kisses, breathy fannings of her skin that tingled and promised without satisfying. Her lips felt bruised and swollen, and she sucked in her lower lip to touch its soreness. She could taste Jeremy on her lip, and she twisted, her mouth blindly seeking his.

His cheek was searing upon her face, his breath heavy and ragged. He began to play her body with his hands, stroking and caressing her breasts, tantalizing the crests to buttons of longing. There was a moist ache between her legs, and his searching fingers found it. She recoiled, embarrassed for him to touch the inexplicable wetness, but he followed her, apparently all the more excited by it. His breath rasped in her ear as he nipped at it, tracing the contours with his tongue and sucking at the lobe. Meredith writhed, almost unable to bear the combined seduction of tongue and fingers.

Jeremy wrenched away from her and rolled onto his back, one arm thrown across his eyes. "God!" He gulped for air. Dazed, Meredith stared at him. What had she done wrong? How had she offended him? "Jeremy?" The tentative question came out almost a croak. "Have I—that is, is there something I should have—I have no experience at this, you know!" she flared in frustration.

He turned toward her and reached out to caress her cheek. "Don't worry. You've done nothing wrong. I'm—too excited. I have to calm down a moment or I'll take you too early, before you're ready."

"It's all right," she assured him, frowning. She had heard men were different, could not contain their passions the way women could. They physically needed the release. "I—I don't want to cause you any pain or—or discomfort."

He grinned. "I'll live. But it's been a long time, and you stir me almost past bearing. Merely looking at you in that gown turned me hard as a brick."

Meredith blushed at his words and glanced away. Her head was swimming with what he said and did to her. Could she possibly excite him? Had she really brought him to this ragged, panting state? Surely not. He said it had been a long time—since what? Since he had taken a woman? Had he and Lydia been unable to meet lately? Was it that he desired Lydia and was using her for an outlet? She had no time to pursue this unpleasant line of thought, for he slid across the inches that separated them and covered her with his large muscular body, pressing her into the feather mattress. It was strange to have his heavy weight upon her, but exciting, too. She could fee the sharp thrust of his pelvic bones imprinting her flesh, and the hard insistence of his masculinity. He ground his body into her, moving from side to side, luxuriating in the feel of skin rubbing skin, while his mouth claimed hers again.

When finally his lips left her mouth and moved lower, Meredith realized she was no longer in possession of her senses. Jeremy had taken control of them, bombarding her with sensual delight. His teeth nipped lightly at her flesh, the tiny pain in erotic contrast to his warm, soothing tongue. He slid his head down until it was level with her breasts, letting her feel every inch of his skin as he moved. Prolonging the enjoyment until it tortured them both, he cupped her breasts and squeezed gently so that the globes overflowed his hands and the peaks tilted up tauntingly. His mouth surrounded one deep pink circle, tugging with the suction of his cheeks as his tongue wetly played with the nipple. Meredith groaned, and he began to suck, sending a wild tremor slashing through her belly. She quivered beneath him, arching her neck as she fought to control the shudders his teasing created. It was delightful, wicked torment, and the throb in her abdomen grew.

Jeremy moved to the other nipple, his lips grazing the creamy, quivering flesh in between. One hand strayed downward, tangling in her curls and locating the slick center of her womanhood. Meredith moaned. "That's it," Jeremy murmured, his voice taut, barely under control. "You're doing fine." One finger slid into the intimate recesses, and she stiffened in surprise. His voice calmed her. "It's all right. Relax. I'll take care of it. Just relax." His forehead was beaded with sweat, but a grin spread across his face. "I should have known. You're well-guarded. Ah, Meredith. What . . . sweet . . ." His mouth dropped onto her flesh between each word, creeping lower and lower. ". . . torture."

It occurred to Meredith she ought to offer him a chance to rest as he had before, but the idea went no further than her mind. She didn't want him to stop. She ached all over, most of all in her very center, where he now worked his wonders. His finger withdrew, then returned, filling her more. She realized what he was doing—loosening the tough seal of her virginity so that his entry would not hurt as much. Tears filled her eyes at the care and time he was taking with her, even though he ached for his own release. But Meredith burned with desire, too. A primitive need to feel him within her body surged through her, making her heedless of the possible pain.

"Jeremy, please," she gasped, past caring what she said or what he thought of her. "Please love me now."

Jeremy's muscles knotted with strain. He wet his lips, and

regarded her. He wanted more than anything to believe her,
but he had little experience with virgins, and he was anxious
not to hurt her. For a moment he hesitated, then parted her
legs with his knee. He simply couldn't wait any longer.
Jeremy probed at the gate of her femininity. Instinctively,
Meredith's long legs went around him, just as in his dreams.
He tensed his muscles and pushed, feeling the membrane rip
beneath his assault. Meredith twisted in surprise or pain, but
Jeremy had gone past attending to her needs. He was carried
by a wave of primal desire, and he thrust in a deep, hard
rhythm, burying himself in her. An animal moan rose in his
throat, ending in a short, hoarse cry. For an instant he hung
suspended above her, his face contorted in an ecstasy beyond
words, and went slack. His breathing slowed as he moved a
few more times. Then he relaxed upon her, his face damp
against her neck.

Meredith encircled him with her arms, stunned by the
experience. The stab of pain had worked against her passion,
but his filling her offered a deeper satisfaction. "Meredith,"
Jeremy breathed into her ear, "are you all right?"

"Yes." She did not mention the faint questing still inside
her loins, knowing neither what it was or what he could do
about it. His weary mind accepted her answer, too spent and
bathed in sweet fulfillment to explore the issue, and he sagged
to sleep. Meredith adjusted slightly to bear his weight and drifted
into sleep more slowly, her numbed mind and senses trying to
absorb what had happened to the body that heretofore had
been hers alone.

Chapter XVII

JEREMY AWOKE in the darkness, confused for a moment. Then he recalled the night before and smiled. He knew an utter peace, one he hadn't experienced in months—if ever. He lay half on top of Meredith, and he slid off gently so as not to disturb her. She turned to snuggle against him, seeking the warmth that had just left her. Jeremy slid an arm under her shoulders and rested her head on his chest. Yawning, he moved his hand over her body, exploring, remembering. Had he ever had a lovemaking as good? As sweet? He couldn't recall one.

He fondled the pillow softness of Meredith's breast. Her nipple tightened at his touch. He grinned in the darkness. How well she responded to him, even in her sleep. God, what wild passion had welled up in her when they made love. A flame he had not expected burned inside her. He had thought it would take a long, aching time and a great deal of persuasion, but she had urged him hungrily to complete the act. Jeremy bent to kiss her breast, his hand roaming lower to the fountain of her femininity. He touched the dried blood on the inside of her thighs and had a moment's regret for her pain. He would make it up to her next time, he promised.

Rising, he went to the washbasin and soaked a cloth, then returned to tenderly lave the joinder of her legs, washing away the blood. Meredith's eyes opened at the touch of the cool cloth on her flesh. "What? Jeremy?" she said groggily.

"I'm sorry, my love. I was washing the blood from your legs. Are you sore?"

"No, I don't think so." Meredith flushed at his intimate touch, even though she had felt his touch even more intimately last night. Last night! Now there was something to blush about. How wildly she had reacted to him, how quickly he had seduced her. Why, she had practically begged him to take her at the end. It was so humiliating.

"Good." He kissed her belly. The soft skin twitched at the feel of his lips. He nuzzled lower, and hastily Meredith twisted away. He chuckled. "Too soon? All right." His mouth came back to her breasts, teasing the crests until they were engorged. He rained kisses over her chest and down her side, ending finally on her derrière. She jumped as he nipped the soft flesh with his teeth. His hands cupped her buttocks, lifting them and squeezing. "Oh, Meredith," he groaned.

"You don't mean to—" Meredith broke off, embarrassed.

"To make love to you again?" he finished for her. "Yes, if it won't cause you any pain."

"But surely last night was enough."

"Uh-uh," he mumbled against her skin. "Never enough. Feel." He grasped her hand and carried it to his swollen manhood.

"Oh!" Meredith gulped. Never in her life had she imagined touching . . . *that*. She could not say it even in her own mind. Yet her fingers curled naturally around it, amazed and delighted by the satin-smooth skin encasing the throbbing rigidity. His flesh quivered in her hand, and she jumped. "Oh!"

"Is that all you can say?" he teased. His lips nuzzled the curve of her neck. Meredith tightened, fighting the treacherous warmth he aroused, but finally had to shiver. A soft moan escaped her.

Immediately his mouth fastened on hers. Meredith found her hands straying over his body, touching the fuzz of his chest, the smooth skin stretched across the hipbones, the hard spine surrounded by his taut back muscles. Jeremy made a noise deep in his throat, and his lips widened over hers, his tongue plunging into her mouth. At last he pulled away, panting. "Touch me, Meredith."

"What?"

"Touch me. Remember I said I would teach you to please me? This is your first lesson. I want you to explore my body, come to know it as your own."

"But where? I don't know how."

"Just do what pleases you. Go wherever you want. Believe me, you'll discover what to do."

Tentatively she continued her exploration, kneading the muscles of his chest, sliding her fingers through the thick mat of hair, even touching his button-hard nipples. Her hands strayed to his arms, discovering the power lying quiescent beneath his skin. Then she went on to his legs, feeling the tickle of the hairs against her palm, the hard bone and thick muscles. Suddenly his hand gripped her hair and Jeremy dragged her up to kiss her, a raw, savage kiss that stamped her mouth as his private territory. He rose on one elbow and pressed her back against the bed. Her legs fell apart naturally, and he moved between them to sink his burning shaft deep into her softness. Meredith gasped at the sweet, sensual beauty of his entry, hardly noticing the brief twinge of soreness.

He began to move within her, but unlike their earlier lovemaking, he thrust again and again. Instead of satisfying her ache, it seemed to make it grow until Meredith involuntarily rolled her head from side to side. Jeremy pounded into her, and she arched up to take him in more fully. She wanted all of him. And something more. She didn't know what, but the urge was deep and driving.

But Jeremy knew. At her whimper of frustration, he began to move faster, his hips churning, carrying her with him to a new universe of blinding pleasure. He hurled her higher and higher, until she was gasping for breath and clutching at his back, her nails digging unthinkingly into his skin. She said his name, almost begging, and then suddenly she felt herself explode deep inside, in the part Jeremy now possessed. The deep shudder sent waves of pleasure crashing through her, and she cried out sharply. A joy Jeremy had never known before pierced him. He had presented her a gift of great beauty, and he thrilled to her response. He came, too, in an earthquake of satisfaction that turned the world black and hot and dark, his whole being centered on their joining.

It was a long time before either returned to the real world. Exhausted, Jeremy kissed Meredith's cheek and rolled off her. Meredith almost cried out at the loss of his body. She wanted to savor his heavy warmth and experience the relaxation of his body. But then Jeremy pulled her into his arms. She snuggled happily against him, not thinking, lying awake, awash in the sensations that a few minutes before had burst through her body.

When Meredith awoke the next morning, Jeremy was shaving in front of the mirror. Sensing she was awake, he turned, a grin slashing across his handsome face. "Hello, sleepyhead," he teased. "Did I tire you out?"

Meredith blushed at his insinuation and wondered why he hadn't returned to his own room to shave. She couldn't get out of bed and dress with him in the room. Even though he had viewed her naked body last night and completely claimed it, Meredith was shy at his seing her in the full light of day and reason. When she didn't get out of bed, Jeremy reminded her, "You better move, my girl. We're leaving for Charleston this morning. Or had you forgotten our honeymoon trip?"

Meredith cleared her throat. "Ah; no, of course not. But—but you're still here."

"What do you mean?" He frowned in puzzlement.

"Well, I mean—I don't have on any clothes," she finished in a low voice.

He shouted with laughter. "What is this sudden modesty? I saw you stark-naked last night. And, in case you haven't realized it, I plan to see you that way often." He pivoted back to the mirror, shaking his great golden head in amusement.

His amusement made Meredith feel silly and childish, so she did not ask the questions she longed to. Would he continue their lovemaking? Was it not to be only on their wedding night? Had he not completed his revenge? And what sort of revenge was it that pleased her so? It was very strange. She studied Jeremy's back and his image in the mirror. It seemed so cold-blooded to appear before him naked now. It had been different last night when his hot eyes ate her up and later when she had been swept away with passion. Then Jeremy had not seemed repulsed by her body, but now, seeing it in the full light of day instead of the softening candlelight, surely he would be disgusted. Tears sprang into her eyes at the frustration of her position.

Jeremy finished shaving and doused his face with water, scrubbing away the vestiges of soap. He swung around to face her again. "Meredith, get up." He dropped a buttonless lawn shirt over his head. Meredith's eyes flickered to the open V of the neck where red-gold chest hairs curled over the material. Jeremy strode to the bed where Meredith lay on her side and whacked her resoundingly on the backside. The force was thoroughly muffled by the thick quilt and comforter, but the familiarity of his gesture made Meredith sit bolt upright, her bedclothes sliding down and exposing her bare torso.

"How dare you!" she exclaimed, then noticed that his gaze had dropped to her chest. His eyes darkened, the lids drooping lower. Hastily Meredith grabbed the covers and attempted to pull them up, but Jeremy was quicker and stronger. He flung the covers to the foot of the bed. "Oh, no, please," Meredith whimpered and closed her eyes in agony of embarrassment.

"No hideous transformation has taken place," he said lightly. "You look the same as last night. Up, girl, or are you unable to walk after my spearing?"

Meredith clenched her teeth and opened her eyes to glare at him. He was too all-fired pleased with himself. "The conceit of men!" she snapped. "I should imagine that one 'spear' is much like another, and all are equally unpleasant!"

His face tightened. "I am sorry if last night displeased you."

"*You* displease me," Meredith corrected, scrambling out of bed. She scooped up her robe and hastily shrugged into it. "I can't conceive why men find so much pride in inflicting indignity and pain upon a woman."

"Indignity!" he exclaimed. "You didn't seem to find it so unbearable last night! Good God, woman, I nearly killed myself trying to make it easy and pleasant for you. I wanted you so badly it was pure torture to hold back; but I went slowly and built your desire so my entry wouldn't hurt you. And now you accuse me of pride in causing you pain!''

Meredith set her jaw mutinously. Jeremy was right. He had gone slowly. She had witnessed the effort it took, the thick bunching of his muscles and his rigid face as he waited, stroking, kissing. It wasn't the lovemaking that angered her. It was his cool teasing, the crude name he had put to it that made it seem low and common. It *was* common to him. That was what really stung. It had been so heavenly for her, and now to hear him joke about it, to learn how little it meant to him, made her writhe with hurt and humiliation. Added to the anguish of his seeing her naked, imperfect body, it was too much for her to bear. So she had struck out at him in the first way that presented itself.

Jeremy sighed and ran a hand through his hair. He had awakened this morning in a soaring mood, eager to share the day with Meredith and even more eager for the night to come. He had expected them to have an easy camaraderie, a warmth engendered by their lovemaking. Instead Meredith had been cold and reluctant even to let him glimpse her body—as if they were strangers! Then she had lashed out saying that their lovemaking was a pain and an indignity. He was filled with a swift desire to turn her over his knee and give her the paddling her spoiled behavior deserved, but the thought of touching her naked, rounded derrière was too much for him. If he started out spanking, he would wind up bedding her, and he wasn't about to do that when she had just claimed to dislike it. So he turned on his heel and stalked to the door, glancing back at her over his shoulder to deliver his parting shot. ''I hoped last night might have sweetened your nature, but I see you're as prickly and sour as ever. You make me wonder if even freedom is worth enduring your acidic tongue.'' He paused. ''I'll wait for you downstairs, since my presence is so distasteful to you.''

Jeremy slammed the door. Behind him, Meredith grabbed her hairbrush and hurled it after him. It hit the door with a thud that didn't bring much satisfaction to her stormy soul. She would have liked to break it over his arrogant, nasty head! Who was he to talk of sweetening her disposition? And how dare he say she was a shrew, sour—Oh! Her hands flew to her face and she burst into tears, the emotional turmoil of the past few days flooding out.

Finally Meredith brought herself under control and managed to stop the stream of tears. She splashed her face with water, then washed and dressed, struggling into her traveling clothes without Betsy's help. She couldn't face the girl's smiles and knowing looks this morning. She forced her thick hair into a passably smooth roll at the base of her neck, then studied herself in the mirror. She looked presentable enough, except for her red, splotched face. Why couldn't she be one of those women who cried gracefully, she wondered, who let great, crystal tears roll down their cheeks, then appeared perfectly calm and beautifully complexioned when the crying was done?

Betsy had packed her bags the day before, so when she was dressed there was nothing else to do but hurry downstairs. It wasn't yet time for breakfast, and fortunately none of the overnight guests were up yet. Lydia waited in the sitting room and scurried out to give Meredith a peck on the cheek and wish her farewell. She searched Meredith's face, her hopeful expression fading at the signs of a recent bout of tears. Lydia bit her lip, but made no mention of Meredith's reddened eyes. "Daniel was too tired from yesterday to see you off."

"I know. That's fine," Meredith reassured her. "If anything should happen, send for me at once. We'll be in Charleston only a few days, but I could come home sooner."

Lydia shook her head. "I'm sure there won't be any need. But if there is, I'll let you know at once, I promise."

"Good." Meredith glanced around. "Have you—a—seen Jeremy?"

"Yes, he's already said good-bye. He's waiting for you at the dock."

Meredith wondered what his and Lydia's private good-bye had been like. No doubt after the scene upstairs he would have been doubly affectionate to his mistress. Meredith's cheeks burned. Oh, God, now she knew exactly what he had done to Lydia, and it made it even worse. How could he share such sweet intimacies with any number of women? She couldn't imagine going to bed with any other man. Meredith stopped short. Good heavens, what was she saying? That she couldn't imagine marrying anyone else? Even Cousin Galen?

No, surely that wasn't true. She tried to imagine what had happened last night transpiring between herself and Galen. No, it wouldn't have been like that. Galen wouldn't have possessed Jeremy's easy expertise, although he would have held more love in his heart. Their lovemaking would have been calmer, more . . . dignified. Meredith bit her lip. She couldn't lie. She had to admit she wouldn't have preferred dignity and calm. And now that Jeremy had known her body, she doubted she would ever let anyone else touch her, even if she should be widowed and have another chance to wed Galen.

Deep in thought, Meredith let the footman help her on with her warm, encompassing pelisse. She tied a short hood on her head, slid her hands into warm leather gloves, and accepted the face mask the servant offered as protection against the sun. Meredith was sure she would be content with the protection of her parasol, but she took the mask because the man expected it. She trailed out of the house, absurdly lonely on the brief walk to the wooden pier. The flatboat that would take them to Charleston had docked, and Jeremy was already on board, conversing with the captain. He politely helped her cross the plank to the boat, although Meredith was sure he would rather have turned his back and ignored her.

The captain of the boat had a small cargo, so there was ample room on the ship and even a chair for her to sit in. She sat there stolidly throughout the journey, her parasol up. She was chilled by the breeze off the water despite her heavy clothing. It would soon be Christmas, and the days had turned cold. Not as cold, however, as the atmosphere between herself and her husband. Meredith thought about the long years that lay before them. It would be a hard life if her husband hated her. She wondered if she should try to heal the breach.

But no, their marriage was too peculiar. It was not based on love or even affection. There was no trust, no compromise, no companionship. It was a matter of trade, a business transaction, a question of payments—Daniel's to Jeremy and hers to Daniel. Their life would never be comfortable or normal. There was no point in trying to make it so.

*   *   *

Jeremy stayed at the opposite end of the boat throughout the trip and glowered at his wife. She was a stubborn, cold witch, and he was quite certain he would never again have any pleasure in her. He had been callously rejected, and Meredith had tarnished the beauty of the night before. Had he considered it, Jeremy would have been surprised at how much her stinging words affected him. As it was, he was too angry to think clearly. Instead he vowed to sell the plantation and depart as soon as Daniel died. That was the only intelligent plan. He'd probably resort to murder if he had to live with Meredith the rest of their lives.

As soon as the boat docked, they walked to The Bull and Boar, a popular Charleston tavern and inn. A black worker at the docks trailed them with their bags while Meredith and Jeremy marched to the inn in icy silence. When they entered the tavern, the host hurried forward, bowing and smiling genially. Although most inns in the colonies were simple, dirty taverns where one slept in a long dormitory room and ate questionable food, large cities such as Charleston usually boasted one or two excellent inns. The Bull and Boar fit into this category. It was a tidy brick building handy to the docks in order to attract travelers, but far enough away to keep out sailors and riffraff. The tavern sported a gracious public room as well as two small private dining rooms. Upstairs there were individual bedchambers to let. Though the furniture was not elegant, the beds were comfortable, and everything was maintained in a sparklingly clean condition.

The host, recognizing quality folk by their clothes, was overjoyed to put them up and quickly led the way to the nicest room available. Meredith was disappointed to find there would be no possibility of sleeping apart from her husband. The inn was obviously filled, and they were fortunate such an excellent chamber was still available. When the host had bowed his way out, Jeremy turned to Meredith with icy politeness. "I am going downstairs to eat. The trip made me hungry. Do you wish to join me?"

It was clear to Meredith that he hoped she would not. "No," she replied in an equally distant tone. "I would prefer a tray in my room. If you would be so kind as to tell the host . . ."

"Of course." Jeremy bowed perfunctorily and departed. Meredith wanted to fling herself on the bed and indulge in another good cry, but she took herself firmly in hand. She couldn't continue to give way to hysterics. Instead she unpacked her clothes and hung up her dresses to rid them of wrinkles. She doubted it would do the trick, and she would probably have to trust her clothes to be ironed by one of the inn's servants, always a tricky proposition with unfamiliar servants.

Jeremy grumpily stamped downstairs and into the public room, where he called for a large tankard of ale. As he drank he casually eyed the notices posted on one wall. There were advertisements of items for sale, notices of runaway slaves or indentured servants and rewards for their capture, departures of vessels for the West Indies and England, and one boldly lettered offer to buy good farmland in the coastal area. Jeremy's eyes narrowed. Had he not happened to see the notice, he probably would have done nothing about his earlier moody decision to sell Bitterleaf. But now he paused, frowning. He felt bitter, wronged, and furious with his stubborn wife. More than that, he realized how foolish he had been to swerve from his original idea of selling the plantation. It meant nothing to him. Meredith Whitney meant nothing to him. He glanced at the name across the bottom of the notice: John J. Emerson, Esq. He motioned to the tavern's owner.

"Yes, sir, may I help you?"

"Yes. Send a tray of food to my wife. She was tired from the journey and didn't wish to dine in the public room."

"Of course, sir."

"And could you tell me the location of this John J. Emerson?" He pointed to the bulletin.

"Oh, yes. He's a land agent, does a lot of buying and selling around here. A straightforward, honest man, too, as land agents go. His office is in the brown frame building next to the Market."

Jeremy's gut tightened. He remembered the Market well. Thanking the man, he tossed him payment for his ale and strode outside. He motioned to one of the street urchins dawdling in front of the inn, hoping to earn a few coins by running errands for its occupants. The lad came eagerly, and Jeremy gave the boy a coin to guide him to the Market.

They were not many blocks from there, for the Market was also near the docks. When they reached the Market, Jeremy quickly spotted the brown frame building on one of the streets surrounding it. He handed his guide another coin, and the boy ran off happily. Jeremy stood for a moment, gazing at the empty platform where he had been sold. Just seeing it, he felt the same sick humiliation in his gut. He couldn't get away from this savage land quickly enough, he thought.

Although it was dusk, Mr. Emerson was still in his small office on the second floor. A portly man with a round, beaming face, he looked innocent and cheerful, almost foolish. However, a few minutes' talk with him revealed a shrewd business mind beneath the mild exterior.

"I understand you're interested in good farmland?" Jeremy began.

"Why, yes. Come in and sit down. Have you any to sell?"

"I will have in a short time. A rather large plantation."

"An entire plantation?" Emerson's eyebrows rose suspiciously. "Is it unprofitable?"

"No. Just the opposite, in fact. I married into it, but I plan to return to England. The climate here doesn't agree with me."

"I see." Emerson pulled a long sheet of parchment closer to him and with his quill began to scratch almost indecipherable notes as he questioned Jeremy. Having maintained Bitterleaf's records for the past few weeks, Jeremy was able to reel off the production figures of the plantation, as well as its size, location, and the number of slaves working it.

"Then you'll be wanting to sell the slaves, too. With the plantation, or individually through a slave agent?"

Jeremy hadn't really thought about that aspect of it. "Oh, I don't know. With the land, I suppose." He was uncomfortable at the idea of selling them in any manner. Was there no other way to run a plantation, he wondered. He had experienced the deep bite of shame at being sold, and he disliked inflicting it upon any other human being.

Emerson remarked that it sounded like an excellent property, his tone implying a suspicion that it might be too good to be

true. Jeremy raised his eyebrows in imitation of his uncle,
Lord Wrexham, at his haughtiest. The other man lowered his
gaze. "I'll get in touch with you later by letter when I'm
certain about selling the land," Jeremy told him and rose to
go. Emerson followed Jeremy to the door and stood there for
several minutes after he left, gazing blankly at the hall. If the
lordly-acting man was telling the truth, he'd have no trouble
selling the land. Perhaps he'd take a little trip up the river and
check out Bitterleaf for himself, discover whether it was
really the jewel it appeared or merely a puff of lies.

Meredith was asleep when Jeremy finally returned to their
room. He had stopped in the tavern downstairs to eat supper
and lingered for several rounds of ale. For a moment he
considered taking the serving wench to bed. She was comely
enough—and he certainly did not owe his wife loyalty after
the way she had demeaned his skill and consideration, he
thought with a blaze of anger. But even the remembrance of
Meredith's contempt destroyed what little desire he had for
the wench. So he slammed down his last tankard in disgust
and clomped upstairs. He banged the door shut, but it didn't
awaken Meredith.

Jeremy flashed an irritated look at her inert form. How
could she sleep so easily? She had no more emotions than a
rock. He was a jangle of nerves. He peeled off his clothes and
hung them on a bedpost, then crawled into bed beside her,
blowing out the short candle that had lit his way upstairs.
The only light came from the unshuttered window, through
which moonlight streamed across the bed. Meredith rolled
toward Jeremy in her sleep, and the cover slid down her arm
to reveal a soft, rounded shoulder. She had dressed for bed in
another of Lydia's gowns, since Betsy had packed no other
kind. This one was of palest blue and had a deep V neck that
exposed a great deal of her rounded breasts.

Jeremy swallowed, the familiar fire kindling in his loins.
He eased down the covers farther and let his eyes examine her
freely. The gauzy material left little to the imagination. Her
breasts were practically falling out of the plunging neckline,
and the dark circles of her nipples were clearly visible. He
glanced at her legs. The gown had ridden up as she slept,

exposing a long expanse of calf and knee and thigh. His mouth went suddenly dry, and he couldn't keep from running a light finger down her side. She twitched a little but did not awaken.

He was a fool, Jeremy thought bitterly. In the morning Meredith would probably remind him how little pleasure he gave her. But right now he could think of nothing but his resurgent desire. He remembered her soft moans of helpless pleasure, and her cry as she peaked when he had loved her the second time. He *had* pleased her. He was sure of it. Her response couldn't have been faked—and besides, when she cared so little for him, why would she even try to fake pleasure?

Shoving down the strap of her gown, he brushed her shoulder with his lips. One breast fell free, a soft, inviting hill with a tantalizing pink crest. His blood thrummed in his temples until he couldn't think. He wanted her. Oh, God, how he wanted her. She was his wife. He had every right to make love to her. Jeremy bent to kiss the nipple. His mouth opened wider to take it in and his tongue began its searing circle. She would want him. Dear God, he would *make* her want him as much as he did her.

Meredith drifted to consciousness in a sea of pleasant sensations. Something was tugging at her breast, and she moaned softly. Her emotions and body more than her mind registered the knowledge that Jeremy was creating the pleasure. Instinctively her hands sank into his thick hair, fingertips kneading his scalp. "Jeremy," she sighed and rubbed her cheek against the top of his head. Then she came to full consciousness and jerked away. "Jeremy! What are you doing!"

He raised his head, his eyes heavy-lidded with desire. "What does it feel like?" he hissed.

Meredith glared. "I assumed that after today you wouldn't care to repeat your performance!"

Jeremy wet his lips, striving to control his temper, and finally managed a small smile. Nodding at her bared breast, he commented, "The style suits you."

Meredith glanced down and gasped to see that a strap had slid down her arm until one perfect globe was revealed. She started to pull up the gown, but Jeremy reached out to stay her hand.

"Why are you fighting it? You know you want to make love as badly as I do."

"That's not true," Meredith protested, her voice breaking on a sob. "Oh, Jeremy, why must you humiliate me?"

"Humiliate you!" he exploded. "Is that what my lovemaking does to you? First you say I hurt and abused you. You inform me I am the same as any other man. Now you tell me it's a humiliation to bed me. Why? Because I'm a bastard? A servant? What? Or is any man's touch degrading? Are none of us as satisfying as your 'dear cousin'?" His voice dripped sarcasm.

"I have no comparison!" she spat. "You know I've never been with any other man."

"Yes, I know it very well. Then it must be only I who am so utterly abhorrent. Tell me, if that's true, what were the whimpers and moans I heard last night? Who put those scratches on my back?"

"Ohhh," Meredith moaned and turned her face into her pillow. "I hate you!" she cried in a muffled voice.

"Why? Because you respond to me?"

"I *don't* respond to you!" she lied desperately.

"The hell you don't." His words were low and thick.

His fingers dug into her arms and swung her back to him. Not giving her a chance to protest, he ground his lips into hers. Against her will, her lips opened, and their tongues clashed in a battle of pleasure. His kiss sucked her willpower from her—her very soul, she thought wretchedly. When at last he ended the kiss, he nipped and sucked at her lips. Then he left her mouth to tease her earlobes and trace the convolutions of her ear with his hot tongue. He rolled the nightgown down her body, following it with his expert mouth. Meredith was lost in a hot haze, all sense of time and reason vanished. She knew only his skin on hers and his hot tongue probing every part of her. She writhed and gripped his shoulders, shuddering in her ache to have him.

Jeremy understood her need, but he was not ready yet to fulfill it. Instead he continued to stroke and torment, lightly fingering the hot chasm of her passions, stroking her hard pleasure button until she gasped and groaned his name, then exploded in shattering pleasure. But still he was not content. His mouth drifted lower, tasting the sweet nectar of her love, gently reviving the pounding hunger his fingers had just satisfied. "No," she moaned. "Oh, no."

"Oh, yes," he whispered back huskily, whipping her into a frenzy of longing with his agile tongue.

She twisted beneath him, her fingernails digging into his shoulders. "Please, Jeremy, please."

He moved to position himself between her legs, his manhood teasing at her gates. "Tell me," he growled. "Say you want me."

"Yes," she gasped. "Yes, I want you. Oh, Jeremy, how I want you. Please love me. Please."

Slowly Jeremy sank into her satiny welcome, and a deep sigh of pleasure escaped her throat. He pulled almost out, then rammed home. He could hold back no longer. Her words melted him, sent hot shafts hurtling through his abdomen. He crushed Meredith to him, his hips churning, pouring out all his accumulated passion and fury and hurt into her receptive womb. "Meredith, Meredith . . ." They crashed together in a white-hot flame of passion, shuddering beneath the force of the collision, so fiercely united there seemed to be not even skin between them. They were one quivering being, melded in the fires of their desire.

Ever so slowly they relaxed, their minds and senses returning from the far-flung stars, and they divided into two people again. Jeremy sank back into his pillow, the sweat on his body cold in the night air. It seemed to take a conscious effort to breathe. He extended a hand to clasp Meredith's and raised it to his lips. He was aware of a hundred sentiments crowding his mind that he wanted to express, but he was incapable of saying any of them. So they lay side by side in a state of bliss, only their hands touching. For a moment they had been so close that no more contact was needed. Their souls retained the oneness.

Chapter XVIII

MEREDITH AWOKE slowly, stretching like a well-fed cat. Then memories of the night before rushed into her mind, and she colored, pulling the sheet up to her nose. My heavens, she thought, she had behaved like an overheated wanton. Oh, how was she to face Jeremy ever again? He knew everything about her, and had her completely in his power. She realized now what he meant by taking his revenge. It was not a physical punishment, but a mental one. He could control her completely by using her desire for him. How he must have laughed inside! Tears crept into Meredith's eyes, and she turned away from Jeremy, lying beside her. It was bad enough to be plain and unable to attract a husband without paying him, but then to give herself to that man so utterly, to expose her innermost feelings, her basest longings! He must despise her. Yet he would continue to bed her just to prove his mastery—and she would be unable to say no.

Callused fingers ran down the column of her spine, and Meredith turned to see Jeremy's relaxed, smiling face. "Good morning, my love."

She blushed and turned back. "Good morning," she mumbled.

Jeremy frowned. Surely Meredith wasn't going to begin the idiotic quarreling of the day before. He nuzzled her neck. "You look lovely this morning. Lovemaking suits you."

253

"Don't." Her voice was low and agonized. "Don't taunt me."

"Taunt you?" he echoed, surprised. "What are you talking about?"

"I know how laughable I must appear to you."

"Laughable! My dear girl, the effect you have on me is anything but laughable." With one strong hand he pressed her firmly onto her back so he could look into her eyes. When Meredith rolled her head to the side, he grasped her chin and forced her to remain still. "Look at me. I want to know what this drivel is all about. Obviously you have some wild, harebrained idea that makes you deny by day everything your body reveals at night. Why? Why did you try your damnedest yesterday to put distance between us? To hurt me so badly I wouldn't ever approach your sweet body again?"

"Hurt you?" Meredith blinked. "What did I say to hurt you?"

"You think telling a man he is no different from every other man in bed will not pain him? Or that it wouldn't cut him to ribbons when you said he gloried in your abuse, especially when he had suppressed his own desire most viciously just to make it good for you!"

Meredith frowned. "I never thought—I didn't mean to hurt you, really. But you were so disgustingly pleased with yourself, whereas I felt so shamed."

"I *was* pleased. Why not show it? I was quite magnificently satisfied for the first time in weeks. Would you rather I pretended to be displeased with you?"

"Well, no, of course not. Jeremy, you're twisting my words."

"No, it's your head that's twisted, not my words. Why did you feel shamed?"

"The way you spoke of it—'spearing,' as if we had been at war and you won. I wasn't a person, but a conquest!"

Jeremy studied her solemnly for a moment. "All right. I apologize for my choice of words. Perhaps I was too crude for a new bride. I didn't mean to make you feel lowered or cheap. I valued you." He grinned. "Oh, Lord, how I valued you."

"How could you?" she cried softly. "What is there to

value in an ugly, hulking female like me!'' Tears suddenly gushed from her eyes, and she raised her hands to hide them. ''Oh, God, and now I'm crying in front of you. You must be thoroughly disgusted with me.''

''Meredith!'' Quickly his arms went around her. ''I'm not in the slightest disgusted by you. Dismayed, yes, for you have the most peculiar notions I've ever heard. But not disgusted.''

''How can you not be? I'm so horribly filled with—with desire!'' Jeremy gaped, momentarily speechless. ''It's so silly for a plain woman to be lusting after a man when no man wants her. It's shameful.''

Jeremy wet his lips, glimpsing the years of hurt and agonizing shyness that lay behind her words. He was flooded with compassion for her. Hugging her closer, he rained kisses on her hair and neck. He could not kiss her face, for she had burried it in his chest in a paroxysm of shame.

''Do you honestly think,'' he whispered into her ear, ''that what happened last night left me unaffected? You weren't the only one to feel lust, you know. I was a throbbing, mindless shaft, driven by pure instinct to find my housing. You say no man wants you, but I wanted you desperately. Are you telling me I'm not a man? It's a point I'll dispute.''

Meredith emitted a small, tearful chuckle. ''No, I don't contend that. I know very well you are a man.'' She paused, then asked tentatively, hope quavering in her voice, ''Did you really desire me?''

''Of course I did! God, how can you ask that? Meredith, I'll tell you something truthfully. I wouldn't have dreamed I'd say this to any woman, but last night when we made love, I reached a place I've never been before. I experienced a sensation I can't begin to describe. I've yearned for you for weeks and weeks, ached for you until I thought I'd die from it. Do you know the first time I wanted you?'' She shook her head in silent wonder. He continued, ''That first day on the scow taking us to Bitterleaf. Your stepfather had purchased me the day before. I sat and stared at you and dreamed about getting you into my bed.''

His statement startled her so that Meredith jerked away to

stare at him. "Are you serious? I thought you hated me, the way you glared."

He laughed shortly. "Well, you certainly put me in my place. I thought I was shooting provocative, fiery looks at you."

Meredith giggled, brushing at the wetness on her cheeks. "They probably were. I was too inexperienced to understand," she said shakily. She moved over in the bed, pulling her knees to her chin and wrapping her arms around her legs. She sank into a thoughtful study. Jeremy admired her naked form, although her hunched posture successfully hid what he most wished to see. Reclining on his elbow, he waited for her to deliver her next bombshell. Finally she resumed, eyes averted. "But why? I mean, I have such long legs and such an ungainly body. I'm not at all attractive."

"Would you let me be the judge of that? I'm a bit more qualified, you know." He ran a hand over the inverted V her legs made. "Your legs are long, but that's not unattractive. Quite the opposite. They're slender and shapely and make a man want to run his hands up the whole length of them until he reaches the treasure. You have beautiful legs. And as for your body, you are statuesque, my love, and not a bit ungainly." His hand insinuated itself between her legs, smoothly stroking until she relaxed and lay back, her legs sliding down into a clean, straight line. He cupped one breast. "Your breasts are perfect—beautiful, touchable, kissable, and exactly the size to fit my palm." He bent to kiss each one. "Oh, Meredith, your body is lovely, and if I continue this praise much longer, we'll not get downstairs to eat breakfast."

Meredith smiled in a teasing way quite unlike herself. "And is breakfast so important?"

He groaned. "Oh, my lovely, lovely vixen." His mouth fastened on hers, and soon they were lost in the ocean of their lovemaking.

A long time later, when they had again scaled the heights that seemed impossible when recalled, they lay together in close, companionable content. Lazily, Jeremy traced the line of her arm with his thumbnail. Finally he remarked, "I've just thought of how we shall spend our time here in Charleston!"

"What do you mean? I thought we were going to see a play tonight." Her voice was tinged with disappointment.

"So we shall. But we have the whole day before us, and while it is tempting to think of spending it in bed with you, I have something important to do."

"Oh," she said flatly. "And what is that?"

"Take you to a dressmaker."

"What? Why? I have plenty of clothes."

"None that suit me. I've been considering what you said earlier. You have a very incorrect view of yourself, Meredith. For some reason, you've come to think of yourself as plain."

"For some reason?" she repeated sarcastically. "You know very well why— it's the truth!"

"It isn't. True, no one sees your naked body, which is your most beautiful aspect—and I'm heartily glad that only *I* shall witness your splendors. But you don't capitalize on your other assets. You try to appear as plain as possible."

"If you were tall and clumsy, you'd do your best to appear inconspicuous, too!" Meredith retorted hotly.

"In case you haven't noticed, my dear, I am tall. And I didn't become a wallflower to try to hide that fact."

"But you're gorgeous!" she blurted, then flushed. "That is, I mean . . . well, you *are* handsome. Surely you're aware of it. Besides, you're a man. It's considered attractive for a man to be tall."

"Look. You are close to six feet tall. There is no way on earth you can change or hide that, unless you'd like to chop off your feet, which I don't recommend."

Meredith had to smile. "And what *do* you recommend?"

"Since you can't fade into the wall, don't try. Do the opposite. Dress with style and flair. Buy beautiful clothes to suit your coloring and show off your figure. Don't skin back your hair into as tight a knot as possible. Let it wave and curl. Pile it on top of your head and show off your graceful neck. Smile. Be proud of yourself. If you're confident, it will glow in your face. Maybe you can't be a pretty porcelain doll like Opal Hamilton"—so he did admire Opal! Meredith thought— "but you can be striking, unusual, even handsome. At the very least, you'll improve your looks." He paused, aware of her doubtful face. "And that's why we are visiting the dress-maker and milliner today."

Meredith would have preferred not to. She dreaded the glazed look that came over a dressmaker's eyes when she was confronted by Meredith's towering form. However, after Jeremy's glowing praise of her figure and the lovemaking that had left her warm and languid, she thought she would have agreed to go anywhere he suggested. Jeremy caressed her hips and reluctantly left the bed. Dumping half the pitcher of water into the basin, he washed and lathered his face and began to shave. Meredith arose and washed with far less shyness than the day before. Jeremy told her an amusing story about his dancing master, and Meredith laughed aloud.

"That's a pretty sound."

"What?" Meredith asked.

"Your laughter. I haven't heard it often. Usually I get the other side of your tongue."

Meredith glanced down, a little abashed, and tried to divert the subject. "And will you hire a dancing master like yours?"

"Why?"

"You promised to teach me to dance."

"And *I* will teach you. Not some vagabond who titles himself a dancing master." He wiped the soap from his face and held his hand toward her. "Here. I shall show you the minuet."

He led her through the steps of a minuet, instructing her where to place her feet and how to curtsy, sway, and mince around him. At first Meredith listened gravely and sought to follow his directions, but soon the humor of the situation overcame her. She burst into a giggle. "What now?" Jeremy asked, arms akimbo, feigning ill humor.

"I don't know. It's a—a trifle unusual, don't you think? To have a dancing lesson with neither one of us wearing a stitch!"

His lips twitched, but he managed to keep his face straight as he replied, "I don't know. It adds a certain flair to our movements."

"Then perhaps I should try it with a dancing master. Or at our next party."

He grimaced and tapped her bottom lightly with the flat of his hand. "Minx."

Meredith hummed as she dressed, and Jeremy smiled to see the glow on her face. Lovemaking had made her almost pretty, put a sparkle in her eyes and color in her cheeks. Once he had her dressed properly, she would be more than presentable. Not commonplace pretty, but unique. Individual. His very own, one-of-a-kind Meredith. Saucy, laughing, frowning, intelligent, impudent, outspoken, kind, shy Meredith.

"Now where is the best dressmaker?" Jeremy asked Meredith as they left the tavern after a hearty breakfast. Seeing her hesitate, he added, "You might as well tell me, or I'll ask the name and directions from one of these good citizens walking by."

"Very well. Her name is Madame Reveneau. She owns a small shop off Broad Street." They started off briskly along the cobblestoned streets, a feature of the city of which Charlestonians were justifiably proud. Charleston was one of the largest cities in the colonies, a major port, and considered to be an art center in the raw land. Its citizens prided themselves on the sophistication and progress of the city, pointing out its cobbled streets, graceful Anglican churches, and the theater that often housed a traveling troupe of actors.

The dressmaker's shop was in a narrow, two-story, white brick building. Madame Reveneau lived in the apartment above the shop. She was a small, plump, bustling woman dressed in dark green, rustling silk. Her dark hair was drawn back in a smooth but elegant style. Jeremy, glancing at her attire and the store, decided she had good taste. The wooden floor was covered by an Oriental carpet in delicate grays and blues that blended well with the pale blue of the walls. A pleasant fire burned in the small fireplace, and before it were placed two wing chairs and a short sofa.

"Madam, Monsieur, welcome to my humble shop. How may I serve you today?" Her eyes flickered over Meredith, assessing the expensive but unattractive brown dress and Meredith's tall form.

Meredith didn't reply, but Jeremy smiled charmingly and

said, "Madame, my wife needs a complete wardrobe, and we are here to place ourselves in your capable hands."

The woman's eyes gleamed. "Thank you, you are too kind. Please sit down." She motioned toward the chairs. "May I offer you tea? Hot chocolate, perhaps? Then we can choose styles and materials, eh?"

Meredith started to decline, but Jeremy responded, "Certainly." He pulled his wife down on the sofa beside him while the dressmaker vanished into the back room of the shop to get the refreshments.

"Jeremy, that is too much!" Meredith protested in an undertone. "A whole new wardrobe!"

"Call it your Christmas present. Don't worry. Bitterleaf can afford it. I'm very familiar with the plantation's profits."

"Well, perhaps we can afford it, but it's needlessly extravagant."

"How could dressing the mistress of the plantation be needless?"

"It's still Daniel's land," she said, trying a new tack. "He might not appreciate your spending his money."

"Then why would he have given it to me? Come, come, Meredith, you know he wouldn't deny you clothes. You're scarcely dressed in rags now, and neither is Lydia. And think of all he purchased for me. Wouldn't he do as much for you?"

"Well, of course, if it were reasonable. But since I already have ample clothes and he bought that ring for my wedding present—"

"That wasn't bought with Daniel's money," Jeremy interrupted almost roughly. "The ring was mine."

"Yours?"

"Yes. Do you think I'm such a poor judge of the size of a lady's hand? It was my mother's, given to her by my father. It was a mere trinket, but the one she treasured the most."

"But how did you keep it? I mean, when those ruffians abducted you, surely they wouldn't have balked at theft, too."

He shrugged. "They didn't see it. The ring was so small I wore it on a chain around my neck. They didn't notice it when they hit me on the head. When I awoke on board and

realized what had happened to me, I secreted it in the waistband of my breeches.''

"But you could have used it to purchase your freedom.''

"I would never sell it,'' he replied, setting his jaw grimly.

"Yet you gave it to me?''

"That's entirely different. You are my wife. You should
have whatever bit of a family heirloom I own. Besides, I
wanted to give you something truly mine, not a gift purchased
with Daniel's money.''

"Oh.'' The idea surprised and warmed Meredith, but she
didn't have time to pursue the topic, for Madame Reveneau
bustled back into the room with a tea tray. While they sipped
the tea, served in rare porcelain cups, Madame Reveneau
brought out several "fashion babies'' recently arrived from
England so that Meredith could select the styles she liked.

As Meredith studied the dolls, Jeremy turned to the other
woman. "What would you suggest for my wife? I imagine
your judgment is excellent.''

"Well,'' the dressmaker said shrewdly, "this one is too
covered with frills and furbelows. It would make you look
fussy.'' She set the doll aside. "But this dress has clean lines,
only two modest bows to hold up the draping of the skirt over
the petticoat. The sleeves aren't overdone and dripping with
lace. A simple dress, but well-suited to a tall woman. So is
this one. Molinist panniers.'' She indicated the swagged material on each side. "Some panniers are so padded and puffed
they make a tall woman seem a giantess. But not these.''

"Aren't the necklines a trifle low?''

"But yes, that is the style. And you, my dear, have a
lovely bosom. No reason to hide it. Let the small-chested
ones fill up the necks with ruffles and lace. You fill it
naturally, and with something more worth seeing. Isn't that
right, monsieur?''

"Indubitably.''

Madame Reveneau smiled. She liked the gentleman. He reminded her of men at home, charming and free with their
money. With him buying, this job would be a treat, even
though the woman was a difficult subject to dress. Actually,
she would be a refreshing challenge—and it was obvious the
husband would allow Madame free rein. She wouldn't have

to accede to the customer's poor taste, as she often did. "I have the very thing for this style. Emerald satin." She rose and went to a table, where she dug through bolts of material, returning armed with a gleaming green satin. Deftly she spun the bolt out across the table. "There. Isn't it superb? Your eyes are green, are they not, madame?" She bent to peer into Meredith's face. "Yes, I thought so, somewhere between green and hazel. This satin will make it obvious they are green, not muddy. A pale green petticoat, I think, don't you? A few ruffles merely, let us say three rows. Here, here, and here." She demonstrated on the doll. "And a stomacher of the same pale green embroidered with emerald thread. I have an Oriental design that will be precisely the thing for it."

"Well . . ." Meredith temporized. She loved the rich green satin. In fact, she was practically salivating at the imaginary gown Madame Reveneau described. But herself in that dress?

"Yes, exactly," Jeremy cut in. "What other treats do you have in store for us?"

Before the morning was over, Madame Reveneau had pulled out rich gold velvet, rose-pink silk, a satin of dazzling white, several pastel Indian cottons and lawns for summer wear, a hand-painted linen of tangled rose vines against an ivory background, and muslin, gauze, and lace for dainty summer dresses and delicate underthings. Meredith's head was reeling at the quantity of material and designs. Not to mention the colors! Never had she worn anything like them. Some were bold, deep colors like jewels, others delicate pastels. The dressmaker assured her she could wear either with flair.

"You have a good complexion for them. Basic, vivid colors and their paler hues. Just don't wear yellow-tinged colors—ochers, olive greens, dead browns. They'll turn you sallow. Pick true shades and lean toward the blue and red tones. They will bring out the color in your cheeks. Your hair can take any hue, as can your eyes. But—if I may be so bold, madame—you ought to wear your hair in a different style. This style harshens the lines of your face. You need a trifle more fullness and softness. A few curls, perhaps a little pouf." Carefully she slipped out a few wisps of hair around

Meredith's face and coaxed them into delicate curls. "There. Isn't that much better?"

Meredith gazed into the hand mirror that Madame Reveneau held up before her. The curls did make her face look softer and prettier. She could wear the style, she agreed, although it seemed too girlish for a married woman. Even some more fullness might be all right, for Jeremy could withstand the extra height it would give her. As long as she didn't dwarf her husband, did it really matter if other men were shorter than she? For the first time, Meredith experienced the security of a married woman. She had a husband, and the opinion of other men no longer counted. She could do as she wished. It was a heady thought.

Madame escorted her charge into the dressing room at the back to take Meredith's measurements. For once, Meredith experienced none of her usual awkwardness in such a situation. Madame Reveneau did not shake her head or click her tongue over Meredith's size, as so many dressmakers had in the past. When Meredith gratefully mentioned it to her, the French woman laughed. "Why should I? There is nothing wrong with your measurements. They are in perfect proportion. It won't be difficult to make your clothes. Those others—they simply didn't have the skill or the perception to dress you properly, so they tried to make it appear your fault, not their own lack of competence."

Meredith had never visited Madame's shop before, believing such a respected modiste would treat her with even more contempt than ordinary seamstresses. Now she wished she had come earlier. It hadn't been a terrible experience, although she trembled inside to think what all those rich colors would look like on her. When she dressed and returned to the front room of the shop, Jeremy paid the woman, and Madame promised full delivery of the dresses to Bitterleaf within a month. "I will set my girls on it night and day, I assure you. It will be a pleasure."

Next they stopped at a hat shop, but here Meredith balked more than at the dress store. She accepted one wide-brimmed straw hat that dipped down all around and was decorated with a trailing clump of bright red wooden cherries. It did not add to her height and would look splendid with the hand-painted linen dress splashed with red roses. She agreed to the soft, dark green velvet cap, boat-shaped with the point trailing down onto her forehead and enlivened by a saucy green cockade, because with it on she remained shorter than her husband. But when Jeremy spied a straw hat covered with a spill of pink satin bows and feathers and insisted she try it on, Meredith blushed and shook her head. It sat on the back of one's head, and the brim tilted up. The profusion of satin and feathers added several more inches to the hat, so that the top of it would be higher than even Jeremy's golden head.

"No. It's impossible."

"Why?" Jeremy protested. "I think it will look charming on you. Try it on."

Meredith plunked it on her head. "You see?"

"See what? I see that it looks adorable on you, and I insist you buy it."

"No! It makes me taller than you!"

He roared with laughter. "My dear Meredith, do you think that *I* will be intimidated because one of your hats happens to reach higher than I? My God, I'm scarcely frightened of seeming short!"

Meredith stared doubtfully at her image. It *was* a darling hat, and it framed her face prettily. She had never owned such a fanciful thing before. And if Jeremy didn't mind . . . "All right," she agreed slowly. "I shall get it."

She grew more adventurous after that, accepting a wide-brimmed, shallow-crowned straw hat that turned down slightly on one side and up on the other, ornamented by a great clump of satin bows on the up side. However, even Jeremy laughingly agreed that the "peasant" hat, which resembled an upside-down bucket covered with linen frills and ruchings, was not for her.

Finally, exhausted, they made their way back to the tavern for a late lunch and retired to their rooms. "What shall we do now?" Meredith asked as she sank into the chair and gratefully pushed off her slippers. "You promised Daniel you would purchase the new seed he needs."

"Later. Or perhaps tomorrow. Right now I have something else in mind." He shrugged out of his coat and began to unfasten the vest buttons.

"What?" Meredith looked up at him and saw the unmistakable light in his eyes. "Jeremy! In the middle of the afternoon?"

"Why not?" He retorted and came toward her, hands outstretched. With a little giggle, Meredith moved into his arms.

They stayed another day in Charleston. Jeremy had business to conduct for Daniel, including buying seed for the plantation and making sure the supply was loaded into the flatboat that would take them home the following day. They also paid a mandatory visit to Meredith's aunt and uncle. Unaware that Jeremy was an indentured servant Hurley had purchased on his last visit to Charleston, the Spencers stared at him in surprise and awe. Phoebe openly gaped. Meredith knew her cousin longed to ask how Meredith had hooked such a handsome, sophisticated gentleman. Meredith was careful not to enlighten them. Their obligations dispensed with, they devoted the rest of their time to enjoying their trip. They attended the theater, where David Douglas's troupe was performing. Douglas maintained a "wandering theater" and had built his own playhouses for his company in several major cities. Even Jeremy had to admit that the performance was "not bad, for the colonies." They dropped by the studio of Jeremiah Theus, the most famous portrait artist of Charleston. Jeremy admired his work and declared that when Meredith's new gowns were ready, he would have the man paint her portrait. "That is," he continued in an undertone, "unless you'd rather wait to be painted with our babes at your feet."

Meredith colored and glanced away. "We may not have any."

He chuckled. "I wouldn't count on it, my dear. Considering the amount of time we spend on the project . . ."

"Hush! What a thing to talk about in public!"

"Then let's return to the inn to discuss it in private."

That was how they spent most of their brief stay, cuddled together in bed, laughing, talking, making love. Jeremy seemed insatiable, and Meredith knew she was equally passionate, though she demurely tried to hide it. She had never known a man's touch of affection. Now, lying within the hard, protective circle of Jeremy's arms, she realized what she had missed—

and would have continued to miss the rest of her life if she
hadn't given in to Daniel. Perhaps her stepfather had been
right. Jeremy did not love her, of course, but he made love to
her splendidly, bringing her a joy she had never imagined
existed. He brought forth her laughter—teasing her, tickling,
relating ribald stories of his life in London, engaging in quick
verbal sparring with her. He even managed to make her seem
small and dainty, stretched out beside his great body. Most of
all, with him she felt special, secure, almost attractive. Jeremy
appeared as enraptured by her body as she was by his.
He would caress her, extolling the virtues of each part of her
body as his hand passed over it. He kissed and stroked,
discovered every tiny spot vulnerable to his touch, and showed
Meredith how to arouse him in turn. Meredith learned eagerly,
although she tried to maintain a modest attitude regarding the
process. It thrilled her to turn Jeremy hot and liquid with
desire. She was astounded that her novice touch could bring a
flush to his skin or cause his muscles to jump and tense or
draw those sweet, incoherent noises of tormented pleasure
from his lips.

Jeremy was fully as amazed as Meredith. Although he had
been hot for her, he had expected his fire to cool quickly.
Instead, he found he desired her all the time. Seemingly, the
more he possessed her, the more he wanted her. At first,
Meredith's reserve had challenged him, but now she responded,
her attempts at maidenly reticence quite transparent. She was
happy to touch and kiss him, with little of the shyness or fear
of many ladies. Meredith had been so gawky as she grew up
that the adults around her hadn't tried to make sure she would
zealously guard her precious virginity. She had not been
badgered and preached to or warned against evil men and her
own frail nature. She hadn't had to hold off too ardent suitors
and suppress her own desires. So now her passion flowed
forth freely—after she got over her initial fear and shame at
her supposed lack of beauty. She was ardent, yet without the
bored skill of a prostitute—a willing, winning bedmate.

It was even more surprising to Jeremy that he didn't tire of
her even when they were not making love. Meredith's conversation was witty and her observation keen. He could speak on
any subject without losing her, for even if it was a matter

foreign to her, she was eager to learn and caught on quickly.
He considered returning to the land agent and telling him he
had decided not to sell Bitterleaf, but he put it off, preferring
to dally in their chamber with Meredith. He had told Emerson
he would contact him when the land was for sale. If he never
wrote the agent, the matter would die a natural death.

The morning they were to leave Charleston, Jeremy awoke
Meredith with a kiss and crawled out of bed to shave and
dress. Meredith yawned, stretching sleepily, and sat up in bed
to watch him. She was naked, her hair tumbling riotously
over her shoulders and partially hiding her breasts, the bedsheets
tangled and rumpled around her. No longer did she feel any
embarrassment at her husband's seeing her this way.

Meredith hated to leave. It would have been glorious to
spend a few more days alone with Jeremy, far away from the
worries and responsibilities of Bitterleaf. She wondered if
they would ever again have this blessed freedom and happiness.
Here they had been released from the roles they had to play at
home. Now she would have to be a lady and mistress of the
plantation. Would that mean Jeremy would no longer want
her to be his wanton, hungry partner in bed? Would he expect
her to be a lady? She remembered what Opal had told her
about men. Did they truly want their wives to be chaste even
with them? Certainly Jeremy had shown no desire for her to
be anything but as passionate as she had been. But that could
have been engendered by the strangeness of their surroundings.

"Jeremy, could I ask you a question?" she began tentatively.
It was an awkward topic, but their relationship here had been
so open and free, surely he would be honest with her. "Opal
told me something the other day, at the wedding party, in
fact. I—wondered if it was true."

He glanced at her in the mirror. "What?"

"Well, she said men expected something different in their
wives. I mean, from what they want in a mistress."

Jeremy casually continued to stroke the razor down his
cheek. "I suppose that's true. Virtue is usually accounted a
more valuable property in a wife. No man enjoys being wed
to a strumpet."

Her throat froze. It was true, then. She almost could not go
on, but she had to know for certain. She couldn't repel

Jeremy by her coarse actions at home if that was how he felt. She would have to dissemble about her desires. "Then—then you would prefer a wife who was not . . . experienced?"

"You mean, who hadn't known another man?" He frowned, trying to imagine his feelings if he had found Meredith not to be a virgin. He was aware of a definite stab of jealousy.

"No. I mean, would you prefer a wife who didn't, well, enjoy the bed part of marriage?"

He spun around to face her, his eyebrows shooting up in amazement. "Lord, no! It's far better to have a woman who wants me, who enjoys my touch." His voice thickened. "The way you do." He paused. "Meredith, what does this inquiry mean?"

"It's what Opal told me. She said I must remember that men like different qualities in a wife. They want a virtuous woman, one who accepts her husband's advances but doesn't take too much pleasure in it."

Jeremy rolled his eyes in disgust. "What tripe. I can't speak for other men, but if you enjoy our coupling and pretend not to so as to appear virtuous, I'll probably snap your neck. Opal Hamilton was merely jealous."

Relief washed over Meredith, but his last words nagged at her. Jealous? Why would Opal Hamilton be jealous, unless she had lain with Jeremy and didn't want another woman to enjoy the caresses she had known. Had he been with her? Meredith longed to ask, but even her boldness didn't extend that far. In truth, she really had no wish to know.

Jeremy finished shaving, then glanced at her still sitting in silence on the bed. "Now what idiotic thing are you dreaming up?" he teased fondly. "I'll tell you the truth, Meredith. If you don't put on some clothes, I'll be tempted to crawl back into bed, and we won't catch our boat."

"Really?" Meredith flashed him a pleased smile.

"Really." Her astonished eagerness for compliments touched Jeremy. What a marvelous woman had been strapped down inside her for so long! Who had encouraged her to value herself so little? Probably those damned Whitneys, he thought darkly, conveniently forgetting that when he first met Meredith, he, too, had labeled her gawky and unattractive. "You are a very beguiling creature, sitting there amidst the tumbled sheets, your breasts peeking out through your hair. It's almost an open invitation.''

"Almost?" She smiled sensually, her eyes promising the delights he knew so well.

"Damn," he breathed. "You *are* a vixen. Now get up and dress before I forget myself."

Meredith slid out of bed and dressed quickly, arranging her hair as well as she could in a way Jeremy liked. When she returned to Bitterleaf, she would ask Lydia to show Betsy how to dress her hair. At the thought of Lydia, her heart plummeted into her stomach. That was something else she had been free of these past few days: her husband's involvement with Lydia. Would he drop Meredith flat and go back to his mistress? Meredith didn't think she could bear it if he did. Or would he keep them both, using either when the fancy struck him? That prospect didn't appeal, either. She wished Jeremy had never met Lydia. He might eulogize Meredith's body now, but he wouldn't when he compared it to Lydia's!

"Ready, my love?" Jeremy asked, holding out her pelisse.

Meredith summoned up a smile. The words "my love" came so readily to his lips, but she knew they had no meaning to him. "Yes. Let's go home."

Chapter XIX

IT WAS dusk when the flatboat on which they rode pulled up to the wooden dock of Bitterleaf. A slave boy who sat on the wharf watching for the arrival of visitors clanged the dock bell as soon as the boat drew close enough for him to distinguish Meredith's features. By the time the boat docked, the overseer was there to supervise the unloading of the cargo. He cast a baleful eye at Meredith and Jeremy and snapped at the slaves to get to work. The slave children had also gathered, eager for the candy Daniel always brought. Not forgetting his custom, Meredith had purchased hard sugarplums in Charleston, and Jeremy now tossed them out.

They had reached the circular pathway behind the garden when Lydia hurried toward them from the porch, arms outstretched. "Meredith, oh, I'm so glad to see you. It's seemed like ages."

Meredith stepped into her embrace, conscious of Jeremy's eyes upon them. She felt at least a foot taller than the other woman. "There's nothing wrong with Daniel, is there?"

"No, I didn't mean that. He's grown steadily worse, of course. It's as we feared. He stored all his energy for your wedding. Since then he hasn't left his bed. I've given him the pain medicine you left, and at least he's slept well because of it." Tears flooded her eyes. "Oh, Meredith!"

"I know. I know." Meredith patted her on the back,

unable to offer any more comfort. She could not believe
Lydia didn't possess a great deal of feeling for Daniel. Why
then had she betrayed him with Jeremy? Meredith supposed it
was Jeremy's great physical attraction, which seemed to over-
whelm all women. After all, consider the way she herself had
succumbed, when she had fully intended to dislike him.

After a moment Lydia sniffed and straightened, dabbing at
her eyes. "I'm sorry. Let's go upstairs. Daniel will be anxious to see you. How was your trip?" she continued brightly
as they followed her into the house. She grinned knowingly at
Meredith. "Obviously marriage agrees with you. You're absolutely radiant."

Meredith's stomach fluttered sickly. Lydia knew all too
well the marvelous effect of Jeremy's lovemaking. "Thank
you. Charleston was very nice."

"I'm sorry you didn't get to stay any longer, but with
Daniel so sick . . ."

"I know. We're needed here."

When they stepped into Daniel's room, Meredith had to
suppress a gasp. Daniel looked at least ten years older than he
had four days ago. His cheeks were ashen, and the dark eyes
beneath the folds of skin were dull, almost lifeless. He was
sliding inexorably toward death. Meredith burned with frustration and anger. With all her skill at medicine, why was this the
one case she could do nothing for? Forcing herself to smile,
she stepped forward. "Hello, Daniel."

"Meredith," he murmured. "How was the wedding trip?"

"Lovely, but it's better to be home again," Meredith lied
valiantly. Stepping closer, she lowered her mouth almost to
his ear to whisper. "And, Daniel, you were right about
marrying him."

The ghost of a smile touched his lips, and he patted her
arm weakly. "I knew I was. I'm glad."

Jeremy came forward to speak to him, and Daniel seemed
eager to hear about the purchases Jeremy had made and the
work he would begin the next day. Despite his illness, he
retained his deep love for Bitterleaf. After a few moments,
however, his voice faded and his eyelids began to droop.
Meredith and Jeremy excused themselves, claiming they had
to wash off the grime of travel. Outside in the hall, Meredith

paused and brushed surreptitiously at her eyes. Jeremy's arm
went around her shoulders, and he squeezed gently. Without
a word, they crossed the hall to her room.

But it was his room now as well. Space had been cleared in
her wardrobe for his clothes and room made in the drawers of
the chest. Daniel's valet, Joseph, came in to unpack Jeremy's
bags. It was strange to watch him lay out Jeremy's shaving
equipment on the tall shaving stand that had been added to the
room's furniture. Strange, but not unwelcome.

There was much to be done around the house and plantation.
Meredith concentrated on putting the household back in order
after the fast-paced last few weeks. She took over the household inventories from Jeremy, who cheerfully informed her
that she could have all the accounts as far as he was concerned.
She was delighted to take them over. In addition to checking
the stock of winter supplies and replenishing as best she could
what had been severely depleted by the engagement party and
wedding feast, Meredith reviewed the books to familiarize
herself with what had transpired since she had last kept them.

There were sick slaves to be tended to, for now was the
season of colds and fevers, except for the deadly swamp fever,
which came in spring and summer. There were also frequent
fires caused by crude fires lit on the cabin floors to keep
warm, or by chimneys that did not work properly. That meant
extra work rebuilding the cabins as well as tending the burned.
Also, Meredith had to supervise the sewing of the warm
winter garments that the women made in the spinning house.

Nor was Jeremy idle. He was constantly inspecting the
fields, giving instructions on preparing for the spring planting
and checking to make certain his orders had been carried out.
Since winter was a slow season for farming, now was the
time to make necessary repairs. Wagons were mended and
harnesses fixed. Tools were made and repaired. Mules and
horses were reshod, as were the few oxen the farm used. The
house and most of the cabins needed work. Although the
plantation had few fences, there were some around the stable
yard and henhouse, and these had to be inspected and fixed
also. The skilled workmen scurried about their jobs, ordering
their less competent help about and checking closely on their
progress. Many of the unskilled workers were set to filling

the deep ruts in the field trails. During the rainy spring and fall, the wagons had bitten deeply into the roads, and they were almost unfit for use.

Christmas passed with a less than festive atmosphere. Daniel was too sick for anyone in the house to feel like celebrating, although they did keep their usual day-long feast and celebration for the slaves. Jeremy gave Meredith a pearl pendant that he had purchased in Charleston. She in return presented him with an elegant leather shaving kit containing an ivory-handled razor and soap brush, a pewter bowl for the brush, and a razor strop. The utensils fitted into carved spaces, and were fastened down with straps. Then the whole case folded over and buckled so that it could be easily carried while traveling. Jeremy thanked her with a warm kiss and asked why she had thought of it. Shyly, Meredith replied, "Because I enjoy watching you shave in the morning."

He grinned. "And I enjoy your watching." Gently he kissed her again, and Meredith was flooded with exultation.

Meredith and Jeremy greeted the Christmas callers while Lydia remained upstairs at Daniel's bedside. Offering visitors eggnog and plum pudding, they forced themselves to smile through the wearying round of social chatter, staving off questions about Daniel and parrying jests about their newly married state. Meredith was hurt that none of her cousins came calling. Bitterly she concluded that Galen and his father had refused Althea permission. It didn't seem fair to see her friend only when Galen or Francis determined it was a suitable occasion. Doubtless Galen had not shown up because he was still angry with her for marrying Jeremy. Althea was right, she thought with a spurt of anger. Galen had had his chance with her many times and had not taken the opportunity. It was dog-in-the-mangerish of him to cry about it now.

But Galen was quickly put out of her mind later that evening when Jeremy led her to bed and made slow, sweet love to her, carefully stoking the fires of her passion. She returned his caresses ardently, her hands running wild across his chest and her tongue teasing his flat nipples into hard pebbles of desire. When she parted her legs, urging him to mount her, he drew back. "No," he whispered. "Tonight I want you above me."

"What?"

"Come here. I'll show you." He lay on his back and guided Meredith's hips until she straddled him. It was strange and exciting to be above him looking down, to watch his face go slack with passion and his eyes close in blissful pain. Meredith sank onto him, feeling a deeper penetration than ever before. She controlled their loving now, and she reveled in it, dipping, churning, rotating her hips until Jeremy moaned aloud and gripped the bedposts so hard the veins of his arms stood out like cords. "Now, Meredith, now. God, I'm dying for you."

She moved quickly then, and soon heaven enveloped them both, ecstasy roaring through them like a fire out of control. Contented, Meredith slipped from him and lay down, letting his arm encircle her. She laid her head in the hollow of his shoulder. It felt so right, so natural. She knew she had never been this happy. She wouldn't allow herself to wonder if she would remain so.

It was several days after Christmas that Meredith started out to the stables, hoping to find Jeremy. She needed to ask a question about a notation he had made in the plantation accounts. She could have waited until supper that evening, but she simply wanted to see him. Quite often she thought of Jeremy during the day and wished to hear his voice or see his face or just know where he was. Paul informed her that Mr. Devlin had gone to exercise Equilibrium. Meredith wrapped a warm pelisse around her and started for the stables.

As she reached the shell-lined driveway, she saw Jackson, the overseer, striding toward her. She checked herself for a moment, considering returning to the house, but decided it would be both obvious and cowardly. Although she didn't like the man, she would have to put up with him until Jeremy could find a new overseer. She nodded a cool greeting to Jackson from a distance and continued toward the stables. However, Jackson loped to catch up with her and grabbed her by one arm. Meredith whirled. "What do you think you're doing?"

He scowled. "Why in the hell did you choose that scum over me?"

"I beg your pardon!"

"I offered to marry you, all right and tight, but you turned me down. Too high-and-mightly for the likes of me. Then you turn around and snap up the chance to marry an indentured servant. An indentured servant!"

"I'm sorry if your pride was offended," Meredith told him icily. "However, whom I marry is none of your concern. Now please release my arm."

" 'Please release my arm,' " he mimicked savagely. "Always so proper, aren't you? But obviously there's a whore's heart beneath your plain, prim skin. Devlin's a handsome hunk of male flesh, isn't he? So you welcomed him into your bed. You were so eager to get a man between your legs, you'd take one your father bought! I'm sorry I didn't know that was what you wanted. I treated you with respect, more fool I. This is what I should have done." He grasped her other arm and jerked her forward, planting a hard, vicious kiss on her lips.

For a moment Meredith was too outraged to do anything, but then she began to struggle wildly, kicking out with her feet and flailing with her hands, twisting her head away. One foot connected sharply with his shin, she was pleased to note. He let out a brief yelp, and his eyes narrowed, a sudden flame in their muddy depths. Raising a hand, he backhanded her, knocking Meredith to the ground. Thoroughly frightened now, Meredith screamed the name uppermost in her mind. "Jeremy! Jeremy!"

She was unable to get out another sound, for Jackson was upon her immediately, clamping his hand over her mouth. She bit and clawed and kicked, her blows frequently landing home. She was a strong woman, and holding her down was rather like trying to subdue a mountain cat. But he managed to keep his hand over her mouth, and since it also covered her nose, he was cutting off her air. Soon black began to swim around the edges of her eyes, and she struggled, not to get away, but simply to remove the hand blocking her breathing.

Then a blur crossed her vision, followed by a tremendous thud, and suddenly her mouth was free. Gratefully she sucked in air and staggered to her feet. Two men's forms rolled along the crushed shells of the driveway, and though she could not see a face, one form was topped by a very familiar bright cap of hair. Jeremy. Thank God. Then her husband straddled Jackson, his huge fists ramming into the other's face. Meredith came to her senses enough to realize that if Jeremy continued, he would murder the overseer. "Jeremy! Stop!" She tugged at his shoulders. "Stop! Please. I'm all right. You'll kill him."

He paused, lifting his face to Meredith. His hair had come undone from its usual neat queue and straggled wildly around his face, matted with dirt. His eyes were afire with blood lust, and his lips were drawn back in a grim, feral imitation of a smile. He closed his eyes, and the great shoulders relaxed. Fluidly he rose to his feet and folded Meredith against his chest. "Are you certain? What happened? I heard you scream and I rode Equilibrium to the limit. I was scared to death I wouldn't get here in time."

For the first time, Meredith noticed the great bay horse nervously dancing nearby. Jeremy must have flung himself off his mount's back onto Jackson. Equilibrium snorted and tossed his head, disturbed by the noise and fighting. Jeremy spoke to him soothingly, quietly approaching the horse. He took the loose reins in his hand, though he did not let go of Meredith, keeping one arm firmly around her shoulders. He turned back to the battered overseer, who had staggered to his feet and was ineffectually wiping at the blood around his mouth.

"I want you off this plantation by evening," Jeremy told the man, his voice cold and hard as flint.

Tenderly Jackson touched his bruised and swollen lips. "You don't have the right," he protested sullenly. "Mr. Hurley hired me and only he can let me go. You ain't master here yet."

"I'm not dismissing you from Daniel's service," Jeremy replied reasonably. "I'm simply saying that if I catch you on this property again I'll break you in half."

Jackson glared impotently and stumbled across the driveway to retrieve his coiled whip, which had fallen from his shoulder during the struggle. For a terrified moment, Meredith thought he meant to turn the instrument against Jeremy. Her husband tensed, his hands knotting into fists and his eyes

gleaming. She rather thought he was hoping Jackson would
do exactly that. However, the overseer only slung the coil
over his shoulder and lurched off in the direction of his cabin.
Meredith had no doubt that he would disappear by nightfall.

"What was that all about?" Jeremy turned to her. "How
did he dare to touch you?"

"A spurned suitor," Meredith replied wryly, trying to
lighten the atmosphere.

"A what? You mean, he actually had the gall to believe
you'd marry him?"

A nervous giggle broke from her lips. "Well, he was
appalled that I had married you instead of him. He thought an
overseer was a better catch than an indentured servant."

Jeremy half laughed, half sighed, and shook his head.

"Ah, Meredith, Meredith, see what a *femme fatale* you've
become. You have the men growling and snapping over
you."

"You make it sound like two dogs fighting over a bone."

He laughed. "There are some resemblances."

"And I'm the bone? Not a very flattering comparison."

"Meredith!" They were startled from their bantering by
Lydia's urgent cry. They whirled to see her flying across the
garden, skirts raised to mid-calf. "Meredith, come quickly."

For an instant Meredith froze. "Oh, my God." One hand
fluttered to her throat. "Daniel."

Jeremy grasped her shoulders and shoved her forward.
"Go on. I'll take my horse to the stable and join you as
quickly as possible."

His movement jarred her from her paralysis. She rushed
forward to meet Lydia. Lydia's face was pale, despite the
unaccustomed exercise of running. She reached out blindly
for Meredith's hands, her eyes blurred by tears. "Daniel—
he's—"

Meredith gripped her hands tightly. "Is he dead?"

Lydia shook her head. "No, but he's breathing so funny.
Please, you must do something."

They ran into the house and up the stairs to Daniel's room,
in their fright still clinging to each other's hands like a pair of
schoolgirls. His bedroom was dim, the drapes closed, and

there was the strong fetid smell of an enclosed sickroom.
"Open the drapes. I can't see."

"Daniel asked me to close them. He didn't like the light."

"Oh." Meredith frowned and picked up a candle. She bent
over the bed, holding the candle so that it shone on his face.
His face was sallow and flaccid, his eyes closed. He appeared
asleep, but his fingers twitched continuously on the bedclothes.
His breath rattled in his throat and chest, but he seemed to be
unable to cough or clear his throat. He sounded as if he was
drowning, Meredith thought.

She rang for Joseph, his valet, and had him turn Daniel
onto his side. They stuffed pillows behind his back to keep
him on his side. He appeared to breathe more easily. Meredith sat down to wait. Her eyes were drawn to his endless
picking at the covers. She was familiar with sickness and
death. She had watched her mother die and also several slaves
whom she could not save. Most terrible of all, she had
witnessed the death throes of children afflicted by one of the
great epidemics of the young—measles or scarlet fever or
diphtheria. She had seen the same gesture many times before
in the very ill or dying: the restless, purposeless motion of
hands and fingers.

Meredith clasped her hands in her lap and stared down at
them, tears flooding her eyes. Daniel was dying. She had
known for several weeks now that it would happen, but
somehow she had kept the truth at bay. She and Lydia had
tended him and given him snakeroot, a common cure for
stomach troubles. She had even tried Stoughton's Cordial
Elixir, although she doubted its efficacy. The only thing that
had helped was Jamestown weed ground up and dissolved in
water. It had eased the pain and helped him to sleep. There
was no remedy, no cure. They had all been aware of that. Yet
she had hoped and denied and refused to accept it. Now she
would have to.

But Daniel did not die that night. Stubbornly he hung on
for two more days, the rattling in his chest growing worse and
worse until no change of position helped. He awoke now and
then and spoke to them, but a fever developed, and soon his
words became senseless conversations with people of the
past, or spoken dreams. Meredith tried to answer him as if

she knew what he spoke of. Often he believed she was her mother, Anne. Later he called her "Mama" several times.

She and Lydia stayed by his side, taking turns watching him through the night while the other slept. Jeremy was beside her at every opportunity, although the demands of the plantation often called him away. Meredith was sitting by Daniel's bed in the middle of the night when suddenly his breathing changed. He drew an odd gasp and then a long shuddering breath. Meredith, half dozing in her chair, sat bolt upright. "Lydia!" she called sharply. She had heard that sound before also.

Lydia was instinctively out of the narrow cot set up in his room and by Meredith's side before she had awakened completely. "What? What is it?"

"I think—I'm afraid—" she stammered, unable to complete her sentence, but Lydia understood. She reached out to clasp Meredith's hand, as icy as her own.

Daniel's breathing slowed and became almost inaudible. It took a few seconds for Meredith to realize what had happened when it ceased altogether. She closed her eyes over the hot tears. "He's gone."

Lydia burst into sobs, sinking onto her knees beside the bed and resting her head on the coverlet. Her hands went around Daniel's, and she cried as though her heart was breaking. Meredith put a hand on her head, knowing there could be no comfort for Lydia. She stroked the shining head, then quietly exited, leaving Lydia alone with the man who had shared his life and wealth with her. Meredith dragged herself to her room, her mind numb. She couldn't think what to do, although she knew there were things that needed to be done. Daniel would have to be laid out, and there would be visitors, and . . . But she could leave it all to Jeremy. He would cope with it.

She opened the door of their room and slipped inside. Jeremy was instantly alert. "Meredith?"

"Yes."

He rolled onto his side, arm extended for her to join him in bed. When she did not, he swung out of bed. "Meredith, what's the matter? Has Daniel—"

"He's dead," she said flatly, then suddenly began to cry,

long-repressed sobs tearing at her throat. "Oh, Jeremy!" She
flung herself against his chest, and he folded his arms around
her comfortingly, one hand stroking her hair and back.

"Yes, my love, yes. That's good. Cry it all out."

"I never—never realized how much I loved him. I always
thought . . ." Her tears choked off the words.

"It's all right. Just cry it out, and then you can talk."

Finally the storm of tears subsided, and Jeremy guided her
to a chair. He sat down and pulled her onto his lap like a
child. She leaned her head against his shoulder. "I used to
tell myself I didn't like him. He was low and presumptuous,
not of my mother's or the Whitneys' class. I tolerated him, I
thought, for my mother's sake, and for Bitterleaf. But these
past few days I've realized how I lied. He was more father to
me than my own father ever was. Benjamin Whitney was a
solitary, bookish man, and I was nothing but an embarrassment or a nuisance to him. It was Daniel who treated me
with love, who gave me presents and taught me things, who
helped and encouraged me, laughed and fought with me. My
father was a shadow, but Daniel was real. But I wouldn't let
myself admit it because of my pride! Stupid! Stupid! Why
didn't I tell him? He never knew, and now it's too late!"

"Don't worry," Jeremy assured her. "Daniel knew you
loved him. He loved you very much, and he never doubted
your affection. Even I knew you cared for him. You were
probably the only one who didn't realize it. It was in your
gestures and words, the way you smiled at him or laughed,
even the way you argued with him. He knew."

"I hope so." Her voice was tiny and forlorn. Jeremy
kissed her hair and wiped the tears from her face with his
large, callused thumbs. Meredith released a shaky little
sigh. It was so comfortable, so right, here in his arms. Thank
God Jeremy was with her, tender and gentle. Her world had
fallen apart, but his stout arms protected her. She fell asleep
curled up in his lap.

Jeremy leaned back his head and sighed. He was torn with
sympathy for Meredith. Her anguish hurt him, and he railed
at his helplessness to change what pained her. He wished he
could take the grief upon himself. He could bear it much more
easily. Kissing her sleeping head again, he rose and carried

her to the bed. After he pulled the sheets up around her, he strode into the hall to rouse Daniel's valet.

Meredith's head ached from crying when she awoke late the next morning. Jeremy was gone. She wished he was there to offer her a smile or a word of encouragement. She rang for Betsy to help her dress, digging out a black cotton gown from the back of her wardrobe. When she was dressed, she sent Betsy to the attic to bring down the trunk of black dresses she had stored there after her year of mourning for her mother. She would have to tell one of the maids to dye a few of Lydia's dresses black. Then she would have to instruct the cooks to prepare food for the many visitors who would come to offer sympathy. Her numbed mind slowly clicked over the multitude of things that would have to be done.

However, when she went downstairs, she found that Jeremy had already taken care of most of them. The servants had been gathered and told of the death, and messages sent to the neighboring planters. The kitchen, presided over by a tearful Dulcie, was humming with preparation of foodstuffs to be laid out on the dining room board for callers and for the customary feast after the funeral. Jeremy had also set the carpenters to building a stout cypress-wood coffin. Paul and Joseph had dressed Daniel's body in his best black suit and laid him out on boards in his room, to be transferred later into the coffin and set in the living room. Although in the hot colonial climate bodies were usually buried immediately and the customary lying in state was often dispensed with, they would have a short period of it, since it was January and the weather was cool.

Meredith was grateful to Jeremy for his quick and efficient handling of the arrangements. It was so nice to give up the burdens and responsibilities to someone else, to not have to be strong and capable. She and Lydia sat in the upstairs sitting room, sometimes crying together and comforting each other, at other times remembering Daniel with tears. She bundled up against the cold and took several walks around the grounds, letting the fresh air sweep away the haze and gloom of her mind. Of course, she also had to participate in the obligatory sitting with the body and greeting the visitors who came to offer their condolences.

Although oftentimes his more aristocratic neighbors had looked down upon Daniel Hurley socially, he had been a powerful man in the area, one of the wealthiest planters and the most successful in his dealings with merchants in both London and the colonies. Many had turned to him for advice or even a loan now and then to tide them over until their crop came in. He was also well-liked in the nearby town of Greenoak, for he had none of the haughty manners of the planters. He was unfailingly polite to those of the middle and lower classes, so tradesmen and laborers also offered their respects, coming to the side door, hat in hand. This part was the most difficult for Meredith, and she was thankful Jeremy remained by her side. Wearily she shook hand after hand, accepted condolences, thanked paople for coming, and offered them a cold repast from the dining board. Jeremy took over many of the civilities, easily greeting and conversing with their guests, always polite, and never at a loss for words.

After a day of such social obligations, Daniel was laid to rest in the Whitney cemetery, which lay to the northeast of the house and overlooked the river. The brief ceremony given by the Anglican priest was well-attended. Even her Whitney cousins came. Meredith knew by Galen's tight-lipped expression that he didn't believe Daniel should have been buried with the Whitneys. But Meredith reasoned that as the master of Bitterleaf for many years, Daniel belonged there. It would have been insulting to his memory to put him in the church graveyard, away from his beloved Anne.

Afterward, at the house, Althea came by to squeeze Meredith's hand and offer her company whenever Meredith needed it. Meredith smiled wanly. Althea was a true friend. Galen, behind his sister, next clasped Meredith's hand. His eyes bored into hers meaningfully. "I'm very sorry, Cousin," he said, but she was aware he didn't refer to her stepfather's death. His gaze flickered past her to Jeremy, and she knew his sorrow was more for her marriage "beneath her" than for the death of a man he didn't like and was convinced she didn't like, either.

"Yes, I shall miss Daniel very much," she replied firmly,

meeting his gaze with her own challenging one. He appeared slightly taken aback. "Daniel was a very good stepfather to me and saved Bitterleaf from ruin. I think all we Whitneys have a great deal to thank him for," she continued. Jeremy, beside her, slipped his hand around hers. It was warm and comforting. Thank heavens I didn't marry Galen! Meredith thought. The idea startled her, but as she ran it through her mind again, she realized how true the words were. Daniel had been right. There was a great deal of emotion in her that would never have been satisfied by her cousin. They had a common heritage, similar tastes in literature and music, and a childhood spent in each other's company. But that was not enough on which to build a marriage. It wasn't enough for love.

She glanced up at her husband and smiled warmly. She loved Jeremy. Strange how she realized it so suddenly and completely. His quick grin, his finely modeled face, his lovemaking, even the sight of him striding across the yard—all thrilled her to her toes. She enjoyed being with him and was lonely when he was out in the fields. He made her laugh and turned conversation into a pleasure. He helped and stood by her and comforted her. That was what she needed in a husband, and Jeremy was who she truly loved. The only problem was that though she had come to love him, she knew that Jeremy did not return her love.

Chapter XX

THE DAY after the funeral, Daniel's attorney, Alexander Carter, rode out from Greenoak to read Daniel's will. He was a white-haired, solemn man who liked to see wills read with full pomp and dignity. Accordingly, he gathered Meredith, Jeremy, and Lydia in the formal drawing room and unfolded the document with great care. Unfortunately for him, his performance was lost on Lydia and Meredith, who scarcely watched, being tired and emotionally drained from the funeral. Only Jeremy noticed, but the gesture only served to bring a twinkle of amusement to his eyes. Mr. Carter cleared his throat ostentatiously and began to read in a sonorous voice. Since he had written the will, it was rife with legal phrases and long words that his listeners found largely unintelligible. However, Mr. Carter was happy to explain the contents of the document when he had finished reading it. "What this boils down to is that after leaving Mrs. Chandler a few enumerated possessions and a nice, though not excessive, sum of money, Mr. Hurley devised the remainder of his wealth and the plantation to you, Miss Whitney . . . er, Mrs. Devlin. He also manumitted—that is to say, freed from slavery—certain of the household blacks, namely Paul, the majordomo, Dulcie the cook, and Joseph, his valet. I am the executor of the estate. Any questions?"

No one had any, so after being offered a warm drink and

politely accepting it, Mr. Carter rode back to town. Jeremy turned to Meredith, his expression thoughtful. "His freeing those three slaves . . . is it common?"

"Yes, fairly. Quite often a trusted, well-liked slave is freed on his master's death."

"What will they do now?"

Meredith shrugged. "They could leave if they wished, go to Charleston or another plantation and hire out. There are several freed slaves living in Charleston. However, I doubt they will. All of them were born on this plantation. They hold rather important positions. We aren't harsh or particularly demanding. I doubt they could improve their lot by moving. I'll pay them servant's wages, and they'll have their papers showing they're free, so no one could sell them."

"Interesting." Jeremy narrowed his eyes. "The major loss to the plantation, then, is a capital asset, not income."

"Of course, there will be a small difference in the income because of the salaries, but it won't be much."

Jeremy knew that was true, for the servants on his father's estate and other noblemen's manors received minuscule wages. "I see. Well, I'm sure they will be most happy."

"Oh, yes. Daniel left them the greatest gift of all."

"He gave it to me as well." Jeremy thought of the canceled indenture lying in a drawer upstairs.

Meredith smiled up at him, bedazzled anew by his handsome face. Since she had realized her love yesterday, she had been acutely aware of her feelings whenever she was with Jeremy—the way her heart lifted and her blood raced at his grin or the swelling joy when he entered the room, the biting anxiety that he would grow tired of her and return to Lydia's bed, the bitter certainty that her love was not returned. After all, he had married her to gain his freedom and a huge plantation. She could hardly blame him. She would have done anything to get out of bondage, too. And she would have done almost anything to keep Bitterleaf. But understanding his reasons didn't help her twinges of pain, or ease her prickling fears. She wished—oh, more than anything!—that her newly discovered love was not unrequited.

"Well, my love." Jeremy raised her hand to his lips. Meredith mused on how sweet and yet how tormenting it was to hear words of love and receive affectionate gestures from him when she knew such things were inspired by habit and politeness or, at most, momentary passion. "I must return to work. Will you be all right by yourself today?"

"Of course, I have a lot to see to as well." Jeremy left. Meredith gazed after his tall, trim figure as he strode down the hall and out the side door toward the study. Since he had thrown out Jackson he had had to do the work of the overseer as well as his own. Although he had been delaying things because of Daniel's death and the funeral, she knew he would be extremely busy from now on. Before long it would be the planting season. He'd better find a new overseer before then, or he would exhaust himself.

It was almost a week later, after midnight, that a huge figure slipped from beneath the covers in one of the slave cabins. He slid on his breeches and picked up a sack, into which he dumped corn bread and a slab of bacon. Quickly tying the sack, he pulled a long, sharp knife from its hiding place behind a loose brick. Then he stood and glided on silent feet toward the door. But the woman in bed, feeling his absence more than hearing a noise, awakened and sat up sleepily. "Neb? What are you doing?"

"Just stepping out for some fresh air. Don't worry. Go back to sleep."

"In January?" she questioned disbelievingly. She rose to her knees, thoroughly suspicious now. "Tell me the truth. Are you meeting somebody else?"

He stared, then burst into quickly controlled laughter. "No. There's no other woman for me. You know that."

"Then what are you doing?"

"I'm going."

"What do you mean, going? Oh, Neb, no!" Betsy understood his intention now, and fear coursed through her. "Neb, you can't. You'll get yourself killed. It's insane!"

"I can't live like this, Betsy."

"Aren't you happy with me?" Tears glistened in her eyes.

"Of course I am. It kills me to leave you behind, but I can't take you. I'd be caught sure if I had a woman slowing me down."

"You're sure to be caught this way!" Betsy wailed. "Neb, you aren't thinking straight. You've only been here less than a year. You don't know the country. The only slaves who escape go deep in the swamp, and they get killed by swamp creatures or die of the fever or drown."

"Maybe so, but I can't stay here."

"But why?" Betsy was crying in earnest now, reaching out to him, tears streaming down her face. "I don't understand."

"I can't live like an animal!"

"You live good now!"

"I'm not free! And that means I'm nothing. Look." He knelt beside the bed and took both her hands in his. "I love you. I loved you the first minute I saw you, slipping in the door behind the white missus. I scared you, but you were brave and beautiful. Even in the fever, I knew I wanted you, had to have you. You've done the best you could. You taught me to talk like a white man, gave me a soft bed and good food, loved me, filled my loneliness, took my seed. I couldn't ask for a better woman."

"Then stay with me. What'll I do without you?"

"The same as you did before I came," he replied roughly. "Betsy, you're tearing out my heart. I wanted to sneak out without you waking up so you wouldn't do this. Baby, I can't be a slave. You say they're good people here. Maybe it's so. You got me an easy job. But I don't mind work, and it doesn't matter that your missy is kind. The fact is, they *own* me, and I can't live knowing that. I got to get away. I got to be free."

Betsy gnawed at her lower lip. She understood what he said. It was that pride and fierce individuality that had initially attracted her to him. He was all man. If he didn't struggle to be free, he would be less than that. But she thought her heart would break to see him go. She almost begged him to take her, but she knew he was right about that. She'd slow him down. He didn't have much chance as it was, but with her along, he wouldn't have any chance at all. "All right," she whispered finally. "Be careful."

"I will." His face relaxed at her capitulation, and he pulled her to him for a long kiss. "I love you. I promise, someday I'll come back for you."

Betsy smiled tearfully. She knew that day would never come. It was doubtful he'd escape, and if by some miracle he did, he couldn't possibly return and spirit her away, too. But it eased his mind to say so. "I'll wait for you. Go on now."

Neb released her and rose in a fluid motion. Opening the door just wide enough to ease out, he slipped into the night, as dark as the shadows around him. It was a moonless night, one of the reasons he had chosen it, for he would not be easily visible. Not that it was likely anyone from the house would happen to glance out a window at this hour. However, he wasn't taking any chances. He soon hit the narrow trail leading to the wharf. His intention was to take the small pirogue always tied there and paddle downriver. They would expect him to run for the swamps, but he would head for Charleston. If he was lucky he'd be almost there by the time they discovered him missing. Of course, Charleston was more dangerous than the middle of the vast, uncharted swamplands, at least in terms of getting caught. But Neb had no liking for any of the unsavory ends Betsy had assured him came to slaves escaping into the swamps. Besides, he had insurance. Joseph had proudly displayed his brand new "freedom papers" to the others, and Neb had laboriously copied them on a piece of parchment he had stolen from the office. Although he couldn't read or write, he was a fair artist, and he was certain he had copied the strokes of the pen well enough for them to pass inspection by some passerby in Charleston. Of course, he would have to leave Charleston almost immediately, for his description soon would be circulated, and he was sure to be recognized.

Neb heard the scrape of a heel upon wood as he neared the docks, and instantly melted into the shadows of the surrounding trees and bushes. Who could be on the docks at this hour? There were no more sounds. After a few minutes, Neb convinced himself it had been only his imagination. Just to be safe, though, he stayed close to the sheltering underbrush as he approached the dock. The stacks of seed sacks unloaded weeks ago still stood on the dock. They loomed up before Neb now, and he edged sideways toward the boat, his eyes roving the expanse of wooden planks and towering sacks. A clink stopped him in his tracks. Narrowing his eyes, he saw a small boat ease away from the docks, a dark figure rowing. Was another slave escaping as well? But no, he could see the huge cuffs of a coat as the man's hand lifted the paddle. Not likely attire for a slave.

He sniffed. There was an odor in the air, a smell of—Neb whirled, his eyes darting, and this time he spotted it. A tiny flame leaped above the others. The sacks were on fire! For a moment he hesitated. The blaze would be seen eventually, but by then the seeds would be destroyed and the dock blazing, as well as the woods around it. The fire would be out of control. Perhaps it would sweep even toward the stately red brick house or the cabins where Betsy lay sleeping. He swallowed. He had an excellent chance of getting away. No one would notice the boat missing in the confusion of fighting the fire. In all likelihood, after the excitement and fear, they wouldn't even notice his absence tomorrow. Then he thought of Betsy and the white woman who had saved his life. He remembered Jeremy's tackling him when he was wild with fever, then carrying him on his back to the cabin. And he remembered cutting Jeremy from the whipping post.

With a muttered curse, he flung his sack deep into the bushes and ran to the huge bell sitting on the dock. He began to pull on it with all his might, filling the night with its ear-shattering clang.

"What the devil!" Jeremy sat up straight in bed, instantly awake.

Meredith roused more slowly beside him. "Jeremy, what is it?"

"Somebody's ringing the dock bell. What in hell is going on?" He padded to the window, but could see nothing outside but pitch-black night. Pulling his breeches from the bedpost, he yanked them on and ran down the stairs, still buttoning the trousers. At the back door, he was met by a breathless Paul.

"It's the docks, Mister Jeremy. They're on fire! That Neb sounded the bell. I already sent some boys down with buckets and kettles."

"Good. Send more. I'm going down there. Oh, send up word to my wife."

"Yes, sir." Paul spoke to thin air. Jeremy was already out of the house and racing for the river.

But Meredith did not need word sent to her. She had jumped out of bed right behind Jeremy and jerked a dress out of the closet. It laced up the front, making it relatively easy to fasten oneself. Thrusting her feet into sturdy shoes, she darted after Jeremy. She met one of the maids on the stairs. "Oh, missy, I was coming to tell you. Master Jeremy's gone to the docks to help. There's a powerful big fire there."

The girl was obviously full of her news and anxious to describe the blaze in detail, but Meredith pushed past her down the stairs and, hiking up her skirts, scampered to the river trail. By the time she arrived at the river, the entire stack of seed sacks was engulfed by flames. Two lines of workers had formed leading from the river's edge to the border of the fire. Closest to the fire stood the similar forms of Jeremy and Neb. The workers handed buckets, kettles, and pots filled with water along the human chain to Jeremy and Neb, who tossed the containers' contents on the flames. Meredith quickly realized it would not be enough. Racing back to the house, she ordered every able-bodied man and woman to hasten to the river, carrying a kettle or other large vessel with them.

With her usual organizational skill, Meredith soon had two more water-tossing rows formed, as well as supplementary runners to carry the empty pails back to the river for refilling, which made the process much faster. However, it was obvious that nothing could save the seeds. Jeremy, waving to Neb, abandoned the line, and two others took their places. They ran toward the outbuildings around the house and returned with two long-handled rakes. They waved the other workers aside. While everyone else pulled away from the docks, knotting into eagerly watching groups, the two men began to push at the flaming sacks with the rakes. Straining the powerful muscles of their shoulders and arms, they thrust them into the water, where the flames fizzled and died out. It was hard, hot work, and dangerous, for they stood perilously close to the leaping flames. However, they managed to escape unharmed until the very end, when an errant spark popped from the fire and landed on Jeremy's leg. Immediately his trouser leg was on fire. Meredith jumped forward, screaming, but it was Neb who reached him first. Throwing Jeremy to the ground, he rolled him across the dock and onto the dirt trail, extinguishing the flames. Jeremy clutched at the ground, his face contorted with pain, while Neb ran back to finish dousing the fire. Meredith knelt beside her husband.

"Are you all right?"

He nodded, tight-lipped. "A little burn, that's all."

But Meredith knew no burn was minor. Burns could cause fevers and horrid gangrenous swelling of limbs until the burned area had to be amputated, almost a sure invitation to death. She whirled. "You," she addressed one of the more powerful workers, then turned to two others. "You, too. Carry him into the house and up to our bedroom. On boards. Don't touch his leg! First fetch several boards and lay him on them, then carry him to the house. Carefully!" While the men ran to do her bidding, she waited beside Jeremy, holding one of his great hands in both of hers.

"What's going on?" he asked, raising his head.

"You rest," Meredith ordered, firmly pushing him down. "Everything's under control. Neb is dousing the remains of the fire. The seeds are a loss, of course, and the dock is badly scorched, burned through in some places. But the pier is intact, and you kept it from reaching the trees and brush."

Jeremy sighed. "Damn! All that seed!"

"Seeds can be replaced. We have the money. Don't worry. *You're* the problem now. You have to heal, or we'll all be in trouble."

He closed his eyes. Meredith was right. He, too, had seen what burns could do, although he hadn't Meredith's experience in nursing. He didn't think he'd been on fire long enough to cause severe damage, but the piercing agony down the outside of his leg belied that notion. It seemed hours before the men returned with the boards and laid them side by side on the ground. But after they shoved and pulled and maneuvered him onto the boards, then lifted and carried him over the uneven trail to the house, Jeremy heartily wished they had never arrived. Each bounce and bump shot pain through his leg.

When at last they reached the bedroom after a harrowing trip up the stairs, Meredith instructed the men to lay the makeshift stretcher on the floor. Setting the washbasin on the floor beside Jeremy, she knelt to cut away his breeches and carefully wash him all over, even the affected limb. He grimaced at the shimmering pain that accompanied even her slightest touch. "Must I be clean to grace your sheets?" he growled unevenly.

"Hush," Meredith retorted stoutly, although tears threatened her eyes. "It's not my sheets I'm worried about. Dirt doesn't help any wound or burn. I don't know why, but it increases the likelihood of swelling and fever and pus. I'm the doctor here, so stop trying to second-guess me."

"Yes, ma'am."

When she was through bathing Jeremy, she directed the men to lift him onto the bed. Then she shooed everyone out of the room and went down to the kitchen to mix a burn poultice. With a mortar and pestle, she ground and mixed molded bread and Jamestown weed, then added flour and water to form a thick paste. Carrying the disagreeable-looking result to Jeremy's bed, she spread it on a cloth and draped it over the burned area. No matter how gentle she tried to be, she knew her touch was bound to hurt, but Jeremy gritted his teeth and said nothing.

"You don't have to be a stoic, you know," she teased, tears clogging the back of her throat. "I won't mind if you holler."

"I know you," he joked back hoarsely. "You're the sort who gets her pleasure from torturing others. I'll not give you the satisfaction of screaming."

"All right, then, spoilsport." Meredith sat back and wiped the perspiration from her brow with the back of her arm. She eased off the bed and covered his naked body, leaving the damaged leg exposed. She mixed more of the sedative weed with water and handed him the brew to drink. "Here. This will ease the pain and let you sleep. It's what I gave you . . . the other time."

"Good." He reached out to clasp her hand. "It still embarrasses you to speak of it, doesn't it?"

"What? The awful, cruel thing I did to you? Yes, of course."

"I don't need or want your guilt, Meredith. I'm sure I

provoked you somehow. It was sheer chance Jackson happened by at that moment and seized the opportunity of your anger. I forgave you long ago for whatever wrong you did me. Besides, you've paid me many times over.'' He smiled crookedly. ''The pleasure's been worth the pain.''

Meredith glanced away, her cheeks coloring slightly. ''Now you need to rest. I'll reapply this poultice in the morning.'' She started for the door.

''Where are you going?''

''To sleep in your old room.''

''But why?''

''Any jouncing or movement will cause you pain. I daren't sleep in the same bed.''

He sighed with mock despair. ''Then I shall *have* to recover quickly, shan't I?''

She shook her head, smiling tearfully, and left the room. Jeremy's head buzzed with thoughts, and he was sure he would never sleep, but within minutes, his eyelids fluttered closed.

Meredith checked on him several times during the night. His sleep was restless, and often he moved agitatedly in the bed, rolling his head from side to side and moaning. However, by morning, he settled down and slept until almost noon. When Meredith peeped in and saw he was awake, she sent a maid for the poultice she had made earlier and entered the room. He turned his head and grinned faintly. ''Hello.''

''Hello, Jeremy.'' Her heart flooded with emotion at the sight of him. Grim lines ran down from his mouth and eyes, and his skin was unusually pale. ''How are you?''

He grimaced. ''Other than the fact that my leg feels like it died and went to hell, I suppose I'm all right.''

Tenderly, Meredith peeled back the poultice and examined his flesh. When the maid returned with the new poultice she spread it on and stepped back, her face alight. ''It looks very good. I don't believe it's a serious burn.''

Jeremy let out a mock groan. ''Well, if this is a comical one, I'd hate to have the serious kind.''

''All right,'' Meredith teased, arms akimbo. ''Enough of that. Would you like for me to read to you, or would you prefer to sleep? How about food?''

"A little dinner sounds good. Maybe beef stew."

"Will soup do just as well? I think Dulcie has a pot of thick beef and vegetable soup."

"Good. But before you send it to me, I want to see one of the footmen."

"Why? Jeremy, this is no time to think about business. The plantation can survive without you for a few days."

"Must you know everything?" Although he meant it teasingly, his voice was irritable from the pain, giving a harsh inflection to his words.

Meredith tightened. "No. Of course not." She left and sent a young footman to him as Jeremy had requested, then proceeded to the kitchen to give instructions for Jeremy's dinner. Her errands accomplished, she went on about her work. Jeremy obviously had no desire for her company.

When the footman arrived in Jeremy's room, Jeremy told him, "Go to the dock and check around—in the water, on the pier, on the ground around the docks, along the trail. Make a thorough search."

"For what?"

"I don't know. Anything out of the ordinary or unusual. An object that might belong to someone—say a pipe or tobacco pouch or a piece of clothing torn off. And set up a guard around the dock. Don't let anybody touch the ashes. I want to go over it myself when this leg's better."

The footman looked mystified, but nodded and set off at once to do as Jeremy bade him. Jeremy ate a lonely meal, wishing Meredith had returned with the maid. What he had said to her had come out wrong, and no doubt she was offended. He hadn't meant to sound angry or irritable. He just wanted to protect her from worry and fear by concealing his thoughts. He might have known it wasn't the way to treat Meredith. Meredith did not return for several hours, but the footman did, bringing with him a sack he had found in the bushes. Jeremy sifted through its contents, then ordered the servant to bring Neb to his room.

"Miss Meredith?" Betsy paused on the threshold of the sitting room, her voice questioning.

"Yes?" Meredith glanced up from her mending.

"I—could I ask you something? A favor?"

"Why, of course, Betsy, come in." Meredith laid aside her sewing, surprised by Betsy's request. The girl seemed nervous. What could she want?

"I—it's about Neb. I'm afraid for him."

"Afraid? Why?"

"Mister Jeremy sent for him a while back, ma'am. Neb's in the master's room now."

Meredith smiled. "There's nothing sinister about that, surely. He discovered the fire, and then saved Jeremy from being badly burned. Jeremy is probably thanking him or giving him a reward. We owe him a great deal."

"Yes'm, but Neb's sure Mr. Jeremy knows what he was doing down there at the docks."

"What do you mean?"

"Miss Meredith, don't you know?"

Meredith stared at her, puzzled. She had been so concerned with the fire and Jeremy's burned leg that she hadn't wondered how Neb discovered the fire. It was strange, now that she thought about it. Why would he be at the docks in the middle of the night? Unless . . . Her eyes widened. "Betsy, was he trying to escape?"

Betsy nodded miserably. "Yes, and now Mr. Jeremy will punish him. I know he will. Nobody could let that pass. He's bound to realize Neb'd try it again. Oh, Miss Meredith, I'm so scared. Neb's been whipped before. His back's a mass of scars. I couldn't bear for it to happen again. Or what if he orders something worse? I've heard of owners chopping off a foot or —"

Meredith clenched her hands. "Hush!" she snapped. "Jeremy won't . . ." But was she really sure what Jeremy would do? Surely he wouldn't hurt the man who'd saved his life, as well as a great deal of his property. But men sometimes were capable of the strangest actions. And she didn't understand her husband, didn't know him, no matter how much she loved him.

"Please, Miss Merry, if you could talk to him before he orders the whipping, he could back down without losing face. Neb's up there now. If you'd go ask the master not to hurt him, he'd listen to you. You're just married. He'd do you a favor, give you a gift. Please."

Meredith wet her lips. She couldn't explain to Betsy that she far overestimated Meredith's influence with Jeremy. He was not a typical bridegroom, so in love with his wife he'd grant whatever she asked. Meredith doubted she could sway him. But she had to try. She couldn't let him harm Neb. She owed the black too much for saving Jeremy's life. "I'll talk to him. Perhaps I can convince him not to hurt Neb."

Betsy's eyes shone with tears. "Oh, thank you, ma'am."

Meredith hurried up the stairs, her mind whirling with arguments to convince Jeremy. She paused at the door and heard Jeremy's voice inside, clipped and deadly quiet. "Answer me, Neb." Meredith knocked loudly and entered without waiting for permission.

Jeremy was sitting in bed, his face pale and set. Neb stood at the end of the bed, his jaw thrust forward stubbornly and his black face as expressionless as ebony. Meredith sighed inwardly. The two men were too alike in disposition. She feared they were on a collision course. "Hello, Jeremy, Neb." She nodded toward the slave and turned to Jeremy. "Dear, shouldn't you rest now? I'm afraid you've tired yourself out already. Why don't I send Neb back to the garden, and you can take a little nap?"

Jeremy's mouth twitched irritably. He couldn't get any answers out of Neb, and his leg was a ceaseless throb of pain. Now Meredith's fussing, so uncharacteristic of her, set his teeth on edge. "Damn it!" he snapped. "I'm capable of deciding if and when I will sleep! I'll also continue to question Neb if I want to." Meredith pressed her lips together, trying to ignore the hurt his tone brought her. She reminded herself that he didn't feel well and that active men did not make good patients. Jeremy turned back to Neb. "Now, I want some answers. I can't imagine what you hope to gain by refusing to tell me. I know you were escaping the night of the fire. Why else would you have been at the docks . . . unless, of course, *you* set the fire."

"If I set the fire, why would I warn you?" Neb retorted scornfully.

"I don't know. Doesn't make much sense," Jeremy

admitted. "But then your refusal to answer questions doesn't make sense, either."

"Jeremy, I need to talk to you," Meredith cut in. "Alone. Neb, would you wait in the hall?"

"Meredith! Stay right there, Neb. Meredith, this is important. We can talk later."

"No, we can't!" Meredith flashed. "I want to talk to you about him!" She jabbed a finger in Neb's direction.

"What about him?"

"Jeremy, he saved your life! And he was the one who cut you down the time Jackson whipped you. He's helped you twice."

"I'm aware of that. My memory isn't impaired by a burned leg."

"Then, please, please, don't punish him." She moved to his side, kneeling on the small stool used to climb into the high bed. She folded her hands earnestly. "Jeremy, we owe Neb your life. Please, I beg you. As a favor to me, don't punish him."

A faint smile touched Jeremy's lips as his exasperation dissolved. His chest felt strangely warm and melting. He stroked her smooth hair. "Why, Meredith, you're asking a favor of me."

"Yes," she admitted, swallowing her pride. "Please, Jeremy."

"I'm surprised. I'd think saving my life would have inspired you to punish him rather than beg to save him," he teased. "Can it be you've developed some liking for me?" He leaned over to whisper in her ear, "Have you discovered you enjoy my presence in your bed?"

She blushed and drew away. "Jeremy!"

He chuckled and relaxed against his pillows. "Well, for your information, my love, I didn't intend to punish him at all—although when I get out of this bed, I may beat the hell out of him if he continues to not answer my questions." Both Neb and Meredith stared at Jeremy. "In fact, Neb, I plan to offer you your freedom."

Chapter XXI

"WHAT!" NEB GAPED. He had expected to be severely punished when he was ordered to go to Jeremy's room, and he had cursed himself for not leaving the place to burn. Now to hear that Jeremy offered freedom instead of punishment stunned Neb so he could hardly think.

"I'm freeing you. In fact, I'm considering you for my new overseer."

Meredith jumped to her feet. "Are you crazy? Nobody's ever—"

"I often do things 'nobody's ever' done before," Jeremy reminded her. "No one could ride Equilibrium, either."

"But Jeremy, a former slave as an overseer?"

"Why not? Did you see Neb organize the fire fighting? He had the line of water going by the time I arrived. He's a natural leader. And he's intelligent. Look at how quickly he's caught onto the language. The day I dragged him to his cabin, he couldn't speak a word of English. Today he speaks better than most of the blacks."

Neb stuck in, "Don't I have anything to say about this?"

"Yes, of course," Jeremy replied. "I presumed you didn't want to argue about it."

"I can't accept it."

"What?" Now it was Jeremy who stared blankly. "I offer to free you and make you an overseer, and you refuse?"

"I can't manage slaves. I won't. I won't lash black backs or shove chained men into the fields."

Jeremy studied him shrewdly. "And what if they weren't shackled? What if there were no lashings? Would you be willing to oversee black *free* workers?"

"Jeremy, what are you talking about?"

"Meredith." He grasped her hands, his eyes boring into hers, willing her to agree with him. "I want to free all the slaves on Bitterleaf."

"Are you serious?"

"Never more so. I've been under the lash myself. I've been chained and beaten, humiliated. I know how it feels to be penned like an animal and sold on an auction block. No man or woman should have to endure it. What if you and I were owned by someone like Neb and Betsy, who could rip us apart any time they wanted? Sell one of us if they chose and leave the other behind? What if any child we created would be a slave as well?"

Meredith's face crumpled in anguish, tears springing to her eyes. "Jeremy, I know. But how can it work? I mean, how could we run Bitterleaf?"

"I've been thinking about it since Daniel manumitted Dulcie, Paul, and Joseph in his will. You explained to me that it wouldn't mean much decrease in income. Wages aren't high. The loss is a capital asset, which is something you wouldn't realize unless you sold the slaves, which I doubt you'd do. Bitterleaf will still produce enough to pay them and make a good profit." Jeremy's voice throbbed with enthusiasm, and he gripped Meredith's hands almost painfully. "If everyone we freed left and we had to get new workers, we'd lose a great deal. But you pointed out the odds are they wouldn't leave. They'll be free and have papers to prove it, but they'll have to have jobs. Why not work here?"

"That's right," Neb broke in, leaning forward against the bedposts in excitement. "Unless they're skilled workers, there aren't better jobs elsewhere. They might as well stay. The cabins, food, and clothes here are nicer than what they'd get from anyone else. Besides, Miss Meredith's a healer. They're less likely to die here."

"That's right. And because of your skills, Meredith, Bitterleaf has a much smaller attrition rate than any plantation. We don't need to constantly buy new slaves because of deaths. I *know* it's financially feasible. Do you realize how much more willing to work a man is when he knews he's free to leave if he wants? Being a slave takes away his motivation and interest. But working for a wage, to support your wife and family—that's an entirely different story. I'm certain we can get the same productivity with fewer people when they're free, not slaves.''

Meredith's heart swelled with love as she gazed at Jeremy's animated face. There was goodness in him that she had never suspected. He remembered his own pain and didn't want others to bear it also. She had always hated slavery herself, but felt trapped by the system. The government in England encouraged it because the slave trade meant a great deal of revenue for its ships. The local planters feared they couldn't grow their crops without it. But Jeremy was willing to risk it because he was kind. Generous. She wanted to fling her arms around him and shout out her love for him. But she refrained and merely nodded. ''Yes. I—you may be right. Perhaps it would work.''

He smiled. ''I'm certain it will.'' He turned to Neb. ''What about you? Will you take the job now? Will you help my experiment?''

''Months ago, when they ripped me from my home, I only wanted to go back. But now I have nothing left there. Betsy is here, and she's everything I possess. I will stay. I'll be overseer for you.''

''Good. And thank you for saving my life.'' Jeremy extended his hand. Neb, startled, slowly reached out to clasp it. ''Now, my love, if you'll excuse us, I'd like to ask Neb a few more things. If you'll be more agreeable to answering now, that is.'' He raised a sardonic eyebrow at the huge black man.

Neb smiled. ''I'll do my best.''

Jeremy settled back in his pillows, and Meredith rose. He had dismissed her again, but she couldn't work up any resentment. His happy, excited face was too fresh in her mind. She ran lightly down the stairs and into the sitting room. Lydia was waiting for her there, small and pale in her

Lisa Gregory

black mourning dress. Since Daniel's death she had been lost and wan. Meredith's heart stirred with sympathy even as she wondered jealously if her husband would return to Lydia's bed. With Daniel dead, there was nothing to stand in his way. He could make Lydia his mistress publicly if he wanted.

"Meredith, I want to talk to you," Lydia began, squeezing her hands together tightly.

"What about?" Meredith sat down and took up her mending.

"I'm leaving Bitterleaf this week."

"Leaving?" Meredith was puzzled. "What do you mean? Are you going to visit someone?"

"No. I mean, leaving permanently. I'm returning to England."

Meredith's jaw dropped. "Returning to England! But why?"

"There's nothing for me here since Daniel died. You were my only friend here, and even you have been . . . cool to me for some time. I'll be happier in London with people I know. Daniel left me enough money to do what I wished. I don't want to stay here."

"But what about Jeremy?" Meredith blurted out without thinking.

Lydia frowned. "What about him? He has nothing to do with it!"

"But—you mean, you won't mind leaving him?"

Lydia's frown deepened. "I like the man, but I don't feel any sorrow at parting from him. I'm much closer to you."

"But you and he—"

"What? Meredith, we seem to be speaking at odds. I don't understand you."

"I'm talking about your and Jeremy's affair!" Meredith exclaimed, angered by her pretense of innocent misunderstanding. "While Daniel was sick, dying, you cuckolded him with . . . with . . . my husband."

"It's not true!" Lydia gasped, white-faced. "Someone lied to you. Who told you that?"

"No one *told* me," Meredith retorted scornfully. "I saw it with my own eyes."

"But how? You couldn't have!"

"I did. I took some old clothes of Father's to Jeremy's

room one day, and I saw you and him . . ." She broke off, unable to complete her sentence.

Lydia stared at her, dumbstruck. Then her face flushed. "Oh. You saw that."

"*Yes*. I saw that. So you needn't bother to lie."

"I wasn't lying," Lydia replied softly. "You didn't stay long enough, Meredith. If you had, you would have also seen that Jeremy and I didn't make love." Meredith raised one eyebrow in clear disbelief. "It's true. I hate to talk about that day, but obviously I must. Otherwise you will believe the wrong thing about your husband and do your best to ruin your marriage. Jeremy didn't take me to bed that day, Meredith—or any other day. I swear to you. I desired him, that's true. It had been a long time since Daniel had been able to make love. Jeremy was virile, attractive. I began to think about him, want him, but for a long time I fought it. I loved Daniel, I truly did. I didn't want to be unfaithful, although Daniel had given me permission. He said he would understand if I sought another man, since he could no longer perform. But I didn't want to! I was loyal, except for that one day. Foolishly I went to talk to Jeremy, and we kissed. But it went no further. I managed to recall my duty, my feeling for Daniel. It's true I felt passion and desire for Jeremy, but we didn't make love."

Meredith bit her lower lip thoughtfully. Was Lydia telling the truth? Could she trust her? She wanted to—oh, how desperately she wanted to! If she could believe Jeremy had not slept with Lydia, her life would assume a new, happier glow. She would no longer feel that awful, gnawing jealousy. If Jeremy occupied no one's bed but hers, might he not stay with her for the rest of their lives, as marriage was intended to be? Perhaps someday he would even grow to love her. She knew she mustn't let herself hope, yet she could not keep from doing so.

Lydia packed her belongings and left Bitterleaf two days later. Meredith experienced a certain sadness at her departure. She had always liked her, and Lydia had been her closest companion for several years. If Lydia had told her the truth, Meredith's recent reason for disliking her was gone. Honest tears welled in Meredith's eyes as she hugged Lydia good-bye and watched her settle herself in the pirogue, her luggage piled high around her. But as the boat moved out into the muddy water, Meredith was also aware of a burst of joy in her chest. No longer would jealousy prick her. She wouldn't worry about Lydia's attractiveness to Jeremy or wonder whether he compared them and found Meredith lacking.

She walked back to the house with a lighter step, certain that even Jeremy's grumpiness wouldn't bother her this afternoon. As she had suspected, he was a terrible patient. Unused to inactivity, he fidgeted and fussed. As his leg grew better, his temper got worse. When the pain diminished, he believed he was healed and should be able to walk and ride about. Meredith's adamant refusal irritated him, but Jeremy respected her healing abilities too much to flout her instructions. Meredith read to him and played quiet, sedentary games with him, struggling to quell her own temper when he snapped and growled.

One afternoon, as Meredith perched on his bed, playing a game of chess on a board lying across Jeremy's lap, his hand strayed to the neckline of her dress. Meredith lightly tapped his hand. "Now, now, none of that."

He sighed. "Why not? Am I denied all pleasure on general principles?"

"I know where it will lead, and your leg shouldn't be moved. It's your turn."

"Damn the game!" He flung the board aside, wildly scattering the pieces. "I'm going mad."

Meredith tightened her lips. "Well, you're certainly acting like it," she retorted tartly.

"And you're the reason."

"Me! Why?"

"You won't let me touch you. You even sleep in a different bed."

"Jeremy, you know why."

"I know it's a damn good excuse to avoid me!"

"I am trying to keep my patience, but you're making it very hard."

He grinned suddenly. "Not as hard as this." Seizing her hand, he pulled it to his lap to touch his burgeoning manhood through the thin sheet. Desire nipped at her loins.

She jerked back her hand. "You're crude."

"Yes, I am," he admitted. "And with all my crudity, I want to bed you again." His hand roamed across the exposed portion of her chest and dipped into the crevice between her breasts. "Meredith, please. I want you. It's been days and days."

"Jeremy! I don't want to risk hurting your leg."

"You could make love to me. Mount me. I'll even keep that leg covered." His fingers fumbled with the laces of her front-opening bodice.

For a moment Meredith hesitated. She refused to hurt his leg, but . . . but if she did as he suggested, they could avoid touching his leg. She had known the pinch of unfulfilled desire herself during his convalescence. Surely it would be all right. She stood and began undoing her laces. Jeremy watched her avidly. Under his gaze, Meredith felt warm and daring. She wanted to tease and exercise her sexual power over him, still amazed at having any. Languidly she eased off her dress.

Jeremy wet his lips. "Teasing wench," he muttered. "Hurry."

But she slackened her pace even more, inching down the top of her shift to reveal her breasts, then pulling it back up and instead removing her petticoats. Jeremy groaned, aware of her game and enjoying the delightful torment to the fullest. It was a new quality in Meredith, a coquettish sexuality that stirred him. Her petticoats joined her dress on the floor, and Meredith returned to the shift, slipping it down with infinite slowness, hands sliding over her body as Jeremy's ached to. When she finished undressing, instead of joining him in bed, she swayed to her vanity table. Sitting down before her mirror, she unpinned her hair and brushed it with smooth, sensuous strokes. Her hair crackled, falling across her shoulders with feather lightness. Jeremy itched to sink his hands into the rich mass. He could see her bare breasts in the mirror, and their slight jiggling as she brushed further increased his ardor.

"Meredith," he warned hoarsely, "I'll pay you back for this."

"Oh? How?" She grinned provocatively as she shook out her fall of hair. He described his intentions in lustful, explicit detail. His words brought a faint blush to her cheeks, but they stirred her as well. Meredith rose and went to him. Kneeling on the bed, she slid his nightshirt up, her hands spread wide to feel his skin beneath. Finally she slipped it over his head and tossed it aside. Jeremy cupped and kneaded her breasts, then took the swollen peaks in his mouth and sucked them to tingling desire. His hands slid lower, eagerly seeking the soft recesses of her womanhood, but Meredith drew back. "No. I am going to make love to you."

She turned down the sheet, carefully draping it over his injured leg, and set to work on his chest. Her lips roamed his skin, sucking the flat nipples, licking, nibbling, arousing him in every way she knew. Boldly she crept lower. Her tongue slipped into the indentation of his navel. He swallowed hard, his breathing suddenly racing. She continued downward, finally pressing her lips against his manhood. He arched upward, groaning, and she explored him with her mouth, her tongue circling the satin-smooth rod from base to swollen tip. He clutched the sheets, his moans turning almost to sobs. "Meredith," he gasped. "Now. Please. I can take no more."

She moved to sit astride him, easing herself onto his hot, throbbing maleness. He lay perfectly still as she pumped up and down, stroking his desire and her own to a mindless, trembling urgency. At last they exploded, scaling the heights of passion, locked in the oneness they had discovered together. Meredith knew with every fiber of her being that she loved Jeremy more than she had ever thought it was possible to love.

Jeremy improved rapidly, and within a few days was able to leave his bed and move around the house, using a gold-headed cane that had belonged to Meredith's grandfather. His mood improved after Meredith returned to his bed, and being able to walk made him almost himself again, although he chafed at his wife's restrictions against returning to riding. Meredith, freed from keeping him occupied, was able to devote some time to supervising the planting of her herb garden, where she grew many of the ingredients for her medicines.

She returned to the house from the garden one afternoon,

tired and wearing an old dress chosen for the task. Her hair straggled damply around her face. When she stepped in the back door, she heard a tinkling feminine laugh issuing from the drawing room. Curious, Meredith strode down the hall to investigate, and came to an abrupt halt in the doorway. Jeremy was lounging on the red velvet sofa, his injured leg lying straight out on the seat. Opal Hamilton was seated nearby in a delicate red velvet chair. Opal, as always, was beautifully dressed, this time sporting a pale pink satin dress as cool as ice and subtly flattering to her complexion. She was smiling at Jeremy, eyes shining and moist lips slightly parted. Jeremy was smiling back, Meredith noted irritably. They both turned at her entrance.

"Why, Meredith, how—how unusual you look," Opal commented. "Whatever have you been doing?"

Meredith glanced down at her old, bedraggled gown, muddy around the hem. She was aware of her mussed, limp hair and sweat-dampened face. Immediately she felt embarrassingly huge, awkward, and unattractive compared to Opal. "I—I'm sorry. I've just come from the garden, and I didn't realize you were here. I mean, I heard laughter, and I wondered who it was, so I came in. I wouldn't have if I'd known it was you." She blushed. "That is, I would have changed first if I'd realized we had a caller." She stumbled to a halt, silently cursing her wayward tongue.

"Oh, that's perfectly all right, Meredith. Heavens, far be it from me to take exception to your attire. Why, we've known each other for years, and I've seen you look worse than that."

Meredith's flush deepened. Jeremy smiled at her and moved his leg to make room. "Come in, love, and join us."

His smile cut Meredith deeply. She was certain he shared Opal's amusement at her ugly garb. "No, thank you," she replied coolly. "I must change for supper. I'm sorry I wasn't here to receive you earlier, Opal."

"Oh, don't worry." Opal smiled archly. "Jeremy has kept me very well entertained."

Meredith managed a stiff smile and retreated hastily, almost running up the stairs to her room. She burned with embarrassment and anger. She'd forgotten Opal in her happi-

ness over Lydia's absence. Foolishly she'd believed she would
have her husband all to herself. But he would always find
some pretty little minx whose company he enjoyed more than
hers. By the time Meredith reached her bedchamber, she had
worked herself into a fury. She ripped off her clothes and
flung them on the floor. Splashing water into the basin, she
washed away the dirt and sweat of the day, then slipped into
fresh undergarments and a clean dress. Looking at herself in
the mirror, she sighed. Mourning did not suit her. Black took
away what glow her cheeks possessed and dulled the luster of
her hair. She decided she resembled a gigantic black scarecrow.
No wonder Jeremy found pleasure in the company of the
dainty, prettily attired Opal Hamilton. Meredith thought ven-
omously that she could have ripped every carefully padded,
wired hair from Opal's head. Why didn't she chase some other
woman's husband?

She heard Jeremy's slow, rhythmic tread on the stairs, and
swung around to face him. He grinned. "You're already
dressed. And here I was hoping I'd get to watch."

"I'm sure it was far more interesting to chat with Opal
Hamilton," Meredith replied frostily.

His smile broadened. "Why, I believe you're jealous."

"Certainly not. Why should I be jealous? I have no claim
on you, and no desire to, either."

"Liar. You *are* jealous. I rather like it."

"I am *not* jealous! I just don't happen to enjoy Opal's
company as much as you obviously do."

"Opal's like the women I knew in London," Jeremy said,
dismissing her as insignificant and boring, but his words
conveyed the opposite meaning to Meredith. Opal reminded
him of what he had known all his life and yearned to return
to, Meredith thought, whereas she didn't in the slightest
resemble the women he had known. No wonder he enjoyed
Opal. Meredith realized she didn't stand a chance against her.
But Jeremy, half turned away and in the process of pulling off
the loose banyan, or dressing gown he wore over shirt and
breeches, didn't catch her defeated expression. He continued
cheerfully, "Well, since you have already dressed, I guess I
am left with nothing to do but go riding."

"What! You'll do nothing of the kind."

"Meredith, I've remained an invalid long enough. It's time I started my life again."

"But your leg is injured."

"It's almost healed. And I don't intend to ride all over Bitterleaf. I simply plan to walk a very gentle horse down the driveway and back, to loosen up a little. I have to use my leg again or it will never be the same!"

"You are the stubbornest man I ever met!"

"Probably," he agreed without heat. "But my leg is nearly well, and I don't see how riding could hurt it. My calf isn't burned, only my thigh. So my riding boots won't rub against it. And neither will the saddle, because the burn's on the outside thigh."

"Oh, all right," Meredith agreed irritably. "Go ahead and ride. It's your leg."

Jeremy chuckled. "I'm glad you remembered. Now, be a love and fetch my riding boots, will you?" He sat down to pull off his soft house slippers.

Casting a simmering glance his way, Meredith stalked to the wardrobe and opened the door, reaching down to yank out his riding boots. Her hand halted in midair, and she stared, shocked, at the small, colorful snake slithering over the top of one boot. Had she touched the boot a moment sooner, she would have been bitten. The thought penetrated her shock. She shrieked and jumped backward. Jeremy was out of the chair and beside her in an instant. "What is it?"

Meredith pointed silently to the snake now crawling across the toes of the boots and out the high wardrobe onto the floor. With one hand, Jeremy flung her behind him, while with the other hand he grabbed the nearest weapon, a heavy brass fireplace poker. He crashed it down on the snake oozing its way toward them. The reptile writhed obscenely and was still. Jeremy whirled, his upper lip dotted with moisture. "Are you all right? Did it bite you?"

Meredith shook her head. She began to tremble. "No. Oh, Jeremy, it was in your boot. I almost grabbed the boot before I saw its head come out!"

He pulled her to him, wrapping his arms around her securely. "It's all right. It didn't happen. Thank God I was here." He brushed his lips against her smooth hair. "I've never seen a snake like that. Is it poisonous?"

Meredith shuddered. "Yes. Deadly. I've seen men as big as you die within minutes after its bite."

Jeremy led her to the chair and sat, drawing her into his lap. Meredith linked her arms around his neck and laid her head on his shoulder. Her irritation with him a moment earlier was forgotten as she luxuriated in the comfort and safety of his arms. Jeremy stroked her back soothingly, but he frowned, his eyes distant and thoughtful.

Chapter XXII

JEREMY'S LEG continued to heal, and before long he resumed his work. Meredith spent most of her time writing out the "freedom papers" for their slaves. Each week they freed more. Although many neighbors were aghast and the others doubtful, their experiment was at least starting successfully. As Jeremy had predicted, few blacks left the plantation, and the productivity of the ones who remained was greatly increased. Free and working for wages, they assumed a far greater interest in the crops. Neb was proving to be a capable overseer, intelligent, hardworking, and naturally commanding.

Jeremy traveled to Charleston for seeds to replace those that had burned. When he returned to Bitterleaf, he brought with him the new clothes Madame Reveneau had made for Meredith. Betsy helped Meredith unpack the elegant dresses, oohing over their style and beauty. "Oh, Miss Merry, you'll look positively beautiful in this!" she exclaimed, holding up a honey-gold velvet gown.

Meredith sighed. They were lovely, and combined with the new, soft way she wore her hair, even she would admit she was almost handsome in them. "Yes. It's too bad I'm in mourning."

"What?" Jeremy was lounging in a chair, smilingly watching Meredith's excited examination of the boxes of clothes. At her words he sat bolt upright, a frown creasing his brow.

"You can't mean to continue to wear that awful black instead of these!"

"But Jeremy, it's been only two months since Daniel died. I can't possibly leave mourning yet."

"I'll not have you looking like a crow any longer," Jeremy announced flatly. "Daniel loved you and he wanted your happiness. You'd serve that wish far better by wearing pretty clothes! I insist you wear Madame's gowns."

Meredith set her jaw mulishly. "Jeremy, it's wrong. It's disrespectful."

"I'm tired of your obsession with propriety and others' opinions. Damn it! You will wear those clothes."

"Are you commanding me?" Meredith's voice rose dangerously.

For an instant Jeremy's jaw jutted out as sharply as hers, and his eyes flamed blue fire. Then he visibly relaxed his face. A smile touched his mouth. "I'd never command you to do or not do anything. I'm merely saying Daniel would have wished it. I didn't realize you were the sort to pay an honor to Daniel that would have hurt him and satisfies only the bunch of pseudo-aristocrats who despised and reviled him when he was alive."

Jeremy had learned a thing or two about dealing with Meredith since their marriage. The major rule was not to back her into a corner or order her to do anything. She would always balk in such a situation. Only reason and persuasion worked with her.

Meredith hesitated. She hadn't thought about her insistence on wearing mourning in that way. It was true that Daniel had not liked mourning. She recalled his asking her to abandon it a few months after Anne died, but she had stubbornly refused. It was what was done in polite society. One wore mourning for at least a year if it was a close relative. She supposed that since Daniel was her stepfather the time could be shortened, but certainly not to two months. Still, it was the social custom of a society Daniel neither liked nor fit in with. He had battled constantly to be accepted by them, and his greatest joy had been when Equilibrium defeated the planters' horses for him. Daniel would have laughed at the idea of her flouting the planters' social strictures. "Perhaps you are right," she murmured, her eyes returning longingly to the colorful cascade of silks, velvets, and brocades spilling out of the boxes.

Jeremy hid a smile. "You know I am. Daniel would be the first to agree you should throw out your black." He selected a hand-painted dress from the pile and tossed it to Betsy. "Here, iron this one." His gaze went to Meredith. "I'd like you to wear it tonight."

Meredith smiled, her resolve to wear black slipping away. "All right. At least here at home I shall leave off mourning."

She felt beautiful and free that evening in her gown. The bright pink roses splashed across the material brought out the color in her cheeks, and the style flattered her figure. Her eyes danced with pleasure at her improved looks and the joyous release from black. Watching her, Jeremy's heart began to thud in his chest. How lovely she was tonight. His mind dwelled with anticipation on the night to come, so distracting him he barely remembered to make civil conversation with her. After they had finished the evening meal, he escorted Meredith upstairs.

"It's a beautiful house," he remarked, glancing around at the painted walls and the fine rugs lying on waxed floors. "And big. Ample room for our brood."

"Our what?"

"Our brood of children."

Color touched her cheeks. "What makes you think we will have even one, let alone a brood?"

His grin was languid and seductive. "I intend to make sure." Possessively he laid a hand upon her flat abdomen. "Who knows? Perhaps our future heir is resting inside you already." Meredith's breath quickened and she glanced away, unnerved by his intense gaze. He gestured toward the rooms in the opposite direction of their bedroom. "That can be the children's wing—safely away from us. First Algernon's—"

"Algernon!"

"Yes," he answered seriously. "The eldest. He deserves a room to himself, don't you think? He'll be a heller, like his father, no doubt."

She smiled, her voice teasing. "You think there'll be no Whitney in him?"

"A little of his mother, probably. Stubborn, tall, argumentative."

"That's *all* he'll get from me?"

"Would you rather he wiggle his hips seductively or spoke in a high voice? Or perhaps you'd like him to possess your skill in sewing?"

A giggle bubbled from her lips. "You idiot."

"Of course, our second, Emily, will be a beauty and very like her mother, with a dash of Irish charm thrown in for good measure. She'll have her father wrapped around her little finger."

"I have no doubt of that."

He led her along the hall he had given to their imaginary children, opening doors and peering in. "This looks good. Add a few frills and furbelows, and it will be perfect for Emily. Next, the twins' room. They'll want to share, of course. One will be very much like Algie, but the other will be as studious and lanky as Cousin Galen."

"Jeremy!" Meredith protested, laughing. He continued his mock tour of the rooms, doling them out to so many children that Meredith lost count. Finally, when they had circled the house and allotted the rooms, they returned to their bedroom door. Meredith tilted back her head coquettishly. "And how, sir, do you think we'll have all these progeny if we spend our time exploring the house?"

He grinned, enjoying her mild flirtation. Meredith was enticing, warm, giving, everything he could ask for in a wife. Suddenly he was very glad he hadn't pursued the idea of selling the plantation. He couldn't imagine being happier than he was here and now. "I'll look into that matter," he promised, bending to kiss her lips, the gentle touch quickly changing into a searing, searching exchange. He crushed her against his chest. "Damn, I want you," he growled, and swept her into their bedroom.

After breakfast the next morning, Jeremy rode out to speak to Neb, who was supervising the spring planting. Meredith retired to the sitting room and began mending one of the long damask board clothes. She sewed away dreamily, her mind elsewhere half the time. She knew it was time to begin spring cleaning, but this morning she felt too mellow and happy to start such a project. Jeremy's torrid lovemaking last night had left her soft and melting and unable to concentrate. He had been tender and anxious to give her pleasure as well as receive it. She wondered if perhaps he had some affection for her. Was it completely foolish to hope he might?

Her daydreams were interrupted by a soft tap on the door. Paul glided into the room. "A visitor here to see Mr. Jeremy on business, ma'am. What shall I tell him?"

Meredith sighed. She hadn't any desire to talk to anyone, but it could be hours before Jeremy returned. She knew more about the plantation than Jeremy did, and it seemed unfair to make the visitor cool his heels when she could discuss it just as well. "Send him in, Paul."

A thick-waisted man with a round, babyish face strolled into the room. He wore a happy, almost silly look that made Meredith wonder how he survived in any business dealings. "John J. Emerson, Esquire," he introduced himself cheerfully, executing a brief, unpolished bow.

"Please sit down, Mr. Emerson." Meredith indicated a chair. "Now tell me, what can I do for you?"

"It was actually your husband I wished to see, ma'am," he began.

Meredith smiled. "I understand. But I'm afraid it will be some time before Mr. Devlin returns from the fields. Spring is a very busy time for him, you see. I know everything about the business, so I'm sure I could help you. Then you wouldn't have to spend a rather boring time waiting for Mr. Devlin."

Emerson smiled benignly. "That's very kind of you, ma'am. It's simple enough. I wanted to ride over Bitterleaf."

"I beg your pardon?" Whatever did the man want? Why should a total stranger wish to roam their plantation?

"Perhaps I should explain. I'm the land agent Mr. Devlin saw on his recent trip to Charleston."

"The land agent?" Meredith felt as though her lungs and heart had stopped. She was suddenly flooded with dread.

"Yes'm. He came to see me on his recent trip to Charleston about selling his plantation. Of course, I was interested in the property from his description, but I like to see a place for myself when the weather's turned decent. Sometimes owners tend to be a bit . . . ah, enthusiastic about their property. So I caught a ride up here with a boat captain this morning. From what I've seen of the house and grounds, it's everything Mr. Devlin told me it was, and more."

"I'm pleased you like it," Meredith uttered through stiff lips. "Are—are you sure you have the right place?"

"Mr. Jeremy Devlin?" Now he was the one to stare at her. "Aren't you Mrs. Devlin? Isn't this Bitterleaf plantation, the old Whitney place?"

Meredith still struggled against believing it. "And you say Jeremy wanted to sell Bitterleaf?"

"Why, yes. I was curious as to why a man would wish to sell such a profitable farm. So I asked him what was wrong with it. He told me how he disliked the climate here and was returning to London." He was silent for a moment, watching Meredith, who had turned as pale as the damask cloth in her lap. "Ma'am, are you all right? Did I say something amiss? I—I'm sure I have it correct. I hope I haven't spoiled a surprise."

'No, you haven't spoiled any surprise, Mr. Emerson." Meredith was seized with cold, deadly rage. "However, I am afraid you've made a wasted trip. You see, Bitterleaf is not for sale. What Mr. Devlin neglected to tell you is that the plantation is mine, not his. It is not for sale and never will be as long as I live. So you might as well turn around and sail immediately for Charleston. In fact, one of our servants will take you there in the pirogue." She rose and rang for Paul, clearly dismissing Emerson. He gaped at her blankly, hardly able to absorb the fact that instead of granting permission to explore the farm, she was tossing him out.

When Paul entered the room, Meredith gave firm instructions to take Mr. Emerson to Charleston immediately. Nodding shortly at the land agent, she swept from the room. Once out of his sight, she almost ran upstairs. Jeremy had lied to her! With every loving gesture and word, he had lied! "On his recent trip to Charleston"—it must have been only a few days ago when he had gone there to buy seeds. He was planning—had probably always planned—to sell Bitterleaf and escape with the money to London to resume his carefree, riotous life at her expense. He had cheated, lied, kissed, and

caressed her while he planned to break her heart and steal
everything she had. There wasn't a speck of truth in the man.
He was a wicked, vicious snake who wouldn't hesitate at
anything to obtain what he wanted. No doubt it had sickened
him to have to bed her the past weeks, but he had done it to
lull her suspicions and make her believe she was safe, even
cared for. All the time that she was falling in love with him,
he was plotting to destroy her, to betray and desert her. It was
as if the enormous love she felt for him now turned to slap
her in the face. If only she didn't care, it wouldn't be so bad.
If only she didn't love him and thrill to his caresses, it
wouldn't hurt, wouldn't slash through her like a knife. Disillu-
sion and rejected love fed the fuel of her anger, multiplying
until she was consumed by fury. She yanked the bell rope
sharply. When Betsy entered the room a few moments later,
Meredith whirled, her eyes bright with unshed tears. "Pack
Mr. Devlin's things and remove them."

"What?"

"You heard me," she snapped. "I want everything belonging to him out of my room immediately! Clothes, brushes,
shoes, everything!"

"But—but where should I put them?"

"I don't care what you do with them!" she almost shrieked.
"Put them in the room he used to occupy. Toss them outside
on the grass. It doesn't matter to me. Just get it all out of
here."

"Yes, ma'am." Betsy bobbed a little curtsy and flew to
work, gathering up Jeremy's belongings and stuffing them in
a trunk, then ringing the bell for a footman to carry it out.
Within an hour she had stripped the room of his possessions.
Betsy was wise enough not to speak to her enraged mistress
again. She didn't know what had happened between her and
Jeremy, but obviously at the moment Meredith despised him.

Jeremy didn't return until late in the afternoon. He roamed
through the house looking for Meredith, then went up to their
room. His hand reached out to turn the doorknob, but it was
locked. His momentum nearly carried him smack into the
wood. Irritated, he stepped back. "Meredith? Are you in
there? The damned door is locked."

"Yes," Meredith replied coolly from inside.

"Well, let me in." There were a few sounds inside the room, and the door opened a crack. Jeremy caught a glimpse of Meredith's deadly white complexion and bright eyes. "What's the matter? Are you ill? Why did you lock the door?"

"I'm not ill. I've merely come to my senses. This is no longer your room."

For a moment he gaped at her, too stunned to speak. Then he growled, "What in the hell are you talking about?"

"Mr. Emerson came to see me today." She paused significantly.

His expression didn't change. "So?" he finally prodded. "Who's he?"

"The man you're trying to sell *my* plantation to," Meredith bit out, her eyes flashing.

Recognition dawned on Jeremy's face, and any last hope that it was a mistake faded. Good God, he had forgotten about the fellow. Jeremy blurted out the first thing that flashed into his mind. "Why the devil did he come here?"

"He wanted to inspect my land before he purchased it. Surely you realized he would want to view it eventually. Or did you intend to sneak him in without my knowing?"

"Now, Meredith," he began soothingly. "It's a mistake. I can explain—"

"Don't bother!" Rage surged in her "How dare you! How dare you think you can sell my land and run off with the money? You're a lying, cheating blackguard! Daniel called you an Irish devil, and he was right. You hoodwinked a dying man and set out to destroy the daughter he was trying so hard to protect. I can never forgive you for that. Never!"

"Meredith, don't. Please, listen to—"

"No!" She jerked away from his hands reaching out to her. "Don't you dare touch me—ever! I despise you. I've heard enough of your lies to last a lifetime. 'Oh, Meredith, how lovely you look in those clothes.' " She mimicked him viciously, the pain of his betrayal tainting her voice with bitterness. "How you panted and moaned in our bed, how you pretended to enjoy my body—and all the while you were preparing to betray me utterly."

"No, I swear—"

"Liar! You were going to sell my land. *My* land. Bitterleaf—
the only thing I love in the whole world."

Jeremy was hot and tired and irritated by her refusal to
allow him to defend himself. Now her words pricked him with
jealousy. He retorted sharply, "Of course—your land. Nothing else matters to you, does it? No mere husband can
compare to this great stretch of land. You'd do anything to
have it—even marry me."

"Yes, but, God, how I regret it now! Let me tell you,
Jeremy Devlin, you may be my husband, but you don't run
things here. This isn't your land to sell. It's *mine!* And,
believe me, I sent your friend packing."

He barked back at her, "You know as well as I that
everything that belongs to you is mine. I have full rights over
it." He would have liked to grab Meredith and shake her until
she cried. How could any woman of feeling stand there
without tears for the close marital communion that was being
trampled beneath her angry words? She didn't give a damn about
him or anyone else. Meredith cared only about her land, her
precious Bitterleaf. She wouldn't even allow him a chance to
explain.

"Under the law, perhaps, but every person on this plantation answers to me, not you. I am the Whitney here. Bitterleaf
is mine. You try to take it from me, and I'll—" She broke
off, fighting her tears. When she had brought them under
control, she continued, "I swear you'll never sell this plantation,
even if I have to kill you in your sleep to stop you."

"I believe you would."

"It would cause me no sorrow to end *your* life. It would
mean no more than stepping on a bug."

His skin seemed to stretch tightly across his facial bones,
paling under his golden tan. He was conscious of a deep, raw
ache in his chest and throat. Meredith hated him, always had.
Briefly her passion had overcome her contempt, but now it
was back in full force. He was the least important thing in her
life. Jeremy sneered, blazing with the need to hurt her as she
had just wounded him. "Thank you for informing me of the
place I occupy in your life. You're the hardest, most vindic-
tive female I ever met. There isn't an ounce of feminine
forgiveness or love in you. Sleeping with you is like sleeping

with a black widow spider. I don't know when you'll turn and bite. Believe me, I'll rest easier alone. I hope your land can keep you warm at night. Good day, madam.'' He turned sharply on his heel and stalked away. She could hear his footsteps thudding down the stairs and the slam of the back door behind him.

Moodily Meredith strolled to her window and gazed out. Moments later, as she stood watching, Jeremy emerged from the stables riding Equilibrium and galloped down the drive. Tears flooded her eyes. She could not stop the images of his feigned passion, of his loving words and teasing charm. She felt as though her heart had been ripped from her chest. How was she going to live without his touch, his companionship? The rest of her life stretched out miserably. Flinging herself across the bed, she broke into sobs.

For the next few days, Meredith and Jeremy managed to avoid each other most of the time. She plunged into the spring cleaning, mercilessly harrying the servants into cleaning the house spotlessly. They took up the rugs, beating them thoroughly, and stored them in the attic. They scrubbed and waxed the floors until they gleamed and laid down the large straw mats, which were cooler in the fierce, damp heat. The draperies were hauled down and cleaned, and the furniture was polished. Mosquito netting was hung on the beds to combat the scourge of the annoying insects that always accompanied hot weather. Not a nook or cranny escaped Meredith's remorseless eye.

Jeremy spent all his time either in the fields or in his office. Although Neb was a natural leader, he was as inexperienced as Jeremy, and they needed each other's help. A curious friendship sprang up between the two men, both large, strong, quick of mind and once in bondage. From the first there had been a rapport between them and, despite their differences, they were quick to understand the other's ideas and usually agreed. Jeremy preferred to take a lunch with him to the fields to eat while he talked to Neb instead of dining in chilly silence with his wife. He also usually avoided breakfast by downing a piece of toast and a hunk of cheese before his early-morning inspection of the fields.

That left only supper when they were forced to be together. Both dreaded it. Meredith, still throbbing with hurt and anger, sat stiffly silent throughout the meal, quelling any attempt at conversation. Jeremy soon gave up trying to talk to her. So they sat with barely a word passing between them, concentrating on their food with an intensity it didn't deserve. Every bitter meal deepened the rift between them. Meredith missed their earlier companionship. She ached to question Jeremy about the progress he was making in the fields. There was so much she wanted to know and share with him. Was the rice planted yet? How was Neb doing as overseer? Were the men working better now that they were free? She realized they had built a life together in the past months, and now she felt as if it had been torn from her. But pride and resentment kept her from asking any of her questions.

Jeremy suffered in much the same way. He wanted to expound on the work and ask her advice. Like a small boy, he wanted to boast that his program with the former slaves was doing well, that they worked with greater efficiency and skill. He longed to see her beaming her approval. More than that, he wished to be back in her bed and to feel her warm body against him. He dreamed of lying with his arm around her once again, one hand casually stroking her bare shoulder, talking and chuckling together about the day's events, their neighbors—anything, it didn't really matter. And after the close conversation, they would make love—fast, slow, hot and churning, languid. Meredith was a constant delight, a source of enjoyment every time they came together. In the months of their marriage, he had never tired of her. In fact, now that he was deprived of her lovemaking, he yearned for it more than before they were married.

At dinner one evening, Jeremy gazed down the long table to where Meredith sat in cold isolation at the opposite end. By placing herself there, she had made any discussion virtually impossible. Jeremy scowled, remembering how she had blocked every attempt to explain. After his anger cooled, he had had to admit that Meredith had good reason to be angry. He had been furious with Meredith when he went to see Emerson, and he had discarded the idea not long afterward, but that didn't excuse him. He had acted selfishly, even wickedly. When he thought about selling Meredith's prized possession and leaving her behind while he sailed to England, the idea appalled him. The action had been a remnant of his old uncaring, bitter self, the aristocratic so-called gentleman who heedlessly sought his pleasures without worrying about the consequences. Now he would never think of abandoning Meredith and Bitterleaf, no matter how she provoked him. It amazed him how he had changed. He wasn't sure what had wrought the transformation. The months of pride-puncturing servitude? Meredith's tart, sweet passion? Or the enjoyment of her witty company? Her compassion for the ill and weak? Perhaps it was Bitterleaf itself, which demanded his heart and mind and muscle and somehow had seeped into his very soul until it would tear him apart to have to leave it. Or maybe it was a combination of all those things. Whatever had caused it, he had changed. He wanted nothing other than what he had, and he despised himself for even considering abandoning Meredith. He wanted to apologize for the wrong and assure her that it would never happen again, to explain the circumstances and the anger that had propelled him to Emerson's office. He wanted Meredith to forgive him and permit a return to their former happiness. But she would not allow it. She cut him off, avoided him, sat so far away they could not speak.

Jeremy rubbed his forehead. He couldn't let it continue this way. It would only get worse. "Meredith, we can't go on like this," he began earnestly. Meredith raised her head, icy slivers stabbing her heart. "I have to talk to you."

She was sure he was about to announce that he was returning to England. Hastily she rose, leaving her dinner half eaten on her trencher. Hardly knowing what to say or do, but too frightened to let him continue, she murmured, "No! We have nothing to talk about."

"Meredith!" She swept from the room. Jeremy slammed his fist onto the table, causing dishes and mugs to rattle. Damn that woman! Why was she so obstructive? So unfeeling? Why wouldn't she allow him to apologize and explain? At first he had thought she merely wanted to make him suffer for what he had done. It was typical of a woman to withhold her sexual favors and smiles when she didn't get her way, punish-

ing her man until he relented or she determined he had paid
sufficiently in pain. He had seen his mother and his mistresses do it often enough. He had waited for her to relent, to
decide his punishment was over, and let him talk to her again.
But now it seemed as though she meant to keep herself from
him forever. Jeremy frowned and ran a hand through his hair.
Damn her. Damn her.

He rose and strode rapidly to his room. But there he had
nothing to do except sleep, and he didn't feel at all like
sleeping. Again he cursed softly and viciously. How did
Meredith manage to keep him in such turmoil? Whenever he
tried to win her back, she blocked him, and he would rebound
into a rage, furious at her stubbornness and cutting rejection
of him. No other woman had so gotten under his skin, been
able to find all his sore spots and make him shout with pain or
anger or frustration—or purr with pleasure. At that thought, a
familiar warmth licked along his veins. Jeremy sat down with
a groan and leaned his head back against the chair. It barely
took anything nowadays to turn him into a pulsating mass of
desire.

At night he dreamed of Meredith—if he was lucky enough
to sleep at all. Too often he lay awake, thinking about her,
recalling their lovemaking. He daydreamed of bursting into
her inviolate bedroom and making love to her with such skill
Meredith begged him to stay. It had been only two weeks
since she had barred her bedroom door to him, but already it
seemed a lifetime. He had taken to stripping and swimming in
the river after he rode home from the fields, but it was not
done just to wash away the sweat and grime of the day. He
hoped the cool water would decrease his aching passion. He
would sit at supper, watching Meredith calmly eat her food.
She refused to even glance at him. She had returned to her
drab mourning—to spite him, he supposed. Though the dresses
heightened his irritation, they did nothing to lessen his desire.
Instead he recalled the succulent body beneath the clothes and
mentally undressed her, with the result that by the end of the
meal, when Meredith left the room, he often remained impo-
litely seated so as not to reveal the thick bulge in his breeches.

Jeremy sighed and glanced at himself in the mirror. He was
thinner, his cheeks hollow and the skin under his eyes darkly

circled. He had worked to the point of exhaustion lately, not only to make the farm succeed, but also to keep thoughts of Meredith at bay. The hard work, brief meals, and lack of sleep had combined to make him look and feel like the very devil. How long did she plan to continue this torture? Never having felt the deep insecurity that Meredith harbored, Jeremy didn't realize how bitterly shamed and hurt she was to discover he had tried to sell Bitterleaf. He considered it an argument about the land, not understanding that it had shaken her confidence in herself and obliterated her trust in him. She retreated into her shell, miserable and lonely, hating herself for having been foolish enough to believe Jeremy had wanted her. Jeremy, not perceiving that she believed his lovemaking had been all lies, regarded her isolation as merely her way of making him pay for what he had done.

And pay he was. Jeremy clenched his fists. Damn! Was he going to sit there and allow a woman—a tall, ungainly, proud woman at that—to rule him? He got determinedly to his feet, his emotions bouncing, as they had all week, from desire to self-dislike to anger to determination. No woman led Jeremy Devlin around by the nose! There was a village less than an hour's ride from Bitterleaf, and where there was a village, there was a tavern. Where there was a tavern, there was a tevern wench. He'd never met a tavern wench yet who wasn't willing to spread her legs for a little silver. Smiling thinly, Jeremy shrugged on his outer jacket and grabbed his tricorn hat. He would ride to the tavern to drink and converse with the other men there, and if the opportunity arose, he would try out one of the sluts who would no doubt be available. Let Meredith find out she wasn't the only woman. He'd ease himself on the tavern wench and allow Meredith to stew a while longer without his lovemaking. They'd see which one broke first.

Chapter XXIII

WHEN JEREMY entered The Blue Ox in Greenoak, he paused for a moment, blinking in the smoke-filled air. At a table in one corner of the low-ceilinged, crude room, Blaine Randall lifted a hand and gestured to Jeremy to join his party. Jeremy hesitated, then strolled toward them. Remembering his plan to tumble a serving wench, he was reluctant to sit with planters who knew Meredith. He didn't want to shame her before her peers, forgetting his earlier desire to retaliate as well as to release his sexual tension.

"Jeremy!" Blaine's face was flushed, and he weaved slightly as he rose to greet Jeremy. "Come, sit down. Do you know my brother Percy? And Kenneth Littleton?"

"Of course. I met them at the race, I believe."

"Yes," Kenneth agreed heartily, heaving to his feet to shake Jeremy's hand. "Beautiful animal you rode. You have an admirable seat, too. Where'd you learn to ride like that?"

Blaine flushed at his companion's blunt question. It was what everyone in the parish wondered, but few were so tactless as to ask. He started to intervene, but Jeremy answered without embarrassment, "In England when I was a lad, at my father's hunting cottage. I frequently visited him there. My father was an excellent horseman."

"I see." Kenneth frowned. He hadn't learned what they had

all wanted to know. If anything, Jeremy's words had deepened the mystery of his origins.

Blaine motioned to a blowsy, dark-haired serving girl and ordered an ale for Jeremy. The girl eyed Jeremy and smiled boldly. Her breasts were full and thrusting, swelling above the neckline of her blouse. She leaned over to remove Percy's empty tankard, allowing Jeremy a long, clear look down her blouse. He noted in surprise that he didn't experience even a twinge of lust. How odd, when he had been so long without sex that even the sight of Meredith's bare throat or slender hand filled him with longing.

"We're celebrating," Blaine informed Jeremy, smiling. "So drink up."

"What's the occasion?"

"Blaine's about to join the ranks of those no longer free," Percy explained.

"Like yourself," Blaine explained, "I will soon be a married man."

"Althea Whitney?" Jeremy hazarded a guess.

Blaine's grin broadened. "How did you know?"

Jeremy smiled. "It's been written all over your face since I first met you."

"She's too long and cool for my taste," Kenneth remarked in his usual blunt way.

Jeremy swallowed, suddenly flooded with the lust that the serving girl's lavish display of her breasts had not inspired. "Don't discount tall, cool-seeming women," he murmured, flashing a knowing look at Blaine. "There's much more to them underneath." Blaine's eyes burned, and he gazed at Jeremy in perfect harmony.

The serving girl made it a point to sway past their table often, each time smiling at Jeremy and brushing him with some part of her anatomy. None of her efforts enticed Jeremy. He told himself it was the presence of the others. He was not a man who conducted his affairs in public, he thought, conveniently forgetting that he had not had such scruples before he met Meredith.

The other men had been at the tavern quite a while before Jeremy. They reached their limit and exceeded it. After a couple of hours, Jeremy, himself unsteady on his feet, had to

help the other three to their horses and into their saddles. He
returned to the table and called for another drink. Now, he
decided, he would begin his flirtation with the maid.

She was eager to respond, but Jeremy found he had little
interest in flirting. She was not an ill-looking girl, though her
full figure bordered on plumpness. But she was dull and
giggling, and there was no wit to her banter. Knowing all the
motions, Jeremy followed them by rote, even though not
inspired. He pulled her between his spread legs and took out a
coin, which he dropped down her blouse between her breasts,
letting his hand linger in the warm crevice for a moment.

The girl giggled and pulled out the coin. "That's a strange
place to put your coin, sir."

"Indeed? I can think of other things I'd rather place there—
and other places I'd rather put things."

She giggled at his coarse insinuation. "Go on, sir, you're
teasing a girl."

"Am I?" Jeremy was desperately bored with the game and
stood up quickly. "Do you have a room here?"

"Yes, sir." The woman was startled and disappointed by
his abrupt abandonment of the teasing. He was a well-featured
gentleman, and she usually didn't get such as he. She would
have liked to continue the play longer. "Upstairs."

"And could you slip off for a few moments?"

"Of course, sir, if you wish it."

"I do."

She hastily returned her tray to the serving bar and whispered to the tavern keeper, then rejoined Jeremy. She led him
out the rear door and up a narrow staircase to the workers'
rooms. Inside her small chamber, she turned, tossing back her
hair, and began to fiddle with the lacings of her bodice.
Jeremy watched in silence, his lack of expression unnerving
her. The taut material fell apart easily, and her full breasts
tumbled out. Jeremy made no move, and she hastily finished
undressing, hoping the sight of her whole body nude would
elicit a response. Her hips were broad, matching the lush
breasts, and though her legs and waist were a trifle thick, her
figure was not unpleasant.

But to Jeremy, recalling Meredith's spare frame, her volup-
tuous curves seemed excessive and coarse. The desire he had

known earlier at home deserted him. Though she smiled and
wiggled her hips invitingly, he felt not the faintest stirring
of passion. "I'm sorry," he told her, blushing a little at
the unusual situation. "I think too much drink has unmanned
me." He dug in his pocket and brought out a coin, which
he flipped to the woman. "Here. This is for your trouble."

She stared at him, mouth agape, the coin clutched tightly in
her fist, as Jeremy turned and thundered down the rickety
stairs. In a foul mood, he shouted for the hostler to fetch his
horse, mounted, and set off down the darkened, rutted lane.
He had drunk a fair amount of ale, but not enough to incapaci-
tate him. No, that wasn't the reason. He knew the cause, and
it made him grind his teeth in rage: he wanted no one but
Meredith. She was the only one he sweated and hungered for.
Another woman wouldn't ease the discomfort. He emitted a
short, bitter bark of laughter as he recalled his thoughts before
their wedding. Then he had figured he would tire of her
quickly and leave. Instead, he wanted Meredith more than
ever. He was like a lovesick lad.

When he reached Bitterleaf, he left his horse with a stableboy and entered the darkened house, climbing the stairs quietly.
At the head of the staircase he paused before Meredith's door.
The desire that had deserted him was now back in full force,
thrumming along his veins and pounding in his loins. What
would happen if he entered her room? Would she shriek?
Cry? Rail at him to leave? Or would he be able to kiss her
awake and feel her arms curve around his neck, her lips
respond to him. . . . He swallowed harshly and reached out
to turn the doorknob. It moved, then stopped. She had locked
her door against him. His hand dropped away as if burned,
and he stalked to his own door, closing it behind him with a
solid thud.

Meredith heard his hand try the doorknob, for she had lain
awake for several hours, unable to sleep, a condition that was
becoming more and more familiar. She had seen Jeremy ride
out from the stables, which he often did in the evenings. She
didn't know where he went, but her jealous heart was certain
he met Opal. Tonight he was gone far longer than usual and,
remembering her fear of the topic he had wanted to discuss at
the dinner table, she feared he had run away with Opal.

Finally, long after everyone else had retired, Meredith forced herself to leave the window and go to bed. But lying in the dark could not compel sleep. Instead, she continued to think about Jeremy and Opal, about what he wished to tell her and how long she could manage to avoid it. Worst of all, she remembered the long nights of lovemaking they had once shared before she found out about his perfidy. She wished fervently, not for the first time, that she had not discovered it. There was much to be said for ignorance. She could have blissfully continued enjoying his caresses, believing he returned at least a part of her affection. She would not have had to lie awake, hating him while she ached for his touch, her hot, bitter tears mingling with the molten yearning in her loins.

The fire of her original anger had burned down, leaving bitterness and disgust, as much at herself for believing him as at Jeremy. She had been a fool throughout the whole thing, and her final, crowning idiocy was tossing him out of her bedroom in that imperious manner. Later, she realized it was probably more a relief to him than anything else. She had not deprived him, only herself. Meredith was the one who ached at night, several times almost going to his room and begging him to make love to her despite the humiliation. She missed his warm, big body in bed, and she missed the delights of his fingers and mouth. She missed their shared laughter, their conversation, their interest in the farm. In fact, she felt utterly alone and miserable. The more miserable she grew, the more she withdrew from Jeremy, fearing her own tears and the treacherous temptation to fling herself into his arms and ask forgiveness.

She hated him, of course, although she noticed it had become more of a conscious effort every day to keep alive her steadfast hatred. But more than hatred, she felt the piercing pain of his betrayal. And more than either, she knew the awful depression brought on by Jeremy's lack of effort to reconcile or to explain his actions. He could offer no excuse and seemed not to care whether he saw her or not. Instead, he spent more time in the fields, and every evening would ride out, doubtless to meet Opal. He didn't care, had never cared. But Meredith was finding out exactly how much *she* cared.

She missed him, she desired him, she loved him. Despite his treachery, she loved him, and was beginning to realize she always would.

Such gloomy thoughts had kept Meredith awake until she heard the jangle of a bridle and the muffled clomp of hooves in the middle of the night. She lay tensely in her bed, hands clasped over her chest, waiting and listening to Jeremy's familiar tread as he climbed the staircase. She heard his footsteps coming down the hall, then a momentary pause. Her doorknob turned. Even though she knew it was locked, she gripped her hands tighter, and her body grew rigid as she waited, heart pounding, suddenly alive with the insane hope that Jeremy would pound upon the door and demand entrance. But he did not. She heard his boot heels on the straw mats as he walked down the hall to his bedroom and the loud closing of his door. She relaxed and closed her eyes, tears seeping from beneath her lids.

As always in the spring, there was an outbreak of swamp fever among the slaves. Meredith began to spend most of her time nursing the black workers, dosing them wih Peruvian bark, combating their chills and fevers, and doing her best to make them drink water and other liquids to replace what they sweated out. Because it made the sick ones easier to treat, Meredith isolated them, quarantining three cabins for the sickrooms. Although she hated the sickness, she welcomed the work. It was so back-breakingly tiring that when she fell into bed at night she slept soundly, dreamlessly. It also meant she could see Jeremy even less and so avoid any discussion of his leaving, which loomed ever more threateningly every day. Though what they had could hardly be called a marriage, she couldn't bear to lose him altogether.

She was sound asleep one night when one of the kitchen servants knocked frantically at her bedroom door. Barely awake, Meredith tumbled from bed and opened the door. The girl's face was contorted with fear. "You gotta come quick, miss. Ben's took sick. A snake bit him."

"A snake?" Fear gripped her. If it was a poisonous snake, there was little hope of saving him. Time was of the essence. Meredith threw on a dressing gown and ran to the small chest where she kept her medicines. She unlocked it with trembling fingers as she asked the servant, "Was it poisonous?"

"I don't know."

"What did it look like?"

"I don't know. I didn't see it. Daisy, Ben's woman, fetched me and told me to run for you. She just said he's snakebit."

"All right. Let's go." Meredith hurried down the stairs, clutching the heavy bag under her arm. For the first time, she noticed that the girl was sopping wet. "Is it raining?"

"Yes'm. Best get something to cover you. It's fierce."

Meredith glanced out the window panel beside the door. It was indeed raining heavily. She jerked open the door of the tall armoire beside the front door and yanked out her cloak. Throwing it around her shoulders, she grabbed the first hat her hands fell on, an old tricorn of Daniel's. She followed the maid out the door, hunching her shoulders against the rain as she ran across the slick grass.

The cabin was one of the farthest away, unfortunately. Meredith knew that if Daisy had not had the forethought to apply a tourniquet, the man was doomed. The girl opened the door of the cabin for her, and Meredith ducked to go through the low doorway, removing her wet cloak and hat as she entered. She tossed them carelessly on the floor and went to Ben. He lay on the bed, moaning, his face contorted with pain, limbs twitching and writhing.

"Where was he bitten?"

Daisy stared up at Meredith from where she knelt on the floor beside Ben's bed. She burst into a flood of tears. "He's done for, miss, he's done for. The snake bit him."

"*Where* is the bite?" Meredith repeated sharply.

"His leg," she wailed.

Meredith's gaze moved to his legs, and she spotted the bruised fang marks on his left calf. She was inclined to agree with Daisy. Ben probably was not long for this world. However, she wrapped a tight bandage around his thigh and slashed the skin at the marks. Taking a small glass tube, she sucked out blood several times, hoping she was getting venom along with it. But she knew the tight bandage should have been wrapped around his thigh as soon as the bite occurred, to keep the poisonous juices from going to his heart. She applied a poultice of snakeroot to the wound and bandaged it, then dosed him heavily with Jamestown weed so that he would rest more comfortably. It was all she could do for the man.

Neighbors had gathered in and around the cabin, and several of the women now comforted Daisy. Meredith knew she was of no more use there. Comforting the grieving Daisy would be the main task, and the woman's friends were more able to do that than she. Sighing, she repacked her medicine bag and put on the wet cloak. Winding her hair around one hand, she shoved it on top of her head and pulled the large hat down firmly so that it shielded her face and neck from the pelting rain. Tucking the bag under her arm, Meredith left the cabin and walked toward the house, head down against the rain.

It was nearing dawn, she guessed. The rain obscured the rising sun, but there was a faint lightening of the sky, especially at the horizon. She wondered if it would be worthwhile to return to bed and decided it probably would not. She was sure she had lost a patient, and she was too sad to fall asleep easily. Besides, it would soon be time to begin her daily chores. It might be better simply to dress and start her day.

As she walked, lost in thought, she heard a sudden loud crack. Instinctively she jumped back and glanced around, startled. The first thing that registered in her mind was that she saw no breaking limbs that might have caused the noise; the second was that there was a large, fresh gash in the tree trunk beside her. Curious, she stepped closer to examine it and found an iron ball lodged in the trunk. Someone had shot a musket, narrowly missing her. Indignation rose in her at the thought that anyone would dare to fire at game so close to the house. She swung around sharply to go on to the house. She would rouse the servants and send them to find the hunter. A second crack sounded. This time Meredith dived for the ground even as she shrieked. Someone must be aiming at her!

She lay face down in the mud, her fingers clutching sprigs of grass. She trembled, her mind hardly able to absorb the fact. There had been a shot, and after that, time for a man to reload and fire again. He had to have seen her before the second shot. It couldn't have been accidental. She didn't so much think the idea as realize it in a flash of internal reasoning. She was too dazed for rational thought.

She had no idea how long she lay there, shivering, before she heard footsteps and voices calling her name. She opened her eyes to see several servants hurrying toward her. They stopped hesitantly several feet away, staring at her prone form. Then Jeremy impatiently broke through the knot of people and knelt beside her. "Meredith!"

He was white-faced, and when he turned her onto her back, Meredith felt a tremor in his hands. He was barefooted and shirtless. The rain coursed in rivulets down his face and chest, soaking his golden hair until it lay like a tight, flat cap around his face. "Meredith, are you all right?"

She nodded weakly, and he ran his hands over her arms and legs, searching for a break or wound. After her fright, Jeremy's touch was too much for her, and Meredith flung her arms around him and burst into sobs. His arms tightened, and he rocked her, stroking her back and head soothingly. For an instant, Meredith was lost in the joy of his sheltering arms, and she clung to him, luxuriating in his strength and warmth, breathing in the tangy scent of his wet skin. She was shaken with love, almost out of control, and she realized that in another moment she would reveal her love and beg him to return to her bed.

Sharply she reined in her emotions. Shoving against him with her hands, she wriggled out of his grasp. "I'm perfectly all right," she told him stiffly, rising.

Startled, Jeremy released her and sat back on his heels, stabbed by her rejection. She didn't want his comfort or protection! She hated his touch, even when she was frightened or hurt. Brusque with relief and hurt, he snapped. "What happened here?"

"How should I know?" Meredith responded. "Someone took a shot at me. There's one of the bullets in that tree."

"What?" He stared at her. "Someone fired at you? Are you sure?"

"Of course I am! I'm not given to hysterical flights of imagination. Someone fired a musket twice, both shots practically hitting me. What else could they have been doing but aiming at me?"

Jeremy went cold inside. Numbly he walked to the tree and peered at the gashed trunk. Sure enough, there was a small metal ball lodged in it. He swallowed. Neb, who had arrived shortly after Jeremy, had been roaming around, searching the ground. Now he mutely held out another ball. Jeremy had heard only the second report and Meredith's scream, but obviously there had been two. Meredith was right. It couldn't have been accidental, not two shots, considering the time and effort required to reload. By the second time, a hunter would have been bound to see Meredith. Jeremy had never felt so lost, so frustrated, so unable to handle a situation. Someone had tried to murder Meredith! Who? Why? How could he catch him before it happened again? His fear summoned up anger, and he whirled on Meredith, lashing out at the object of his fear. "What the devil were you doing out at this time of morning? Decent people are at home in bed! Or were you in bed, just not at home?"

"What! How dare you—what are you implying?"

He strode forward and grasped her arm so hard it numbed her. "Where were you? Who were you seeing? Dear Cousin Galen, perhaps?"

"You—you idiot! How could you possibly think that I—Your mind is in the gutter. I was tending a sick slave—I mean, worker. Ask Daisy if you doubt me. You are the lowest, vilest creature imaginable! Someone just tried to kill me, but all you think about is whether I had a 'rendezvous' with Galen. Thank God I don't have your sick, calculating mind."

As soon as he had uttered the words, Jeremy regretted them. It wasn't what he had intended to say at all. What he really wanted was to shake Meredith for running around in the middle of the night without protection, and then to crush her to his chest. Instead he had leaped on her with angry accusations, much as a parent harangues a lost child the moment he is found, love and fear pouring out in anger. "Meredith, I—" He started toward her, hand outstretched, but she whirled and stalked away. He followed her, but Neb's voice called him back.

"Mr. Jeremy." Neb juggled the musket balls in one great hand, frowning. "I need to tell you something."

Jeremy sighed and turned to Neb. Neb might have something important to say about Meredith's safety. "Yes, what is it?"

"I've been thinking. Miss Merry had on a long cloak down to her ankles. A person standing, say, in those trees behind the main house—they couldn't tell if she had on a dress or breeches."

"So?"

"So it's dark, and she's a tall lady, tall as most men. And she was covered by a cloak, with a man's hat on her head."

"I see. So you think someone mistook her for a man?" Relief flooded Jeremy.

"Yes, sir. It makes sense. More sense than somebody trying to shoot Miss Meredith. Who would have known the missus was going out to tend somebody at this hour? If a person was lying in wait so early, more likely they're expecting a person they know will leave the house at dawn because it's his habit. Then they see a gentleman walking toward the house. They don't know why he's there instead of leaving the house, but they aren't about to pass up the opportunity, so they shoot."

"Thinking it's me, you mean."

"Who else would be around the house at this hour dressed in a gentleman's hat and cloak? What other white man is here now?"

"You're right." Jeremy's heart began hammering with excited relief. "Of course. They weren't aiming at Meredith. No one would want to kill her. But he could have mistaken her for me." He grinned. "Thank you, Neb. You've just eased my mind a great deal."

Neb raised an eyebrow, obviously questioning the intelligence of a man relieved to discover he was the target of a killer. Jeremy laughed at his expression. "Don't you see? It means Meredith's out of danger. I don't have to worry about her. As soon as it's light, search everywhere within firing range, see if you can find any footprints or something to indicate who it might be. With this mud, there should be some tracks."

"Yeah, if the rain doesn't wash them out," Ned said pessimistically.

"And don't tell anyone. The less said, the better chance I

have of catching him.'' Jeremy turned and strode to the house, his step jaunty. It was strange, he supposed when he reflected on it, that he should be relieved it was himself who was the object of the killer's attempt. But he didn't feel the same heart-stopping fear he had when he believed someone had fired at Meredith. He remembered how his heart had frozen when he dashed out of the house and saw her inert form on the ground. For a moment he thought she was dead, and he couldn't breathe, couldn't think, could hardly walk. The terror had consumed him again when she told him she had been purposely fired at.

Jeremy stopped, hands on hips, heedless of the rain washing over his bare face and shoulders. He loved Meredith. He was madly, hopelessly, desperately in love with her. That was why no other woman would do. It explained his jangling, illogical, wildly swinging emotions ever since she had kicked him out of her bed. He was so in love that her rejection wounded him past bearing, made him want to strike out at her in retaliation. No wonder he never before had acted so foolishly or been so miserable. He never before had been in love. Jeremy shook his head, chuckling. Meredith, Meredith. Willful, sharp, warm, loving—except with him.

Slowly he started walking again, lost in thought. By God, he wasn't going to allow her to get away. The only problem was, he didn't know what to do. Love was a foreign emotion. Succeeding with women had always been easy, and if he lost out, it didn't matter because he didn't care about them. But now he had to win Meredith. If he let her slip through his fingers, his life would be over. So he must do everything exactly right. He had to convince her to love him. But how? Should he seduce? Cajole? Storm? Explain? What would it take? Or—the thought brought him up short—had he already thrown away his chances? Had he so disgusted her that she would hate him forever? He frowned. No. He couldn't accept that idea. He would tread gently. It wasn't his way, but he had to do it this time. He would be patient and wait for his opportunities. He would study her and learn how to win her heart. No matter how long it took, or how much he had to bend, he would make Meredith love him.

*   *   *

Meredith ran for her room as if it were a haven. Betsy, who had been drawn to the scene along with the other servants, followed on her heels. She helped Meredith out of the soggy nightclothes and washed her muddy face, hair, and hands. She brushed her damp hair dry, all the while droning on in a soft, monotonous voice, saying little, but gradually relaxing Meredith's nerves. After a while, her involuntary trembling stopped, and her mind returned from its blank, horrified state. She crawled into bed and pulled a pillow into her arms. By the time Jeremy opened the door to look in on her, she was fast asleep.

When she awoke, her head was much clearer. She was able to sit up and consider what had happened. Someone had tried to kill her. That was the first, unchangeable fact. She must find out who it was and somehow thwart another attempt. But who would want to kill her? Chewing at a thumbnail, she thought of everyone she knew: friends, relatives, acquaintances—none of them had anything against her. There were those who were not particularly her friends, but surely they did not hate her, either. Of course, there was Opal. She probably resented the fact that Meredith had married Jeremy. Meredith had become convinced they were lovers. But even if Opal was having an affair with Meredith's husband, would she really shoot Meredith? After all, Meredith wasn't any competition for her. She wasn't even sleeping with Jeremy. Perhaps Opal wanted to marry Jeremy, but there would still be the problem of Opal's husband. Would she kill two people just to obtain the man she wanted? The biggest argument against its being Opal was simply the fact that Meredith couldn't imagine her knowing how to shoot a musket, let alone lurking around Bitterleaf in the dark and the rain on the chance she might get to take a potshot at Meredith.

No, it was too random. The killer had to be someone who had heard or seen her when she raced to Ben's cabin. Someone on Bitterleaf. One of the servants? Unlikely. As far as she knew, she was well-liked by them, especially since she and Jeremy had set them free. No. It was ridiculous. They had no motive to shoot her—nor did anyone, for that matter. Except, of course, Jeremy.

Her mind skittered away from the thought, but she made

herself examine it logically, coolly. Jeremy would inherit a great deal when she died. Since they had no children, by law all her property would pass to him. True, he was wealthy now. He controlled her property. But she opposed his selling Bitterleaf, had even threatened to kill him if necessary. With her out of the way, there would be no one to object to his plans. Besides, he wouldn't have to put up with her in order to have the property.

Desperately she sought another person with equal motive or someone with a grudge against her, but only Jeremy would profit from her death. He easily could have heard her leaving her room to tend Ben and realized it was his chance to get rid of her. He could have slipped outside and hidden, then fired at her. When she saw him push through the servants to reach her, Meredith assumed he had come from the house. But he could have dashed around the side of the house. No one would have noticed. Everyone's eyes were on her.

She remembered the time he had asked her to take his boots from the wardrobe. A snake had crawled out of one, but it was merest chance that she had seen it. If it had remained coiled at the bottom and she had grasped the boots, it would have bitten her. She would have gone to her death as quickly as Ben no doubt had. Meredith closed her eyes, suddenly shaking uncontrollably. No, no . . . it couldn't be Jeremy. He had tried to sell the plantation, but surely that was the extent of his greed and treachery. He couldn't have slept with her for weeks, made passionate love to her, whispered sweet words in her ear—and been plotting to kill her! Jeremy wasn't so villainous. He couldn't have done it. Or was that merely wishful thinking? Only Jeremy would want her dead.

Chapter XXIV

During the next few days, Jeremy tried to woo Meredith. Instead of avoiding her, he made it a point to be with her. His manner was sweet and light, flirtatious, as if he were a swain instead of her husband. He turned the full force of his charm upon her, subduing his desire with an iron hand, just as he controlled the irritation and anger inspired by her cool, stand-offish attitude. He tried his utmost to make her love him, and Meredith couldn't help but be swayed by his words and smiles. Yet, even as her heart swelled with love for him and her loins ached for the fulfillment he could bring her, she feared him. His ingratiating ways frightened her more than full-blown rage. She suspected the switch was an effort to make them appear to be a happy, normal couple, newlyweds very much in love, so that when she was "accidentally" killed, he would not be accused. The servants would shake their heads and assure everyone that Mr. Jeremy had been kind and solicitous, that "he and the missus were always laughing and kissing." That was his reason for wooing her.

To make it all worse, there was no one to whom she could confide her suspicions. Althea called to inform Meredith of her engagement to Blaine Randall, and for a moment Meredith considered exposing her thoughts to her friend and cousin, but she could not. Even though she suspected Jeremy of trying to murder her, the words stuck in her throat. Loyalty and love would not allow her to condemn her husband to another—especially since Althea might tell her brother. Meredith wouldn't give Galen another opportunity to revile Jeremy. So she remained silent, listening with patience and determined smiles to Althea's effusive descriptions of her loved one's many admirable qualities, and of the small party she planned to have to announce the engagement. "It will be only a few friends and family," she assured Meredith. "A sitdown supper, very small and informal. Truly, it will be perfectly proper for you to attend despite your mourning. Mama and I planned it that way."

"Why, Althea, how kind of you to consider me at such a time."

Her cousin smiled. "Of course I would consider you. Your presence is very important to me. Since we'll be engaged for probably a year, by our wedding day you'll be out of mourning and can be my bridesmaid—I mean, matron. Oh, Meredith, tell me truly." She leaned forward earnestly and clasped Meredith's hand. "Is it nice, being married?"

Meredith almost laughed. What a question to ask her now! Yes, it was nice, except that she did not trust her husband and wouldn't let him into her bed. Yes, it was marvelous, except for her fear and doubt and the painful knowledge that Jeremy had married her for her land. Slowly she answered, "When two people love one another, it's the nicest, closest relationship one can have."

"Well, then, I don't have to worry, do I? Blaine and I definitely love each other." Althea's gray eyes sparkled. She continued to chatter in a lively manner for a few more minutes, then noticed the time and rose with a sigh. "Oh, dear, I'm afraid I must leave. Mama's at home with all the invitations, and you know Mama. If I don't relieve her, she'll have a migraine for a week."

"I'll walk you to the dock," Meredith offered, rising with her.

Spring was upon them in full force. The trees were lush and green. Azaleas bloomed in fountains of color, vibrant in the strong sunlight. The women carried parasols as they walked the short distance to the dock. Althea stepped into the small pirogue and the slaves poled away from the dock.

Meredith waved as she watched the boat disappear, then strolled back along the path. When she reached the garden, she turned aside to the small herb garden she maintained beyond the driveway. Desultorily she ambled through it, observing the growth of the green shoots poking above the rich soil and stopping to yank up a weed here and there. She glanced down at her gloves and grimaced. As usual, she had carelessly soiled them. There was no getting around it. She simply was not what a proper lady should be.

Suddenly her spine prickled, and she turned. Shading her eyes, she gazed into the woods beyond, then turned in a semicircle toward the house. It was strange, but she sensed a—an antagonism toward herself. Crazy, for there was no one around. But she could not shake the feeling. There was a definite malevolence in it, a hatred and ill-wishing. She shivered, a chill darting down her back and spreading outward.

The trees were quiet, unstirring, the air as hot and somnolent as on any spring day in South Carolina. She spotted no person or animal standing among the trees. She glanced nervously toward the main house. It was a long way to the house, really. It lay past the stretch of driveway and the flower garden. No one would hear her if she called. But then, perhaps home was not safety for her. Perhaps it was from there that someone watched, hating her. There was a flicker of movement at an upstairs window. A person looking out? Observing her? Had that been a flash of gold hair she had seen?

Meredith felt peculiarly suffocated and numb. She wanted to turn and run, but she didn't know where. Wetting her lips, she forced herself to tilt back her parasol and even give it a twirl as she moved on leaden feet toward the house. Just as she reached the flower garden, the door swung open, and Jeremy emerged. He ran lightly down the steps and crossed to meet her in the garden. "Hello, my love. Taking a stroll among the flowers?"

"I think that's obvious, isn't it?" she responded tartly, hating her treacherous heart for the way it pounded at his approach.

He shrugged. "I suppose. But you aren't the easiest person in the world to make idle chatter with."

"Why should you want to?"

Jeremy kept a determined curb on his temper. It was growing more and more difficult to do that where Meredith was concerned. She seemed bent on infuriating him. His nerves were already raw from weeks of involuntary celibacy. When Meredith held herself aloof or answered sharply, it was like salt to a wound. At times he glimpsed something in her eyes that made him hope she returned his love, but as soon as he saw it, she would toss out a tart remark and turn from him. He wondered if her coldness and surly words were a screen to keep him at a distance, to prick his irritation so that he would lash out at her instead of seducing her. Or was it a defense against herself, to make sure she did not go soft and weak? He didn't know. All he knew was that she made it almost impossible to talk. It exacerbated his already frayed nerves to the point where he sometimes was sure if he stayed around her another instant he would strike her—or drag her into his bed. For his passion was as difficult to subdue as his irritation, and the two seemed to feed upon each other.

Jeremy abandoned his original tack. "I saw the Whitney pirogue."

"Yes, Althea was here to tell me she's engaged."

"To Blaine?"

"Yes. How did you know?"

"I saw him at the tavern in Greenoak. He was celebrating with Percy and Kenneth Littleton."

"They're having a party two weeks from tonight, a small sit-down supper. Althea thought it would be proper for me to attend in mourning. I'd like to go—that is, if it's all right with you."

Jeremy chuckled. "You mean you ask my permission?"

"Well, you are my husband." For a brief, unguarded instant, Meredith's face flooded with yearning, begging to be convinced Jeremy was faithful and innocent of plotting to kill her. Jeremy blinked in astonishment and took a step toward her.

"Meredith . . ."

She whirled, remembering the malevolence she had sensed earlier in the herb garden. She could not give herself into Jeremy's hands if he was the one watching her—and who else could it be? She almost ran from the garden and Jeremy, darting up the steps into the house, pursued by the demons of her fear and desire.

The situation between them did not improve in the two weeks before Althea's party. If anything, it deteriorated. Jeremy's temper grew so short he snapped at everyone, including Meredith. One evening at the supper table, he barked at her so sharply that Meredith slammed down her tankard of cider and swept from the room, leaving her meal unfinished and Jeremy filled with chagrin. Everything he did, it seemed, made his cause less likely to succeed. It was most unfair that he could charm any woman but the one he loved.

But, he excused himself, Meredith could make a saint snarl. Being around her was sheer torture. He could smell her soft scent, a combination of roses and her skin, which reminded him with debilitating clarity of how she looked and felt and smelled as she lay beneath him in their lovemaking. Once he entered the study and found her standing on tiptoe on a short ladder, reaching for a topmost volume. Her movement exposed her ankles, and the mere sight of them made his palms sweat. He knew her body by memory, knew the weight of her breasts in his hands, the sharp points of her hipbones, the delicate spots behind her knees and elbows that when touched spiraled her passion. Though he saw her fully clothed, he could imagine perfectly how she looked without them. There was nothing about her that did not arouse him now, and he thought he must either go mad or rape her if she did not soon return to his bed.

Both Meredith and Jeremy were happily anticipating Althea's party. It would be a change from the constant tension between them. There would be other people to converse with and to take their minds off each other. Meredith hoped she would gain more perspective about him when she saw him beside other men. And Jeremy dreamed of taking her out on the dance floor and holding her in his arms as they moved to the music, for she could not object or escape before all those people. So when the afternoon of the party arrived, they were both filled with anticipation and eager to get started.

Jeremy dressed more quickly than Meredith, bathing and

donning an elegant dull gold satin coat and waistcoat and black satin breeches. Lace frothed down the front of his shirt and out his cuffs. The gold satin coat was edged in black, with black froggings to hold back the turned-back skirts of the jacket. Securing his white wig and adding the pearl stickpin that was his wife's wedding present, he strolled to Meredith's room to find out when she would be ready. He walked in without knocking and stopped short at the scene before him.

Meredith was bathing in the tiny half-tub, her long legs ludicrously cramped. But he did not see the humor of the situation, only her white breasts bobbing at the waterline, the pink tips blurred by the water, and her creamy-skinned, slender legs naked to his view after months of deprivation. Desire hit him like a rock in the stomach, and he wanted her so suddenly, so badly, he could hardly speak. Meredith gasped at his intrusion and crossed her arms to cover her bosom. "What are you doing here?"

"Why bother to conceal yourself?" he rasped, struggling for control. His fingers itched to pull her from the tub and take her right there, heedless of his clothes, her wetness, and the proximity of servants. "I've seen you before."

"I expressly forbade you to come into my room."

"I wanted to ask when you would be ready." Jeremy turned partially away to hide his obvious desire. He could not force her. He could not. He might lose her forever if he did. Yet he wanted her so much, he thought he would die if he did not have her. "Obviously it will be some time yet."

"The longer you remain here, the longer it will be," Meredith warned.

"I'll wait downstairs." His voice was clipped.

Only by carefully avoiding looking at her again was he able to leave the room. His wait downstairs seemed endless, although actually Meredith's agitation was so great that she immediately popped out of the tub, dried off, and dressed with tremendous speed. She was ready in record time. Clutching her fan as if it were a lifeline, she swept down the stairs. Jeremy, sitting in the drawing room, jumped to his feet when he saw her, a frown marring his features. "What the devil! Why are you wearing that?" He pointed contemptuously at her high-necked black silk gown.

"Because I'm in mourning."

"No! I forbid it. You left mourning. God knows why you saw fit to return to your crow's attire, but I'll be damned if I let you appear in public that way."

"I will wear this dress," she countered adamantly.

"Like hell. You'll change even if I have to drag you upstairs and dress you myself. Now, which will it be?"

For a moment Meredith stared him down. He grasped her arm harshly and pulled her upstairs, bellowing for her maid. Meredith surrendered quickly. Tonight it was easy to imagine Jeremy's doing her physical harm, even killing her. There was something wild and barely under control about him. She wouldn't be surprised if he throttled her in front of the party-goers. "All right, I'll change clothes," she gasped. His fingers relaxed on her arm, and she tore herself from his grasp. He quickly recaptured her arm. She whirled in astonishment. "I said I would do it."

He didn't smile, but his lips barely parted, showing the tips of his teeth, reminding her of a wolf. "I'll not have you going into your room and locking the door, then refusing to come out. I'll stay with you."

"I wouldn't—" she began to protest.

"I don't trust you," he replied shortly and propelled her into her room. Releasing her arm, he strode to the wardrobe and rifled through her clothes until he found the one he sought: a vivid emerald-green satin gown with an Oriental-design stomacher and pale green petticoat. He tossed the dress onto the bed just as Betsy hurried into the room, eyes wide with interest. "My wife has decided to change her attire," Jeremy told her. "This is what she'll wear. And redo the hairstyle, too. I want it as she wore it on our wedding day."

"Yes, sir!" Betsy immediately set to work unfastening Meredith's buttons. Meredith stood stiff and straight as a mannequin beneath Betsy's hands, refusing to glance at Jeremy. It was degrading to have to dress in front of him. Humiliating. And yet she could not restrain a ripple of desire at the idea of him watching her.

It had been a mistake to stay, Jeremy knew. He should have trusted her to do as she had promised, but his anger had carried him away. Now he was forced to endure the torture of seeing Meredith strip to her shift and underpetticoats. After she undressed, she sat down before the mirror while Betsy rearranged her hair. Then the maid carefully dropped the brilliant green dress over Meredith's head, arranged its panniers and drapings, and fastened the tight bodice. It fitted Meredith like a second skin, a tribute to Madame Reveneau's dressmaking skills. Feminine without frills, its color blazed against Meredith's pale skin and turned her eyes sparkling green. She was vivid, striking, unbearably desirable. Jeremy ran his tongue across his lips. He pulsed with longing. He clenched his hands to control their trembling. When he spoke, his voice was hard with repressed passion. "Are you ready? We're already late."

Betsy fastened a pearl necklace around her throat and added the finishing touch of a small, soft velvet cap with a pale green cockade. It gave Meredith a saucy, beckoning quality. Jeremy stood aside to let her pass through the doorway, and she swept by him haughtily. He caught a faint whiff of her fragrance, and his eyes closed briefly. This was going to be a very long night indeed. While he would have the exquisite pleasure of watching her and holding her as they danced, he also might explode before the night was over. He followed her down the stairs.

They sat in complete silence on the short boat trip to Four Oaks. Jeremy was drunk on the scent and sight of her. He couldn't speak. Meredith avoided looking at him, although she sensed his continual stare. She was furious—and he frightened her. And he was so unfairly handsome in the dull gold satin. The black breeches looked glued to his muscular thighs, and his calves bulged beneath the thin white stockings. Surreptitiously she peeked at his large hands resting on his knees. Just the sight of them shot a frisson of desire through her. She remembered the way they covered her breasts, the calloused tips rubbing her nipples to hard swollen points. She also remembered them between her legs. The thought brought the familiar wetness there. She swallowed and chewed at her underlip.

When the dock of Four Oaks came into sight, it was a distinct relief. Meredith scrambled out, hardly giving her hand to Jeremy to be helped out, offering only her fingertips.

His fingers slid down to grasp her palm firmly, and even through her gloves, his touch burned. Though they approached from the docks, they circled the house to enter by the front. Althea received them warmly, as did her fiancé, but there was a definite coolness emanating from the rest of the Whitney family. Althea whispered to Meredith that she was absolutely lovely, and Meredith noticed that Galen stared at her in stunned disbelief. When she took her husband's arm and stepped into the drawing room, she was gratified to note that everyone gaped at her with the same amazed stare. Meredith sneaked a glance at herself in the mirror. Even she had to admit she looked . . . well, striking. There was something different about her, a life, a flare that added to her appearance. In the past, her reticence had reduced her good features to insignificance. She understood that now.

Opal Hamilton shot her a venomous look, and Meredith nearly giggled. No doubt Opal was incensed that any woman should steal her thunder, especially a plain thing like Meredith Whitney—no, Devlin now. She stopped to greet a friend, and Jeremy released her arm to join a group of horsemen. Meredith followed him with her eyes. That was the important difference in herself, she thought—the fact that she was a Devlin now, not a Whitney. Jeremy was responsible for the improvement in her. His ardent lovemaking had given her confidence, and it showed in her carriage and her ability to converse without blushing and feeling she was making an idiot of herself. And all this was due to Jeremy Devlin.

As the evening progressed, Meredith conversed congenially, surprising several women who had thought her tongue-tied. As she drifted about, she could feel Jeremy's eyes upon her, even during the supper, where the place cards had separated husbands and wives for variety's sake. Once she turned to look at him, but she quickly averted her eyes. The way he looked at her took her breath away. It was almost frightening.

After the plentiful repast, the dancing began. Jeremy led Meredith onto the ballroom floor, firmly disregarding her protests about the impropriety of dancing while in mourning. Being looser and more confident, Meredith discovered that she danced much more gracefully. It was actually enjoyable to move with the music, guided by her husband's expert hand.

When the dance ended, she flashed him a smile that left his knees melting and strolled out of the ballroom to the refreshment table. Picking up a glass of wine, she turned and almost ran into Galen, who smiled thinly at her.

"Meredith, I hope you are enjoying the party."

"Oh, yes, it's most pleasant. I'm so happy for Althea."

Galen shrugged. "I would have wished for a different husband for her. Blaine is a trifle rough to suit a woman of her sensibilities and education."

"I confess I was surprised when she told me about her affection for him, but now that I see them together, I can tell they're very much in love."

"Love fades," Galen pronounced pedantically. "Similarity of interest does not."

Meredith remembered what Jeremy had retorted when she had made a similar remark to him—a pet dog could provide gentle companionship. But she did not utter the thought aloud. Galen would have been shocked. He was dear to her, being her cousin and lifelong friend, but she could no longer speak freely with him. He disapproved too much of her husband and current life. He would probably faint if he knew how she had reveled in Jeremy's sexual education. Still . . . he was her best friend besides Althea, and, being a man, he could do more to help her concerning Jeremy's attempts on her life. Perhaps she ought to confide her fears to him.

"I had hoped Althea would choose our cousin on Mother's side, James Warren," Galen said.

"The attorney in Charleston?" Meredith asked in surprise. Warren seemed an excessively dull person. How strange that Galen would think Althea might fall in love with him. Blaine was much more virile. He would give her pleasure and children. Meredith almost blushed at her thoughts. Once she would have declared that such things weren't important in a marriage, but now she knew differently. The bedroom figured prominently in wedded bliss or sorrow. She was all too aware of it.

"Yes, I get along very well with James. A good fellow."

"Yes, but it's whether your sister would get along with him that's important, don't you think?" Meredith pointed out tartly.

Galen seemed taken aback by her comment and quickly

changed the subject. "You're looking very—full of life tonight, Cousin."

"Thank you. You know, Galen, I'm more confident than I used to be. I have more pride in myself, and I find it easier to talk. It's because of Jeremy, I think. He's made me see myself differently."

"I rather think I preferred you the way you were," Galen remarked sadly.

Meredith's eyes widened. Did he really mean that? Had he preferred her shy and awkward? She realized suddenly that his friendship with her had been selfish, like his attitude toward his sister. He wanted them tied tightly to him, comfortable only around him and eschewing all others. No wonder James Warren seemed to him such a perfect choice for Althea. She would have been so bored and lonely married to Warren she would have remained as close to her brother as before. But Blaine Randall would take Althea away, just as Meredith's newfound confidence and better looks took her away.

No. She couldn't reveal her fears concerning Jeremy. Galen would say nothing pertinent. He would urge her to flee Jeremy and come to his family. He would try to suck her back into her drab old self. Meredith felt a sudden determination not to allow that to happen—ever. No matter what took place between her and Jeremy. She and Jeremy were bonded in a way she could never be with anyone else. Even if she feared him; even if he despised her; even if she had to defend herself against him. It was between the two of them, and it must remain so. She was irrevocably tied to Jeremy. He had changed her. He was a part of her, as she was a part of him. They were blended, joined forever, like Dante's Pyramus and Thisbe. They would swirl together forever in the flame of either love or hatred. She loved only him, wanted only him. She would do what she must to protect herself, but she couldn't bring another person into their private struggle.

As if her thoughts had conjured up Jeremy, she saw him striding toward them from the ballroom. His face was dark and drawn in harsh lines, the sensual mouth pulled tight. When he reached her, he grasped her arm, his fingers biting cruelly into her flesh. His eyes blazed, as blue and shining as star sapphires. "Meredith," he ground out through clenched teeth, "I'd like to speak to you."

Fear swelled her throat, mingling with a curious excitement. Meredith lowered her gaze to hide both emotions. "Of course," she murmured. "Excuse me, Cousin Galen."

Jeremy marched her onto the veranda, which ran across the house. It was deserted, but Jeremy made even more sure of their privacy by dragging her to the far corner, which the bright slats of light from the ballroom windows did not penetrate. A tall hedge of azaleas grew on the other side of the railing, enclosing the corner and flooding it with the flowers' heady scent. Afterward Meredith couldn't smell the flowers without recalling that moment when her husband backed her into the corner, tall and menacing, his hands going out to grasp the railing on either side of her. "What the devil do you mean by consorting with him right under my nose? Do you feel so confident that you can make me dance to your tune?" he growled.

"I don't know what you're talking about." Meredith was so chagrined that her voice shook.

"Don't lie. You know it very well. Your love for Galen Whitney. The way you hang upon his words, your eyes shining with adoration."

"I did no such thing!" Meredith cried hotly, too angered by his ridiculous statement for fear.

"I have eyes. And ears. You've always wanted him. But you're my wife, however little you like the notion, and I won't be cuckolded!"

Meredith gasped, her outrage beyond expression. Jeremy made a peculiar sound deep in his throat and plunged his hands into her hair, jerking her to him. He kissed her hard, demandingly, his lips sinking into hers almost savagely. He pressed his body into hers, pushing her against the column. Crudely he ground his pelvis into her as his tongue reclaimed her mouth. He groaned out her name. "Meredith. Meredith!"

One hand slipped inside her bodice, seeking the fullness of her breast and fingering the diamond-hard nipple. Meredith felt herself succumbing, slipping into the wild vortex of sensual pleasure. She ached for him, the center of her desire a throbbing torment in her loins. She realized that in another moment she would be responding to him, returning his flaming kisses and thrusting her body up against his. She didn't doubt that she would be capable of lifting her skirts and begging him to take her right there, heedless of privacy. But she must protect herself. She couldn't give in to him until she had thwarted his plans. But oh, God, surely he did not want to kill her—not the way his hands roamed over her body, the way his mouth clung to hers. But she must not trust him, she reminded herself. She had seen the evidence. No matter how much she desired him, she had to ensure that he would not kill her later.

She wrenched herself out of his arms, leaving Jeremy gasping and blindly reaching for her. "No!" She dodged away from him. "I'm not falling in so easily with your scheme."

"Have mercy, Meredith," he rasped. "You're killing me."

"*I* am killing *you!*" she flared, her indignation giving her the strength to withstand his pleading voice, raw with sensual longing. "Don't you have that backward?"

"What do you mean?"

"I mean your plan to murder your wife and gain a plantation. I wouldn't let you sell Bitterleaf, so you decided to get rid of me."

He blinked uncomprehendingly. "You're mad. What—"

"I *know* about it, Jeremy. I'm not entirely stupid, although you appear to think so. Nor am I blinded by your charms."

In an agony of frustration, he grabbed her arms and shook her. "What in the hell are you blathering about?"

"You shot at me. You tried to kill me. You had me fetch your boots that time a snake just happened to be coiled inside. It's only sheer luck that I'm not dead already."

His hands dropped away, and he stepped back. "What? You think those were attempts on *your* life?"

"Of course I do. You're the only one who would benefit by my death. It had to be you. But you needn't bother to try again. Nor do you need to lull my suspicions by making love to me. I—I told Galen about it. I even wrote it all in a letter that I gave him to hold. If something happens to me, accident or murder, he'll take my letter to the authorities. You won't get away with it, and you won't inherit a cent. More than likely you'll be hanged." She paused, almost panting from emotional exhaustion. She was bluffing, of course, making a desperate bid to block him—and giving him a chance to prove her wrong. If he were not guilty, he would argue and explain. He'd exclaim in horror and offer proof that he could not have fired the shot. She waited expectantly, her heart knocking against her rib cage. Her whole world rode on his answer.

For a moment Jeremy couldn't speak. Anguish gripped his vitals. He loved Meredith with all his being, trembled and burned for her—and she despised him. She believed him capable of murdering her. Sweet Jesus! His heart had almost stopped when he thought she had been shot. He had turned himself inside out the past weeks trying to prove his love. But she knew him not at all, loved him not at all. In the midst of his most ardent passion, she had coolly pulled away and accused him of seeking her death. And she had confided her suspicions to Galen! Her dear, beloved cousin, the idiot she had wanted to marry instead of Jeremy. She had exposed Jeremy to his rival's ridicule, put him in the man's power. She trusted Galen—and feared himself.

Jeremy half turned to conceal the unaccustomed moisture in his eyes. His voice was lifeless. "Make your farewells. We're going home."

Chapter XXV

He HAD not even tried to deny her accusations! That was the most horrible aspect of it, Meredith thought, slumping against the porch railing for support. He had ceased his pretense of desire and strolled away without offering explanations or denials. Obviously he had done it, or he would have exploded with indignation. He would have ranted and raved about her ridiculous suspicions. But he did not. He was guilty.

Meredith made an effort to pull herself together and walked unsteadily into the ballroom. She sought out Althea's mother, who, after one look at Meredith's pale face, readily believed her excuse of sudden illness. Meredith went into the cloak-room and pinned on her saucy little scrap of a hat, her face beneath it a sad contrast. Jeremy waited for her by the front door. He did not offer her his arm, but stepped back to let her exit and strode stiffly behind her to the dock. Meredith's back prickled with anxiety. What did he mean to do? Was he inventing a new scheme? Had he accepted that she had outmaneuvered him—or was he so inflamed with rage that he would murder her out of hand when they reached Bitterleaf?

They rode home, as they had come, in silence. The boatmen's figures were barely visible in the vast, moonless night. Only Jeremy's white wig caught and reflected the faint starlight. His face was blank and shadowy underneath. Meredith shivered and looked away from him. When they docked at

Bitterleaf, she forced herself to move up the path to the house at a sedate pace. She wouldn't let Jeremy know how frightened she was. Inside, she hurried up the stairs to the haven of her room. Behind her, Jeremy tossed his hat at the waiting footman and headed for the sitting room. He shrugged out of his jacket and waistcoat and threw them onto a chair. He tore off his carefully set wig and hurled it across the room, satisfying his pent-up anger slightly. He shoved both hands through his hair, pressing his fingertips into his scalp as if to hold the turbulent thoughts inside. Flinging open the doors of the liquor cabinet, he jerked out the pewter container of burgundy and a wine cup of the same set. Pouring himself a healthy dose of the liquid, he downed it in a single tilting of the cup.

Slamming the cup down on the top of the cabinet, he poured another drink. He had drunk sufficiently at the Whitney mansion, trying to take the sharp edge off his desire and jealousy as he watched Meredith talk to Galen. He knew it was his overheated imagination that made it seem they were flirting. Not the proper Meredith. Not the proper Galen. They'd freeze their own hot juices before they slid a step from the path of rectitude. He downed his second glass almost as quickly as the first and poured another. Raising it in salute in the general direction of Meredith's room, he executed a mocking bow. "To my lady wife," he murmured. "Icy and inviolate."

His hands clenched the stem of the goblet. Dear God, how was he to bear it? To love Meredith and know she hated him, to live with her suspicion and love for Galen, all the time wanting her so badly, loving her so much he was a mass of quivering jelly inside. Jeremy slumped into a chair and stared moodily at the wall. Gradually, as he drank, his aching sorrow changed to anger. How dare she accuse him! How dare she tell Galen Whitney he was a murderer! Had she revealed all their private lives to the man? Described his lovemaking, too? He was torn and furious at the thought of her betrayal. But overriding his thoughts was the picture he couldn't obliterate from his mind: the moments on the veranda when Meredith had trembled in his arms, quivering, desirable, her mouth answering his. His hand remembered her soft breast beneath it, the rigid protrusion of her nipple. His mouth again tasted her lips, her skin, the astringent trace of perfume below her ear.

Jeremy swallowed convulsively and rose to pour another drink. His walk was unsteady, not quite weaving, but off balance. The glasses of burgundy on top of the rum punch he had consumed at the party buzzed in his head and throbbed like fire through his veins. He started to pour another drink, intending to send himself into drunken, careless unconsciousness, but instead he slammed the cup down on the cabinet, knocking it over. It rolled off the edge and bounced across the floor, staining the carpet with its dregs, but Jeremy didn't notice. He was halfway across the room, heading for the stairs.

When Meredith had reached the safety of her bedroom, she found Betsy curled up in a chair, dozing as she waited for her mistress to return. Meredith gratefully turned the lock behind her. Even with Betsy's company, she didn't feel entirely safe. Her maid jumped at her entrance, blinking. "Oh, Miss Merry, I'm sorry. Lord, I must have slept a long time."

"We returned early," Meredith explained. "I'm very tired."

Taking the hint, Betsy hastened to unfasten her gown, keeping her usual chatter to a minimum. She helped Meredith undress, hung up the elegant gown, and took out one of Meredith's old nightgowns. "No," Meredith decided. "I'd rather wear one Lydia made. It's too hot for such heavy nightclothes."

Betsy eyed the other woman speculatively, but refrained from commenting. She tucked the high-necked gown back into its drawer and pulled out a sheer pink gown slit high on both sides to reveal the thighs. She wondered if this attire meant the master would be visiting Meredith tonight. Betsy hoped so. Both Meredith's and Jeremy's tempers were far too sharp of late. It would be a relief to everyone when they called off their bedroom war. Meredith sat down at the vanity. Betsy unpinned her hair and began to brush the thick mane with a heavy, silver-backed brush. Meredith closed her eyes. Her temples were pounding, and the rhythm of the brush soothed her. The tingle of its bristles over her scalp was strangly pleasurable. It seemed as though her nerves lay on the surface of her skin, alive and trembling, sensitive to the slightest stimulus.

Suddenly there was a heavy stamping on the staircase, and Meredith jumped. She forced herself to relax. She didn't want Betsy to know her fear. Her door was locked; Betsy was with her. There was no reason to be frightened. She heard a periodic metallic click coming nearer, louder, and concentrated on it as if it meant her life. What could it be? It was with great relief that she finally recognized it as the sound of a ring upon the wooden banister as a hand grasped the railing. Tonight Jeremy had worn a gold ring set with a single star sapphire the color of his eyes. Why had she noticed that detail? Why remember it? She didn't know, any more than she knew why it was important to identify the sound. She only knew that such things kept life normal, acceptable, preventing it from bouncing out crazily and rolling along bizarre, foreign paths. She was capable of rational thinking, of memory. The world was normal. Jeremy wasn't really trying to kill her. It was a great hoax that would soon be explained. She gripped her hands together tightly and listened to his tread, the clicking of the ring.

Inexplicably it turned ominous. Steady. Closer. Why would Jeremy have to grip the railing? Was he drunk? Mean drunk, she thought. Crazy drunk. Betsy continued to brush her hair as though nothing was wrong, but Meredith became tauter and tauter, until the steps ended outside her door, and the doorknob turned. Meredith jumped so much Betsy inadvertently banged the hairbrush into her head, sending brief, smarting tears to Meredith's eyes. The door was locked and did not open. Betsy pivoted toward the sound, then back to her mistress, her eyes questioning. Meredith shook her head, and Betsy frowned.

Then suddenly, so loudly the door shook beneath the force, Jeremy thudded his hand against it—once, twice, three times. "Meredith!" he roared. "Goddamn it, open this door!"

At the sudden blare of noise, both women flinched. Meredith wet her lips, and Betsy glanced at her nervously, eyes rounded. Meredith made no answer, and the knock was not repeated. She began to relax, thankful, yet strangely disappointed, too. With a crash the door burst open under the force of Jeremy's foot, and he filled the doorway, huge and overpowering. His eyes glittered midnight blue. His face was flushed. Meredith was very aware of the bulging muscles of his arms and legs. His jacket was off and the sleeves of his shirt rolled up. The red-gold hairs covering his arms caught the light. Beneath them, the veins of his arms stood out like cords, tightened by his clenched fists. His heavy breathing filled her ears, harsh, almost panting.

"Damn it, don't ever lock your door to me again!" His voice was low and all the deadlier for it.

Meredith swallowed, dredging up her last ounce of courage. She had to face him down now or she was lost. "Stop it. You're drunk. Don't make a fool of yourself in front of the servants."

His eyes flickered briefly to Betsy. "You're right. I am drunk. I am also master in this house, and you are my woman. I've let you make a fool of me for weeks. But no longer." There was no threat in his voice, only calm purpose. It made Meredith tremble. He turned to Betsy and jerked his head toward the door. "Get out."

Betsy stepped closer to Meredith, raising the hairbrush with a trembling hand. The master was drunk and crazy. She couldn't leave Meredith alone with him, although he scared Betsy silly. She wondered whether Neb would hear her if she screamed his name. Jeremy's lips curled, whether in contempt or amusement, she wasn't sure. He looked straight at Meredith, his message clear. This matter was between them alone. Meredith longed to clutch Betsy's skirt and beg her not to leave, but she couldn't expose the girl to possible danger. With a curious resignation, even in the midst of her fear, she realized she had to meet her fate with Jeremy. "It's all right, Betsy. Go back to your cabin."

"But, Miss . . ."

"It's *all right*." Her voice was firm. Betsy glanced doubtfully from Meredith to the man in the doorway. "I can handle it." Biting her lip, Betsy scurried past Jeremy out the door. She hated to leave Meredith for even a moment, but by doing so she could fetch Neb. He was the only person capable of subduing Jeremy.

Jeremy closed the door after the girl and leaned against it, arms folded, his heavy-lidded eyes roaming down Meredith's form. Meredith rose, backing against the vanity table, while her mind raced to recall what lay on the table that she could use as a weapon. But that was ridiculous. Jeremy was far too strong for her. He would quickly render any weapon useless. All she had to fight him with was reason. "Jeremy." She struggled to keep her voice even and calm. "Think. You cannot. All the servants will know."

"I don't give a damn what the servants know," he replied thickly. He was almost insane with desire. Meredith's thin nightgown revealed her body through a haze, hinting at the smooth line of her legs, the patch of hair where they joined, the dark circles of the aureoles. He could hardly speak, or even think, for the blood pounding in his brain, the breath rasping in his throat. He clenched his hands and began to walk toward her.

Meredith swallowed, first edging away, then breaking and running mindlessly. There was no escape, but she could not control her flight. Jeremy was on her in two steps. With one iron hand he grabbed her wrist and flung her onto the bed. Immediately she rolled, trying to rise, but he shoved her back. She kicked out wildly, flailing her hands. He covered her legs with his weight and circled both wrists with one hand, forcing her arms above her head. His breathing was loud in her ears, his face flushed. Meredith's heart tripped in terror as he brought one great hand to her throat. But he stopped short, hooking his hand into the low neckline of her gown and tearing it down. It split with a satisfying rip. His eyes blazed, and he made a noise deep in his throat, animalistic, hungry. Meredith stared, numb with terror, incapable of taking in what he was doing.

His face loomed closer and closer, and his mouth met hers. His tongue shoved past the barrier of her teeth, and she tasted burgundy as he possessed her mouth. His skin was damp and hot, and the smell of sweat and cologne and, deliciously, Jeremy's own familiar scent filled her nostrils. Desire mingled with fear, taking off its edge, and Meredith was able to think again. She realized finally that he was trying to bed her, not kill her. She went limp with relief. Her lips began to return his pressure, and she jerked her arms against the restraint of his fingers, wanting to free them to hold him.

Jeremy tore away with a half sob, half groan, releasing her. "Oh, God!" He lurched to the window, his arms wrapped around his stomach like a man in pain. He leaned his hot face against the cool panes of glass. "Oh, Meredith, forgive me." His voice was so low and broken she could barely understand what he said. "Christ! I almost raped you. I'm sorry. I'm sorry. I wanted you so. I thought—I thought, she's mine, my wife. I can take her if I want. I was going to *force* you. I didn't care that you didn't want me, that you fought me." He drew a long, shuddering breath. "I want you so much, sometimes I think I'll die from it." He laughed harshly. "And you hate me. That's the real jest. You despise me and love Galen. You don't want me in your bed. The only way I can taste your sweetness is to violate you. . . . God, Meredith, I'd rather you put me back under Jackson's lash than torture me like this."

Meredith sat up in amazement and stared. Tears started in her eyes, and she was flooded with love and wonder and compassion. "Oh, Jeremy! I don't love Galen." She stood, not considering her boldness or her earlier fear, and went to him. Pressing her body against his back, she ran her hands down from the sharp points of his collarbone over his ribbed chest and across the muscular wall of his abdomen, caressing his hard, jutting hipbones, and ending on his thighs. At her touch his entire body jerked convulsively. A primitive sound choked his throat. "I don't love Galen," she repeated softly, "and you wouldn't have to force me into your bed."

"Meredith," he breathed, clutching the drapes on either side of the window. "Don't toy with me."

"You mean you aren't my plaything?" she teased, her hands drifting across his thighs and converging on the hard bulge between his legs.

He sucked in his breath sharply. "Stop," he warned her without conviction. "You'll bring me to my peak before I can enter you."

She kissed the sweat-dampened shirt, her teeth nipping at his back beneath the cloth, while her hands busily unfastened his breeches. "And have you only one peak in you the whole night? Have you changed so much?"

"I have enough in me to love you all night long," he growled.

Meredith giggled, heady with her sudden freedom from fear. She didn't question or think, simply acted with a woman's instinct. Her fingers finished with the buttons of his breeches and moved up to undo his shirt. Jeremy stood still under her ministrations, barely breathing. He wondered if he had passed into a drunken hallucination. But no—the hot touch of those supple fingers was real, as was the fiery pleasure they evoked wherever they roamed. He gripped the curtains tightly, his anchor in the dizzying world of sensations Meredith plunged him into.

After she opened the shirt, her hands crept beneath it, crossing over his chest. She caressed him, feeling each rib, tangling her fingers in the fine hairs, rolling the pointy nipples between her thumbs and forefingers. While her hands played with his front, her mouth roamed his back. At first she kissed and bit through the cloth, but finally she stopped the movement of her hands long enough to roll up his shirt and allow her mouth to run wild over his skin. Licking, nipping, rubbing with her velvet lips, she traversed the ridge of his spine from his shoulders to the deep dimple above his buttocks. Jeremy rose on tiptoe, his chest tightening and arms bulging with the effort of control. "Have pity," he murmured.

"Pity isn't what I want to have," she retorted, nuzzling the flesh beneath one shoulder blade.

"And what is it you want?" he played along, although his voice was breathless and jerky.

In answer, Meredith shoved down his loosened trousers and curled her hands around his manhood. Sparks burst behind his eyes, and Jeremy bit his lip until it bled. He wanted to delay the joy, to wallow in the sudden, ecstatic change of circumstances. Meredith's fingertips ran lightly over him, then slid away, caressing the smooth skin of his abdomen and coming around to cup his buttocks. She squeezed, and Jeremy moaned, bracing himself against the wall. "Meredith," he gasped. "Ahhh—you're killing me. Where did you learn this?"

"I had a very talented teacher—and an imagination. What do you suppose I've spent my nights thinking of the past few weeks?" She caressed the taut, muscular buttocks, his rock-hard thighs, stealing back to his stiff rod.

He emitted a tormented groan. "Meredith, I can hold back no longer."

She dug into his pocket and pulled forth a large linen handkerchief. Stroking and wrapping him with one hand, her other crept between his legs. He writhed, but moved his legs farther part to allow her access. Cradling his bulging sac tenderly while she stroked with the other hand, Meredith introduced Jeremy to a world beyond pleasure, almost beyond sanity. He clenched his hands and stiffened all over, a prime-val cry bursting from his lips. When it was over, he sank to his knees, resting his head against the window. Meredith knelt behind him, wrapping her arms tightly around his chest as if she would never let him go.

Outside the door Neb and Betsy halted. Neb turned to Betsy, his grin splitting the darkness. "Baby, I think you got it all wrong," he whispered. "She's the one's got *him* scream-ing like a stuck hog."

Jeremy had no idea how long they remained kneeling at the window before his mind gradually returned from the deep, black, joyous space it knew for a few moments. He turned and sank onto the floor, pulling Meredith into his arms. "You're a witch, woman," he murmured. "No courtesan could manage what you just did to me."

"Good. Then you won't need to try one." She rubbed her cheek against his damp chest. How good, how familiar he smelled and felt and tasted.

"I told myself I was master in this house, that I would bend you to my will. Instead you beat me—no, you broke me."

"Not broke."

"Broke," he repeated firmly. "You turned me into a quivering, mindless chunk of flesh. I'm jelly beneath your touch."

She giggled. "You didn't feel like jelly. I was reminded more of—say, a stone."

"Teasing wench." He nipped lightly at her shoulder. His mouth came up to touch hers briefly, then again, deeper and deeper, his tongue softly wooing hers, winding and circling, stroking, breaking away to trace the ridged roof of her mouth. Her lips tasted salty, and he realized the salt came from his own skin. The thought excited him. His mouth widened, burrowing into hers. "You proved you rule me, Meredith," he whispered huskily. "So, like a good subject, I shall adore you."

He pulled her up so that they knelt, facing each other. His hands wandered over her, rediscovering the hills and valleys, the plains of her body. He cupped her breasts, murmuring, "Do you have any idea how my hands have yearned for this?" His thumbs circled the crowns of her breasts until they tightened, then continued to explore every inch of her flesh, caressing even the soles of her feet. "I think," Meredith told him shakily, "that you're a subject who pays homage very well."

"I've only begun," he replied thickly. "You satisfied me, and now I plan to spend a long, long time on you."

He kissed her neck and ears, returning now and then to taste the honey of her mouth. Her lips were slightly swollen from the earlier force of his kisses, and he nibbled at them tenderly, lightly licking with the tip of his tongue. He moved to the nape of her neck, massaging the sensitive skin between his lips. She shivered uncontrollably as he mouthed the tender flesh over her spinal column, at the same time covering her breasts with his hands, raising the nipples to thrusting rigidity. He commanded her to stand. "Remember, it's proper for a subject to kneel before his ruler."

"And doesn't the ruler have the choice?"

"Not this one," he growled.

"It places your lips at a—very unusual level."

"That's where I intend them to be."

"Oh! Oh, Jeremy."

"Move your feet farther apart. Ah, there. A succulent morsel."

She moaned and shifted. "Jeremy, please."

"Please what?" he mumbled, his tongue busily at work. His fingers dug into her buttocks. "Am I not pleasing you?"

"Ah! Oh, yes."

He pulled back. "Shall I stop?"

"No!" She reached out blindly, digging her fingers into his hair and tugging. "Please, don't stop."

But he did not return immediately, instead tracing the insides of her thighs with his finger, then tongue, coming back at last to the hot center of her passion. Her legs trembled under the force of the desire building in her, so that his arms beneath her buttocks had to hold her up. Expertly he brought her to the brink, then retreated, until she was almost sobbing with pent-up longing. At last he took her even higher, and the joy exploded within her, rippling out through her body. She sagged weakly in his arms.

"Oh, no," he chuckled softly. "You're not done yet. Feel what you've done to me." He guided her hand to his swollen staff. Meredith smiled and lay back upon the floor. The straw mat scratched her slightly, an erotic contrast to his soft, teasing mouth. He began to roam her sensitized skin, gently and tenderly arousing her once more. When again she began to writhe and moan, Jeremy slid into her. Meredith sighed with satisfaction. Now she was complete, fitted to the other part of herself. Supreme happiness washed over her, and Meredith wriggled beneath him. Jeremy drew in his breath sharply and began to stroke, smoothly lifting them ever upward. Meredith moved, matching him, then thrusting in counterpoint, returning what he offered her measure for measure. A tremor began deep inside her, triggering his explosion, and they crashed together into the blissful unity they had missed for so long.

Chapter XXVI

MEREDITH STRETCHED and rolled her head on the pillow, utterly at peace. It had been a long time since she had awakened this way, happy, content. She turned her head to look at the blond head on the pillow next to hers. Jeremy lay facing away from her, one arm curled around his head. Smiling secretively, she admired his broad, tanned back and tousled hair. Jeremy wanted her. She was certain of that. No one could be such an excellent actor. And he hadn't tried to kill her. She had realized it viscerally when he had whirled away, berating himself for almost raping her. He wouldn't harm her, even by taking his marital rights by force. His wasn't the behavior of a man capable of murder.

As if he felt her gaze, Jeremy rolled over, one blue eye opening blearily. When he saw her, he smiled and raised the other eyelid, his arms reaching out to pull her into their circle. Meredith went willingly. He yawned so wide his jaw cracked. "Ummm. You tired me out."

"*I* tired *you* out!" she retorted with mock indignation.

"I may stay abed this morning."

"You ought to," she agreed seriously. "You're exhausted. You've been working far too long and hard."

"It wasn't the work that exhausted me. It was lying awake at night thinking about you." She had no reply, and for a moment they lay together in silence. Finally, he said,

"Meredith, I—you must believe me, I never tried to hurt you."

"I know."

"What? But last night you accused me of murder. You said you gave Galen Whitney a letter."

"Oh, I made that up."

"You what!"

"The letter, I mean." She sat up, leaving the circle of his arms in order to see his face. "I wouldn't have revealed such a thing to Galen. I couldn't. If he knew my suspicions, he'd have urged me to leave you."

"I should hope so."

"Well, I couldn't expose you to his comtempt."

"Even though you believed I wanted to kill you?"

She shrugged. "I'm a loyal wife, I hope. And I wasn't sure. All the evidence pointed that way, but I didn't want to believe it."

"But I've never harmed you. How could you so easily conclude I'd shot at you?"

"It wasn't just the shots. There was the snake in the boot you asked me to pick up. And you were the only one who would profit by my death."

"Did it never occur to you that perhaps it wasn't *your* death that was sought?"

"What do you mean?"

"I mean that the snake crawled out of *my* boot and that you were shot at while you were wearing a man's hat and a cloak that completely concealed your feminine form."

Meredith stared at him, shock punching her in the stomach. "You mean it's you! Someone is trying to kill *you*?"

He nodded. "I think so. I didn't want you to worry or be afraid, so I didn't tell you. God, if only I'd known what you would conjure up in your head!"

"But who? Why? What reason would anyone have for killing you?"

"Revenge?"

"Revenge! Who would seek revenge on you—except maybe Caleb Jackson, but he's been gone for weeks." Jeremy said nothing, just cocked an eyebrow at her. "You mean he's still here?"

"I learned that little tidbit of information from Opal Hamilton the day she visited me in the drawing room. You remember, the time you were so jealous."

"I wasn't jealous," Meredith retorted automatically.

He snorted. "Anyway, she informed me that Jackson was hanging about in Greenoak, staying at The Blue Ox and trying to find another job in the area. He never found one, but reports are he's still at The Blue Ox. I'm almost certain he's behind this whole thing. When the dock caught fire, it was no accident. Neb saw a figure sneaking away from the blaze. As soon as I found out Jackson was still in the neighborhood, I realized it must have been he."

"Still, it's quite a leap from arson to murder," Meredith mused.

"One I'm sure he's capable of making."

"Yes, you're probably right. But, Jeremy, if you think he's tried to kill you, why haven't you done something about it?"

"Because I can't prove it!" He slammed down his fist on the bed. "Dammit, I haven't a shred of evidence. Neb saw someone, but he couldn't identify him. The night you were shot at, we found horse tracks and a man's footprints in the woods behind the house. The tracks led to the main road, where they mingled with other tracks and became untraceable. There was nothing to identify them as *his* tracks. I'm working solely on supposition. Neb's had men on watch since then, but we don't even know exactly what to look for. He could strike anywhere in any way. It's maddening."

"And even more maddening when your wife accuses you of being the murderer?" Meredith teased.

"Yes," he growled. "God, Meredith, how could you think I did it?"

"Tell me the truth. Did you never have even the tiniest suspicion that perhaps it was I who was trying to do you in? I mean, I could have hired Jackson, and he simply made an idiotic mistake in firing at me—or I could have been setting up an alibi, that I was almost killed, also. After all, I'd threatened to kill you if you tried to sell Bitterleaf. Didn't you think any of it, even once?"

He glanced at her out of the corner of his eye, and his lips twitched into a grin. "I ought to lie, but, yes, in one of my blackest, foulest moods, I lay on my bed wondering if you wanted me dead. But I didn't retain the idiotic notion longer than a second!"

"You had more information than I did." Her expression turned serious, and she gripped his upper arm tightly. "Oh, Jeremy, I'm so dreadfully sorry I distrusted you."

He caressed her hands. "It's all right. Last night it cut me to the quick, thinking you hated me, that you'd told Galen. But I'm less . . . ah, tense now. I see things more clearly. You were confused and frightened. You had proof of my untrustworthiness because of the land agent. Meredith, I want to explain about that."

"It doesn't matter." Somehow his attempt to sell Bitterleaf seemed of little importance now.

"Yes, it does. You were angry with me, and rightly so. I behaved like a dishonest fool. You see, I've never been a paragon of virtue. I lived a spoiled, moneyed life without enough money to maintain it. I did several less-than-upright things to maintain my status. I was considered by some to be 'an unsavory character'—and they were probably right. Anyway, when Daniel told me his plan for our marriage, I knew I wanted you and the land. But I'd never been content with anything long, and I was afraid it would be the same with both you and Bitterleaf. I didn't realize how much I had changed or would change. I thought if I grew bored, as I must surely do, I could sell the land and return to England. It was something to be kept in reserve. Then, after our wedding night, when you told me I had abused you and was like all other men, I was so furious I went to the land agent."

"You mean when we were first married? I thought it was when you went to purchase seeds!"

"Oh, no. Long before the seed trip, I had decided I didn't want to leave and wouldn't hurt you in that way. I wouldn't have done it, Meredith. I swear. Even at the time I felt guilty. I went only because I was so angry with you. I'm aware that doesn't excuse me. It was wicked to even think of it. I was wrong, very wrong. That's the truth, Meredith. Will you forgive me?"

Her hands cupped his face, thumbs caressing his bristling

cheeks. "Yes, I forgive you. I'm sorry I acted so precipitously. I didn't give you a chance to explain, but I was hurt—and last night when I accused you of trying to kill me, I thought your quiet was proof of your guilt. I—I'm sorry." He caught one of her wrists with his hand and turned her hand to place a kiss in the palm. She smiled softly, but her voice turned brisk and practical. "The thing we have to think about now is how to trap Jackson. You can't simply wait for him to try again!"

"He won't get me. Better men than Caleb Jackson have tried and failed."

"But you can't trust in blind luck forever. Jeremy, something just occurred to me."

"What?"

"There has to be another person involved."

The muscles of his arm tensed slightly. "Why?"

"Because Jackson wouldn't have the money to stay at The Blue Ox so long without getting a job. He cheated Daniel, I know, but I suspect he spent most of that on drink and women. He couldn't afford such a long, drawn-out revenge."

"I'd thought of that."

"And?"

"And I imagine you're right. There must be someone else behind him, giving him money." He watched her, his eyes hooded and dark.

"The only one I can think of who'd wish you harm is Angus Hamilton. He's dreadfully jealous, and he's bound to have guessed that you and Opal were—" She stopped, coloring slightly, unable to continue. She hadn't meant to confront him with his affair with Opal. Such things were best left unsaid. She knew now that she could have a closeness with Jeremy, and she must not spoil it with jealous accusations.

Jeremy stared, his brows drawing down ominously. "That Opal and I were what?"

"Well, you know. . . ."

"No, I don't. What?"

"Having an affair," she said in a rush.

"Good Lord, woman, every time I turn around you're accusing me of another betrayal. I have not had an affair with Opal Hamilton!"

"Jeremy, please don't lie. I—I can accept it, I think, but I'd prefer you didn't lie."

"I'm not lying," he muttered through clenched teeth. "Meredith, look at me." He grasped her shoulders. "I am *not* lying."

"But she's so pretty, and she chased you terribly!"

"That doesn't mean she caught me. Her prettiness is common. I knew a hundred like her in London."

"But all those evenings when you rode off—weren't you meeting Opal?"

"Your imagination ought to be locked up!" he roared. "I was doing exactly what it looked like I was doing! I went for a ride, hoping the physical exercise would wear me out enough so I could sleep. I was trying to relieve the torture of living with you, seeing you—even in those awful dresses— and not being able to so much as touch you. You were driving me insane! Riding was one method I used to combat it. One of those evenings—*one*—I went to the tavern in Greenoak and met Blaine Randall there. That evening, drunk and angry and hurt, I gave one of the serving wenches a few coins to let me bed her. But I couldn't do it. I didn't want anyone but you. Meredith, I love you!"

She blinked rapidly. "No. You couldn't."

"Will you kindly stop telling me what I do and think and feel? I know more about it than you. And I say I love you!"

"But that's impossible." She ached to believe him. His words opened up a glorious vista. However, a life of self-dislike wouldn't let her accept it. "I'm not pretty. I'm clumsy and tall. I make you angry."

"That's true. You're doing it right now, in fact. But anger doesn't mean a lack of love. And maybe you aren't pretty. But I light up inside when I see your face. I've never known before the sweet lovemaking I've had in your bed. You *aren't* clumsy, and why should I care if you're tall? So am I!"

"You married me for my land. For your freedom."

"Yes. And because I wanted you between my sheets. If I loved you then, I confess I didn't know it. But love can grow. It doesn't have to burst upon one immediately. Meredith, you suit me. Whatever combination of qualities you have, it's what I need and want. I've never loved before, but I love you." One hand whipped out to cup the back of her neck and drag her to him. He kissed her deeply, his lips moving over hers with infinite passion and love. Meredith melted, her lips responding and her tongue slipping out eagerly to meet his. Jeremy groaned and pushed her back onto the bed. Gently, without a word, he loved her.

When it was over, he lay back with a sigh. "I've always had your desire," he murmured, "but never your love."

"That's not true!" Meredith denied spontaneously, then stopped, realizing how much she had revealed. Now he would have complete power over her. Jeremy smiled and pulled her onto his wide chest, reaching up to kiss her lightly.

"Then if it's possible for you to love me, why isn't it possible for me to love you?"

"It's not the same." She frowned.

"Why?"

"It just isn't!" she snapped, irritated by the way he compelled her to believe him, to go against all the truths she had held about herself. No man as marvelous as Jeremy Devlin could love her, she reminded herself. And yet . . . he said he did. She jerked away, hopping out of bed.

"Meredith, come back."

"No! I have to think, and I can't do it around you. I'm going for a long ride."

He flung aside the covers. "I'll come with you."

"Alone," she replied firmly.

"Damnation, woman, what will it take to convince you?"

"I don't know," she replied miserably.

Jeremy's lips twitched. He didn't know whether to laugh or scream. Meredith was the most exasperating female he'd ever known. But she was his . . . and he had a whole lifetime to convince her of his love. He smiled. That wasn't such a bad prospect, if it meant more nights like the last one.

Meredith bathed and dressed quickly, Jeremy good-humoredly acting as her maid. She ate a hasty breakfast in the kitchen, blushing at Dulcie's blunt statement that from the rosy glow in Meredith's cheeks it was obvious the master had returned to her bed. She strode to the stables, unable to keep from humming under her breath. In the past twenty-four hours she had experienced such a deep change of emotions she could hardly take it in. But she was happier than she had ever been in her life—and yet more frightened, because now she had so much to lose.

"Miss Merry!" Sam exclaimed upon seeing her and hurried forward. But he lacked his usual grin, and his forehead was creased with worry. "Ma'am, am I glad you came in!"

"Why, thank you. I think I'll take Mercy for a little canter, if you'll have her saddled."

"Yes'm." He shouted to the stableboy to saddle the docile mare, then turned back to Meredith. "Ma'am . . ."

"Yes? Sam, what's wrong?"

"Well, ma'am," he said. "I'd like you to look at something, Miss Merry. I didn't know what to do when I saw it. Neb told me to let him know if I saw something unusual, but this is too important for him. I was wondering whether I ought to tell the master himself."

"What, Sam?" Fear gripped her stomach. "What is it?"

"I'll show you." He hurried away and returned with a bridle in his hand. "Equilibrium's bridle, ma'am. Look, here by the bit." He turned the bridle to the inside, revealing a narrow slash in the leather. "It's been cut. That'd break at the first hard tug, and with a wild animal like Equilibrium, there's no telling what could happen. The master would lose control of him completely."

Meredith swallowed, fear spreading, almost immobilizing her. Had she needed any confirmation that it was Jeremy the killer sought, this was it. What was she to do? She was flooded with the need to protect him and also with a conflicting desire to seek the safety of his arms. She gnawed at her lip. "Tell the master about it. He'll want to know. You're a wonderful man to check the equipment so closely."

"That's what I do, Miss Merry."

"Then you keep on doing it. Don't ever let Jeremy ride out unless you've checked the bridle and saddle yourself."

"Yes'm, I won't. Here's the mare, miss."

"What? Oh, yes." He led the horse to the mounting block, and Meredith climbed into the saddle. Her head was spinning, and there was a cold lump in the pit of her stomach. But she knew the ride would help sort everything out, including this new information.

She rode aimlessly at first, busy with her whirling emotions and thoughts. She was terrified, gripped by a fear even deeper than what she had felt for herself. Someone was trying to kill Jeremy! Who? Angus? Was he really that jealous? Could he murder a man over Opal? Perhaps. She had seen his black eyes shooting fire at Opal and Jeremy as they stood laughing together at her engagement party. He had looked as if he'd like to choke Jeremy right then and there. Yes, she could believe Angus capable of killing Jeremy in a flash of rage. But would he order a man murdered—slyly, secretively? It seemed crazy. But she didn't know him. He might do anything. And who else could it be? Surely Jeremy's uncle had not decided to do away with him forever, reaching clear across the ocean to order it done. Perhaps he was afraid that if Jeremy survived his servitude, he would return to London and reveal what his lordship had done to his flesh and blood. Could the man dread scandal to that extent?

Meredith realized that under her slack grip the gentle mare had ambled to a halt. She glanced around, orienting herself. She was on the familiar road to the long meadow where she and Jeremy had ridden when he was teaching her. She smiled, remembering those times—her fears, her reluctance, her deeply hidden love and fire. How Jeremy had changed her. Did he love her? Truly love her? Was her refusal to believe him simply a clinging to her old frightened self?

Meredith tapped Mercy with her heels. This way was as good as any. She could turn back when she reached the meadow. That would give her ample time to think. Or . . . the meadow lay about halfway to Four Oaks, the Whitney plantation. Perhaps she could go on and visit Althea. Althea was a soothing person. Maybe she would be able to calm Meredith and help her sort out her feelings. Wait! She could do more than that! Galen would be there, and though she no longer felt as she once had about him, he was still her closest male relative, the only man she could turn to besides Jeremy. And she needed a man to perform the task she had just conceived of. The surest way of discovering Jackson's backer *and* preventing another attack on Jeremy was to have Jackson followed. He would presumably visit the other man for money or instructions and would lead them right to the villain in the shadows. Even if he did not, at least they would always know where he was and what he was doing.

However, she couldn't set Neb on the task, for a black would be too noticeable to follow Jackson successfully. She would have to hire a white man, but she hadn't the slightest idea how to go about it. That was where Cousin Galen could help her. Men did that sort of thing—went to taverns and hired other men, something she could not do even if she knew whom to hire. Galen would help her. He didn't like Jeremy, true, but he would be appalled at the idea of murder. She rode on at a faster pace, encouraged by her decision. With a man watching Jackson and all the servants on the alert at home, surely they could keep Jeremy safe until they obtained evidence of Jackson's villainy and the identity of the man behind him.

Her mind slightly freed by the solution, she returned to the problem that had first sent her out to ride: Jeremy's declaration of love. Should she believe him? Why would he lie? He had the land. He had her love and passion. Saying he loved her gained him nothing. Rather, it brought her joy. She said she loved him, but didn't loving someone mean you trusted him? Trusted him to tell her the truth when he said he loved her. Wasn't her love big enough for faith?

Joy welled in Meredith's heart. She realized it had been fear that had held her back. She was afraid to give herself completely to Jeremy, to invest her heart and mind and soul in their marriage. If she believed him, she would have to give herself utterly into his keeping, lay herself open to be destroyed should his word prove false or his love fail. But as long as she refused to believe him, she could withhold a part of her being, keep something safe. That was not complete love. If she loved Jeremy, she must believe him. She smiled, sure now of her answer when she returned home.

Meredith was almost cheerful by the time she clattered into the stable yard of Four Oaks. A stableboy ran to take her horse and help her dismount. She hurried through the back door into the house without knocking, as she always did. Eager to speak to Galen, she headed straight for his study without looking for Althea or her mother. She heard voices inside the study as she approached and paused, uncertainly.

She didn't want to eavesdrop, but there was no nearby room to wait in. She started to turn back to the sitting room when she heard Galen's voice rise in unaccustomed anger. ". . . what I'm paying you for!"

Meredith stopped, startled by his rage. Then the other man spoke, and she frowned. There was something familiar about the voice, even muffled as it was through the heavy oak door. "It's not my fault. He's too damn—"

"I don't want your whining excuses!"

"Mr. Whitney, we both want the same thing," the other man said placatingly. Meredith still could not place the voice, but she realized that she was doing precisely what she didn't wish to appear to do: eavesdrop. She tiptoed down the hall and into the open door of the music room. No one was inside, and by standing slightly to one side of the door, she would be able to see when Galen's visitor left without the other person catching her lurking in the hall. She didn't have to wait long. Only moments after she entered the music room, she heard the door to Galen's study open and close, then a rapid tread down the hall. A man passed the door, face twisted in angry frustration. For a moment after he passed, Meredith remained frozen in place.

Galen's visitor had been Caleb Jackson!

Chapter XXVII

GALEN WAS the man behind Jackson! Galen was trying to kill
Jeremy. It was almost too much to absorb. Her cousin. Her
lifelong companion. She would have sworn Galen was the
last person in the world to do anyone harm. He disliked
Jeremy, of course, but in trying to list Jeremy's enemies, she
hadn't even considered Galen, because she couldn't imagine
him helping a killer. She remembered Jeremy tensing when
she began speculating on the backer's identity. He had suspected Galen but refrained from saying so, knowing it would
hurt her. Jeremy was the truly kind one. He possessed the
compassion of a man with emotions, a man who loved and
hurt and fought and did things he was ashamed of. He
understood the emotions of others. Galen's equanimity was
not the kindness she had always believed it to be, but simply
cold lack of feeling.

Rage washed her, sweeping away her shock and galvanizing
Meredith into action. She snapped her riding crop against her
booted leg and strode down the hall, hands clenched at her
sides. She burst into Galen's office without knocking. He was
standing at the window and whirled at her loud entrance. His
jaw dropped. "Meredith! What is it? What are you doing
here?"

"No, I'm the one with the questions, and you're going to
answer me!"

If possible, his jaw sagged even lower. "Meredith!"

"What was Caleb Jackson doing here?"

"Who? Oh, him. He's doing a little task for me. Why?"

"A little task? Such as murdering my husband?"

Galen drew up stiffly. "I don't know what you're talking about."

"No? Then what were you angry about? What had he failed to do? Wasn't it that he was unable to kill Jeremy?"

"Meredith, please, calm down. You're hysterical."

"Of course I'm hysterical! I trusted you. I thought you were my friend as well as my cousin. And now I discover you're trying to destroy me!"

"Not you, Cousin," he hastened to assure her. "When he fired at you, it was an idiotic mistake. I gave him a good tongue-lashing for it."

"A good tongue-lashing?" Her voice rose. "For almost killing me, you spoke harshly to him? God, Galen, but you're a cold snake."

"Meredith! I don't understand. I didn't tell you because I knew it would upset you. It's only proper for a lady to be offended by such gruesome matters. But I thought you'd be glad to be rid of the husband you didn't want. I know you were forced to marry Devlin. He's crude, animalistic—your life must be a constant hell, living with him."

"I was not forced to marry Jeremy!" she shrieked, raising her riding crop and smashing it down onto a nearby chair with all her might, splitting the leather back. "I love him! You kill him, and you destroy me."

She thought Galen's eyes would pop out of his head. "No! I can't believe—"

"Well, do believe. It's true. He's my husband. More than that, he's my life. He makes me happy. He makes me laugh. He gives me pleasure you couldn't even dream of. Everyone in the parish can see how I love him. Ask Althea or your mother. So don't ascribe your evil plans to some noble motive to help me. You were trying to get rid of a man you despised because he is all the things you are not. You didn't want me. I think you would have preferred to have no wife, wouldn't you? But you were planning to bravely grit your teeth and someday marry me to obtain Bitterleaf. That's what you wanted, my money.''

"Meredith, that's not true!"

"Isn't it? I'm surprised you didn't instruct your flunky to do away with me as well. That way you'd get the land without having to marry me. Or hadn't you thought of that possibility?" She drew a long breath and released it slowly, forcing her fury to abate. "All right, Galen, I'll tell you what's going to happen now. I hate to see the Whitney name besmirched. Althea doesn't deserve the shame. I'm sure Jeremy would agree with me. So I won't tell anyone what I just overheard. However, I'm going straight home and write down everything. I will give the letter to my attorney to be opened if Jeremy and I die, even accidentally.''

"My God! I would never harm you! You're my cousin, a Whitney. Devlin is—vermin. I was simply using one vermin to get rid of another."

"Another thing, Galen," she went on, ignoring his interruption. "You're to call off your dog Jackson immediately. Pay him and send him away. After that, you're leaving Four Oaks. I think Charleston would be a better place for you to live. Perhaps James Warren, the cousin you admire so much, will take you in. Or, on second thought, farther away might be better. I might have to see you in Charleston. Virginia is nice.''

"Don't be ridiculous. I have no intention of moving from Four Oaks.''

"*I* intend for you to move. And if you don't, I'll tell everyone what you tried to do, starting with your sister and mother. I won't rest until the whole parish knows you hired a man to kill Jeremy. Do you think you'll receive much respect after that? You'll be ostracized, despised, even by your own family. Wouldn't you rather leave than face the shame, Galen?"

His face was white as parchment. "Meredith, you wouldn't—you couldn't do that to me!"

"You'll find out, if you stay here," she warned grimly. "I'm going now. I suggest you do as I've told you. If I haven't heard you've left Four Oaks by the end of the week, I'll make a public announcement of your cowardly, murderous plans. Good-bye, Galen." She whirled and stalked out, a little surprised to find that her feet and legs worked normally. They felt so rubbery and trembling.

She almost ran down the back steps and across the lawn to the stables. The stableboy was obviously amazed at the brief time she had spent in the house after such a long ride. He had barely unsaddled and rubbed down the mare. He resaddled the horse and led her out for Meredith to mount. Meredith climbed into the saddle and set off, her heels digging into the mare's sides. She wanted to rush home as fast as possible. There was so much to tell Jeremy, and right now she needed the shelter of his arms. Oh, Jeremy! What an idiot she'd been for so long. Distrusting him, fighting him—and all the while having faith in a snake like Galen.

The return trip seemed to take ages. She felt as if she should be home already, yet she had barely reached the edge of Corley Woods. The rutted track sliced through the tall, thick trees of the undeveloped stretch of land. The trees joined overhead, hung with gray moss, shadowing the bright afternoon. She shivered—a delayed reaction from the shock of her discovery, she supposed. But no, it was more than that. Her spine prickled, reminding her of the day in the herb garden when she had felt someone watching her malevolently. At the time she had assumed it was Jeremy staring out a window at her, but she realized that wasn't true. It must have been Jackson in the trees, watching and hating the woman who had rejected him.

Meredith glanced over her shoulder. It was foolish, of course. There was no one behind her. But the feeling persisted. She urged her mare into a trot. The road curved in front of her around a huge oak. Just before she reached the curve, a man stepped from behind the tree into the middle of the road, his musket leveled at her. Meredith shrieked, and her hands automatically jerked back on the reins. Docilely the mare stopped. Later Meredith realized it was the worst thing she could have done. She should have spurred and run him down, taken her chances that he would shoot her as she charged at him. Instead, she had stopped and was caught.

"Well, well, Miss Whitney. Oh, excuse me, *Mrs*. Devlin, isn't it? You must be proud to wear the name of Irish trash."

"Get out of my way," Meredith ordered, assuming as

grand and aristocratic an air as she could. Perhaps she could bluff the man.

He grinned. "I don't think so. Get off your horse, or I'll have to shoot you off."

Meredith clenched her fists around the reins, furious and frustrated. Why hadn't she been more careful? She should have realized Jackson might have seen her standing in the music room. Why hadn't she left her mare at Four Oaks to be collected later by one of the servants? The Whitney boatmen could have taken her home on the river, and this wouldn't have happened. Too late to think about it now. It wouldn't help anyone, neither her nor Jeremy, if she died. Sighing, she dropped the reins and slid off the horse.

Jackson waved her to the side of the road, never taking the gun off her. When she was several feet away, he walked over to Mercy and swung up into the saddle, awkwardly riding astride on the sidesaddle. "All right, now straight ahead." He pointed with the gun.

"Into the woods?"

"Yes, into the woods."

"Why?"

"Because your husband's got that damn place too well guarded. I haven't been able to get close enough. So we're going to bring him out in the open."

"I don't understand."

"You don't need to. Just start walking."

Mechanically Meredith obeyed him, following a narrow trail deeper and deeper into the woods. Finally the trail disappeared altogether, and she wound through the trees, scrambling over logs and fighting through underbrush. Thorns tugged at her clothes and slashed her face and hands. Behind her Jackson chuckled. "Not so high and mighty now, are you? You know, I kind of like this. Me riding and you walking."

Meredith ignored him, keeping her back straight and head high. Finally she reached a small clearing where a horse was tethered. A black boy sat on a log. He sprang up when he saw them. Meredith saw blind fear in his eyes when he looked at Jackson. Jackson ordered the boy to tie Meredith to a tree, which he did. Jackson kept the gun trained on her until she was securely bound, the rope tied around both wrists and circling the tree. The position was both uncomfortable and debasing. Meredith felt utterly helpless, which was no doubt what Jackson wished. The best thing was to pretend confidence. That might unsettle him.

"You never were particularly bright, Jackson," she began. "And now you've committed another stupid act."

A light flared in his eyes for a moment. Sarcastically he asked, "Have I? And what is that?"

"Galen won't pay you a farthing for harming me. He's fond of me—and he has to marry me to acquire Bitterleaf."

"Him." Jackson dismissed his employer scornfully. "He won't raise a fuss no matter what happens. He'll be too scared I might tell everybody he paid me. Anyway, I know enough to know he's your next of kin if your husband's dead. He'll be content with getting your money that way. 'Sides, I'm not necessarily going to kill you. Oh, I'll make you pay for turning me down, all right, but I may not kill you. Right now, you're the lure."

"Lure?"

"Yeah. Bait for the trap." He gestured to the waiting black boy. "Okay, Joe, now here's what you do. Hop on this horse and ride to Bitterleaf. You know how to find it, don't you? All right. When you get there, say you have to speak to Mr. Jeremy Devlin, nobody else. He's a huge blond fellow. Tell Devlin this: I have his wife. The fact that you're riding her horse is proof. If he wants her alive, he's to follow you. He can't bring anyone else or any weapons, either. Got that?"

"Yes, sir."

He tossed the boy into the saddle. "Now, hurry."

Fear tightened Meredith's stomach, but she refused to let it show. "You prove your stupidity more with every passing minute," she snapped. "Why should Jeremy risk death to save me? He married me for my land, you know, not my looks. It's no loss to him if I die. He'll get the farm and the money. You'll get nothing. Galen'll get nothing."

"He'll come," Jackson retorted. "He nearly choked me to death for trying to kiss you. He'll come."

He must not come. Jeremy wouldn't be so foolish as to walk into a trap, Meredith assured herself. And yet, if he didn't, what would happen to her? She closed her eyes, praying Jeremy would stay at home, wouldn't endanger himself. But another part of her called out to him, certain he would rescue her.

After Meredith left, Jeremy rose and dressed leisurely. He spent the morning in his office, though he didn't get much work done. Instead he recalled the night before and wondered what Meredith's thoughts were as she rode alone. She didn't return for lunch, and a little, niggling worry began to grow in him. She had been gone an unusually long time for a mere ride. Of course, she could have decided to visit someone while she was out, but that wasn't like Meredith. Her only close friend was Althea, and the Whitney plantation was closer by water than by the road. He knew quite well she wasn't the best of horsewomen. If Mercy had been startled and shied suddenly or reared, Meredith could have been thrown. She could be lying out there somewhere, hurt. . . . He wondered if she had had the sense to take a stableboy with her, sure that she had not. She had wanted to be alone. Jeremy went to the stables to ask. Sam told him she had ridden out alone, then showed him the cut bridle. Jeremy glanced at it and thanked him for his caution, but his mind was on Meredith, not his own safety. "Send a couple of lads to look for her. She's been gone too long," he ordered and returned to the house.

It took the length of the walk to the house for Jeremy to decide he should go looking for her himself. He had entered the back door and headed for the stairs when he was intercepted by the majordomo. "Mr. Devlin, sir, Mr. Randall's waiting for you in the drawing room."

Jeremy grimaced and strode to the drawing room. "Blaine, nice to see you."

The other man rose and shook his hand. "Jeremy. I hope I haven't come at an inconvenient time."

"No, of course not. I was about to go for a ride. Care to join me?"

"Some other time perhaps. I plan to go on to Four Oaks after I talk to you."

Jeremy's eyes twinkled. "Can't wait even a day, eh?"

Blaine's tanned face darkened; on a lighter-skinned man, it would have been a blush. "Frankly, no."

"All right. No more teasing, I promise. What did you want to see me about?"

"Equilibrium. I have a lovely mare, Elizabeth's Fancy. Good stock, same dam as Chimneysweep. I was wondering if you'd consider putting your stallion to stud."

"I hadn't thought about it. I suppose so." They settled down to a discussion of bloodlines and breeding, so engrossed that neither noticed the minutes slipping away. Half an hour had passed when suddenly the back door crashed open and feet thundered down the hall. "What the devil!" Jeremy jumped up and rushed into the hall, almost colliding with Neb. "Neb! What's going on?" He glanced down in confusion at the small black boy whom Neb held tucked under one arm.

"He rode into the fields, asking for you," Neb began breathlessly, letting the boy slide to his feet on the floor. "He was riding Miss Meredith's horse."

"What!" Jeremy's eyes widened, and he grasped the boy by the shoulders, kneeling so as to be at eye level with him. "Where's Meredith?"

"I don't know," the boy answered. "Is she the lady on the horse?"

"Yes. Where is she?"

"With my master. He said I was to bring you to them."

"What happened? Is she hurt?"

"No, sir, not when I left. Mr. Jackson had me tie her to a tree, but he hadn't done nothing to her."

Ice encompassed Jeremy's heart, and his fingers clenched involuntarily. The boy winced, squealing, at the pressure of his fingers. Jeremy forced himself to relax. He must remain calm. "Where is Jackson?"

"I'm supposed to take you there, where he and the lady are. He says you have to come alone. And you can't bring no weapons."

"I say, Jeremy, what's going on here?" Blaine stood in the doorway, frowning. "Has something happened to Meredith?"

Jeremy rose slowly. His face was pale and set. "Our ex-overseer has her. He's threatened to do her harm." Jeremy turned to Neb. "Send a message to the stables. Tell them to saddle Equilibrium. I'll put on my riding boots. Excuse me, Blaine, I have to leave."

"But wait!" Blaine protested. "You can't mean to go alone! The man sounds insane."

"He'll kill you," Neb warned darkly. "You know that's why he wants you there."

"I know." Jeremy paused, then shrugged. "But if I don't, he'll kill Meredith. What choice do I have?"

The other two men began a chorus of protestations, but he ignored them and climbed the stairs to his room. There he tugged on a pair of riding boots, loaded a dueling pistol, and slipped it in the back of his breeches' waistband. He knelt on one knee to slide a long knife into his boot. Thrusting his arms into an outer jacket, he hastened down the stairs. Blaine and Neb greeted him with another round of arguments, but he shoved past them, grabbing the child by the wrist and hustling him out the back door. "Sorry, gentlemen, I haven't the time to reason with you." Neb and Blaine turned to each other in consternation.

Meredith wriggled restlessly. Her back was hot and stiff, her arms scratched by the rough bark. Her fingers had grown numb, and the deadness was creeping up her arms. She wet her lips and wondered how long it had been since the child had left. It seemed hours, but she knew the discomfort and waiting made it feel longer than it really was. The heavy growth of trees blocked the sun, so she could not tell how late it was. She glanced at Jackson. He was lying on the ground asleep, secure in the knowledge that she couldn't escape. Meredith glared and twisted her wrists for the thousandth time. The boy had tied her well.

She heard a noise in the trees and tensed. Perhaps it was Jeremy. If he approached quietly enough, he might catch Jackson literally napping. On the other hand, it could be merely an animal roaming the woods. She strained her ears, but couldn't hear another sound. Suddenly Jackson sat straight up, clutching his musket. He peered through the dim forest for a moment, then walked to Meredith's side and placed the end of the muzzle against her temple. The quiet ended. She heard the definite cracks of twigs breaking. Soon the black child walked into view, and behind him a tall blond man leading an elegant bay horse by its reins.

"Jeremy!" Meredith cried out, torn between joy and despair. He had come for her! He had loved her enough to risk his life for her. But he was killing himself! She would lose him forever. "Jeremy why did you come? You should have stayed away."

He moved into the center of the clearing, dropping Equilibrium's reins. "Did you honestly think I could?"

Meredith noted his careless handling of the reins. Equilibrium was anything but a docile horse. He was aristocratic, nervous, and just plain mean, not the sort of horse one allowed to stand about casually untied. Even the dangling reins could be enough to panic him. Meredith realized Jeremy was hoping the horse would create a diverson. But for once in his life Equilibrium seemed as placid as his name.

"Jackson, you know how insane this scheme is, don't you?" Jeremy asked conversationally. "Blaine Randall was with me when your message arrived. If you kill me, he'll know it was you. You'll be caught and hanged."

"Randall wouldn't waste his time on a dog like you," Jackson replied.

"I wouldn't count on it. He's awfully anxious to breed a mare to my stallion," Jeremy responded lightly.

Jackson sneered and snapped at the boy, "Search him for weapons!" The child found the dueling pistol hidden at Jeremy's back and carried it to Jackson. "I knew you wouldn't do as I instructed," he told Jeremy, setting aside the musket. "But thank you, this is a much handier weapon." He dismissed the child, instructing him to wait at the tavern, and the child darted away eagerly. Jackson smiled. "Well. Now we're alone. I think I'm going to enjoy this very much. Devlin, take off your coat and throw it on the ground. Now, back up against that tree."

Jeremy did as he was told, never taking his eyes from the pistol Jackson held to Meredith's head. Jackson pulled a knife from his belt. Jeremy sucked in his breath sharply and tensed to fling himself at the man, thinking he was about to use it upon Meredith. But Jackson merely sliced through the rope binding Meredith to the tree. Still holding the gun to her head, Jackson propelled her to his horse and yanked a length of rope from his saddlebags. "Here. You're going to tie up your lover."

They walked to where Jeremy stood, and Jackson stood back, his gun leveled at Jeremy's chest. Meredith uncoiled the rope slowly. She was delaying—she didn't know exactly for what, but it was all she could think of to do at the moment. If enough time went by, perhaps somehow a miracle would happen and they would be rescued. She tied one end of the rope around Jeremy's wrist, looping it as large as she could without Jackson's noticing. Perhaps if his bonds were loose enough, he could pull free. She circled the tree to his other wrist.

"No!" Jackson snarled. "I want his arms back farther, tighter."

Tears in her eyes, Meredith tautened the rope until it strained his chest and arm. She raised his other arm to the same position and tied the wrist, again making the loop as loose as she could.

Meredith turned to Jackson. "There's no reason to do this. You wanted to marry me to get Bitterleaf. Well, I'll give it to you."

"Meredith!" Jeremy exclaimed, warmth invading his chest. She would give up her precious land for him.

"I'll sign over the deed to you. We'll go back to the house, and I'll sign it."

"I'm not fool enough to be caught by your tricks."

"It's not a trick, I swear it. Send someone for the deed and have it brought here if you're afraid to go to Bitterleaf. I'll give you all my jewels, too, the money, the silver plate—whatever you want."

"What I want is *his* skin, strip by strip. I'll take care of you later. I'll make you regret refusing me." He picked up the rope he had sliced through before. "Now, come here."

Meredith pressed herself against Jeremy, raising her face for a final kiss. He mumbled against her lips, "Right boot."

She frowned and stepped back, biting her lip. "Come here!" Jackson repeated impatiently. "Do you want his flesh even when he's dying?"

"Yes!" Meredith shrieked, startling even Jeremy. "Yes! Yes! I love him." She bust into huge, racking sobs and dropped to her knees before Jeremy, wrapping her arms tightly around his legs. Shielded by her body, her fingers dug into his boot and found the handle of his knife. Carefully she slid it out and curled her fingers around it, still sobbing.

Making an impatient sound, Jackson strode to them and jerked her to her feet. Unexpectedly, she turned as she rose, and her right hand thrust out hard. Had she been lucky, she would have stabbed him through the heart. As it was, she hit a rib, and the knife was deflected. It sliced through his skin and sent blood gushing over his shirt, but caused little real damage. Jackson shrieked with surprise and pain and began to grapple with her. He clutched her wrist with both hands, squeezing until the knife dropped nervelessly from Meredith's fingers. Still she struggled, kicking and flailing, ripping at his face with her fingernails. Jeremy watched their struggle helplessly, straining against his bonds, his hands squeezing and tugging, trying to pull through the loops Meredith had made.

Jackson slapped her hard, sending Meredith tumbling, and Jeremy let out a hoarse cry of rage, lunging futilely against his rope. Jackson threw himself on her and though Meredith fought with all her might, he managed to turn her face down on the ground, his legs clamped around hers, and forced her hands together behind her back. Grabbing the rope that he had dropped in the struggle, he tied her hands, then rolled her onto her back. "Bitch!" He slapped her again.

"Goddamn you, I'll kill you!" Jeremy roared.

Jackson staggered to his feet, tearing aside his shirt to look at his wound. "Look what you've done to me, you filthy slut!" He ripped off a hunk of Meredith's skirt to wad up and press against the wound until the bleeding stopped. "Damn near killed me," he muttered.

"What else do you think I'd try to do?" Meredith lashed out, panting, her cheek aching, but still defiant. The fight had ripped free several buttons of her dress, exposing the tops of her breasts, which rose and fell heavily with her panting breaths. Jackson, reassured he wasn't about to bleed to death, paused and looked at her. He licked his lips.

"Just you wait. You and me are going to have a fine time

after I play a little with your husband first.'' He picked up the pistol and stuck it in his belt. He strolled to the horse and grabbed his coiled whip. Smiling, he let it play out, then snapped it experimentally. ''I never got to finish that lashing I was giving you, boy,'' he told Jeremy, his eyes shining with an unholy light. ''Nobody around to stop us now. 'Course, after your doxy cut me, my aim may not be too good. I might accidentally slice open that handsome face of yours.'' He swung to Meredith. ''How will you like your lover then, huh? Nose split, blinded, skin all stripped away? Not a pretty sight.''

''No!'' Meredith screamed and struggled to her feet. He had bound her hands, but not her feet. She could run, and she did so now, crashing into Jackson with all her force. He went down, but she was helpless against his retaliation, and he shoved her aside, striking her so hard her head buzzed and she saw nothing but shooting sparks of colors.

Jackson laughed. He straddled her. Her lush breasts were almost falling out of her bodice. With both hands he kneaded her breasts harshly. ''No. I think the lashing can wait. I wouldn't want to kill you, Devlin, or blind you before you see me teach your wife her lesson. I'm going to use her, Devlin, right here in front of you, so you can watch. You'll learn how a real man handles a woman. And she'll learn the feel of a real man.'' Slowly, in vulgar detail, he began to relate the perversities he would perform on Meredith. Jeremy cursed loudly and foully, lunging and struggling to break free of the heavy rope. Meredith screamed, hoping to incite Jeremy's sensitive horse to action. Her screams and Jeremy's curses did indeed excite Equilibrium. He plunged and stamped, circling nervously and whinnying. But he did not distract Jackson from his purpose, as Meredith had hoped. Jackson tossed up her skirts, exposing long, shapely legs, and grasped her underclothes to tear them away. Suddenly, with a tremendous yank, Jeremy's hands slipped through the knots, leaving much of his skin behind. He threw himself at Jackson, knocking him off Meredith. The air whooshed out of Jackson, and the gun flew from his belt. Jeremy crashed his fist into the man's jaw, and Jackson went limp. Jeremy would have liked nothing more than to beat his face into a pulp, but his concern for Meredith overrode all else. He rose and rushed to her and pulled her into his arms. "Meredith, my love, are you all right?"

"Yes. Yes. Oh, Jeremy." She burst into real tears now. He set to work on her bonds, his hands trembling so much he could not untie them. Neither one saw Jackson rise stealthily to his hands and knees. Silently he crept forward until he could stretch out and grasp the knife lying forgotten on the ground. Raising it above his head, he launched himself at Jeremy's unprotected back. At the sound, Jeremy whirled instinctively, thrusting Meredith aside. Jackson crashed into him, but the knife merely sliced through Jeremy's sleeve.

Meredith rolled away and staggered to her feet, watching with horror as the men wrestled on the grass. Jackson struck again at Jeremy, but Jeremy caught his wrist and forced it away. Though Jeremy was by far larger and stronger, Jackson fought with the fervor of a man in danger of his life. Slowly Jeremy pushed him up, then, bringing up his knee, shoved Jackson from him. Jeremy bounced to his feet as Jackson came up in a crouch, knife poised for Jeremy's rush. Suddenly a loud crack split the air.

Jackson fell back, blood spurting from his throat. Jeremy and Meredith whirled. Blaine Randall and Neb stood at the edge of the clearing. Blaine brandished the other dueling pistol of Jeremy's set. Neb carried a long, wicked-looking knife, which he now sheathed.

Jeremy relaxed with a sigh. "Thank God." He sank to the ground.

Blaine stuck the pistol back in his belt. "We followed you. Neb and I agreed you weren't in full possession of your senses."

Jeremy gave a shaky laugh. Neb jumped off his horse and neatly cut through Meredith's ropes while Blaine went to examine Jackson. "Dead," he pronounced with satisfaction. "Neb, help me tie him on his horse."

Meredith, on being released from her bonds, fell into Jeremy's arms. He held and rocked her until the shaking in both of them had died down. Jeremy kissed her hair and buried his face in it, breathing in the familiar scent. "Oh, Meredith, my love, I thought you might be dead," he whispered. "I died a thousand deaths when I got Jackson's message."

"Oh, Jeremy, I love you, I love you." She cuddled against him. "Take me home, please."

"Of course." He picked her up in his arms as though she were feather light and carried her to his horse. Equilibrium, after all the excitement, shied at having a passenger placed upon him, but Jeremy's stern voice held him still. He vaulted into the saddle after Meredith and, cradling her in his arms, led the others out of the woods. Meredith said nothing on the way home, and neither did Jeremy, their clinging arms expressing everything they felt. When they reached the house, Jeremy left Blaine to take care of the legal matters regarding Jackson. He carried Meredith upstairs and laid her on the bed. She would not let him leave her even to remove his boots.

"Oh, Jeremy, I want you near me." Smiling, he sat beside her.

"There's nowhere I'd rather be." He cupped her face and kissed her mouth lightly. "If I had lost you, I'd have died myself!"

"Jeremy! Your poor wrists!" She grabbed his arm and stared at the raw, bloody rings where the ropes had rubbed away his flesh in his wild struggle to break free. "I must put something on them."

He chuckled. "Ever the healer."

She scrambled off the bed to get her bag, then tenderly bathed the wounds and dressed them. "I can't let them get infected. I'm sure Jackson's rope was dirty."

Jeremy laughed. Meredith raised one eyebrow in mock anger. "Just what is so funny?"

"Nothing. Probably an overload of nerves. But when you said his rope was dirty, as if that were the vilest thing he'd done . . ."

Meredith smiled, too, and hugged her husband fiercely. "It scared me so when you came to rescue me. I was afraid he'd kill you. Jeremy, I won't ever let anything come between us again." She paused. "I—I went to Four Oaks today."

"Oh?" A certain wariness crept into his voice.

"Yes, and I found out—I found out that Galen is the man

behind Jackson.'' She paused, but he made no comment. ''Did you know it?''

''I suspected. Angus Hamilton would have been more likely to come after me with dueling pistols than set a killer on me. It was a cold act, not a heated one. And Galen was the only one who could profit by my death. I used the same logic you did, my dear.''

''I'm sorry I doubted you.'' She kissed him lingeringly on the lips. ''I told Galen to leave the parish—the colony, in fact—or I would reveal what he'd done.''

''Would you?''

''In a second. Otherwise, he might try to harm you again— more successfully, perhaps. But I pray he'll leave. It would be a terrible scandal and would hurt Althea so. You don't mind, do you?''

''No. I wouldn't want to hurt Althea, either. She is your dear friend, and therefore dear to me.''

''Not *too* dear,'' she teased.

He laughed. ''No, not too dear. One Whitney female is all I can handle, believe me.''

Again she kissed him. ''I love you.'' She stared earnestly into his eyes.

''And I love you.''

''I know,'' she replied simply, her whole heart in the words.

He understood her meaning. She believed him, trusted him completely. His throat ached with a happiness so great it was almost painful. He drew her to him for a deeper kiss. ''I'll love you forever,'' he murmured when at last he released her. Meredith sighed with contentment and sank back into the bed, holding out her arms beckoningly.

''Then come here and prove it. Opal Hamilton was right. I should take full advantage of my indentured servant.'' Jeremy growled mockingly and rolled on top of her. For a moment he gazed down at her, drinking in her features. Then his lips came down, sealing the promise of their words.

Fiery Tales Of Forbidden Passion And Shameless Desire

by LISA GREGORY